I0583816

So She May Grow

by
Jaimie Thomas

So She May... Book 2

Published through IngramSpark

So She May Grow

Print edition ISBN: 9780975665121
E-book edition ISBN: 9780975665138

Printed by IngramSpark
First IngramSpark edition: April 2025

Names, places and incidents and either products of the author's imagination
or used fictitiously. Any resemblance to actual persons, living or dead
(except for satirical purposes), is entirely coincidental.

Contains mature content.

What did you think of this book?

I love to hear from readers.
Please visit the website and send a message...
https://www.jaimiethomas.com/contact

To everyone who has spent years of their life commuting
to and from wherever you may need to go.
Embrace those daydreams.
The books you've read will never leave you,
and let the stories you've made flourish.

This book was written on a bus, and yours can be too.

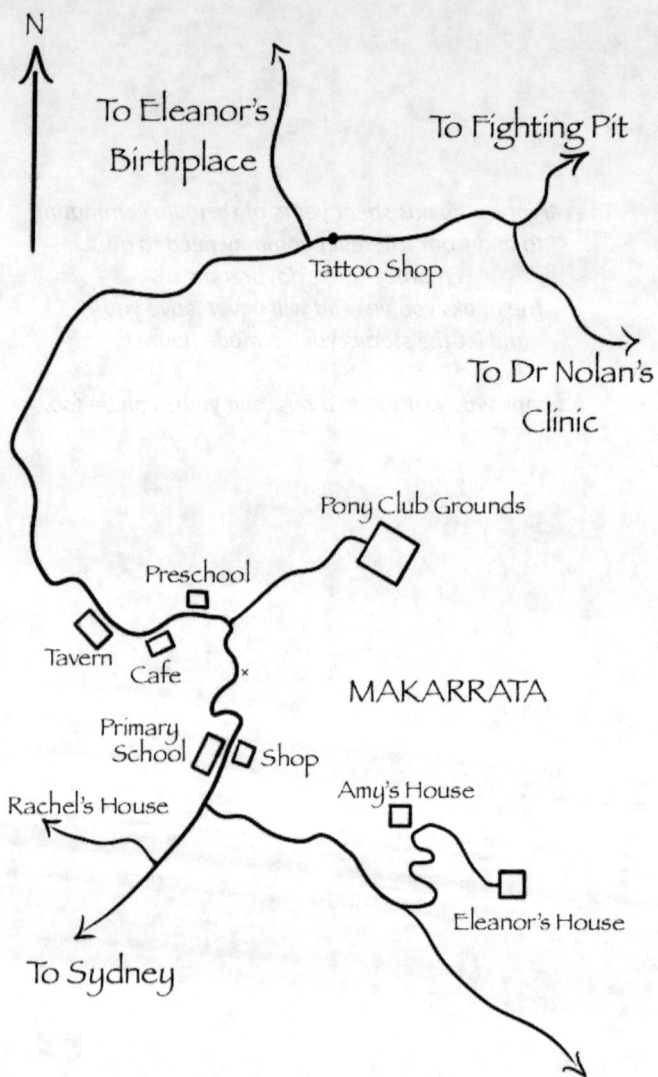

Chapter 1

The van rattles along the road, jostling the NAP strike team as they approach the most recent attack alert. Within, the team sombrely watch the security feeds as the brutality is displayed across the set of screens before them. Michael can barely keep his eyes on the bloodshed, pure rage painted across his face as a blur of green cuts through the men before him.

The anger is not isolated to Michael as sour expressions pin on Kenichi and Kaylee. Nikolas pauses slightly to look up at the camera, in his eyes is apology and heartbreak, but the tale of anguish does nothing to soften the displeasure radiating within the van. Kaylee barely needs to raise her voice as she calls for the driver to hurry up, but nothing else can be done to place them on a suitable interception path.

Nikolas had planned this little tirade perfectly. Just close enough that driving would be quicker than preparing the jet, but far enough that the alarm could be raised, and he could get out with enough time to avoid them completely. They all understand this of course but nevertheless, are racing along in a desperate attempt to recapture the wayward Prince. After the pain of nearly losing his Geminae, he used the distraction of Eleanor leaving to escape, then offered his services to the Daemones as a sacrifice for hiding the truth of her life in Australia. Any trace of Nikolas was lost past the destroyed ankle bands. This was the first time he has resurfaced, their first chance to give Eleanor a bit of her life back.

The close confines of the van allows little room for the frustration bubbling under the surface to be released, instead they continue to watch the slaughter with disbelief. Nikolas weaves in an out of view of the cameras as if a conductor for the symphonious blood bath, holding every ounce of the grace and power his Angeli heritage allows him.

"I can't believe he would do this..." Zach mutters, the one least affected by the discovery of Nikolas's return to evil, "everything he has done in the last few months has pointed towards remorse."

Kenichi – ever the expert on Eleanor's whims, and thus Nikolas's emotional attachment – sighs as he breaks his focus from the feed. There is a weariness in his eyes, mostly prompted from the late nights he has spent on the phone to Eleanor, in various states of explaining their efforts to find her Geminae and convincing her to take care of herself. Adelyn is happy, as ever, but Eleanor has always sacrificed her own needs for the sake of self-imposed punishment.

"Neither of them thinks like us. They don't trust, they are incapable of believing anyone's word," he says. "If I'd thought at all, I would have seen it... he will do anything to keep her safe."

Kaylee ducks her head fiddling with the weapon in her hands as she joins the conversation.

"The worst thing was that she didn't expect it," she whispers. "Eleanor was happy. He broke her heart."

Every part of Michael is tensed as he listens to the conversation, about ready to snap as Kenichi agrees with a solemn nod. Their attention returns to the feeds as the radio gains volume.

Nikolas walks out of the building, unhindered.

"How far out are we?" Michael bites out the words, stern focus on the driver as he delivers the bad news.

His grip on his rage slips as his Herculean hand slams into the wall beside him and the yell that echoes around the cramped cabin makes everyone wince. Kaylee gives the instruction for the driver to continue to the site as Kenichi considers the lingering glance they had been confronted with earlier.

"This was never about us having a chance to catch him, all he wanted to do was let us know that he is with them now," Kenichi explains. "He wanted us to know that he was doing what he could to keep her safe, in the only way he knows how."

Michael bristles, attention snapping to the doctor.

"He knows many ways that don't involve treason, ways that don't taint my word with his foul ideations," he says, lips turning as he watches the screen, now empty. "A quiet life was never what he wanted; he will always choose the dark path just to spite me."

Kenichi can't stop the exasperated sigh that escapes him as Michael's declaration lingers in the already tense air. It takes all his focus to level his tone as he replies, however a fire begins to spark in his eyes.

"Nikolas will choose the path that keeps Eleanor happy. She'll learn to live with Adelyn, and he thinks he's giving her the chance to. He doesn't realise how much she began to love him... he can't of," he explains.

Though Kaylee's attention is conflicted between Michael's rage and Kenichi's disappointment, she addresses both simply.

"The major thing we need to consider is that this is what Nikolas *thinks* will be best. We have all seen how Eleanor is now, but you didn't hear the betrayal in her voice when she made that call." Kaylee shudders, looking away from them all. "We all give her more credit than she is due, including him. She is still a child. She is ill. Nikolas thought that protection from within the Daemones would help... maybe it will. We all have different opinions, but I think the most important one is that Eleanor needed to be away, no matter what that meant."

"You said yourself that she is still a child, how can we expect her to live alone?" Kenichi argues. "She's barely well enough to care for Adelyn at the moment, let alone herself..."

With measured calm, Kaylee says, "she will learn, just like we did. Let it be her choice what happens from here on."

Chapter 2

A part of me hopes that Nikolas someday watches the footage of the day she got his letter. That day and the next week, in fact. Watching it now, I can't see how she ever forgave him but then, there is a lot I still don't understand. Even so, his abandonment makes me mad.

At the time I was unable to express those feelings, I didn't quite understand what was going on between them. Eleanor and Nikolas – in her own words – were always very complicated. They kept to themselves, and I think it was just their way.

You could say the National Agency for Protection team weren't happy, in fact they were furious – each for varying reasons – but Eleanor's sadness was the worst. For a week she never let herself stop moving. She was waking up multiple times through the night, having to sleep with headphones on so that she could get her eyes shut. The only time she ate was when she started to feel like passing out, which was about once every two days. The wound on her throat had been hurting but hadn't reopened, luckily.

It's because of this that Kenichi decides, after finishing a phone call with her, to move her first session with her therapist closer.

On day eight of living in Australia, she gets in the car, baby Adelyn strapped in the car seat, and is off to her appointment.

~

It doesn't surprise the psychiatrist as she spots her newest – and potentially most complicated – client walking across the road ten minutes early. Nor is it surprising that after dropping her daughter in the provided day care, Eleanor hangs in the doorway until she is addressed.

"Come in and take a seat," she offers, standing up to fill two glasses.

In silence, Eleanor perches awkwardly on the edge of the firm grey couch, face refusing to budge from a blank stare, as the woman places a glass of water in front of her.

"It's nice to meet you," the woman smiles, "I'm Doctor Nolan, but you can just call me Vanessa. I know everything your American friends do, so could you please tell me your current name, and your actual name?"

For a few minutes, Eleanor just sits, watching the woman with a set to her jaw. But the therapist doesn't pressure her, instead watching as Eleanor scans the room, skipping over potted plants and neutral paintings to focus on the occasional radio and the decorative lampshade.

Eleanor's skin is paler than normal, an almost grey pallor and she sits with a slack expression, as if she is too tired to bother holding her face together. Dark bags hang under her bloodshot eyes and the blue of her irises are a dull, murky grey. Though it was hard to tell through the thick turtleneck, she looks too skinny, as if the only thing keeping her upright, is muscle. She looks terrible, to put it simply.

Her bony fingers tremble slightly as she sits there, refusing to tap out a tune like they would normally. Lips cracked and pale, ashen hair limp and unkempt, thrown into a loose bun as she left the house.

Eleanor is a complete mess.

Opting to redirect her, Dr Nolan pushes the glass closer.

"Please have a drink, you look thirsty," she says, keen brown eyes waiting for a reaction.

Eleanor's head tilts, but her attention draws onto the woman.

"My current name is Diana Evans, my actual name is Eleanor Beck," she replies, voice tired and raw. "I am agent 828, codename Kitten."

Dr Nolan smiles, sitting back a bit to allow the girl to have space.

"Why did you include the last two?" she follows.

"They were what I was called for most of my life. In fact, I've been called 828 for longer than I have ever been Eleanor," she blinks, voice still thin.

"What would you prefer I call you, Diana or Eleanor?" Vanessa specifies with eyes kind.

Quietly, she replies, "Eleanor."

"Can you tell me your daughter's name?"

The doctor stays alert and careful trying to make herself friendly. It was certainly a task, understanding the psychologies of an assassin.

"Ady, Adelyn," Eleanor says, "my sister and I, our names are both classical. Eleanor and Kate. I figured hers should be as well."

"That's nice. What about middle names?"

Before her, Eleanor drifts off, eyes glazing over as her head tilts slightly. Her pale lips are barely moving, and no sound comes out.

"Eleanor," Vanessa tries, smiling slightly as the girl's head snaps to her, a smile forming easily.

The change in Eleanor's mannerisms comes as a shock, but Dr Nolan doesn't let that show as Eleanor starts to speak.

"Mine is Violet, and my daughter's is Lily," she says. "My sister was Kate Iris. My mother's name was Rose, she wanted to keep the flowers in our middle names."

"Why did you continue the tradition?"

"I don't know, just felt like it..." Eleanor shrugs. "At the time I was choosing I had gained access to my file. I didn't know what my middle name was, or my parents' names. Nikolas, he helped me to unlock some of my memories so that I understood why we matched."

Other than a slight pause, there is no heartache on Eleanor's face. She just sits and waits for the next question. Kenichi had mentioned the mental wall to the psychiatrist before Eleanor's session, explaining how she locked off when she was scared or unstable. Though he didn't know what it was and hadn't had enough evidence to ask her about it either.

"Do you have many nicknames? Ones you remember from your parents, maybe?" Dr Nolan asks, trained eyes keeping track of the girl's movements.

"A fair few. My parents used to call me Ellsie, and the team call me Ellie when I'm behaving..." Eleanor answers, pausing slightly to observe the woman. Her guard drops as she continues, eyes casting towards the floor. "I don't let people who know me now call me Nora, but in the Agency the two I lived with called me that. And Mein Vater called me Kleiner Fuchs: little fox. Nikolas called me Dulce Meum for a while, and Incaendium, when I was being a pain."

Now the reaction Dr Nolan had expected earlier rises, Eleanor drawing in on herself, fingers raising to her throat. The distant look in her pained eyes.

"What do they mean, the two names he called you?"

Eleanor scoots into the back of the chair, knees tucking to her chest and a hand moving into her hair. She cradles her head, eyes almost rolling back as she starts to rock in her place.

"I don't know," she whispers. "It's Latin. I... it's one of the languages I do not know. Michael refused to let me learn it, I'd assume because he didn't want me to... I don't know why. I wanted to learn it though."

"You speak a lot of languages." A statement. "How many was it, again?"

"14. Though I'm only fluent in about nine of them, the rest I can get by on."

"What are you fluent in?"

An innocent question. But also, an answer to something the team had been asking for years. They only knew of six. Figuring out exactly where Eleanor could run to is an important part of building her file, but so far, they had been completely unsuccessful. Eleanor's gaze focuses on the woman opposite her, the bluntness of her stare causing Dr Nolan to falter for a moment.

"So, they did give you a list of things to get out of me," Eleanor says with worrying clarity.

"They did." No point in lying to her, she figured. "But I'm also curious. I've never known someone who could speak so many, so well."

After a few seconds of silence, Eleanor shrugs. Though her face is still sunken and pained, her mind has been distracted from the previous conversation. With a roll of her neck Eleanor scans the room once more before she begins.

"English and German are my most used. But I'm also fluent in; Spanish, French, Japanese, Russian, Mandarin, Swedish, Italian and Hungarian," she lists, pausing for Vanessa to write them all down. "Places I fit in well, which is why I don't know many South

Asian, African or South American languages. Though I am decent in Portuguese and my Latin American Spanish is passable. I also know the common dialects so can do lots of accents. I can pass as a local in most of Europe, so I spend more of my time there or in Western countries. There are other agents who fit into other cultured countries, so I have no need for learning those languages."

"What about the ones you aren't quite fluent in?"

"Portuguese, Polish, Danish and Greek—" she almost chuckles as she says the last two "—though I doubt I would pass as anything more than someone who has lived there for more than two years. I don't get much chance to practise."

"I don't think anyone would blame you for not being fluent in 14 languages. I can only speak two," Vanessa smiles *(English and German, they decided it was best to have someone who could speak Eleanor's comfort languages)*, only noticing her mistake as Eleanor flinches away slightly.

"They would. They did. The Agency were never forgiving."

Those who knew Eleanor well, knew that the punishments the Agency had inflicted on her projected in little abnormalities in the way she went about things. Those who cared enough might notice how she never tripped up or got caught on her words. While others thought her smart or lucky, friends knew she feared the beating that came after a mistake.

It bled into other behaviours as well. When she was sassy about a question and someone got annoyed at her, she would flinch away. Both actions were responses to her training as a child; the need to be in charge, and the fear of her superiors. Ellsie did those things less; considerably so but little Nora fell back on the actions as a crutch.

Deciding to test the limits, Dr Nolan follows the statement with a heavy question.

"What would they do to you, when you did something wrong?" she asks, holding the 18-year-old's gaze. The defiance lurking behind the blue of Eleanor's eyes forces her to raise her shoulders as she continues, "I don't plan on letting you coast through these sessions, Eleanor. You need help with your past and I will give it to you. But that does mean I will ask you to tell me things, so could you please answer the question?"

Cleverly hiding the tremor in her hands, Eleanor clenches her jaw and returns the woman's gaze. Ellsie had risen once again. Protective as always.

"You just have to tell me something in regard to the question."

Vanessa understands what she is doing, as Eleanor forms fists with her hands, head trembling in its place.

After a long pause and just before Dr Nolan goes to speak again, Eleanor breaks.

"Tasers. They needed to keep my skin pretty for when I was older," she says. "My handler was the worst, then the dance teacher; I heard rumours he took a fancy to some of the girls. Not me though, Mein Vater always made sure he was there to pick me up early."

"He cared for you, your Vater?"

Eleanor glances away swiftly, eyes focusing on something else.

"I was like a daughter to him. I don't know why, but he did care," she murmurs. "He's disobeyed orders multiple times because he couldn't bring himself to kill me."

It takes a moment for Vanessa to process her response, entirely unused to the calibre of Eleanor's mind. But as she watches the assassin roughly stitched together, she asks her question based on most power abuse cases.

"Would you have killed him if you were ordered to?"

It was important for Vanessa to judge Eleanor's response; to reveal the extent of her training and what mental barriers had been formed in the time she had been with the team. How much they could truly trust her instincts.

"Even if I tried, I wouldn't succeed. He is a better fighter than I am, and it is much easier to defend than attack," the girl answers, gaze turning weakly back to the woman.

"But would you try?"

Eleanor straightens again, eyes narrowed on the woman.

"I would," she says, confidently. "Whether or not I would let myself fail would depend on my mood. Sometimes, when I fight, the people around me blur into faceless things. If I had proper motivation, I could find it in myself to kill him."

Though Dr Nolan tries her hardest to hide her surprise, Eleanor can still read it on her face. The cocky mask falling into place. Her muscles tighten with the excitement of power, but she holds herself back as Vanessa struggles to find the words.

"You thought I'd say no," she chuckles. "I am a woman willing to kill myself to keep my daughter safe. Do you think I wouldn't eliminate him if he became a threat to Ady? You think I wouldn't eliminate anyone who became a threat to her?"

"Why do you say eliminate not kill?" By now the woman has regained her composure, ready to make use of the more confident Eleanor.

"It's more formal. Makes me seem like I know what I'm doing. Which I do, but sometimes people have trouble believing that," Ellsie laughs, a hint of psychopathy dancing on her tone. "How do you think I got the name Kitten? So small and insignificant, with a roar bigger than her bite. But I assure you, my bite is fatal enough."

Another distinct choice Kenichi made in hiring Dr Vanessa Nolan to be Eleanor's therapist; she served in the army for a long time. She had seen things in her time which many never cared to think about. Death was not a new subject for her, and she had experience with soldiers who had taken too much of a liking to killing humans.

Ellsie's intimidation techniques would not work as well as she thought they would.

Before Dr Nolan can reply, Eleanor droops slightly, the tremor returning to her hands. Her eyes look away, cast to the floor in shame. Her fingers inch to her throat.

"Sorry, that was rude," she says. "And eliminating makes them less like living beings, more like a line through a word. It's easier to bear the guilt that way."

However, in her time in the military Vanessa had never worked with someone with a split personality like Eleanor's. The quick changes stumped her as both Ellsie and Nora were revived. Confusion was written all over the therapist's face.

Dr Nolan glances at her watch, realising at the same time as Eleanor that their meeting was over.

As Eleanor stands, about to walk away with a brief farewell, Dr Nolan says, "I'll see you in two weeks, and I'd like you to make an effort to eat a little more, please?"

Eleanor's blue eyes glance back for a second, searching the doctor's brown ones.

"See you in two weeks."

Chapter 3

The drive home from the therapist is about an hour and a half, during which Adelyn, from the backseat of the car, mutters on about nothing in particular. The sound soothes the wild turning of Eleanor's mind and allows her to keep her focus on the twisting road before her.

As the road quality steadily decreases, bitumen turns to dirt and Eleanor pulls into the start of her driveway – a small private road twisting through a collection of ghost gums and iron barks. The towering trees leave the air with a sweet scent of eucalyptus and host a wide variety of birds, flitting though the dense branches. Even the dashes of movement well above her sets Eleanor on edge as if each flick of movement were a drive to attack her. If Adelyn notices her mother's raised stress levels, it was impossible to tell, as the child continues to rattle off little observations.

Two other properties share the little side road that their new house is accessed by. The family that she had met on the first day and an old man, who had been living there longer than her own house had been built. His was the first house on the road and his cattle grazed in the paddock she had to drive through. The man himself was a bit of a recluse, which Eleanor was more than happy about.

Completely opposite, Amy and James's house, just over a rickety bridge, is a wealth of activity. The bridge itself was held over a creek that was dry more often than it was full, but nevertheless the grass held a slight green tinge in the shaded areas. Amy's yard is littered with children's toys and pieces of half-working machinery in a scene of organised chaos.

Eleanor's property is the furthest, up the rough dirt track. Completely hidden from public view, her house is tucked into a hill, protected on one side by a towering cliff at its back. Making use of the steep slope, it stands two storeys tall with a spacious attic in the A-frame roof. Stone terraces support the hill beside the house, with room for cars to park, and a series of gardens in tiers, up the hill. With the car open to the elements, Eleanor had already found two big blankets to throw over her black, four-wheel drive ute, if it ever decided to hail (or needed camouflaging). She was far enough north that it didn't snow in winter, but not so far that the summers would be overly sweltering, a few days in the 40°C range were to be expected.

While decorated by a wooden deck, the underlying structure is made of strong steel beams that support the whole house including both the top and lower decks. Wisely, the walls are made of light blue painted bricks, allowing for the trees growing close by to remain, as brick doesn't burn. The corrugated iron roof is a greenish colour that makes it harder to see from above, with extra support from the towering trees the house is nestled into.

In front of the house, only 50 metres further down the hill, the property opens onto wide fields, before the valley wall rises again in dense bush. A sharp turn in the valley keeps the paddocks hidden from view, and the stretching valleys provided many places to explore – as Kenichi explained it, Eleanor favoured the term 'hide'.

A walkway, ten metres of wood boarding with tall handrails to stop Adelyn or any small child from falling off, rises from the car park to meet the house's main level. A collection of tools and firewood sit organised against the wall from the last owner, but Eleanor passes them by to enter the building.

Within the house, the open plan helped her to relax into the lack of confinement. The kitchen has only a long bench to separate it from the dining room, which has a sideboard backing a lounge onto the living room. A fireplace sits opposite the television to heat the house during winter; an effort to reduce the amount of electricity used. Empty bookshelves line the walls, wooden much like the other furniture to contrast the tile floors. A bathroom sits furthest from the door, just past the staircase that takes them down to the bedrooms.

Downstairs Eleanor's room is smaller than the one in America, with a large wardrobe, but no walk-in and sliding glass doors out onto the lower deck. Adelyn has the same in her room next door. There is a guest bedroom on the opposite side of the hall next to another small bathroom for late night needs and the laundry. The lower level is much cooler, perfect for avoiding the summer heat.

The attic space was for Eleanor alone. In one half, it harboured a stash of weapons and the ability to train with them. A punching bag and dummy, as well as a small target for throwing knives. There was a pull up bar downstairs already. In the other half of the attic are canvases, paints and sketchbooks. Art supplies and a place to hide them all if people came over. Her personal belongings had been sent over from America so the storage in the attic was already filling.

At the top of the staircase to the lower level was a baby gate so Adelyn wouldn't fall. Eleanor was very careful of her daughter, always watching her while they were outside knowing that a trip to hospital would complicate things.

Eleanor's favourite place to sit – legs crossed on one of the lounges – allows her to watch as Adelyn crawls around and plays with her toys. Already, Eleanor had started to teach her two languages. She made use of Ady's impressionable mind in order to set her up to understand potential threats made against her later in life.

Most of their boxes were already unpacked, due to Eleanor's constant state of movement, but the space still seemed empty. She had yet to order enough furniture to fill the room and only her books had joined them, so the rest of the bookshelves were waiting to be filled. Over the coming month it started to feel more homely.

After two more sessions with Dr Nolan, two ideas were proposed.

The first, Eleanor is to get a service dog. It is quickly accepted within the NAP team, since Eleanor needs something to pick up on shifts in her behaviour and stress levels and be able to calm her down. A service dog could do just that. Her eating habits also needed to be policed, as she still hadn't been eating enough. The dog could, and would, be trained to handle any of her episodes. To take her down without harm and keep people away from her as well. And to protect Adelyn when she was unable.

The second was her getting a job. She needed an income, and while she would always be partially financially supported by Zach – who felt for the girl completely alone in the world – they decided it would be best if she earned her own income as well. Nothing too big, just a job at the local general store and café. It would also allow her to get to know some of the locals.

A nanny was hired, to watch over Adelyn while Eleanor was working, but once she started preschool that would occupy much of her time.

The day she starts at the Makarrata General Store and Cafe is slow, the clouds holding the humidity into the atmosphere in preparation for a storm. An ever-attentive student, Eleanor only requires an instruction once before she can replicate the process but remains in stoic silence. However, the other waitress was more than happy to fill the silence – only two years older than Eleanor she knows nearly every person who walks in the door. Glowing with the health of her environment, Rachel was the polar opposite to Eleanor's gloom.

"How's your friend, the one you said was coming to live with you?" she asks during one of their breaks, having been the one to welcome Eleanor before she found the note – the apology that Eleanor had refused to show to anyone in America.

Eleanor pauses for a second, but Ellsie is quick to take over as Nora loses the words.

"He didn't make it. We decided it would be better for him to stay away," Eleanor says. "I have a complicated past, but this is my new chance, far from it all."

Clever techniques she had picked up long ago to stop people asking questions. Mention trauma, they clam up instantly.

"Oh! That's no good," Rachel replies, bubbly demeanour flattened a little. "At least you have a nanny to look after Adelyn, and she can start preschool next year, can't she?"

Just as planned.

"Yes, she is already very talkative so I have no doubt she will figure it all out quickly." The smile Eleanor pulls onto her face appears genuine but fades as Rachel turns to serve a new customer.

The bubbling blonde introduces her to many people – mostly locals – throughout the day. It surely surprised a great many people when Eleanor remembered their names without a thought, but none thought it weird enough to ask.

It took a few weeks, but soon enough, Kenichi paid his first visit, to take her to get her service dog.

Chapter 4

Eleanor – accompanied by Dr Nolan and Kenichi – keeps Adelyn on her hip as she follows the two doctors into the building. A few faint barks can be heard from further into the compound and Adelyn immediately begins to grin but keeps herself quiet as her mother had instructed. She had already been talked to about not patting their new family member unless she was told she was allowed to.

In conjunction with Kenichi, Dr Nolan had had no issues in diagnosing multiple disorders that would qualify Eleanor for a certified Service Dog (as was the law in Australia).

Firstly, her eating disorder and overworking both impacted her physical and mental health, and these were things they quickly decided she needed to have support in managing.

Then came her mental illnesses. While neither of the doctors could pinpoint her split personality, it mattered little. Complex post-traumatic stress disorder – CPTSD – was the major one. She still reacted badly to dreams and loud noises. More importantly, her reactions were dangerous to others.

Which is why they had decided the dog should be a German Shepherd, much like Zach's dog. Easily trainable, loyal and protective, but still able to notice anxiety. And large enough to knock Eleanor down. He would also stay in her room with her, to assist with nightmares, so a friendly disposition was important.

They had driven quite far to find a dog already trained to handle her specific problems, since she needed him to work without having to train him too much. But they had found one, a four-year-old who was ready to start his work.

"Diana, could you come sign these please?" Kenichi calls, the girl nodding obediently as she steps up.

The ink flows easily, her cursive script neat as she finishes. The woman at the desk smiles widely as she places the pen down, filing the papers easily.

"Brilliant, we have put him in a room already, if you'd like to follow me..." she says, beginning to walk down the hallway.

Kenichi pauses, taking Adelyn out of her mother's arms before gesturing for Eleanor to walk in front on the way down. Holding a door open, the woman gestures for the group to enter the room, Eleanor first. A dog is sitting attentively next to his handler, large, with beautiful brown eyes and a tan coat. Black marks his back and face, ears pricked in attention.

Eleanor cannot help but smile at him.

"His name is Captain. He is very loyal and will attach to a new owner incredibly quickly. Once you take him home, he will realise you are now his handler and love you forever." The woman smiles, gesturing for the man to bring him closer. "He's very attentive and can tell if someone has eaten recently enough without problem."

The man stops about a meter away, hand still on a short lead.

"Feel free to give him some pats when I pass his lead to you, it will put his attention properly on you, since you will hold his lead," he says. "He should still alert if you are patting him."

He carefully passes the lead over to Eleanor, who crouches down to greet the canine as he sits in front of her. Letting him sniff her hand, she kindly scratches his head, stopping as he bumps his nose against her knee. When she looks up, the handler is rolling his eyes.

"That's his alert for food," he says as her head tilts in question. "Have you eaten today?"

Eleanor pauses before answering, somewhat quietly, "no."

"He won't stop until you eat, he's gone at it for an hour before," the man chuckles, grabbing a snack from the table and chucking it to her. "Though, it was a good way to prove my point."

With a glance at Kenichi – who is scowling at her – Eleanor finishes the muesli bar quickly looking back to the dog as he wags his tail.

"How do I reward him for doing the right thing?" she asks quietly, still crouched.

"Tell him he's a 'good boy' and give him a few pats, and you should get a clicker that tells him he did the correct thing as well. Occasional treats are fine, but we'd suggest getting a toy for when you know you won't be triggered, he likes tug of war toys," he replies. "He'll get in your way, or bark if you are overworking yourself, annoy you enough to stop. If he feels you getting anxious, he will paw at your leg. If you believe you can handle it, tell him you're okay in a strong voice and hold out an open hand to his face. If you do not improve or get worse, he will alert again, or if you get significantly worse, he might put himself in your lap or jump to put his paws on your shoulders."

Eleanor nods in understanding, letting the dog come closer so she can pat his side.

"If he senses your becoming violent, or panicked, he will move anyone nearby away from you. I believe your doctors are devising ways to manage this occurring, so whoever is trained to do that will be known to him. If you are in control of yourself, you can say his name forcefully with your hand out. He will also go with someone else if you tell him to. Say, your daughter needed to go somewhere while you were doing something safe for you, you could send him with her," he continues. "If someone attacks you, he will place himself between you and the attacker but will only guard unless you give him the command which is his name and attack. He will only follow that order if he trusts the person."

"Good," Eleanor nods, standing up again. "What are his commands for everyday things?"

The woman explains quickly, handing over a small booklet of information. She suggests introducing Adelyn.

Smiling gratefully, Eleanor hangs Captain's lead over his back, telling him to stay as she steps away to take Adelyn back off Kenichi. She kneels back in front of Captain, waiting for a few seconds as he stays perfectly still, eyes only on her.

"Okay," she says softly. "Come here, gentle."

He makes no noise as he pads closer to them, Eleanor placing a hand on his vest as he extends his nose carefully to Adelyn. She waits patiently, looking towards her mother, who nods in assurance. Adelyn's small hand strokes Captains snout, the dog lightly exhaling a breath as he nuzzles her, very gently.

They stay for a few more hours, going through all his commands. Dr Nolan leaves much earlier than everyone else, but Kenichi waits with her until they finally leave. Captain takes his place, buckled in behind the driver's seat with Adelyn in her seat next to him.

"Shall we stop for lunch?" Kenichi asks as they pass into a town on their way back to Eleanor's home.

"Sure, just find a café somewhere," Eleanor shrugs, "I have some food for Adelyn in my bag."

With a nod, they find a nice café, Captain sticking loyally to Eleanor's heels as they walk in and find a seat, placing Adelyn in a highchair as they sit. Eleanor can feel the weird glances she's getting, her turtleneck (she wore them most days, in place for covering her scar with make-up) snug around her upper half. She ignores them, ordering a plain burger and chips.

"Have you made some friends?" Kenichi asks as they wait. "Met people?"

"I see a lot of people at work, so I know quite a few, and I'm friends with maybe two," she replies softly. "Amy is my neighbour, works for ASIO. But I'm being careful not to let her in on anything. She isn't working much at the moment anyway. The other is a girl I work with, Rachel. She's a few years older than I am, very talkative, but I like that she holds conversation. She is way too bubbly for her own good."

Kenichi chuckles, shaking his head at the girl.

Pausing slightly, he asks, "ASIO?"

"Australian CIA, except they do a decent job of keeping their existence secret."

He left early the next day, returning to America before he would be missed. The search to try and track down Nikolas was in full swing, Angeli Terra heavily on Michael's case as they continued to find no leads. The King was not happy.

Captain settled in well, very quickly discovering his new owner's behaviours. Eleanor would have sworn he found too much joy in alerting her need to eat, bumping his nose against her leg until she gave in. It was working though; she was putting on a little weight. Her portions still weren't large, but he would make sure she ate three times a day.

And he had quickly gotten used to sleeping on the end of her bed, jumping awake when she did and burying himself into her arms. Not to mention, she made a point of letting him out whenever she woke.

Chapter 5

No one had told her that there would be canine units patrolling this particular event. Lots of guards? Yes. Stringent security checks? Also, yes. Canine units that would be able to smell her on the assassinated person? Nope. No mention. Not a peep.

If they had told her, she would have gone for a sniper shot, even if it were messier. In hindsight, being chased through the woods in a dress is also messy.

The dogs had arrived after the discovery, while she was still hanging around to create deniability of her sudden disappearance if someone ran into her as she left. The minute the dogs showed up, she started to slip out the back door, away from the opulence of a ballroom and through the gardens. It was far too early to call in her driver, and that would arouse suspicion of course, so Eleanor makes her way into the dark forest with a vague plan of making it to the highway on the opposite fence line.

Her pair of beautiful heels get discarded in a creek as she breaks into a jog through the twisting trees. From the house, a set of dangerously excited barks echo into the woods. The jog turns into a sprint as she attempts to distance herself from the crime scene.

Unfortunately, the barks get louder and human yells follow her into the woods. Eleanor had experience with dogs, even canine units, while training, therefore knew that they would not stop hunting her if she stayed on foot. With one hand grasping the bottom of her dress, she sprints faster over the uneven ground towards the slight flashes of light now peeking through the trees. Even still, the dogs sound closer and closer.

She breaks through the tree line with a flurry of limbs as torches appear behind her, close enough that if they were in the open, they would have an easy shot. With the promise of imminent death on her mind, Eleanor begins to sprint down the highway, waving her arms and running just enough into an oncoming lane for the biker in it to stop violently. She drags him off just as the dogs break through the trees and is riding away before their handlers get the chance to spot her.

As she arrives at the arranged spot, long having abandoned the bike for another in a shopping centre, a scowl fixes on her face.

She faces her handler and says, in German, "you didn't tell me there would be dogs!"

With a nonchalant shrug, he replies, "we didn't know."

Eleanor keeps her fury on him but doesn't bother arguing as he ushers her into the car and hands her the simple little pill, as always.

Chapter 6

I must give Vanessa Nolan some credit. She discovered Eleanor's secret quicker than anyone else. Even Nikolas. However, she was also a trained professional who was literally taking notes on her behaviour. But she realised exactly what was different about Eleanor.

It terrified Eleanor, of course, but making her squirm was the point of her therapy, to find out what makes her upset and work on it.

"Eleanor, could you tell me why you never touch your cup of water?" Dr Nolan asks as the girl settles into her seat.

She had long figured out that she needed to warm Eleanor up into her sessions. Anything too deep too quick sent Eleanor into a mental spiral that usually ended with threats of violence. Even still, Eleanor remains completely uncomfortable as she considers the question.

"I don't trust it's not poisoned," she answers. "I mean I know you wouldn't poison it, doesn't mean someone else hasn't. It's a bad habit."

"I've been thinking..." Dr Nolan starts, "about your wild moods. Before I propose my idea, do you have anything to tell me?"

Eleanor answers without a thought, as she always did when she was concealing something.

"No."

"Can I count on you to tell me the truth, even if I am correct?" she asks next, receiving a nod before she continues. "It had me stumped for a while, but then I realised. Extreme traumatic event at a young age. Need for survival. Extreme environmental shift. Abusive treatment. Fast forward to today. Extreme mood shifts. Almost as if there are two of you. The frequency threw me originally, you are not like any recorded case. But I truly believe you have dissociative identity disorder."

Vanessa watches as Eleanor's face pales.

"There are only two of you. The girl who lost her parents, who doesn't want to murder anyone. Who is hurt, and upset, and wants to punish herself. Then there is the one who enjoys the fighting. The killing. Who will protect her other side to the grave. Do they have names?"

Eleanor's eyes lose focus, staring blindly into space. Her lips move only slightly, as if talking. Then her gaze turns to the woman.

"You promise me you will not tell anyone, not even Kenichi. I will tell him myself, at some point. Just, keep this to yourself, please?"

"I promise…"

There is a pause as Eleanor takes a breath.

"Nora and Ellsie," she whispers. "I'm Nora, the first one. Ellsie is the second."

"And how did you discover her?"

"The first time they wanted me to shoot, it was just a target, but I couldn't pick up the gun. Too scared," Eleanor explains. "She appeared, took over. It was like I was watching what was happening through a screen. She killed the two men beating us. Then she started talking to me, consoling me. I called her Ellsie, because my mother used to call me that when I needed to be brave. She called me Nora, because that's what Kate would call me."

"So you two can communicate?" Vanessa asks.

"Yes. And she can hold my hand, when I'm in control. Lend me some of her confidence. I… Ever since she arrived, I haven't ever had full control over us, not a day where I cannot hear or feel her. She was… most of the time between eight and sixteen Ellsie was in control," Eleanor says, hands finding Captain's head as he paws once at her leg.

The uncharacteristic stumbles in Eleanor's speech puzzles the therapist. She hadn't expected it to be so easy to make Eleanor admit to the illness.

"How did you wake up and take back control?" the doctor presses, deciding it to be her last question on the topic before giving her a little space.

"When I was raped. It pulled me, Nora, to the surface. I took full control when I found out I was pregnant. I was conscious of everything that Ellsie did, even clearer than she was herself," Eleanor answers honestly. "Nikolas—" she takes a slow breath "—he proposed that my drawings were a way of me handling the pain. That that was me breaking through slightly. The crosses on the forehead were all Ellsie though... Taking pride in her work—"

"I was not taking pride in my work, I just did it because it helped to release the fight in me, once I had finished."

Dr Nolan looks on in curiosity, but true to her plan, doesn't ask any more questions on the topic.

"Thank you, for being honest with me," she says. "Now, how's Captain been going?"

"Ellsie," Eleanor mutters when she finally gets to her room. "How did she figure it out?"

The other personality takes over, watching herself in the mirror.

"She is a trained professional, she would have to be familiar with the concept," Ellsie replies. "And we were being quite erratic. I thought she would find out quicker. But I mean, three months is quicker than he did..."

They go quiet, laying back on their bed and glancing at the hoodie dumped on the other pillow. It was way too warm in November to wear, but the smell still helps her to sleep. That and the lavender bear that sits on her bedside table. She had heated it a few times during the winter, but even spring was too warm to consider heating it. But having the weight on her stomach helped anyway.

Adelyn would also occasionally join her mother. The child had already developed a keen sense for when her mum was upset, so every so often she would slink into her mother's bed to sleep. Or if they were still awake, make her way to where Eleanor was sitting and curl up in her lap. Eleanor loved to hold her daughter close, read her stories to get her mind off other things. And Adelyn understood that she still needed to sleep in her own bed most of the time, so there was really no consequence to holding her daughter close every so often.

Adelyn had started picking up German quickly and had figured out to only speak to her mother or Dr Nolan – who she didn't see often, but enough to make the connection – in the language. For a nearly two-year-old, she was a quick learner and could hold enough of a conversation that Eleanor wasn't worried about her starting preschool at the start of the New Year.

It would just be the three of them – Eleanor, Adelyn and Captain – for Christmas – Kenichi is required to go to visit his parents this year – and the decision was made for everyone else to stay in America. Upon hearing this, Rachel – who had decided Eleanor was now her friend, and as such couldn't miss having a traditional Christmas Lunch – invited her and her daughter to have lunch with her and her family (just her parents and brother's family, which included a two-year-old for Adelyn to play with). After double checking, Eleanor finally agreed to go.

They opened their presents at home, mostly books and art supplies for Eleanor, and toys for Adelyn, before leaving around 11 to go to her friend's house. Adelyn had a great time playing with the other child, and Eleanor found she enjoyed the lunch more than she thought she would. But with still no word from Nikolas, she found she was missing his presence more than usual.

Captain stayed at her side the entire day, even as another dog tried to play with him. He held no care for anyone that wasn't his owner or her daughter. When she was working, he would settle into his dog bed in the corner of the shop, constantly watching Eleanor. She hadn't had a proper episode, luckily, but she always made sure to carry headphones, for the loud dry thunderstorms that rolled in during the spring and summer evenings. She also made a habit of ensuring she was home during these times, so no one could see her. What they don't know won't hurt them.

Chapter 7

The decision for Adelyn to start preschool just after her second birthday was an easy one, even though it was generally considered a year early for a child to start preschool. It ran each day of the school week, but only for a few hours, and while Adelyn was the youngest one there, her understanding of her two languages was more than enough to get her by. Riley – their neighbour's daughter – was eight months older than Adelyn and would be starting this year as well.

Eleanor knew that it was the right decision. But the anxiety building up in her chest and running through her mind a thousand miles a minute was unavoidable. Inescapable. So many variables messed indefinitely with her head, that the assassin's mind was unable to allow for organic changes in her life.

But it was the best choice for Adelyn. The best choice for her, in the long run. So, Eleanor forces a smile onto her lips and lifts Adelyn out of her car seat and places her on her hip. She calls Captain out after her, vest on but no lead attached as Eleanor's other hand grabs Adelyn's bag.

"Are you ready Ady?" she asks, bouncing the grinning two-year-old on her hip. Even if she was completely unsure of sending her daughter off on her own, she could certainly act the part.

"Yes!" Adelyn replies, looking across the road to the school.

With a nod – to herself really – Eleanor crosses, Captain close on her heels. She swings open the little gate and walks closer to the other adults. Their children already playing.

Eleanor recognises most of them – only by name, however. One of them has a dog, already straining at his lead as Captain ignores him dutifully. But refusing to take a chance, Eleanor swaps Adelyn onto her other hip and moves him onto her other side, placing herself between the two dogs.

At least the owner has the dignity to look sorry as her dog continues to strain at its collar.

"Diana, isn't it?" Amy – her neighbour – asks as she stops at the group. For the benefit of everyone else, Eleanor is sure.

"Yes, Adelyn is starting today," she smiles, forced. "I must say I'm more nervous than she is."

"Haven't been away from her much?"

"No and, when I have, she has been safe at home," Eleanor admits, "but she is much more social than I am, so it wouldn't be fair to keep her at home until she's three."

Amy smiles kindly, turning to introduce her to the rest of the group. There was something about the way the woman considered her that put Eleanor on edge. It probably had something to do with her occupation, but it was clear enough that Amy thought something was off.

"This is my neighbour Diana, she moved in mid last year to Tony's old place," she says. "Though I'm sure you've seen her around, she works at the shop."

A few nod in recognition, a few greeting her as one of the teachers walks up.

"Is this Adelyn?" she asks, attention solely on the child. Eleanor had thoroughly screened her over the holidays, nothing was found out of order.

"Yes, she's very excited," Eleanor grins, placing the girl on the floor with a kiss to her head.

Adelyn takes her bag without problem and says a cheerful hello to the teacher. Before she walks away, Eleanor crouches down, hugging her daughter again. The hold lingers for a few seconds, the mother having to force herself backwards.

"Be good," she tells her in German.

Adelyn answers in the same language, "I will Mummy!"

"Okay," Eleanor smiles, back to English. "Love you."

"Love you!"

Eleanor stays crouching until she is a few meters away, giving Captain a look as he slowly raises a paw. She jumps up before he can hit her, scratching his head quickly before asking him to sit. As she turns back to the group, she finds them watching her in interest. Half an eye stays on her daughter. So very protective.

"You speak German?" the red head named Marie asks.

"Yes, I spent some time there as a child," Eleanor answers. "I decided to teach Adelyn, since learning multiple languages is easier as a child and can increase their ability to learn." A lie. It was so Adelyn could translate her ramblings if she needed help.

"Does she know how to differentiate?" another asks, and though Eleanor searches for malice in the polite tone, she resigns to find none.

"Yes, she knows only to speak to me in it, and I have a friend in America who does as well," Eleanor answers easily. "She's quite smart, really."

They smile, starting to say their goodbyes as Eleanor lingers, Captain starting to bump his nose against her thigh. Attempting to stop him, he just starts hitting her hand.

"You are a pain in my ass," Eleanor mutters, adjusting the strap of her singlet as she begins to walk away.

"A few of us are going to get drinks and a bite at the café next door, if you'd like to join us?" Amy asks as she starts to walk, having waited for her.

"Is the other dog going to be there?" Eleanor asks in response, hand still trying to stop Captain from making a wet spot on her shorts.

"No, they don't allow normal dogs."

As if trying to prove a point, Captain bumps her as soon as Amy finishes and receives a rather irritated glare from his owner. She plants the smile back on her face to respond.

"That would be nice, thank you. I'll just go grab my purse," Eleanor agrees.

She takes note of Amy's happy smile as she crosses the thin road.

Purse may be the wrong word, as she pulls out a large tote bag, stuffed to the brim with items Dr Nolan had suggested may be of use in the event of an episode. She takes out the jumper and places it the back seat – not before her face presses into the familiar softness and she takes a deep breath. Eleanor secures Captain's lead to his vest as she shuts the door, locks the car and jogs back across the road to meet Amy. Captain, content with her intention to get food, stops alerting, however, sticks close to her heel as they enter the small café and Eleanor's muscles begin to tense.

The town is small, built more for tourist day trips than extended stays with one street running through and a few cafes and gift shops on either side. The post office has a small general store built onto it as well and most of the buildings are heritage listed from the early colonial days. For the most part it was quiet, but a nice weekend could get a lot of traffic. Mostly Eleanor stays in on those weekends, but exposure in small doses was good for her.

The other two who spoke to her earlier are already sitting at a table for four, and Eleanor takes a seat backing onto the wall, on the outer edge so Captain can lay next to her out of the way. There is little conversation as they decide their orders – a decaf latte with one sugar and a serve of scones with jam and cream for Eleanor – but as they hand over their menus to the waitress, chatter starts. Mostly directed towards the one they didn't know.

"Where did you move from?" Donna asks kindly.

"America, I was living near Washington DC until I finished school last year," Eleanor answers easily, she was well used to using a cover story, especially as this one was based on truth. "I wanted to move back to the country I was born in."

The women look surprised. Probably because of her age.

"Why were you in America?" Marie continues.

"My mother had friends there. We were living in Germany when my parents died, I spent some time in the foster system there, but things happened, and I was sent to America. I was glad to leave," Eleanor explains. "The family I got placed with are quite rich, and they were happy to pay for my move here. Really, it was a giant legal nightmare, but it happened, somehow."

They seemed happy with the answer, and while Eleanor can feel Captain watching her, she is confident enough that he doesn't get up. Nevertheless, her knuckles are white beneath the table, straining to keep her hand from rising to her hidden scar. It was aching – as it did whenever she even thought about the months before her move – just enough to be distracting.

"Are you here alone?" Donna questions, receiving a short nod. "Where is Adelyn's father?"

Captain sits up from the floor, a movement noticed by them all, but he lies back down as Eleanor tells him to.

"Prison," Eleanor replies shortly, lips pursed slightly. "I have sole custody, and he isn't allowed to see either of us."

Blunt. Shut down. The tension pinning Eleanor's face in a tense scowl finishes the conversation, but the two she had just met share a slight look that doesn't pass Eleanor's notice.

The waitress returns, the drinks being dispensed with promises of the food coming soon. Eleanor is glad for the interruption, taking a long sip from her drink before placing it back down.

"It's quite isolated to be living alone..." Donna worries.

"I was going to be joined by my boyfriend, but it was decided he shouldn't come. I have a lot of people who do not like me," Eleanor continues, Ellsie absolutely fine with covering this weakness. "But I'm safe here, so that's nothing to worry about." Though somehow, even Ellsie seems unsure as she speaks. Her eyes focus on something in the back of the room for a second and Captain finally places his head under her hand as she shakes herself back into reality.

Peace was settled, and at least she wouldn't have to tell anyone else. The mothers would do that job for her. She hangs in town for the rest of the day, anxious eyes continuously scanning the people around her. No one asks why exactly, but the lingering focus on the small, sandstone preschool was clear enough if you knew her. It would take a while for her to be able to relax while her daughter was away.

Chapter 8

Something most peculiar happened in February, on Eleanor's birthday in fact. This peculiarity would become a normality over the next period of Eleanor's life.

There is an attack on Florida, like there was most months. Ever since the first attack, it had become clear that Nikolas had integrated back into the Daemones seamlessly, planting the story that he had so carefully crafted from the burning pain of betrayal they found him in. Eleanor had not been able to be revived and had died on the way to Angeli Terra. They brought him back as a sympathy. He had spun it into more hatred for his brother, who couldn't save her, and they allowed it. He slipped right back in as if he had never left.

But after this attack, the NAP strike team finds a present, left out of the sight of cameras, but easy enough for the team to find when they arrive. Wrapped in delicate paper, and with a string tied in a bow around it, the small present waits for attention. In beautiful cursive on the front the present is dedicated to Eleanor. Nancy Randall runs every test she can think of on the small package, but once it was decided there were no trackers or potentially harmful objects, she has nothing left to do with it. Kenichi is the one who argues for it to be sent to Eleanor, in fact, he accompanies it – along with other gifts from the team – to visit her.

Eleanor is neither excited nor mad, just quiet with broiling acceptance. Her night is spent curled up in her room, the weight of her lavender bear on her lap and the book in her hands as slow tears trickle down her smooth cheeks. By morning, she shelves it with some others and moves past the present. The gift was a hardback copy of 'The Librarian of Auschwitz', in the original Spanish. She reads it the day after Kenichi leaves, while Adelyn is in preschool.

Kenichi can't afford to stay long, there is still work to be done, so the visit is brief. However, the familiar face builds a little bit of Eleanor's confidence back up and returns just a little colour to her face.

Even with the visit, and her regular therapy sessions, Eleanor's nightmares are getting much, much worse the later it gets into February. Captain had become more attentive each time she went out, constantly on her heels and prepared to step between her and a potential trigger. She makes sure she has the few days before and after the anniversary of her parents' death off work and manages to avoid a major episode as she comes into the date. Both Amy and Rachel notice her clear distraction, but don't dare to ask her as Eleanor continues to retreat from society.

Eleanor is tired. With only a few hours of sleep a night, and still not eating enough – Captain was trying his hardest, but when she kept risking throwing up, there was only so much he could force – the mental toll of keeping herself constantly in check is exhausting her. Ellsie was getting horrendously restless as well. Neither of them would admit it, but the bloodlust that had kept her alive for so long has built up more than she would admit. Nora knows of course, which only pushes her further into exhaustion as she refuses to let her violent side loose.

Dr Nolan is the most worried, seeing all the progress they had made together disintegrate into a puddle of anxious mess. The only suggestion she can make is to let Ellsie have a safe outlet for her rage: boxing, karate, or the like. Eleanor starts to search for an option, but there is the ever-present fear in the back of her mind that Ellsie might go too far and accidentally – or worse, purposefully – hurt someone.

For the next few weeks, she only emerges from her house to drop Adelyn at preschool and pick her up, spending the rest of her time painting, drawing, or training – which she can only do so much of before Captain stops her. Adelyn cuddles up to her mother each night while they watched TV, but Eleanor makes her sleep in her own bed.

It isn't too surprising when Eleanor starts to get physically sick after the anniversary has passed. She brushes it off, but Kenichi keeps a close watch on her vitals through the band on her ankle, merely a black strip of hardware the size of a watchband with patterns etched into the metal.

~

A fist slams into her ribs, making her splutter out her breaths in thick coughs that tear up her throat. Her eyes are watering, and her head is swimming as she straightens up to face her Vater again. The coughing doesn't stop as she does so, unable to redirect the movement through her heavily blocked nose.

"Please…" she manages to get out. "I am going to pass out."

The Dunkler Bischof merely continues, though pulling his punches slightly. On instinct Eleanor deflects them, movements sluggish and weak.

"An ACE must be able to fight in all conditions. Being sick is not an excuse your targets will accept to let you kill them easier," he mutters. "You have to fight through it."

"A sick agent cannot do their job as well, why would they send us on assignments sick?"

He pauses, gripping her chin to make her look at him.

"Sickness is weakness. Agents must never be weak. You will not be weak, understand me? Get sick too many times and they will eliminate their problem. You are merely a machine, machines can be replaced," he explains roughly. "Now get over it and fight."

~

While Eleanor isn't working, she stops at the shop on the way home, planning to get some milk. Her head is swimming with fever but growing up in the Berühmte Söldner means she ignores the sweat on her brow and her weak limbs and walks through it. Really, it isn't healthy, but she cares little.

Rachel is working as she enters the shop, Eleanor moves to the fridges, offering a weak smile. As she makes it to the counter to pay, her friend frowns.

"You look like crap," she mutters, taking Eleanor's cash.

"Just a little head cold, and I'm pale normally," Eleanor assures, but Captain starts to whine, pawing at his owner's leg. He always seems to know.

When she tries to brush him off her head starts swimming, Eleanor braces herself to walk and Rachel quickly realises that she is much worse than she said. Jumping quickly around the counter, the blonde takes her friend's arm as they step out of the shop. Captain is trying to paw with both legs, almost pouncing on Eleanor's feet as he does so.

"I'm not sure you can drive home," Rachel mutters as she steers Eleanor towards a seat, now having wrapped an arm around her waist to help her walk.

Rachel is able to keep Eleanor on her feet as she slumps, calling for someone to grab a chair as she gingerly lowers Eleanor onto it. As soon as she is down, Captain places himself between Eleanor and everyone else, refusing to let anyone near. He stops only so Rachel can get the ringing phone out of his vest, answering it in confusion.

"Hello? Who is this?" she asks, Captain nudging Eleanor's limp hand.

"I'm Dr Kenichi Tanaka, I'm a friend of Diana's from the States," the man on the other end of the phone answers. "Is Diana with you?"

"Yes, she just passed out at the shop. I think she's got the flu or something," Rachel answers. "How did you know to call?"

"The band on her ankle reads her vitals, just like a Fit-Bit, we get notified if she loses consciousness," he answers. "Did she say anything before she passed out?"

"Just that she had a little head cold. Captain was going berserk," she says. "And he won't let anyone near her now."

"Yeah, he's trained to do that..." the Doctor goes quiet, thinking, "she will freak out if she wakes up in a hospital, so you can't take her to one... And she won't accept medicine off anyone but me." He sighs deeply. "You're Rachel, right?"

"Uh, yes. How did you know that?" the 20-year-old frowns.

"Diana calls me weekly. Are you able to contact her neighbour Amy Williams and get her to drive Diana home and watch over her?" he asks, already starting to move as he speaks to her. "I will be there in about 15 hours, so someone will have to pick up Adelyn as well."

"I can, but she really needs to go to the hospital," Rachel answers worriedly.

"She can't. If she does, she will undoubtably create a scene when she wakes up, and in her state, she will either pass out again, which could put her in a coma, or she may try to fight her way out," Kenichi explains. "People could get hurt, and she just needs to be calm. She really doesn't like hospitals. Will you do this for me?"

"I will, Amy just pulled in, so that should be easy enough. But Adelyn probably won't let anyone other than her mother pick her up…"

"Just tell her purple irises are beautiful, she'll go with you then. But make sure you assure her that her mother is okay," Kenichi sighs, "I'll be there as soon as I can."

As the call hangs up, Amy jogs up the stairs in confusion, eyes on Eleanor.

"She's sick and passed out. Her doctor friend in America just called and said we cannot take her to the hospital 'cause she'll freak out, so he is coming and will be here early tomorrow. He wanted me to get you to take her home and watch her until he arrives," Rachel relays. "And apparently she won't take any drugs off anyone but him…"

"I can do that, when do you get off your shift?" Amy agrees, realising it was better not to argue.

"Soon, I was going to pick Adelyn up, he gave me something to tell her to get her to come. I'll take Eleanor's car as well."

"Okay then…"

Kenichi was in California, in fact, had just finished working when he gets the alert. Luckily, they were able to get him on a plane over to Australia within an hour (it was a stretch, but he wanted to get there as quick as possible). Everyone knew her aversion to doctors, and if she was at the point of passing out, he needed to treat her before she got too sick.

He knocks on Eleanor's door around midnight, being greeted by her tired neighbour.

"She is such a pain in the ass when she is sick," Amy mutters after he introduces himself, waving him in. "'I'm not sick', 'I'm fine'," she mocks.

"Why do you think we got her the dog? He's the only way we can get her to consistently eat," Kenichi mutters, already finding his way downstairs. "She still got a fever?"

"39°C, hasn't risen but hasn't lowered either. And she won't take any Paracetamol," Amy fills him in. "Has she never been sick before or something?"

"Very little, and there's problems in her past around sickness so she will never admit she needs help. Moreso, she refuses to take drugs off people other than me because they could be trying to poison or harm her," Kenichi replies, pausing outside her shut door. "Thanks for your help today. You can go home now; I've been taking care of her for a while, so I know what lies ahead. Adelyn asleep?"

"Has been for a few hours. Captain wouldn't get off Eleanor's bed," Amy answers, starting to walk away.

"Thank you. You're a good friend," Kenichi finishes, slipping into Eleanor's room. "Now, now. What's happened here?" he asks as the girl groans.

"You took less time than you should have," Eleanor frowns, voice a faint moan as she rolls her head to look at the clock.

"Yes, I was helping clean up a little mess from your boyfriend in California," he replies, sticking a temperature gauge in her mouth before she can reply.

As he pulls it out, she mutters, "he's not my boyfriend."

"Yes, sure. If you had the option he would be, thus, nickname," Kenichi returns. "39.2, take this."

She eyes the pills he holds out.

"I have liquid form, and I will shove it down your throat. So, take the damn pills," he growls, smiling happily as she takes them and swallows them dry. "Brilliant, now, why did you ignore my instructions to take some medication earlier this week?"

Eleanor rolls her head away, cheeks sucking in in shame.

"I didn't know which you meant," she admits. "I've only ever been given nameless pills."

Kenichi sighs, sitting lightly on the edge of the bed.

"I'm sorry, I should have been more specific. I should have realised," he apologises, placing his hand lightly on hers. "Panadol, for fevers and pain. And otherwise just ask, Eleanor. Buying medicine from drug stores is fine, they can tell you what to get, but if you must ask me that is fine."

Eleanor nods slightly, eyes still turned away.

"And if you are sick you need to admit it, Eleanor. You are allowed to be sick, it's normal," he continues, "and if Captain starts alerting, you need to listen to him. He can tell when you are unwell."

She stays quiet and faced away, eyes blinking blearily as Kenichi stands, grabbing the water bottle off her bedside table. He sits back down, gripping her upper arm carefully.

"Sit up, you need fluids," he says, supporting her with one arm, while the other lifts the bottle to her lips. "You weren't sleeping enough earlier this month, were you? You were so exhausted your immune system couldn't handle it."

As the bottle lowers, Eleanor leans forward, letting her head rest against his shoulder. Kenichi places it on the bedside table, wrapping an arm around her waist in comfort.

"I should have come, I know how you react," he whispers. "You need company."

"I do not need your mothering," she replies, though the retort is half-hearted.

"You need a shoulder to lean on," he returns softly. "I know you miss Nikolas more than you will admit. I saw your face when you received his present, you fell in love with him."

Eleanor doesn't move, eyes shut tight.

"Maybe. It was stupid to hope," she says. "There's no point in wishing what could have been. There is just what is."

"Sometimes it is only the dreams that can keep us afloat."

"My dreams serve only to drag me down."

Kenichi pulls back slowly, lowering Eleanor back onto her pillow.

"Get some sleep, I'll check your temperature in an hour," he says. "You will most likely dream, but Captain refuses to leave your side, and I will just be next door if they get bad. I'll see you in the morning."

She nods weakly, eyes already drifting shut. But her hand stays linked in his. He waits at her side for a while, until he decides the drugs have kicked in and he checks her temperature again.

It was lower, but still high. Acceptable, he decides as he stands. He pauses slightly at the door, to glance back at her and after a moment, he passes through, shutting it quietly behind him.

"Is she okay?" a small voice calls from a few metres away. Adelyn.

"She will be," Kenichi assures. "Now aren't you supposed to be in bed? It's late."

"I heard you arrive..." she answers. "She said she was okay."

Kenichi smiles softly, walking over to the girl.

"She says a lot of things to try and protect you. Don't worry, I know to keep a little closer watch now," he says. "Now, off to bed. Or I'll tell her you were awake late."

To his surprise, Adelyn fixes him with a smouldering glare. And with all the sass of a two-year-old turns on her heel and stalks back into her room. Kenichi huffs a laugh, turning on his own heel and dropping onto the guest room bed.

Chapter 9

In her fevered state, Eleanor manages to sleep through the night, Kenichi rising well before she does. Even Adelyn is awake before her mother, finding only her 'uncle' in the kitchen.

"She's on the mend, sleeping nice and sound," he explains, moving over to lift the girl up into her seat. "What would you like for breakfast?"

Adelyn takes full advantage of his offer and is happily munching away on pancakes as her mother drags her leaden limbs up the staircase. Kenichi grins as he sees her, offering a plate in her direction as she kisses Adelyn's head and sits gingerly next to her.

"We only have pancakes on special occasions," she mutters, grinning on the side to her daughter.

Adelyn looks very pleased with herself as Eleanor pokes her side.

"I'll take her to preschool, you rest," Kenichi says, already packing her bag. "We'll talk when I get back."

Eleanor nods slowly, standing weakly to start brushing through Adelyn's dead straight hair. As the pair leave, Kenichi sends her a look, she hadn't finished her breakfast.

She does, if only to skip that argument, and washes the dishes. When he returns, Eleanor is sitting with a foot tucked underneath her, reading a book. Waiting until he has settled in a couch across from her, Eleanor speaks without removing her eyes from her book.

"You drugged me," she mutters, Kenichi tensing a little.

"I did. You needed to properly rest," he replies. "It wasn't a heavy dose."

"I have a particular hatred for sedatives," Eleanor continues, now glancing across to him. "You know that."

"I'm sorry, but it was necessary. You needed to stay asleep," Kenichi sighs.

"You should be glad I didn't throw up the minute I smelled food," she mutters in response, getting only an eyeroll.

Eleanor goes quiet for a few minutes, the doctor frowning slightly as Captain rises from his bed across the room to sit quietly next to her, large head resting on her thigh.

"You said it was *his* attack? Why you were closer…" she asks a few seconds later, hand already rubbing circles onto his head.

"Yeah, nothing too major," Kenichi answers. "He is leaving them alive, which is why I have to keep travelling so much. I was trained as a field doctor anyway."

Eleanor whispers so quietly he can hardly hear her, "they won't like it. He needs to be more careful."

Kenichi grimaces, desperate to take Eleanor's mind off it, but finds himself unable to stop himself as he says, "as much as I hate to say it, Nikolas can handle himself. He will adjust if he needs to, he will do anything to keep you safe."

Silence falls upon them as Eleanor reaches to pick up a distraction, but her hand stops partway there, hovering in the still air as her mind turns over. Kenichi leaves her to decide what she wants to do as her hand slowly withdraws and her young eyes – for they had never seemed so young before now as she looks towards him with simmering question.

"Your family is Japanese right?" Eleanor asks quietly and continues after he immediately nods. "Then why do you speak German?"

Against his better judgement, Kenichi laughs.

"I never considered that you wouldn't know that," he says with a grin covering his face. He forces himself to sober before he continues. "My parents were humanitarian aid workers my entire childhood. They worked freelance as doctors and since they had studied internationally, had friends in Germany when the wall fell. I grew up there with them as they provided free medical assistance and taught the children pro-bono while the Government was righting itself. They moved just after I left for university."

Eleanor stews over his response as he watches her closely.

"That's why you knew how to treat me. You grew up with people scarred by violence…"

Kenichi nods, a faint smile returning to his features as Eleanor scans the room. He'd long noticed that this was her way of finding the words to say among the millions within her head.

"I wanted to do some good, like my parents did. That's why I don't work clinically. When Nancy needed to make a team to accompany Michael, I was the best option as I can mediate better than most of them," he offers, however hesitates before he continues. The thought seems to appear in both their minds at the same time as their eyes meet sharply. "No, I don't have any contacts in Germany anymore. I never had many friends there anyway. Most recently I was there to provide care to the Syrian refugees in 2015, I only returned to work on the team."

Eleanor visibly relaxes as Kenichi once again laughs, this time at their similar line of thought.

"Imagine if all this time I was a Berühmte Söldner spy, wouldn't that be a lark," he chuckles, but even still he keeps a wary eye on Eleanor. "You think that if I was, I would tell you I was in Germany for such a long time?"

"No, I don't," Eleanor replies quietly. "If I did, you would know about it by now."

"I know, Ellie. I know."

All that is left to handle, once Eleanor was feeling better and Kenichi returns to America, is Rachel. Amy had been fine with the answers she got, but Rachel hadn't been told anything. Luckily, it was a slow morning when Eleanor finally returns to work.

"You can ask, I know you want to," Eleanor eventually says, looking across the counter from where she was restocking.

Biting her lip, Rachel gives in.

"Why did your friend say you couldn't go to the hospital? Or take medicine?" she asks quietly.

"The hospital: I can go if I take myself there, and am fully conscious, but waking up there… Being unconscious in a hospital bed was how

I got pregnant with Adelyn, it triggers too many things in me," Eleanor explains, passing Captain a treat as he alerts. She was ready to handle it this time. "And I have an immense lack of trust for all people. I'm working on it but taking medicine from people is a little bit of a sore spot. Kenichi is my doctor, so I trust him, other people, not so much."

"Thank you, it was just confusing me," Rachel smiles. "It's understandable, though."

"I am a very confusing person, just ask my therapist," Eleanor half jokes. "You can ask about those things though, if I can't tell you, I will let you know, but it is good for me to talk about it."

Ellsie was speaking, of course. But Nora was relatively calm anyway, Captain not feeling the need to alert again. Her control wasn't completely gone, it seems. Or, at least, her control in that area.

Chapter 10

Captain takes his time finding and settling into his spot on the edge of Dr Nolan's office, careful to keep an eye on Eleanor as he doubts her judgement – as he often does – at sending him away. The carpet where he lies is darkened by his fur, making a bed for him to sit in as Vanessa straightens in her seat.

"Have you noticed anything Captain alerts to that we didn't originally get him for?" Dr Nolan asks as Eleanor delicately places her hands on her neatly tucked in skirt. "Movements he interrupts or any times he introduces himself into a situation?"

Eleanor's eyes stray to the dog and an unconscious smile faintly pulls onto her face as his tongue lolls out of the side of his mouth, perfectly content in the crisp autumn air.

"Some. He has a way of noticing when I'm zoned out," Eleanor shrugs, playing with her shortcut nails. "...he'll place himself on top of me if I've been in one place for a while."

"Are their particular movements?" the therapist continues, pen perched on her notepad.

"Twisting my fingers, clenching my fists. Tracing my stomach..." Eleanor answers, flexing her fingers as she speaks, "playing with my fingernails."

Taking a sip of her water, Dr Nolan gestures for Eleanor to continue.

"I get restless, when I get restless, I twist my fingers or play with my fingernails, sometimes so hard it can damage my joints. I'm not supposed to do it, and he interrupts," she says. "I trace my stomach subconsciously because of Adelyn, usually it shows I'm thinking too deeply. And I clench my fists to stop myself from showing weaknesses, which is a cause for alert."

"Good," Dr Nolan smiles, noting down the response on her paper. "Do you know what weaknesses you're trying to suppress?"

Even in conversation the haze of distraction in Eleanor's eyes is clear. The absent movements that entrap her hands like a second hand on a clock, superfluous but always ticking.

"Touching my throat..." she says quietly. "The scar."

"Why do you stop yourself from doing that?"

Eleanor bites her cracked lips, breath shallow.

"It will draw attention to it, and I don't want to get asked about it," she answers, eyes still unfocused, "neither of us like talking about it, really."

The psychologist frowns slightly in surprise, noting down Eleanor's admission before she asks, "even Ellsie?"

It was odd to find something the daring personality was averse to. So adverse that Dr Nolan can sense the discomfort radiating through their mask.

"Even Ellsie. Possibly even more so Ellsie," Eleanor admits, voice trembling with the control she so clearly is holding – whether on her emotions, or Ellsie, Dr Nolan can't be certain. "She thinks she has to be perfect. It shows she isn't."

"Can I talk to her?"

The request feels strange coming out of Vanessa's mouth as she asks it, like asking a child to please eat more candy or telling a dog to bark all it likes.

With only a blink, Eleanor's back straightens, and her eyes sharpen on the doctor with a cold blankness.

"I am not the one who needs help, doctor," she replies, but her mechanical stiffness worries Dr Nolan. The Ellsie she had come to know was never this proper, never this focused on manners – which is the whole reason Vanessa had begun to worry.

"I don't believe that. You are not exempt from trauma," the woman reprimands. In the face of the murderer, Dr Nolan's words are far less personable than with Nora, her focus never lapsing, and words carefully measured. "It is perfectly acceptable to be worried or scared by something."

"The whole point of me is to be the one who isn't ever scared," Ellsie bites. "I am fine."

"You nearly died. That impacts everyone," Dr Nolan replies calmly, "especially when you are unable to prove yourself again. If they knew anything about the psychology of soldiers like yourself, they never would have pulled you from the field like that..."

"I'm fine," Ellsie insists.

"Then why don't you like to talk about what happened?"

Ellsie cracks her jaw as she considers the hard stare meeting her from the other side of the room, ignoring, but not oblivious to, the shift in Captain's posture as he too considers the tension floating in the air around them.

With a snake-like twist of her head to the side, Eleanor replies, "it is embarrassing..."

"Only to you, Eleanor. People would not be ashamed nor discredit you for saving a school full of people."

Ellsie – to both Nora and Dr Nolan's surprise – stays quiet, the words twisting in her brain as she tries to determine the words she wishes to say. For a girl raised on lies, the truth was often hard to come by.

"But I am ashamed. I failed to keep us safe. It was my fault," Ellsie says. "Never before have they even come close to hurting us like that. They're growing stronger and that... scares me."

"You are allowed to be scared," Dr Nolan says smoothly. "Do you often find yourself thinking over what you could have done differently?"

"I know what my mistake was, it was not a choice I made," Eleanor says. "Being made into an ACE isn't just practical, I spent a fair bit of time learning about mission related mental issues. I can identify and handle blaming myself for decisions. Of course there are other things I could have done, but they are inconsequential. What happened happened, and it went wrong, there is no use in hoping for a different outcome, because it was my choice in the moment that led me there, and instinct is near impossible to shift."

Dr Nolan narrows her eyes but lets the comment slide.

"What scares you about that day?" she asks instead.

"I am weak. Not in a way anyone would notice outside of the Agency, but ever since I had Adelyn, I've been weak. She makes me hesitant, and hesitance is dangerous. And physically I am weaker, my fighting is less refined. The thought of her in my mind means Nora cannot detach herself fully, which means I cannot fully focus like I once did," Eleanor explains. "The things they would do to her if they managed to get a hold of her terrifies both of us to bits. I worry I cannot protect her. I am but one person, they are a system."

One of her hands moves to rub the other, almost as if Nora was comforting her other personality.

"They do not know where you are, Eleanor. You do not have to protect her," Dr Nolan tries. "You are all safe."

With her hand raising towards her throat for just a second, Eleanor shakes her head.

"As much as I trust Nikolas to do that for us, being paranoid has kept me alive for the last 13 years," she shrugs. "Something you've relied on for so long is hard to let go of."

"And when you feel you've failed at it, it hurts more, doesn't it?"

Eleanor looks away face held in perfect immobility, not an inch of weakness to be found by a stranger.

"Yes."

Simple, clean speech. A window into her way of life.

"Do you think it would affect your ability to complete a mission in your normal efficacy?"

A pause. Then, like a robot rebooting, Eleanor's face straightens into the mask of a machine.

"I have heard this before..."

Only a flick of confusion forms on Eleanor's face to represent the human within. Beethoven plays on her leg in silent contortions of her fingers.

"Where?"

"At the Agency, Mein Vater asked it of Sebastian," Eleanor breathes. "I only caught the latter part of conversation as I was playing piano."

Dr Nolan, with her limited knowledge of Eleanor's relationship with her fellow trainee, has to ask what the assassin thought they may be talking about.

"Me. Seb and I were... close. He was less reserved about being close to someone than I was," Eleanor sighs. "He's a second-generation agent... which basically means his parents were both ACEs who survived long enough for the Agency to harvest their reproductive cells and implant them in a surrogate. He knew who his parents were, and his mother had a soft spot for us. She offered to harbour Adelyn and I when I was pregnant. It was probably a trap, but he didn't think so."

"He was asking if his emotions for you would affect his work…"

Eleanor nods slowly, the tightness on her muscles not receding.

"He assured Dunkler Bischof he would be absolutely fine. But Mein Vater wasn't sure, he talked to him again later. He knew I was listening," she says. "He never talked to me about it though."

The doctor has no issues determining why, as the blank look stays on Eleanor's face.

"Would your feelings for Sebastian make a difference?" Dr Nolan questions anyway.

"Only if it was safe to. If there was any doubt, I would leave him behind." Harsh words, so much so Nora slips back in. "We care for him a lot, we want to protect him… but if it was us or him, we would always choose us. That's why Mein Vater never questioned us about it," she says.

Glancing at the plain clock across the wall, Dr Nolan sighs. Their time was up.

"You deflected my question earlier… would it affect your ability?" she says in way of finality.

Eleanor answers almost too quickly.

"No."

Chapter 11

*A*ll efforts within the NAP were focused upon finding Nikolas and returning him to confinement, and in the process destabilising the Daemone forces. Only issue with that was that the Daemones – and Nikolas – were rather good at evading capture. If you remember that they only really were noticed because Eleanor handed herself in, and Nikolas followed, then you may understand the exorbitant amount of time the team spent sitting around reading through files.

Michael was poor at this, of course, so often ended up on loose end missions that did nothing to help find his brother and merely added to his ire. Kaylee often followed to ensure nothing too important was damaged and to provide support to the emotionally tired Crown Prince. Kenichi was stuck between checking in on Eleanor and providing much needed medical aid at attack sites long after the rest of the team had returned home.

Zach however seemed at a loose end most of the time. His expertise as socio-political assistance – as had become his role since Michael's arrival – was unnecessary on dead end missions, and his weak stomach and lack of any medical expertise meant he was of no help to anyone at all. He found himself the receiver of Dr Nolan's fortnightly reports on Eleanor's mental state. (Kenichi of course also read these, though gained most his knowledge through conversation with the assassin).

The reports started to make more and more sense to Zach as he shifted through more of them, and then looked back on the psychological analysis reports that they had performed on Eleanor when she first arrived. The connections were clear, and more so, he found the connections to his own sister – Bella's – struggles after the attacks on their corporation that had left her a paraplegic almost frighteningly obvious. One night, at dinner with the team – a practice they tried their hardest to continue as much as they could – he is reading through one of the reports, the most recent, on his phone.

Having been completely silent the entire meal, the team looks over to Zach in surprise as he puts down his phone and looks up for a chance to interrupt the conversation.

"After Bella had her run in with the Berühmte Söldner, she mentioned the impact that even conversing with them had on her..." he starts, glancing down at the page again as he speaks. "I had put it down to the traumatic events that made her unable to recall it clearly, but I remember her telling me that they seemed to be like live wires in a conversation. Always ahead, and always at risk of flipping at any moment. When she said she thought they looked unstable, we always assumed it was psychopathy..."

"Most people would," Kaylee interjects. "Normal people don't harm others like that."

While she says her words with conviction, she doesn't return to her meal after delivering them. Rather continues to watch Zach as he aimlessly scrolls through some of Eleanor's files.

"That's the thing... normal people do, when absolutely necessary," he says, frown stitched onto his brow. "Vanessa Nolan has been reporting a level of mistrust in Eleanor's judgement that Eleanor herself suffers from. She overthinks everything that she does, to the word, but refuses to accept that anything is changeable, because her first response must always be correct."

Kenichi glances up from where he had been continuing to eat.

"She's always said that the only thing she relies on is her intuition," he says in way of stopping Zach's line of thought, but the man merely shakes his head in amusement.

"That is what she thinks... it's what they all think. But it's all just a trauma response to the pressure to be perfect little agents that they have felt growing up. Everything is too quick for them to really process," he explains. "I'm saying this to suggest that when Eleanor is here, we should try and slow everything down a bit more. She can't heal her mind without a chance to slow down a little."

"I thought you were of the opinion that all this business was a fruitless venture?" Michael mutters from the other end of the table. Without Nikolas and Eleanor to fill up spaces, he has isolated himself to a brooding corner that had led to everyone forgetting he was there.

Zach sighs, clicking his phone off in irritation.

"What I'm saying is that Eleanor isn't really that bad... morally. She just has never been allowed to develop the step in her brain that hesitates to reconsider things. With a bit of time, she might be able to slow it down enough to make her just like the rest of us," Zach explains softly. "And it might be the same for all of them, from what my sister seemed to express. The Berühmte Söldner might not be an agency of highly trained assassins, they might just be the creators of people who don't know any better."

"Maybe," Kaylee replies, voice quiet and focused on Michael's tense posture at the other end of the table. "We just have to see. Let's not dig ourselves too deep of a hole to get back out of, okay?"

For a moment, it appears like Zach might wish to argue, but the careful warning on Kaylee's face makes him pause before he does so. He lets the conversation lapse, but the idea lingers in his mind as he reads further and further into Eleanor's mental state.

Chapter 12

It was becoming increasingly apparent as April continued that Ellsie's bloodlust was rising to a point that basic interactions in public threatened to send her over the edge. The only technique for mitigation that Eleanor had managed to find was a small but popular bare-knuckles boxing gym two hour's drive away. It took longer to find a suitable babysitter to watch Adelyn while she was gone.

The girl had passed a rigorous background and personality check before Eleanor had even approached her. Even though she is 17, she had already made it clear she was going to stay close to the valley instead of going to university in the city – which meant Eleanor wouldn't have to start all over again in a year's time– and was more than happy to drive out to the house for the price Eleanor was paying her.

Captain remains close to Eleanor's side as she pushes open the fly-screen door and enters through what appears as a maintenance door in the industrial district around them. From afar, Captain appears totally out of place in the maze of mix of brick, concrete and tin, but while Eleanor scans the rooftops nearby as she shuts the door behind them, she appears surprisingly relaxed. Within moments of entering the building, Eleanor has mentally catalogued the faces around her, and she keeps her chin up as she stands in the entrance. The front desk is small – merely a table with a sign in sheet – and unoccupied as Eleanor looks it over in amusement. Her lips twitch with a smile of familiarity as the thick and slightly musty air meets her senses.

Distantly, it reminds her of the dirt, blood and sweat of the Berühmte Söldner, but at the same time it felt just a little like home.

Her body couldn't decide between revulsion and relaxation, so she met it in the middle with a balanced focus on the people within the room.

A stout ginger haired man, having stopped talking to another man across the gym, makes it over to her shortly after her entrance, though every step he takes is overwhelmed with a reluctance that begs for a taunt. Similar to her quick assessment of him, Eleanor can feel him scanning her and how his attention lingers on the dog at her side.

"What can I do for you, love," he says, having to look up to her as she straightens her back.

"I'd like to train here," Eleanor replies, voice smooth as butter. So much more poised than she was often given credit for.

The man looks a little bored as he asks, "we don't do self-defence classes. And we are a boxing gym, you should look elsewhere."

"I assure you, I am fully trained," Eleanor smiles, face almost too sweet. "I'd just like to be able to blow off some steam once a month, surely some of your ring fighters could benefit from a different practice partner."

Shock hits the man's face for two reasons; first being the fact the ring fights were supposedly secret, only those trusted in the area could put up their fighters. It was the whole reason Eleanor had come so far, for the pure brawling fights that Ellsie begged for. And the second, longer lingering reason is his disbelief the girl could fight well enough to be put up against his fighters.

"I'm not sure how you know about that," he starts cautiously, "but a slight thing like you couldn't keep up with those fights. And I don't particularly want you to get hit and have a problem."

His eyes flick to Captain again, who is sitting calmly beside Eleanor.

"I have no problems being hit; he is a psychological service dog. He steps in if I lose it," Eleanor explains, "and let me have a go in the ring, I'll prove myself. You fight bare knuckled, yes?"

"We do. But I'm going to need your name if you want to be let in the ring," the man grunts, still having trouble believing her claims.

"Ellsie," Eleanor supplies. Untraceable. "I'll go put my bag down, if you have a fighter ready."

Still in disbelief, the man gestures for her to enter the room and Eleanor strides past him to place her bag against the wall. Her shoes and jumper join the bag, leaving her in only her tights and sports bra. Her knuckles get wrapped in cloth; her muscles quickly fall into their rather short stretching routine.

Captain sits on the edge of the mat, attention on Eleanor as she bounces lightly on the blue flooring. Two men, the ginger and the other a burly brunette fighter join her, both clearly double taking as she grins across at them.

"What are the rules?" Eleanor asks politely, watching the fighter carefully as he stands opposite her.

"Ten seconds on the ground or tap out. No weapons, everything else is allowed. Keep fighting until someone loses," the ginger says, affronted as Eleanor quickly crouches and sheepishly pulls out a flat blade from her tights. Whether it had been left intentionally, or honestly forgotten, it is impossible to tell. He turns to his fighter just before he steps off the mat, "go easy, wouldn't want to injure the little lady."

The fighter nods, raising his fists as Eleanor steps a little closer, keeping her hands loose in front of her face.

He initiates, stepping into the fight with a half-hearted right hook. Eleanor dodges the first few throws, analysing his patterns as he lets himself be lead in a circle around the mat. As he grows frustrated, unable to get a hit on her, she finally slips under his guard, landing a forceful punch to his gut before dancing out of range.

She grins as he stumbles back, cracking her neck as he straightens and comes forward once more. This time, as he sends a punch towards her, Eleanor steps past it, slamming her elbow into his shoulder to send him off balance before spinning around her left foot to slam her right into his exposed side. As he sprawls onto the floor, she pounces forward, one knee on his throat and the other securely on his wrist.

"I think you can fight better than that," she teases, keeling backwards as he taps out.

The gym owner looks suitably surprised.

"Where did you learn to fight like that?" he questions, almost threatening.

But Eleanor holds still, grin wide.

"Not in this country," she teases. "Now, will you give me a better fight than that. Honestly, I'm a little bored."

Another fighter, who had been watching closely from the other side of the room, walks over, standing proudly next to the owner.

"I'll fight you," he offers. "We need to see what you're made of..."

Eleanor opens an arm to the floor, taking herself back to the edge as he steps forward. He doesn't give her much time, sending a kick towards her stomach as soon as he's in range. Eleanor wisely dodges it, taking advantage of him being off balance to send a left-handed punch directly to his sternum. With his next punch he manages to clip her shoulder, but she recovers quickly using his next extended arm to swing herself onto his shoulders. With her legs linked under his chin, she swings herself to the side, leaving only one leg around him as he stumbles and – as he is about to fall, Eleanor pushes herself back off him. She regains her footing as he lands on the ground, ready to pin him when he quickly rolls away.

His hand grabs her ankles, swiping them out from under her and pinning her arms above her head. The owner starts the countdown, but Eleanor slams her knee into his nuts and rolls him over. She sends five punches to his face in quick succession, almost continuing after the call, but Captain runs over, shoving himself between them. Eleanor rolls backwards, pulling her t-shirt out of his dog vest and stuffing her face into it.

Her opponent offers her a hand up, which she takes, tucking the shirt into Captain's vest before smiling tightly at him.

"Sorry 'bout your face. Lost it a little," she mutters, trying hard to keep her accent at bay. "Really needed to find this place earlier than this."

"You fight... like you fight professionally," he replies, watching her curiously as she chuckles.

There is a distinct smile to his gaze that relaxes Eleanor as he unknowingly confirms his lack of allegiance to her old owners. Or even his lack of any knowledge of them at all.

"Not in the way you are thinking," she says, turning towards the owner.

"Are you willing to fight in an underground competition?" he asks outright. "It's not illegal, but it's not on the books. You could make some good coin."

"I would, once a month. Preferably on Saturdays," she answers, "and any money I make you are to distribute evenly between your other fighters. I have an income, and I don't need anyone wondering where extra money is coming from."

The man shrugs, not caring too much about what she did with it.

"Every fourth Saturday of the month alright?" he asks, pulling a card out of his back pocket. "It's at that same location each time."

"Perfect," Eleanor grins, taking the card which only had a phone number and the address on it. "This yours?"

"Yes, just in case you need to skip a fight," he replies. "The name's Barney."

"Well, Barney, if you could enter me under the name Elizabeth that would be appreciated. And I will be fighting in a mask," Eleanor says. "A girl's got to protect her identity."

He nods in acceptance, still standing in shock as Eleanor stalks out of the gym, bag in hand.

Chapter 13

The fights were the high of Ellsie's month. Better, she had been given permission to conceal their little excursion from everyone else, and the assassin delighted in being able to hide something again; Dr Nolan was only told that she had found solace in Tai Chi.

The therapist knew she had found a way to fight. She understood more than Eleanor ever figured out, but luckily it was never to anyone's detriment that both parties could keep their secrets. It was allowing for them both to heal, to get a sliver of reprieve, so she kept quiet. Dr Nolan was a very smart woman.

It was Nora, however, who suggested the next form of not quite illegal, but not particularly favoured, activity.

Tattoos.

She did already have one, the Agency stamp on her lower back, but she wanted some for herself.

The next week Eleanor walks into the parlour, dark walls covered in artworks. Much like the fighting gym, the shop is hidden at the far end of the shopping precinct, bordering on the suburbs of their nearest town. With a beat-up roller door not quite all the way open and a near black tint on the windows, it was completely concealed from the outside world. Since Adelyn was at preschool for most of the day, Eleanor had enough time to drive into town and back without being missed.

No other customers are within the store, so there is no one in the front of the store – housing only the front desk and a couch – when Eleanor walks in. The bell rings loud as Eleanor taps it, smiling as a heavily tattooed man walks out from behind the partition.

He is quick in his assessment of her – a wrong one – but it serves her for the time being. Captain is happy sitting in between her legs, taking up as little room as possible, but his vest is still visible to the tattooist.

"What can I do for you?" he grunts, sitting in the chair behind the desk. His nametag reads Baz, and Eleanor is not at all surprised.

"I'd like a tattoo, if that's alright," Eleanor answers bitterly, she had little time to bother being overly sweet to men who underestimated her. "You can do that, can't you?"

He nods in answer, gesturing to a booklet on the desk. Ideas.

"What would you like done, and I'd suggest looking over this sheet for placement. It is best to start in a low pain area," Baz offers, seemingly bored.

"This isn't my first time getting a tattoo," Eleanor mutters, "and, either way, I have an exceptional pain tolerance." She continues without looking at the ideas, "I would like four short words written in capitals along the inside of my index finger."

A simple tattoo, sitting on her trigger finger.

I AM MY OWN.

"I can do that, but it will have to be in black, the area will fade in colour," he tells her, "and the pain will be extreme."

"I can handle the pain, and it's fine in black," Eleanor assures. "Can you do it in the next four hours?"

"Definitely. I can do it now if you'd like."

It seems Baz had warmed up to her.

"Brilliant."

The back part of the shop was much like the front, with two adjustable chairs, like the ones at the dentist, and another two with arm rests. A set of rolling stools hang around them, likely for the tattooists.

~

The bench is cold, but the vinyl grabs at the bare skin of her stomach as she readjusts her position. Her head rests on her arms, and she forces her breaths to remain even as the tattooist steps towards her.

"Ultraviolet, yes?" he confirms with her handler, watching from the edge of the room.

"Yes, no name yet. We still have to test her out," the man replies. "Get on with it, I have better things to do."

The tattooist nods, beginning his work on her lower back. Eleanor doesn't flinch, she doesn't whimper – much to her handler's annoyance – laying perfectly still until it is done. Merely a mark on her skin. What more should she have to worry about?

The door shuts behind her as she returns to the apartment, a tear rolling down her face to spite her. The Dunkler Bischof steps forward to greet her, wiping the stray tear away in silence.

"Welcome to the Berühmte Söldner," he murmurs as he leads her further in. "You are one of us now."

~

Baz directs her to one with arm rests, grabbing a seat and machine for himself. She gets Captain to lie under the bench in front of her, placing her bag on the floor. She has to show him her ID – to confirm she is in fact over 18 – before taking the waiver he hands her. She scans over it quickly, before signing at the bottom – with her new signature, specific to her new name – and giving it back over.

"What words?" Baz asks easily, preparing to type into the machine, "and are you wanting a particular font?"

Eleanor relays her message, wanting just plain Arial in uppercase. With a raised eyebrow, he enters it into the machine, measuring quickly her finger length and width before printing out a transfer strip.

"This is so I can trace it, if I could have your finger..."

Eleanor is silent as she gives it to him, keeping still as he transfers it over. It takes a minute for her to find a remotely comfortable spot to put her arm, but she does and settles back into the seat.

"You got somewhere to be?" Baz asks as he prepares the machine.

"I have to get groceries before I pick my daughter up, but really I'm just a hyper-efficient person," she answers easily.

"And any reason you're getting this on your trigger finger?"

Eleanor doesn't answer, giving him a look as he shrugs and starts the machine up.

"Not my business, I know. Just a little odd for a young thing like you with a daughter to come in and be so casual," he shrugs, finding a good position before glancing up one more time. "You ready?"

"Get on with it," Eleanor mutters, face not flickering an inch as he starts.

He seems surprised, raising an eyebrow as he continues.

"That always gets a reaction out of people," he adds, pausing his work to look at her curiously. As he starts again, he mentions, "and its odd to find someone with deadly sharpened blades holding their hair in place. You know they're illegal to carry in this country."

His assumption that she is international surprises her just a little, so Baz receives a much more focused look as she reassesses him. Eventually she drops the inspection and sighs.

"Even you must admit this place looks a little dodgy, and I'm not one to take chances," Eleanor answers smoothly, grinning at the man. "Would it help if I said I used to be in a sort of gang?"

"Only if you assure me you're not anymore," he replies slowly.

"I'm not. Different country, different life," she grins. "I'll probably be back, in a month or so."

"Planning on getting something bigger?" Baz asks in interest.

"No, I like to be able to cover anything I get done if the need arises," Eleanor answers. "You the only one who works here?"

"I have a partner, but I work Tuesdays by myself since it's so quiet."

Eleanor smiles happily, letting the silence settle in as he finishes.

It doesn't take long, the tattoo only small. He covers it and gives her care instructions for the next few days, eyes lingering on Captain as she pays.

"You can give him a pat, if you'd like. I'm sure I can survive for a few seconds," she offers as she hands over a thick wad of cash.

He does so with thanks, watching curiously as she walks away.

Amy frowns at the bandage on Eleanor finger when she arrives to pick up Adelyn. Ady knew about the tattoo already, so barely looking at it twice as she makes her way to her mother.

"What happened?" Amy asks as they walk out of the preschool.

Eleanor grins as she answers, "tattoo. First of probably many."

All the older woman can do is raise an eyebrow as Eleanor proudly walks back to her car.

Eleanor got two more that year, one on her wrist – a rose with its stalk in an infinity symbol – and 'I'm Sorry' just beneath her Agency tattoo. Baz, who had done both, noticed the uneven skin, but didn't comment on it. Eleanor also made sure it was high enough he didn't see the two burns only a few centimetres further down.

Dr Nolan was in full support of the choices, knowing that it could help to remove some of the pain Eleanor felt. That, and it showed Eleanor was willing to make changes to her appearance. Vanessa had noticed how she always kept her hair the same length, kept only her one set of ear piercings. Small things to make her adaptable but indistinguishable. Like an agent.

Chapter 14

As the year progresses and Eleanor becomes more familiar with everyone around her, everything starts to relax a bit. One weekend, Rachel invites Eleanor and Adelyn to watch a horse competition she has entered, and Eleanor's love of animal compels her to agree against the screaming warning in her head that being around so many people from so far away was a bad idea. It isn't long until Eleanor finds herself with a pair of horses for herself, finally making use of the paddocks and shed on her property and giving herself something else to focus on – other than consistently worrying about Adelyn's safety.

One was just a pony, short and fat, with an abnormally sweet disposition – for a pony. Adelyn loved to be led around on her, and when she was old enough to be off the lead, the 15-year-old Shetland could teach her to ride for herself. She was named – much to Michael's annoyance and Eleanor's subsequent delight – Angel.

The other was significantly larger, standing about the same height as Eleanor with a patchy black and white coat. Though he had started out with enough education for anything that Eleanor wished to do with him, the extended amount of time she spent with him meant he was learning quickly. He didn't quite have the presence Nikolas's mare had, nor the quick mind, but it would be hard to find a horse as simultaneously sweet and wild as Ferox.

They had joined the local Pony Club where Eleanor often spent the morning leading Adelyn around different activities, before riding herself in the afternoon when Adelyn got too tired. The younger kids would go off to play while the older kids were out jumping their horses which left her able to ride in the arena with some of the other adults, before they too had a go at jumping and some of the games set up around the area.

Some of the instructors, upon seeing Eleanor's ability to ride a horse, suggested she enter some competitions, or get out to clinics, but she assured them quickly that she was happy where she was. Frankly, she wasn't quite sure she could trust herself to stay calm and kind in such a competitive environment, but she didn't mention that to anyone. Captain had adapted to watching Eleanor ride, and her horse – Tucker – had adjusted to him sitting at the edge of wherever they were riding and though he would very occasionally alert while Eleanor was riding, Tucker similarly noticed and was unconcerned by the dog arriving at their side.

Amy also had a pair of ponies, a larger for Owen, who was the instigator of the purchase, and a smaller one for Riley. She and Eleanor often spent the morning walking around the Pony Club together while their girls chatted happily. Rachel occasionally arrived in the afternoon to get her younger horses out for some exercise.

It was one such day, when the cold morning had given over to late October heat, that they first found out about the scar – Eleanor had done a very diligent job at hiding it over the past year.

Having removed Adelyn's jumper an hour before, Eleanor quickly realises her mistake in not bothering to put makeup over the scar on her throat that morning. There hadn't been any indication that the heat would get this high, so she had been lazy in her morning prep... though not so much that the scars on her back weren't covered.

She pulls the hoodie over her head – having wedged the lead to the pony between her legs – and carefully ties it around her waist. The possibility that they might not even notice occurs to her, but as Adelyn frowns up at her in concern, the possibility gets smaller and smaller.

"Mummy..." she starts, knowing her mother had always hidden the scar public.

"It's okay, Ady," Eleanor assures, pulling her attention away from her train of thought as it becomes her turn to trot the bending poles.

It's as she walks Tucker out of his yard, Rachel on one side and Amy arriving to take Adelyn off her hands, that the ASIO agent notices the silvery ridged line along the 19-year-old's throat. She frowns deeply and within moments Eleanor finds Captain at her side.

"What's that?" Amy asks cautiously, cutting off her path on instinct, "on your throat."

"A scar," Eleanor answers quietly, eyes averted and hand already reaching for the shirt piece in Captains vest.

"Yes, I figured that much, where did you get it from?" Amy replies tersely, though an echo of worry shadows her tone.

Rachel frowns as well now, eyes on the line.

"A knife. Just before I came here," Eleanor says, pressing the fabric to her nose and taking a deep breath.

More than anything else, the scar on her throat still shook her. The memories that shadowed its presence. The thoughts. The aching.

Her eyes trying their hardest to ignore their surroundings.

"How come we've never seen it before?" Rachel follows, after Eleanor has lowered her hand.

"I hide it so that people don't ask questions," Eleanor replies. "Can I please go get on? It's there, it has been there this whole time. I'm fine."

Rachel shrugs, walking away herself, Amy stepping to the side shortly after. Gladly, Nora escapes the confrontation, tucking the fabric back in Captain's vest and clipping her helmet under her chin. Rachel smiles encouragingly as she enters the arena, Captain laying easily in the corner as Eleanor pulls herself into the saddle.

It hadn't gone nearly as bad as she thought it would.

"They found out about my scar today," Eleanor tells Kenichi when she calls him later that night.

It was early morning in Washington DC, the doctor having just arrived at work. He had found himself particularly empty of schedule, so was able to take an extra call to what was generally scheduled between them.

"Did they?" he muses, focus split between the conversation and something on his computer. "Who asked questions?"

"Amy and Rachel," Eleanor answers, "though others were looking at it."

"What did you tell them it was from?"

Through the phone, Eleanor can hear the concern in his voice.

"I said it was a knife before I arrived here," she answers.

"That's fine, and now they know, you don't have to cover it all the time," Kenichi replies, covering the phone to talk to someone for a second before returning. "How did you handle it?"

"Captain alerted; I stuffed my face into the shirt scrap I have in his vest. It made me miss him more than usual," she admits, glancing down at the oversized shirt she has on. "I'll sleep in one of his shirts, but I'll probably get a nightmare anyway. The scar is aching slightly."

"Call again if it's bad, we're doing nothing at the moment," Kenichi says. "Have you thought over where to move the horses to if the fire season doesn't go well? Aren't they predicting a bad one?"

"They are. Drought does that," Eleanor huffs. "Rachel's place is prepped for horses, she said they can stay there. My place is too closed in for them to stay here."

"That's good," Kenichi notes. "Now go to sleep, isn't it like, nearly eleven there."

"Shut up, asshole," Eleanor mutters good-naturedly. "Goodbye."

Chapter 15

By mid-November – barely a month into the fire season – the heat is stifling, and nearly every day is a total fire ban. Eleanor's anxiety had risen early in the season, when multiple days were declared catastrophic, and Adelyn was kept home from school. When the school reopened, however, Adelyn remained at home to keep the child's day to day routine as steady as possible. Eleanor finds it infinitely harder when bushfires spark up nearby.

The smoke triggers horrible flashbacks of burning buildings, bedrooms, the like. Burning plazas, screaming people. And as images come out from the fire fronts, Eleanor's mind turns to their own safety, hidden up in the bush. As such, the horses are moved early to Rachel's place, leaving an eerie quiet to the valley and their home.

Two days after additional firefighting units from surrounding areas arrive, Eleanor has her fortnightly therapy session.

Dr Nolan – as always – is waiting in her office as Eleanor walks in. Instantly, the psychiatrist notices Captain's close focus on Eleanor and his strict heel as she walks to her seat. Once sat, Captain remains posed at Eleanor's side, large head on her knee and brown eyes staring up at her.

"How are you today, Eleanor?" Vanessa greets.

"I don't think I can stay in my house any longer," she states, a blank stare in her eyes that doesn't quite meet Vanessa's eyes, then as if realising who she was talking to, "actually Nora can't stay in our house anymore. She won't admit it, but we can't sleep with all the smoke. I mentioned it to Rachel, and she said she was fine taking care of my horses until it's calmed down. All the out-of-town crews risk exposing us and that stresses me out. I can't track their faces, and any one of them could be easily an undercover agent."

"Okay then." Vanessa nods, but her eyes never leave Captain's position at Eleanor's side. "Why do you feel the need to tell me this?"

"Aren't I supposed to tell you my inner emotions..." Eleanor mutters, rolling her eyes as she flops backwards to lean against the back of the couch.

"Yes," Vanessa nods, leaning back in her chair. "Now, can Nora tell me why the smoke is triggering her?"

The girl shifts, and when she stills again, her legs are tucked up under herself and Captain has jumped up onto the couch to keep his head close.

"I just smell the smoke of the bombing," she says, "or things Ellsie set fire to, buildings, rooms, the odd person. Gunsmoke." She pauses for a few seconds. "The smoke from the pipe our handler used to blow in my face when he saw me."

"Does he come up often? Your handler?" Dr Nolan asks.

"Not really. Killing him..." Eleanor pauses, focus shifting between Vanessa and the window with a dragging screech in her mind. "I have no qualms with killing him. No nightmares. But I still get nightmares of him beating me," she admits, voice quiet. "Sometimes I imagine him beating Adelyn. That scares me more than anyone can know... it makes me glad that I killed him."

The therapist scribbles something down, watching Eleanor as the girl dutifully ignores the water. Her fingers start to play but stop abruptly as she realises what she's doing.

"You still haven't played the piano, have you?" Vanessa asks carefully, once more forgoing the illusion that their sessions were private for the sake of Eleanor's progress – after all, the fact never seemed to be far from the assassin's mind.

"I can't. It reminds me... of how happy I was..." A look akin to anger flicks through the anguish that painted her face "...how naïve. I don't want to remind myself of that. Of him. The books are enough weakness. Enough indulgence. I don't know how many times I've read over the messages. It makes me wish I could talk to him. Talking always helped."

Dr Nolan smiles kindly, letting the girl run her hands through her dog's fur for a minute or two, before adding her piece.

"You are allowed to be reminded, to remember the good times," she says. "It helps you be the fullest version of yourself. It is all a part of you, and sometimes we do need to remember the past to make our own future happier."

Eleanor smiles tightly, hand shifting to raise to her throat for a second, before she drops it again.

"I know," she shrugs, taking a breath in as if she was sucking in her entire soul, "it's just hard, sometimes."

Rachel held to her word to look after the horses, so it was easy for Eleanor to leave the country. They all understood that she was having a hard time of it, didn't understand exactly why, but bushfires spark a lot of uncertainty in people. Adelyn was pulled out of school early for the year, but many weren't sending their kids anyway, opting to keep them close by just in case the wind changed.

They were on a plane the next day and free of the permanent smell of smoke the tension in Eleanor's shoulders releasing a little bit. They travelled first class so that Captain could lay at Adelyn's feet with as much room as he wished, and enough of Eleanor's clothes were in America so they only packed two suitcases. Valuables like technology, backups and Adelyn's favourite toys included. The wooden box that Eleanor kept under her bed and the books from Nikolas made the cut as well, sitting snug against the bottom of a bag with her mask — forever within her reach.

Her house wasn't suspected to burn, but she brought them just in case. Her special things.

She wore a wig and contacts through both ends of the airport, Adelyn wearing just a hat. Kenichi was waiting in the car at the other end, helping Eleanor — though she didn't need it — place the bags in the boot before Adelyn was placed in a car seat and Eleanor slid into the passenger seat.

"Easy flight?" Kenichi asks as they pull out, the slow traffic allowing for slow conversation.

"Yeah, a few upset people flying on other people's money that thought I was different from them, but other than that fine." Eleanor shrugs. "Things at the house okay?"

"Kaylee's excited to see you, Michael is a bit tense, and Zach, as always, indifferent," Kenichi replies with a flicker of amusement. "I'd stay out of a fight with Michael, he's getting a tonne of heat off his father for Nikolas escaping. I've told him to leave you alone but if you get in a fight with him, I won't be able to help much."

"You can help fix his asshole face once I beat it to a pulp," Eleanor mutters in German beneath her breath, but he hears anyway, glaring lightly.

"Don't you start," he returns, in English — he always preferred English, only indulging her German when he had to, "and don't lose your own emotions in Nikolas's."

Eleanor scowls playfully at Kenichi but her face falls into a shallow stare as they continue driving. She doesn't pull off her wig, or the contacts, until they are in the driveway, eyes focusing blandly on the green landscape. Kaylee greets them at the door of the manor, smile wide as she hugs Eleanor, then picks up Adelyn to spin her around with more glee on her face than Eleanor thought she could ever muster.

Since they had landed late in the afternoon, dinner was already prepared and waiting as they get well within the confines of the building. Adelyn – while she should have just woken up back home – had been kept awake on the flight, so is extremely tired as Kaylee carries her into the dinner table. Meanwhile Captain had never been to the house, so Eleanor lets him off, chucking him his toy to tell him he could relax as she sits down to eat. After a few moments, Bronte discovers a new canine in her house, the pair matching as they run around.

Everyone else was out, it seemed, and after very quickly finishing, Eleanor calls Captain back to her, which he responds to immediately with his toy half falling out of his mouth as he grins at her. Adelyn takes the guest room next to Nikolas's which had been prepared for her and Eleanor walks into her own, her bags opened on the floor as she quickly changes.

It is hard for her, being back in the manor without Nikolas there. She kept looking up to catch a reassuring smile from him and meeting empty space. The slight edge of comfort that she had always felt here was gone, and it felt so much quieter. Everything was so much quieter.

Eleanor slides down her shut door, head heavy in her hands as the loss hits her in a new wave that hadn't appeared since the first book had arrived. As if the realisation that she was actually, truly, alone had finally hit... or perhaps it was a final acceptance that there was no truth in the lies she would tell herself in the darkest nights, that he maybe was just visiting the compound for a couple days. Captain drops his front half into her lap, wet nose snuffling up to her face as he tries to get her to respond.

Weakly, Eleanor lets her hands find his face instead, hiding her face in his silky fur. It takes a while for her to sit back, eyes finding her bed then giving up on the venture. The time was nearing midnight, the entire house silent as she eases open her door. In three quick steps, she is across the hallway and pushing through the door to the empty room. Captain slips in behind her, pausing as the door shuts behind him.

The room still smelt like the things he had been taught not to touch. Nearly every surface lingering with that very particular scent that those items of purity had most strongly, and that his mother always carried, just slightly. Eleanor calls him softly, already having climbed into the nearly identical bed. Captain stays on the floor, as she instructs, curled tight against the bedside table.

Eleanor sleeps on his side of the bed, face pressed deep into the pillow as she curls around it.

Only Adelyn notices she didn't sleep in her own room as she spies her mother slipping back across the hallway early the next morning. She doesn't mention it though, returning to her bed to wait for Eleanor to wake her. Her mother does shortly after, fully dressed for the day and held together by the pressure of all those around her watching.

Eleanor stays away from them all as much as possible, hiding in her room or in the library. The piano is ignored, and while she visits the horses once or twice, seeing them all raises her worries about her own pair.

Rachel calls to keep her up to date each day, usually early in Eleanor's morning, and she is glad to be kept informed. Kenichi watches her each morning as she paces back and forth on the grass, a hand in her nearly permanently loose hair. The news from Australia so far hasn't been good.

Wind was still blowing, and in the dead environment, fire had no hindrance. Rachel was confident her place would be fine, as the two bushfires were both on the other side of the one major road through town, an easily defendable spot. Eleanor's house however was in the line of fire.

A few days after she had left, the flames were within two kilometres of the fence line her house sat against. But luckily for them all, the wind died. It didn't double back, which they had been hoping for since burnt land can't burn again, but the fire front was moving slow enough for firefighters to start to set up defence lines.

It was three weeks from her leaving that they declared her house was no longer at risk, but with the wind still dead, the smoke was hanging in the valley. Eleanor wouldn't return home yet.

The shift in her is obvious, most of the team glad to see her talking more, meeting their eyes and coddling Adelyn. She chats with Kaylee, lets Zach stay in casual silence – even if his gaze on her had been so much more focused since her arrival – and avoids Michael, who does the same to her. The silence between them is icy – neither making any attempts to talk to the other, Nikolas's absence weighing on them both.

Eleanor called Barney, cancelling for the rest of the year, and Kaylee became her new sparring partner, an exercise Eleanor had come to enjoy. Of course, she held back – they didn't know she had been underground fighting and being perfectly in shape was not a good way to keep her secret.

"Captain's been working hard..." Kenichi notes as Eleanor runs her hands through Captain's coat. They were all having breakfast on the last day before she returned home – Christmas had just passed, and Eleanor was itching to be out of the manor again.

"I'm quite stressed. Being here is harder than I thought it would be," Eleanor admits. "I'm missing my therapy sessions as well; my head is not benefitting from it."

"You've been sleeping in his room. Adelyn told me," he says, watching her carefully. "I thought you were working on letting him go..."

"It's hard, alright," she snaps. "It's my life. Let me make my choices."

The doctor's lips pull tight, but he allows for her to fall silent on her own accord.

"It is hard to let go of someone you love," Eleanor whispers, "especially when you know they are still out there."

"Are you worried he can sense you're on the continent?" Kaylee asks from across the room, careful, but confident.

Eleanor doesn't reply immediately, focus scanning around the room before she finds it within herself to answer.

"He knows," she replies quietly. "After my first nightmare, I could feel him checking on me. Just the barest of touches on my mind. I assured him I was okay. He was gone a few seconds later."

Kaylee smiles sympathetically, returning to her food without another word.

Eleanor reaches out to the table, cup warm in her hand as she places it back down. But the doctor frowns as she pulls her left hand back in to her body. He stands and holds a hand out, waiting for her to tentatively offer it forward before grabbing her wrist to turn it over.

A thumb rolls over the tattoo, Kenichi's gaze rising to meet Eleanor's annoyed one.

"When did you get that?" he asks shortly.

"About August, Dr Nolan approved. Suggested it even," Eleanor replies.

"Do you have any more?" he continues, eyebrows pinched.

"Two," Eleanor shrugs, flashing the one on her trigger finger to him. "The other is below my Agency tattoo. It says, 'I'm Sorry'. Why? Have a problem with tattoos?"

He mutters something unintelligible, before asking louder, "why would Dr Nolan suggest it?"

Before Eleanor can answer, Kaylee speaks from across the room.

"Can't work as a spy with tattoos. Means you can be recognised even if you change your appearance. It's a way of distancing herself from that life." Her gaze locks on Eleanor for a moment with a playful smile. "It's autonomy."

"And they're permanent reminders, permanent apologies," Eleanor adds quietly. "I'm going to get some for my family, as well. Just haven't decided what or where."

"Who do you get to do it?" Kenichi questions, without response to her previous question.

"Just a guy in town, I go in during the week while Adelyn's at school and only he is working," she says. "He's chill."

"Good," he mutters, dropping beside her as he releases her arm.

Adelyn appears down the staircase – well able to manage them as she neared three – running around to jump onto her mother. But Eleanor is ready, catching her before she can knock the wind out of her and carefully placing her in a sitting position.

"What's up, Ady?" Eleanor grins, poking her stomach lightly.

"You promised we could go for a ride!" Adelyn replies, trying – and failing miserably – to sound serious.

"I said we can go for a ride as soon as we get home," Eleanor corrects kindly. "I'll come up to pack the last of your stuff away in a second, hmm? Then once we have dinner we'll head to the airport."

Nodding in understanding, Adelyn relaxes into her mother's chest, head cradled carefully by Eleanor. Kenichi smiles softly at the pair, standing up to go talk to Kaylee when Eleanor calls out.

"I wasn't hiding them from you," she says. "I just didn't mention it because I was worried you'd be mad."

"Your life is your own, Eleanor. I may dislike the practice, but I won't yell at you for it. Just... don't go getting any on your face," he replies, smiling as Eleanor does.

They flew home that night. Much of the drive back to their quaint little town was drastically changed, a landscape of black, brown and beige. Amy drives up to see them an hour after they arrive, Eleanor relieved to see her property still in one piece. They pick up their horses the next day, and as promised, go out on a ride together, Adelyn's little pony tottering along behind the bigger horse.

A fire season survived.

Chapter 16

Not even in their own files did the Daemones record their locations, so I have very little to go on when trying to track Nikolas's actions over this time. Not at all surprising considering the Berühmte Söldner were able to hide their own little secret in their files for decades. Misinformation should have been the Daemones' prime focus, since they excelled so well in it.

Somewhere far out in America, Nikolas glances over the reports set out in front of him. Various are Berühmte Söldner, conveying dangerous information that he barely can focus on. Politicians corrupted and government files stolen, none of it really matters to him. But organising attacks where it mattered was his job, so he looks them over anyway.

His room is bare, empty but for a bed, desk, and wardrobe. The dark stone appears just a little too much like Angeli Terra's prison, and the chill in the underground base seeps into his bones. Though the bed is piled with blankets to combat the freezing night temperatures he is never comfortable, tossing and turning late into the night.

Not only do the conditions make it hard to sleep, but the nightmares that torture his mind, whenever he does have time to get some rest, persist like a stubborn flu – easing for a day or two before flaring up again. Most are of Eleanor, of course. The gruesome slice across her throat opens again, pouring crimson blood. The others are a plague of death caused by the unwavering steel of his blades. Nikolas understands he must kill the people he attacks to keep his Geminae Animarum – his twin soul – safe. It doesn't make it easier to cut them down, but he does it for Eleanor.

She who plagues his thoughts almost constantly. She who still sends waves of pain through his chest at random times. They were getting less frequent and more numbing than sharp, but the punishment for hurting his Geminae never discriminated against her feelings.

His hands freeze on a file, the name plastered on the front shocking. 'Sleeping Beauty Protocol: Extracted from AUS'.

Just as he knows her identity under any alias, there is a distinct wave as he looks at the new name. There doesn't seem to be any connections made between the protocol and Eleanor, not yet at least, but it's a threat he doesn't need. It's a threat she doesn't need.

But the report has no other files connected to it, and the fact he was allowed to see it suggests they don't have any leads further than its name and origin. Past that, there is nothing there. He puts it down, ensuring not to spend too long looking over the paper as he moves onto the next.

There is an uneasy feeling in his chest, reading through the information he really should be ignoring. In his mind, the files are all just more information, but he knows that the betrayal of the deal Angeli Terra had given him pushed him closer and closer to death every day. There is enough intelligence that he knows they are looking for him. That his brother is trying his hardest to recapture him and send him right back to Exilium Terras. But the intelligence hasn't noticed that every so often Kenichi flies to Australia, or that the manor had extra residents not that long ago. For all their trying, they can't find any trace of the child, whose name they still hadn't been able to verify. According to him – as it was one of the first questions they asked – Adelyn's name was in fact Isabella and having been unable to hack into the manor or compound security systems since he disabled the bug, they have very little they could use to prove him wrong.

A few times they have found something, a whisper of a nickname, but he is always quick to wipe the evidence from their minds, and then from the system. Each day, his Aspect grows in power, some of that power imbued in his gifts to her and the rest used to hide her from the Daemones.

There is something changing in their desperation to find her. When he had been there the first time they wanted her for her ability, yes, but also to stop her from stopping them. The Daemones merely offered brawn and had no real care what happened to her other than to shut her up. It is different now though. They have their own motive to capture her, not kill her. A motive that he hasn't been able to decipher, and a position he wasn't entirely sure he was happy with. They want her for something; to do something or be someone, all his searching underground has not allowed him to see what, but it is there.

The few interactions he's had with the Berühmte Söldner only confirm it, their General – a brutish Daemone referred to only as Salkmal – growing almost frantic in his belief that Eleanor isn't dead. The looks he gives Nikolas are what scare him most about being back in hell on Earth. Hungry and powerful, General Salkmal is the only threat to Eleanor's safety that he cannot control, no matter how hard he tries.

The book tucked under his bed – one waiting to be written in and wrapped – calls to him as he lies down for the night. He aches to scrawl any series of words that would help her, or help him, he can't tell. He wants to tell what he knows: her boss's name, his face. He wants to tell her to move somewhere much more obscure, where they would never find her, but he doesn't. With the charm on his books, he cannot find her himself, and the last of his self-control is put into not risking his position. The torture strains on his heart, wearing his expression thin and manner quiet.

It was for her, though, so he would endure it all. For Eleanor he would do anything.

Chapter 17

Eleanor throws a small party for Adelyn's third birthday, holding it in the local park with the other children from the preschool. With every passing day, Adelyn grows more and more, both in size, but also in intelligence. Occasionally she would give her mother a discreet hug or keep everyone else's eyes off Eleanor for long enough that her mother could regain her senses, as much as Eleanor tried to hide her struggles.

Similar to Adelyn's birthday, Eleanor's 20th birthday was simple, just a few drinks at the tavern – non-alcoholic for Eleanor, since drunkenness only leads to Ellsie forcing control over them both. All her presents arrive from overseas. Mostly gift cards to buy art supplies, but with them is another book, left behind at an attack. A special edition of Little Women. Inscribed of course.

That month, after winning her fight – as she always did – Barney approaches her. He was getting glorious profits off her wins, often with outstanding odds, and was more than happy with pairing her up with difficult fighters for the fun of watching her beat their asses.

"Are you ever going to tell me where you learnt to fight?" he starts, ignoring the looks Eleanor gets in the locker room.

She fought with a singlet on to hide the scars on her back, but that had been ripped off during this fight. Nevertheless, the mask she had decided on – a neck tube that held tight on the bridge of her nose – stayed up as it always did until she had driven away.

"No. I wear this damn thing to stop people from ever finding out," Eleanor mutters, not even pausing to stop packing her bag.

"And are you sure you can't swap onto the first or third week? Just once! People are already talking about you going up against this really popular fighter, but he only fights then," Barney tries, but it falls on deaf ears.

"He can swap to my week if he wants to fight me, but you know I'm not in this for money or popularity," Eleanor returns, now finished and throwing her bag over her shoulder.

Captain stands from his place under the benches, staying out of the way of the fighters. He had grown extremely capable of distinguishing between a good level of adrenaline and the dangerous amount that put everyone nearby at risk that he barely has to rise from his normal place at the edge of the arena, until Eleanor finishes and needs assistance forcing her heart back to a normal rate.

"So, you'll fight him if he fights on the same day as you?" the excited man asks, taking the wholly wrong message as Eleanor starts to walk away.

"That's our agreement, is it not?" she calls, flipping a dagger into her hand and placing it on the throat of the man too close behind her. "I could legitimately kill you where you stand, learn some damn manners," she hisses, grinning as he nods in submission.

With a flick of her hair, she disappears into the dark.

"Do you think she can win? No one has been able to so far…" another man, a trainer, asks.

Barney glances over quickly.

"I hope so. Got a lot riding on it," he answers.

"He was watching her fight tonight. I saw them discussing something as they left."

To his credit, Barney doesn't balk.

"Those tattoos are just superstition, there's nothing special about him. She can take him down."

Barney is not entirely sure.

Chapter 18

As luck would have it, a few weeks later – before Eleanor even gets the chance to fight her new competitor – the world shuts down. Global Pandemic.

Eleanor is more than happy to stay in her house as the sickness spreads. Keeping Adelyn away from it all didn't even counter a second thought. And thus, she misses the next fight and the next. One more just in case.

It does allow for Eleanor to relax through the anniversary of her parent's death. She doesn't get sick afterwards, instead she forces herself into a state of numbness for the weeks before and after. Though Kenichi attempts to convince Eleanor to continue her therapy sessions online, she refuses to even consider the idea without the incredibly intricate encryptions on Kenichi's computer. It would be far too easy for the call to be hacked, and her secret revealed.

Eleanor thought nothing of teaching Adelyn herself, not for the basic things her teacher assigns. In fact, it just gave her the opportunity for the German lessons to increase as well and Adelyn quickly becomes fluent in both languages. All this, and she still spent more of her time peering across at her mother's Latin textbooks, than doing her own work. Since Michael could no longer block Eleanor from doing so, and she is determined to learn the language her Geminae Animarum had grown up speaking before she needs to face him again. She was getting there, and with so many derivative languages, a fair few of which she spoke, most of the terminology was easy to pick up.

Missing the fights had been impacting her, the itch growing more and more infuriating as time passed, but Eleanor holds her grip, focusing on teaching Tucker new moves – he could now be ridden at a canter while she was shooting arrows – and exercising herself while Adelyn was watching television.

Going shopping was stressful for her, however. Captain stayed close to her heel, being careful to watch her anxiety with the face mask over her mouth. Nora had problems with the stifling piece of cloth, and Ellsie wasn't to be trusted when they hadn't fought for so long – a truth that somehow, they both agreed on. More than once Captain alerts, jumping up onto Eleanor's shoulders as she catches glimpses of people that are no threat to her, but merely look like someone from her old place of employment.

One such time, when Adelyn was being looked after by Amy for a few hours, Captain had the opportunity to demonstrate the full extent of his abilities as a service animal.

A woman is causing a raucous at the front of the store, mad at being confronted about not wearing a mask. The yelling, on top of the mask pinching at the bridge of Eleanor's nose, makes her heart quicken dangerously. Eleanor tries to walk further away, but she knows she had to keep eyes on the situation, otherwise it would get worse. Knowing is always better than isolating.

Security guards come over shortly after the confrontation starts, physically blocking the woman from entering the store. Unable to draw her eyes away, Eleanor's breathing starts to tighten, the baton on the security guard's belt holding her attention. He doesn't move to draw it, but as the woman starts to try to fight her way through, eyes landing on the paling girl as she does so, Eleanor unconsciously starts to massage her throat.

~

The Dunkler Bischof raises the hard-shell mask to her face. It clicks into place a few moments later. For a few moments Eleanor holds onto his arm, using it to steady herself as her eyes adjust to the dark mesh.

It takes a few attempts to speak without pressing against the hard shell, and she learns to limit the movements of her face to avoid scratching herself.

"I don't like it," she says quietly, looking up to him. "It's hard to breathe."

"I know. But you'll get used to it, even start to like wearing after a while," he replies. "It's easier to wear this than have people beg for mercy because you look like a sweet child. You are faceless, nameless and merciless, yes?"

"Yes, Mein Vater."

~

Captain alerts with his paw, trying to get his owner to respond as she pulls off her mask for more air.

"Ells, I can't do this," she barely whispers, to no avail.

Ellsie could fight her way out of any situation, the mask triggering her fight response more than anything else.

A shopping centre was not a place that was an option. They couldn't trust themselves.

"She doesn't have a mask on!" the woman yells, pointing aggressively at the now shaking Eleanor.

Eleanor's legs give out from under her as the security guard looks at her in annoyance. Captain is in her lap in a second, trying to push her hands away from her throat with his nose.

"Lady, you need to leave. You are disturbing other customers and putting their safety at risk," the guard orders the woman, who finally gives in.

She is still swearing her mouth off as she exits the plaza but doesn't return to hinder anyone as the security guard steps away from the entrance. He walks towards Eleanor, aiming to assist her as she hyperventilates.

But as he gets within a few meters of her she flinches away, Captain leaving her lap to place himself between her and the guard. With a low growl, he returns to check on Eleanor, who has curled into a ball with her back facing the man.

He tries to approach again, but Captain returns to his spot, barking twice in warning.

"Come on, Buddy. I just want to help her," he tries, but the protective German Shepherd stays in front of his owner, only leaving as someone tries to approach her from the other side.

They finally seem to get the message, everybody around backing off a little as Eleanor runs a rough hand through her hair. Someone new approaches, having heard the barking from the back of the store. Her tattoo artist: Baz. He starts to cautiously walk up to her, eyes on Captain as he runs back and forth from keeping them away to check on Eleanor.

The memory of the four words he had tattooed on her finger rise to mind as he spots the security guard hovering around her and begins to understand Captain's hyperactivity.

"You all need to get well away," Baz instructs, eyes focused on the guard. "He needs to do his job, and you are stopping him."

"We're trying to help calm her down," the guard returns. "This is none of your concern."

"I know her. She's having a panic attack," Baz enforces. "People scare her, yelling and attention can trigger her. And she's had bad experiences with men who look like you, you are making it worse."

Seeing the serious look in his eyes, the guard walks back a few meters, people on the other side copying, but less to be helpful, and more in fear of the German Shepard and the tattoo artist. Carefully, Baz starts to edge closer, watching Captain as he quickly runs to check on Eleanor before running back to get between him and her.

"Captain, I'm here to help her," he says cautiously. His hand trembles as he holds it out for the dog to sniff. "You know me, I'm just here to help."

Captain moves back to Eleanor, allowing the man to come closer. He tries to think back to what Eleanor had mentioned she needed if she was having a panic attack. The jumper. It's easy to find it in the tote bag Eleanor carries everywhere, the black hoodie laying in his hands as he moves to her side. Her throat is red from her scratching, the scar visible in dots beneath her scratched off makeup. Captain was attempting to force her hands off her neck, face pressed close against the spot as Eleanor tries to push him away to no avail.

Baz lightly places a hand on her shoulder, snapping it back as she flinches away. He tries again, introducing himself carefully. She stays still this time, Captain moving back so he can pass her the jumper.

Almost immediately she starts to relax, hands clutching at the jumper in her hands to her face.

The crowd starts to disperse – as if guilty at their interest in her pain – eventually leaving only Baz, the security guard and the store manager as she gingerly puts her mask back on. She takes her tattoo artist's arm to stand – the jumper now enveloping her body – and keeps her other hand on Captains head.

"We are extremely sorry for any disturbance we may have caused you," the manager says as soon as she turns towards them, head still swimming. "Is there anything we can do for you?"

Eleanor shakes her head weakly, "she was in the wrong, and I acted out of proportion. Usually, I can handle confrontation better than that but being locked in my house has meant I haven't been able to practice my coping methods."

The manager smiles and nods, clearly glad she wasn't mad at the store.

"Your service dog is very protective, he wouldn't let anyone near," the security guard mentions, almost saying it as if it's a bad thing.

"He is trained to do that," Eleanor answers. "People I used to know could easily cause a scene to trigger an attack for me, and it's his job to keep everyone away while I cannot protect myself. He will not attack anyone unless I order him to. Now, if it's okay, I need to go to my car."

"Of course, we can return the things in your cart," the manager replies instantly. "Once again we are sorry for the disturbance."

With a nod, Eleanor takes her bags from the cart, leaving it there as she starts to walk away. Baz follows her until they're out of earshot of the two employees.

"Thank you," Eleanor turns to him to say. "Captain couldn't work properly with them all so close."

"It's fine, Diana. They should read the situation a little better," he chuckles, "go relax."

"When your place is opened up again, I have another idea for a tattoo..."

"I'll call you," he assures. "Now go, they might start worrying you want to file a lawsuit."

With a slight chuckle, Eleanor says goodbye, letting Captain lead her to her car.

She went to the tattoo parlour four weeks later, gaining a cross on her left hip. In each corner went the letters L, R and K. Luke, Rosalie, Kate. For her family. Later one more would join it.

Chapter 19

By the end of June, Eleanor returns to the fights, having missed three in the short stint of the Australian lockdown. Word had gotten out quickly after she notified Barney to enter her and written next to Queen Liz – the adapted name that had arisen out of a few of her fights –on the match board is 'The Crier'. No one expected her to win. The odds were heavily in her opponent's favour.

But Eleanor Beck had trained with the best.

She arrives early, scanning the fight board to find herself entered twice. She held favour in the first match, an easy one – she had fought him before – but she second, she did not. They had convinced him to change weeks, it seems.

Captain is watching lazily as she stretches and warms up, eyeing off the other men as they started to approach to give him a pat. But Eleanor would snap a quick 'hands off' before they could, giving them a glare that sent them running. She is glad she wears a mask all the time anyway, as many of them wear flimsy ones until they get into the ring. Apparently, they were charging a spectator entrance fee now, which severely reduced numbers.

She wins her first match with ease, limbs loose as she gets called forward to fight her new opponent. She hadn't been able to find him in the locker room – obviously because he wasn't there she realises as she steps into the ring.

He was huge, taller than both Nikolas and Michael, but only by an inch or two, and just as buff as the latter. Tattooed tears sit in drips beneath his light green eyes, the obvious origin of the name. A cross sits on his throat, solid and unavoidable. And on his hands are matching tattoos, almost a cuff around the wrist, angel wings along the lower back of his hand which reach along his thumbs. A ring sits in the middle, made to give the effect it was glowing by blank space in the otherwise solid black ink, which continues to his fingers, where it stops in dribbles made to look like blood. As he turns around to speak to a woman carrying the same markings, she spots an intricate upside-down-V tattoo on the bridge of his back.

The slight fear builds in Eleanor's chest at the distinct otherworldly edge she gets from his presence in the room. Somewhere in the back of her mind she realises she's felt this exact feeling only one place before – the yearly Berühmte Söldner ball. But his clear attachment to the woman is enough to keep her from running immediately, the Generals never had friends.

He turns back to face her, taking in her small stature with a grin. He thought she would be easy. But for a few seconds confusion clouds his eyes, considering her with a look almost akin to admiration. His partner lets her gaze linger for a moment longer, so many conflicting emotions swimming through her deep navy eyes.

Oblivious – for once – Eleanor only thinks of the fight. He would be a challenge, but beatable – she figured she had taken down Michael on multiple occasions, and he couldn't be harder.

They start to fight as soon as the buzzer goes. He launches into the attack, more than confident he can get her pinned. Eleanor darts out of the way, spending the first few seconds getting a feel for his fighting techniques.

Her deduction: she is in deep, deep trouble.

The man moves with almost unnatural grace, completely sure of all his extremely accurate movements. His muscles held the same level of augmented strength as the Angeli Princes, but his punches were thrown with more purpose than any she had ever received from them. It was as if he had trained for thousands of years instead of decades.

Realising he could fight for longer than she, Eleanor moves onto the offensive. Able to duck under his guard as he lunges for her once again, she puts all her strength into a punch to his throat, grinning as he stumbles away coughing. Not allowing for him to recover, she continues, kicking hard into his tailbone and swiping his legs out from underneath him.

He recovers quickly enough to spring out of the way of the foot she sends towards his face. Grabbing it as she tries to pull away, he uses his strength to throw her down onto the mat.

The crowd is screaming in encouragement, others watching on in worry as the girl rolls out of his reach and flips onto her feet. For a second they circle each other before Eleanor decides to go for it again.

As he blocks off her attack, he gets enough of a grip on her arm to halt her for a second.

"I didn't know the Berühmte Söldner sent ACEs into petty fighting rings," he mutters just as she slips from his grasp, "or are you the bitch who escaped them? Last I heard she was dead."

In her surprise, he manages to clock her in the face, sending her flying to the floor. With her head spinning he manages to pin her, grinning as he reaches around under her singlet, fingers rubbing over the tattoo. He grins, starting to move his hand upwards when she growls.

"I'm the bitch. The one who befriended the Angeli Princes and Princess," she mutters, hearing the seconds being counted. "Fallen Angel."

Now it's his turn to be surprised and Eleanor uses it to flip him onto his back. One knee waits just over his balls, the other wrapping around one of his legs, and locking it in place. She locks one arm around his and places the other on his throat, growl hanging in her throat as he stares at her in horror. Unable to get her off, the ten seconds pass, her win being declared.

Eleanor stays there, though.

"Do I need to kill you?" she grits, keeping her arm pressed to his throat.

"No," he grunts.

"Your friend?"

Though he pales slightly, he answers, "no. She doesn't know anything."

Enough of an answer for her, Eleanor peels herself away, Captain instantly arriving to place his paws on her shoulders. Her breaths are shuddering, muscles tight as she grips his coat. It takes a few seconds longer than normal before she can step away, walking out of the ring with her head high. It's only as she enters the locker room that she notices her nose is gushing blood underneath the mask, broken. She gets multiple surprised looks as she pulls it down to spit blood out of her mouth.

"Anyone got a mirror I can reset this in?" she calls, someone passing nearby holding one out for her to use.

They continue to look on in surprise as she puts it back in its place, careful to ensure there would be no mark (this was not the first time Eleanor had reset her nose). With a thanks to the man who held it, she grabs a handful of tissues and starts blocking it with one hand.

With the other she quickly packs her bag, Captain still pacing at her feet.

"You should probably get out of here," her opponent mutters as he walks towards her, friend watching her curiously. "The bookies aren't exactly pleased and there are some very drunk, rich assholes who just lost their money."

"How nice of you to care," Eleanor returns bitterly. "We need to talk, your friend included."

He nods carefully, the woman smirking. Something about them puts her at ease in a situation where she should be anything but.

"We were planning on catching a bus back to my place, would you like to give us a ride?" he suggests. "There's a park across from my block, no one is there this time of night."

"Sure," Eleanor mutters, shutting her locker quickly and starting to jog outside, "but I'm going to need to make a call."

Eleanor throws her bag on the back seat floor, Captain jumping up easily and moving over to allow for the woman to take a seat. She shuts the door and runs around the other side of the ute. The male Fallen Angel has already slid into the passenger seat as she jumps in and starts the car. Just as people burst from the building, she pulls the car onto the street. She speeds out of the alley and into the flow of cars before she turns her lights on, confident no one would be able to catch up to them.

He tells her where to go, raising an eyebrow in surprise as she pulls a handgun from under her seat. Her bloody tissues are stuffed into the door, the blood flow now stopped.

"Those are illegal to carry in this country," the woman says.

"It's fully loaded, and I have no qualms with putting a bullet in your head. Or four. How many does it take to kill your kind?" Eleanor returns. "And if you even think about reporting me, be prepared for the Crown Prince to come arrest your ass."

"You like your threats, don't you?" she counters.

"You learn that when you grow up in a compound full of murderers," she returns. "Now, shut up, I need to call someone."

She'd get cash on the way home, she figured.

Her babysitter picks up on the fourth ring.

"Hello?" she asks cautiously.

"Hi, it's Diana. I'm going to be late home, I'm sorry. I'll pay you double, and you can sleep in the guest room. I'm really sorry but things have come up," Eleanor replies, voice ten times kinder than it had been a second ago.

"That's okay. Can I stay until morning? I don't drive very well early in the morning. You don't have to pay me for once you get home. Adelyn's already asleep," the girl answers.

"That's completely fine, thank you so much. Bye!" Eleanor finishes, waiting for the girl to respond before hanging up.

"They're still teaching you to be spies, I see," the man grins. "I never quite understood how you all could do it. Be so utterly cheery and innocent after murdering hundreds of people. Made it really hard to trust motivations."

"Compartmentalising," Eleanor returns in a bitter tone. "Can I trust you both?"

"Are you going to trust us if I say you can?"

"Probably not."

The two share a not-quite-grin and Eleanor finally pulls into the parking lot of the park they had arrived at.

She is about to step out of the car when he mentions, "no matter how many times you shoot us, we'll recover perfectly after a few days. You must either decapitate, crucify, or burn us to ashes. They really meant eternal when they gave us eternal punishment."

"That seems like more of a benefit," Eleanor says, opening the door for Captain and slipping around to the back of the car. Her eyes stay cautiously on the woman. She was the only unknown variable in this encounter.

Eleanor emerges with her twin blades swinging them thoughtfully as she catches up to the pair. But she still hangs back, eyes flicking around the park for any other movement and keeping the two Fallen Angels constantly in her view.

For once the glimpses don't haunt her. She is lucky; or maybe the steel in her hands keeps them away. Maybe it was the ethereal presence.

"Not when we are used to being effectively bulletproof with extreme power. A life for eternal inferiority to the Angels and their kin," the man replies, passing his gaze over her in the dark. "Nice swords, also not legal in this country."

"The Americans care more about me being able to stop myself from being taken back by the Agency than the laws of this country."

"I'd say there are people who would wholeheartedly disagree with that."

The woman sends Eleanor a grin as she speaks, her previous confliction forgotten to cocky confidence. Women were always so much more irritating; but then again, Ellsie lived off being irritating so she couldn't exactly fault the woman.

"Oh definitely, but they can say so to the International Criminal Court," Eleanor grins. "What are your names? I'm assuming you're actually thrown out from Heaven since you're immortal."

"We were a long, long time ago. But like all good punishments, our memory does not fail us," he says. "I go by Lachlan, have since about 2010. We manage about 15-year blocks before we have to leave a place and find a new name. Botox has been helpful in extending that timeline, though."

"And I am Lucy, seemingly tied eternally to this ass," the woman follows. The swing of her hair – cut into a long, angled bob – emphasises her words perfectly.

"What were your original names?" Eleanor prods, grinning at the man as he sends both the women a glare in turn. "What? I must collect my intel. And I know how alias's work. Untraceable and all."

"I'm Lahash, she's Lerajie," he offers. "That enough to trust us. I've told you our names, how to kill us... I think we deserve a little in return."

"Tell me what my name is," Eleanor says, lips tight as she watches them sit lightly on a park bench, blades still in her hands.

"You go by Elizabeth when fighting. You called yourself Diana earlier," Lahash lists. "Safe to say, I doubt that's your actual name. I seem to remember your name being... Eleanor. Yes, Eleanor Beck, the lone member of the Beck family that was never found."

Though it shouldn't surprise her, she still pales a fraction, keeping her breath measured.

"You should be 20 by now, quite a skilled little ACE. Got pregnant – raped I'd say – got out of the Agency. Somehow got picked up by the Americans," Lerajie continues. "It's how and why the Crown Prince didn't hate and kill you for your crimes that I don't understand."

"Cause I'm just charismatic," Eleanor bites, before amending. "You know what Geminae Animarum are?"

They both frown deeply, eyebrows knit close. They did, and it worried them more than they will ever admit.

"You're human, or if you have any blood its very little. If you were the Geminae of a Prince, they would never let you fight in a hole like that. It doesn't seem plausible," Lahash mutters. "And the impacts on your mental state could be catastrophic if the connection was entertained and broken."

"I am the Geminae of the exiled, younger Prince. The bastard of the Queen. Michael – firstborn – took pity on his brother and tried to give me another chance. But Nikolas made it off Exilium Terras and went after Michael. Learned about me. We never went very far, so I'm only slightly mad." Her tone almost elicits a chuckle from Lerajie, but she quickly hides the amusement. "If he finds out that I got hurt, he'll... not take it well. And I can very easily report that there are two first generation Fallen Angels here and there will be a legion of Angeli Terra soldiers – probably led by Michael – that will come to find you," she explains. "I trust you do not want to spend the rest of your life locked in their prison."

"No. I quite like being able to see the sky," Lerajie mutters. "What will it take to stop you from telling them?"

"Not all that much. I mysteriously go missing and they will search my house. Until I trust you properly, I'll keep a note somewhere they will find it telling them you exist. Also, if I find out you've spilled to the Daemones or to the Berühmte Söldner, I will find you and keep you alive long enough for Michael to take over. Possibly even Nikolas. He won't take very well to that at all," she grins. "I would quite like to have you both as friends, being able to talk to someone about the secret problems in my life would be good and I am inclined to trust you, for some reason. I already know he's a brilliant fighter, I'd assume you are as well. I find it hard to manage my bloodlust. Having nearly invincible sparring partners would be useful."

"How do you know we're not working for the Berühmte Söldner now?"

"You would have called me 'Kitten'. All those assholes do. And you wouldn't have had to ask who I am. My hair colour is fairly distinctive, and if they sent one of you after me, I would be dead or captured by now," she shrugs, glancing over at Lahash as he grins at her. "And I have a feeling she wasn't in the Agency at any point."

"I wasn't, we got separated for a while after the Second World War. I knew there were Angeli still creeping around, so I hid while he played villain," Lerajie smirks, flipping back her ebony hair. "He still gets Christmas cards; I accompany him when he decides to entertain their parties."

Lahash adds, "ditched them a while back, got bored. They're a little overbearing for my taste. Visiting keeps me up to date with the up-and-coming ACEs. If I remember correctly, I watched you steal a ring off a boy last time I was there. I figured it would do no harm not to dob you in," Lahash says, chuckling as he finishes. "You fight like you were trained by one of my students. Who trained you?"

After a pause, Eleanor answers, "Mein Vater, his code is 613. Dunkler Bischof."

Lahash chuckles, nodding.

"He always held promise. Didn't ever seem to have a soft spot for murderous girls, though," he frowns.

"I think he more had a soft spot for the soft part of me. I am not a normal girl. They broke me harder than they realised, he understood that, taught me how to control it all. I am like a daughter to him," she admits, checking her watch quickly. "I need to get home. But I'd like to stay in touch with you. I need to talk about things. But if you are happy with your current company, I can leave you alone."

"No need. We rather like having someone new to talk to as well," he grins, handing over his phone for her to copy his number. "Do you speak Latin?"

"I'm learning, the Crown Prince wouldn't allow me while I was in America," she mutters crankily, finally breaking a chuckle from the Fallen Angel. "Can you help me? To learn?"

"If only so you can shove it up his ass," Lerajie replies.

With a roll of her eyes, Eleanor gently asks, "which name do you want me to use?"

"Our original," Lerajie answers. "And you what name shall we call you?"

"If we're alone, you may call me Eleanor, otherwise, Diana please. I must keep up appearances," she requests.

Eleanor stands quietly, throwing the phone lightly back to him. With barely a goodbye, Eleanor moves to her car, Captain obviously glad to take the passenger seat once again. Her blades are lazily thrown onto the back seat, and her car pulls away.

The two Fallen Angels stay sitting in the park for many more hours. Finally, as the sun starts to rise, Lerajie breaks.

"What do we do?" she asks. Disbelief has returned to her.

"Support her. Help her. If she is..." Lahash stops his sentence early. "Do we tell her?"

"There's no reason to. It's safer for her and her daughter if they don't know," Lerajie sighs. "I always thought there was something more to her actions, I never thought it might be this..."

"The Archangels are very complicated beings, you know that."

Chapter 20

"Dr Nolan," Eleanor grins as she walks into her therapy session – they had already had two since lockdown lifted, but today Eleanor was in a rather chipper mood.

An oddity for the usually morose girl, but last night was her fight night. She had fought Lerajie this time. More importantly, she had won... the second round. It was more fun than Ellsie had had in a long time. And Nora had relinquished control so her other half could gloat it out. Censored of course.

"You seem happy," the psychiatrist returns. "Perhaps you had Tai Chi last night?"

"Yes, Tai Chi," Eleanor smiles – fighting, was what they both meant. "I made two new friends, who can challenge me. She is like me, it's fun to talk with her and he's fun to beat."

"A man? Describe him to me."

With a roll of her eyes, Eleanor drops herself onto the couch, crossing one leg over the other.

"To answer your actual question, no I do not want a relationship with him. We are friends nothing more. I have no want or need to find anything else," Eleanor returns, haughty smirk clear on her face.

"And what in his appearance makes you say that instead of answering my question?" Vanessa grins, holding the glare Eleanor sends her. "On a scale of one to ten?"

"It's impossible not to admit he's at least an 8.5, probably a nine," Eleanor answers bitterly, "though if you don't like tattoos he probably would drop to a seven. But someone could easily look past that."

"You feel no attraction to him?"

"No. I don't want anyone else, except… him," she replies softly. "I like having friends who are my friends first, not Nora's. Everyone always takes her side, only Mein Vater, Seb and Nikolas ever showed me acceptance."

"Can you describe Sebastian to me?" Dr Nolan prods, watching her carefully.

"Dirty blonde, grey eyes, not quite as silver as Nikolas's. He was wider in frame than him as well – though I haven't seen him in a while now – stronger jaw and face than Nikolas's. Probably 5'10," Eleanor lists after a few seconds. "He was kind, let her hold onto him when she needed to, and was able to keep up with my banter. He wasn't as skilled as I was, but he was going to become an ACE, probably has by now. He was never jealous of my relationship with our trainer and took the cane for me more than once. I was always getting in trouble; I doubt I would be able to walk if he didn't take the blame for a few things."

"You compare him to Nikolas a lot…"

Eleanor glances away, almost guilty.

"They are quite similar in appearance. I guess it's my type, since I'm Geminae to Nikolas," she shrugs, Nora now starting to restrict her control. "But they are from different times in my life, I try to keep them separate in my mind."

"Why do you do that?"

Eleanor must think for a few seconds, eyes glazing over as she shifts back into her seat. A leg tucks underneath her as she answers.

"I think it's because I don't want to feel… I don't want to miss Seb as I think I would if I talked about him more," Nora breathes. "And I don't want to hold onto him when I know I will probably never see him again. I don't want to cloud the memories I have of Nik with the ones I have of him. Both relationships were so different from each other."

Dr Nolan thinks for a second, contemplating her options.

"How so?" she ends up asking. "How are they different?"

"With Seb, we didn't talk all that much. We traded banter more often than anything else, and it just formed as we got older. We never slept together – in that way – but we made out a lot. I feel like we were only so close because we were the only ones we ever had," Eleanor replies. "Whereas Nikolas. I wanted him, even though I could have had any of the boys at the school. We spent most of our time talking, sharing secrets. He had a game for when I lost focus because of something I was thinking about, it was like we were trading admissions. I still have the pennies. Our relationship was all about proximity and comfort, and we understood each other more than anyone else. And we were extremely protective of one another. Me, when it came to Michael, and him just in general. Although that protectiveness did kind of end us up in this situation, but I can understand why."

"What do you understand about it?"

"He is sacrificing his happiness with me, to allow for me to be safe for longer – even if it affects me and I miss him. It's the exact same thing I plan to do for Adelyn, what I have planned to do for her since I found out she existed," she admits. "Except she will never get to see me again, she will never be able to find me. I will be completely gone. He made me a promise to be with me at the end. He sends me books, lets me know he is okay. It hurts a lot, but I understand why. I can't hate him for it."

"And you need to take advantage of the opportunities he gave you," Vanessa finishes, tone kind as Eleanor looks away. "No one could blame you if you decided to... take some pleasures for yourself."

"I do not want to... I like my life as it is, even without that kind of love," she notes, pausing as Captain slinks closer. "I think a small part of me is hesitant. That even if Nikolas was here, and there were no extra complications that came with having sex with him, I still wouldn't be in any rush."

"Because of Adelyn's conception?"

~

Other than just before giving birth, Eleanor never spoke about, that, with anyone. Not to me, although that I can understand, but not even to her friends, not to Nikolas or Kenichi, Lahash or her Vater. I don't think anyone ever got close to that kind of intimacy. Any kisses she shared with Nikolas never went that far.

You will learn more, as you continue, but let me just say, her easy life does not last.

~

Eleanor shrugs, hand running over Captain's head as he alerts. Dr Nolan decides to retreat from the topic.

"So, what are the names of these new friends?" she asks.

"Lucy and Lachlan."

Much like herself, their real names were kept private.

Chapter 21

"It's so good to be able to have so many people over," Amy grins as they mill around in the large living room of her house.

Some people are out on the deck, most of them with drinks in hand. The children had already started a movie, the setting sun casting long shadows on the spring grass. Food had already rotated past them, only a few people still eating. Some of the older kids had gone for a swim, but Eleanor had stayed out of the water, she didn't really want all the people around to see the scars littering her body. Or to see how truly skinny she was.

"I'm sure a lot of people are glad about that," Eleanor replies, "though I must admit, limited travel is making me much more relaxed."

"Don't you miss that doctor friend of yours coming over?" Amy asks casually.

"I still call him every few weeks. He thinks it's beneficial making me have to take advice from others." Eleanor chuckles quietly as she swirls the drink in her hand.

Amy grins but after a few seconds a frown forms on her face. A car was driving up the road.

"Everyone's here..." she mutters, starting to walk towards her parking area.

With a quick assessment, Eleanor sends Captain to Adelyn.

"It's a hire car as well," she adds, hand lightly checking for the blade held in the secret pouch in her pocket. "Male, strong build, unfamiliar with the area."

Amy nods in agreement before she stops short and spends a short second looking at Eleanor in surprise.

"I trained for years to be able to do that..." she says carefully.

Eleanor replies under her breath, "so did I."

The man climbs out of the car slowly, obviously taking the time to observe the crowds before his eyes land on Eleanor.

"Oh, I swear..." she growls as she finally realises who it is.

"You know who it is?" Amy asks, raising an eyebrow. "And where's Captain?"

"With Adelyn, I thought it might be a problem," Eleanor mutters. "And yes, I do."

"Who is he?"

Fully in view now, Michael tries his hardest not to shy away from the glare Eleanor is sending him. But he was here with a purpose.

"My ex's brother. My bet is he's trying to get information out of me about the location of his brother," she replies. "I put five dollars on Kenichi not knowing he's here."

"How would he be able to get in? They still aren't allowing people into the country."

"Because he has very high security clearance and won't have been in contact with any cases," Eleanor hisses. "Still doesn't mean he should be here."

Wisely, he stops twenty metres from the two women, crossing his arms.

"He is not to enter your house, I'll deal with him then send him up to mine," Eleanor says. "He can sit on my deck for a while."

"You don't seem to like him very much."

"I'm not his biggest fan. Believe it or not we used to be close, but he's been a bit too rude about his brother recently and ambushing me in my hometown is not something I put up with well."

Eleanor leaves the conversation at that, stalking down to where he is standing and streaking straight past. They needed to be further away to talk – Amy suspects a little too much about her already. As they stop, both faces matching as they face each other, Eleanor slaps him.

"What the hell are you doing here!" she growls. "You aren't supposed to know this location, or visit it, you could completely ruin my cover or lead the Daemones straight here!"

"I didn't, I promise," he returns. "Came to deliver this in person and get a straight answer out of you."

He thrusts a book into her chest, without wrapping paper. They always came with wrapping paper. Eleanor knowing it's from Nikolas, shoves down the wave of loneliness for the moment.

"Straight answer to what, Michael? If I know where the hell my Geminae is? If I'm purposefully punishing myself by not being with him?" she snaps.

"Yes. There is no way you don't know more than you've told us about the location of the bases," he returns.

"I don't know, Michael! You don't think if I did, I would have told you all so you could take them down! They ruined my life, killed my parents. I want them to burn in hell!" Eleanor yells. "All I know is the base I grew up in was in the Bavarian Alps, and once a year we went to a ball, each in a different place. They never told us exactly where, or the exact date, and the date changed every year.

"But he isn't going to be holed up at the Berühmte Söldner base, he will be with a faction of Daemones, in a base in America. I don't know where any pickup spots are, any runways or anything else. We get drugged coming into the country and stay that way until we are at our unique deployment zone, and when our handlers come to pick us up, in goes the sedative until we wake up in Germany."

Michael balks at her tone, the rage in her eyes.

"He sends you books multiple times a year, we have no idea what they say. He could be passing you information, telling you where he is if you need him," he continues anyway.

"They are books, fictional stories! The inscriptions read the same as this one probably does. I'm sorry. I'm safe. Forgive me. He knows I can't know where he is, because I will go to him and make him leave. He is hurting, Michael. It isn't easy for him!" she bites, anger plain in her tone. "I know you think the worst of him, but he just wants to help me, help Adelyn, in the only way he knows how. He has made himself a villain so he can sacrifice everything to keep me safe, to do things no one would allow. A Prince cannot do that. He knows how to keep me safe, and to do that he has to break laws. You've made him the villain in your mind, you have since your mother died. Because dishonourable actions trump honourable morals. You don't let yourself see past that."

The argument that had been hanging off her tongue for years.

"He is a bad person, Eleanor! He is murdering people," Michael argues.

"Because if he doesn't, they will beat him. Even kill him if he does too many things wrong. They don't care who does their dirty work, just that it's done to their standard. They could replace him with an ACE in a second, and then it would all be for nothing," Eleanor barks, having to reign in her anger as she remembers where she is. "How did you even find me? You weren't told my address."

"I used your tracker," he replies, quieter than earlier.

With a crack of her jaw, Eleanor turns away.

"Go back out the last gate you came through, continue to follow the road further into the valley until you reach a brick house on the side of a hill. The house is locked, don't try to get in. You can wait in your car until I decide to come home. You leave tomorrow," she orders, fists clenched tight. "Understood?"

Michael answers to the affirmative, watching Eleanor as she walks back up to the house.

For a second her steps stutter as she glances back, past him. A yelp of terror barely held behind her lips. She refuses to look back again. She refuses to let anyone notice her weakness. But the shadows keep reaching out to her, calling for her.

"Everything okay?" Amy asks as Eleanor breaches the front of her porch.

"Just brilliant," she replies bitterly. "He just had to ruin my night."

"You can stay here tonight if you'd like."

"It's fine, but can Adelyn stay over tomorrow night? I'll need to get my emotions in check, and I can't do that with her in my care."

Amy looks at her curiously, but nods.

"Thank you."

Eleanor goes to find Adelyn, slipping in the back of the room as quietly as possible. Captain, of course, notices her first, moving back over to his owner only as she softly calls him. Adelyn glances back in confusion, frowning at her mother.

"Are we okay?" she asks sweetly.

"Yes, just a visit from Michael," Eleanor assures her. "Come out once the movie is over, okay?"

"I will Mumma."

With a loving smile, Eleanor slips out of the room once more. Her fingers tap over her phone screen like lightning.

Eleanor

I need to rant.

And punch something.

Can we meet tomorrow night, normal place?

Lahash

Of course, what am I but a brilliant punching bag…

What has you in such a mood?

Eleanor

An Asshole Crown Prince who thinks it's okay to show up unannounced and question me about his brother.

Don't worry. He's going back to America first thing tomorrow.

Lerajie

I'd come punch him for you, but once again, I quite like fresh air.

Eleanor

I would expect no less.

See you tomorrow.

If Michael had expected to get away with his little visit, he was sorely mistaken. He got in a multitude of trouble from Colonel Nancy Randall, who was just about ready to skin him alive when he landed back in America. Eleanor did not forgive him quickly, choosing to hold her grudge for over a year.

He didn't dare question her again… about Nikolas at least.

Chapter 22

"So, an asshole Crown Prince?" Lahash grins as Eleanor arrives at his private training ring.

The space was large, hidden in the middle of a residential area. But most importantly, had no cameras. Neither Eleanor nor the Fallen Angels were particularly fond of there being evidence of their existence.

Lerajie stayed hidden in the corner, methodically cleaning her blades.

"He reached a new level of idiocy," Eleanor mutters in response, already starting to advance on him. "Tracked me to my friend's house, ambushed me there, so we had an audience and pretty much told me he thought I was plotting with Nikolas so he could kill people, and I could raise Adelyn." Lahash blocks all her advances, smirking as she grows more and more frustrated. "Thought I withheld locations of the Agency bases because I was still loyal to them. Thought I would be purposefully staying away from Nikolas when I am legitimately crazy without him nearby. Because, you know, I would let myself have horrendous nightmares each night just so my Geminae could go and help the people who ruined my life and murdered my family achieve world domination." Lahash nods along with what she is saying, still blocking her attacks. But they were getting closer to the wall. "And he was saying that Nikolas – who is only killing those people because he must, otherwise he will die – is doing it all because he is an evil person and is still telling himself that Nikolas is the villain, not his asshole of a father! Stop dodging!"

"Eleanor, you are fully capable of landing a punch on me, I'm just putting up a mediocre defence," the Fallen Angel taunts, grinning as the girl's eyes darken.

The grin drops as she punches him straight in the face. Three times.

"See?" he groans, flicking his head back up in pain. "Easy."

"You are infuriating," Eleanor hisses, spinning on her foot to kick him in the side. "Like, who would even think of doing that in the car park of a party he isn't even invited to? Michael, that's who. He thinks he's so special, set to take the throne he doesn't even want, while his sister who is so much smarter than he is, gets sidelined to be a broodmare. He didn't even think enough to worry about her as she was married off to his best friend! He is always calling Nikolas the villain, but Nik's the only one who cares about what Anastasia wants, he's the only one who cares if she's happy."

"He's 30 now, isn't he?" Lerajie calls from across the room, Lahash now attempting to land a few punches on Eleanor.

"Yes…"

"Why isn't he married yet? And why is he still in the human world, they usually only stay for a year or two…"

"He hasn't married because he likes a human girl, and since he's the 'only eligible heir to the throne' his father is willing to let him play around until he becomes king. And he's still here because he doesn't want to be King. He just wants to lord over everyone but have no responsibilities," Eleanor bites. "He wants to play around at being the hero."

Lahash swipes her off her feet, grinning down at her as she scowls. But she doesn't get up, content to lay on the floor. Across the room, Captain gets up from where she had told him to lay. He plops onto her stomach, using his weight to draw her back to her senses. As she does so, he bops her with his nose. Multiple times.

"Do you have any food?" Eleanor mutters at the still grinning Lahash. "I haven't eaten for a while."

He raises an eyebrow, but nods. A few seconds later he holds two options: an apple and a packet of Oreos. Eleanor manages to get a hand free to point at the sweeter option, catching them an inch from her face as he throws them towards her.

Captain gets off her, relaxing at her side as she sits up to eat. Lerajie abandons her work, walking over and dropping in front of Eleanor. Lahash takes the place on her other side, waiting expectantly for her to pass him one of the biscuits. Passing one over begrudgingly, Ellsie stretches out her legs.

"How come he is trained to alert to you not having eaten for a while?" he asks as she does so, edging off the topic of the Crown Prince.

"They used to refuse to give us meals if we misbehaved," Eleanor answers. "I guess I kept doing it to punish myself even after I got out. It got bad when I first got here and Nikolas left, so we made sure to find a dog who was taught to read whether I needed food. Captain did and had the other requirements too, so we drove quite a way to get him."

Lahash accepts the answer, but it's clear Lerajie is a little less accepting — she was much more despising of the Agency — both watching the dog that had placed his head in Eleanor's lap for attention. About to speak again, he stops as Eleanor does.

"Are you two romantically involved?" she asks, confident in her question.

"Hell no," Lerajie answers immediately, her laugh almost defensive. "We slept together once or twice thousands of years ago, but he is not to my taste. Though he goes for pretty much anything."

Lahash rolls his eyes, but a little hurt lies behind them. A little disappointment.

"Why have you never tried to, sleep with me? We've been plenty close enough times for you to have tried something, but you never have," she says, cautious. "Not including the first time we met."

He can't help the surprise that jumps to his face.

"You're the Geminae Animarum to an Angeli. I've seen what unmated Geminae have done if someone touched their partner. And I also have seen you punch quite a few men for trying to touch you up," he shrugs. "If you had started something I would have gone along with it. But you've never once seemed like you have wanted to."

Eleanor smiles gratefully, glancing around the dark room.

"I haven't. I was just wondering." Pausing to send him a cocky smirk, she adds, "it seems I'm pretty irresistible for most people."

"I wouldn't say most," Lahash taunts, taking another Oreo off her. "Just the fighters who get off on domineering women."

"Domineering?"

"Though I'm sure the Agency would have taught you to manage that if you stayed until graduation."

Both women roll their eyes.

"And to think that if I had stayed and aborted Ady then I probably would have been taught even earlier," Eleanor mutters. "I heard rumours some of the graduated ACE women have the 'immense privilege' to be in the boss's bed. Often without choice."

Lahash is the one who chuckles at that, glancing across at her in amusement.

"I never was quite fond of that practice," he says. "The lack of choice part. Had plenty of fun with some of the fully willing ones, but I could tell when they didn't want to do it. Some made fun of me for it, but I guess my previous angelic chivalry stuck around."

Eleanor frowns somewhat, glancing away as she thinks. Her head stays upright, though, a conversation with Nora running rampant in her head. Captain notices her dissociating, lightly pawing at her thigh to regain her focus. Carefully she turns back, patting the dog gratefully and turning to look at her companion. Lerajie holds a knowing smile as Eleanor starts to talk.

"Can you promise me you'll never become like them? Force girls to do, that?" she says, eyes hard on his. "That you'll always make sure they truly want to do it, even if they change their mind in the middle?"

Lahash doesn't hesitate as he answers, "I promise. And where I can I'll stop others from doing it as well."

It isn't hard for Eleanor to find the sincerity in his eyes, the assurances in his movements as he holds out a pinkie. She takes it quietly.

"Thank you."

"I promise, Eleanor, I am not as bad as many others make my kind out to be. Sure, there are a lot of assholes who really should be rounded up by the Angeli, but there are some who truly want redemption, and there are others, like us, who just are happy living our lives. Who knows, if the Angels ever return to Earth, I may just offer my services," he says, winking as he finishes.

"We may," Lerajie amends, looking to Lahash for a moment.

Kinship. They had walked side by side for millennia.

"Do you think they'll come anytime soon?" Eleanor asks, purely curious.

"I don't think the pricks from heaven will, no. But I think that there will be a battle against the Daemones. It doesn't happen often, but maybe an Angel will be born of it. You never know," Lahash shrugs, laying back on the floor while Eleanor crosses her legs.

Lerajie adds, "he's quite fond of his prophecies."

"Whose side will you stand on?"

"If the Angeli stand a chance of winning, we will aid their cause. But if hope seems lost, we will stay impartial until someone can convince us to the side of the Angels," Lerajie answers slowly. "I've tried to make it my duty never to kill an Angeli, but it would be nice to see some of my old friends. I've lost quite a few to them over the years. If the Angels walked this Earth once again, I'm sure they would make use of their prison guard to fight, I'd fight alongside my brethren, even if it meant being lost to that place."

"Fallen Angels work in the prison?"

"Some. The decent ones. Of course, there are others who make it their life's purpose to wipe out the Angeli, but I care little about those," Lahash chuckles, he had a better sense of humour of the two, Lerajie barely putting up with his antics. "Pretty sure they have Lucifer and Beelzebub locked up in the depths of that cavern. They lost a pretty big war to the Angels a thousand or so years ago and have been suspiciously silent ever since."

Eleanor returns his grin, flopping backwards again.

"Thanks for putting up with me..." she offers.

"Anytime, Regina Tenebris," he grins, poking her side in jest as he flamboyantly bows.

Queen of the Dark.

It makes me sure the Fallen Angels had an idea of what was to come. This would not be the last time Eleanor was crowned with the name.

Chapter 23

Another thing that I have to mention is Eleanor's continued correspondence with Anastasia. It was rare that Anastasia was able to get messages out on the single computer in Angeli Terra, but Eleanor's was always one email she never failed to respond to.

Whether it was merely discussion about Anastasia's life on the island – for she and Markus had settled into married life quite well – or quiet mentions of Nikolas and whether or not Eleanor had heard anything, they always found something to discuss. Most recently, it had been history, comparing human events to the Angeli version, and often finding answers to the discrepancies that troubled Eleanor.

The other topic of discussion was, of course, Adelyn. The Princess was always happy to receive photos of the young girl, or if photos weren't particularly interesting, Eleanor would recount stories in great length.

I won't bore you with one, since there is nothing groundbreaking in any – both women knew far better than to record stuff like that – but I thought it would be important to explain why the Princess always protected Eleanor's wishes.

Chapter 24

Her fight the month after was a difficult one for sure. Both she and Lahash were blindfolded for their match, the two landing more hits each than normal. She would be sore tomorrow, that's for certain.

Eleanor slips through her door, making sure to keep her hood up as she makes it into the living room. Captain, toy in his mouth, trots over to greet the occupants of the house, tail wagging. Quietly, she calls out to the babysitter, surprised to find two people sitting on the couches, instead of one. The teenager jumps up and walks over to her, apology clear on her face.

"I'm sorry, Diana. He kept insisting he was a friend of yours. I made Adelyn go to bed early and kept an eye on him since he arrived," she rushes, seemly worried to find her employer's face so bloody. "Are... are you okay?"

"I'm fine, Piper," Eleanor assures, handing over her payment, along with some extra, "for your troubles. And thank you, you did the right thing. I can handle this from here."

With a hesitation, the girl thanks her and leaves, Eleanor ignoring the extra person as she moves into the dark kitchen and grabs a bag of peas, pressing them to her shoulder.

"She's a good babysitter," the person calls. "I tried to pay her early and put Adelyn to bed myself, but she wouldn't let me."

Kenichi. It comes with no shock to Eleanor as he walks closer. He had nearly caught her a few months ago.

"You didn't tell me you were coming," she calls out. Voice cautious as ever. "I would have ensured I was home to greet you."

Her friend scoffs, moving to block her way out of the kitchen as she attempts to slip away.

"Of course you would have. That's why I didn't tell you," he says, flicking the light on as Eleanor turns towards him.

For a second, they shut their eyes against the light, before Kenichi pulls back her hood and cracks his jaw in anger.

"Where the hell do you disappear to every month? Don't think I haven't noticed it on your tracker," he demands, taking her by the upper arm to drag her to her room.

"Ensuring I don't accidentally kill someone," Eleanor returns as she pulls out of his grasp and walks herself. "I didn't think you needed to know."

"Why not, Eleanor?" he snaps. "Does Dr Nolan know?"

Eleanor pauses slightly, swallowing before she walks into her bathroom and brings out a first aid kit. Kenichi turns on her light and shuts her door, sitting with her on the bed and taking the kit out of her hands.

"Somewhat. She told me to do something to get the violent tendencies out. To let her—"

She cuts herself off, standing abruptly to walk to her window. Her lavender bear is in her arms as she looks out into the darkness. He didn't know, yet. But if he was to understand, she had to tell him.

"Dr Nolan has kept a secret for me, for a while now," she whispers as she turns back around and sits on the opposite edge of the bed. "I begged her to. And even though she agreed, she made me promise to tell you soon. That was, two years ago."

Kenichi nods slowly.

"I have two questions," he says carefully. "First, what is it you have been doing? And does what you are going to tell me change the state of your legal case?"

"I have been attending monthly, underground fights, bare knuckle rings. I compete with my face covered, and with most of my scars covered. It's safe, that way. And it shouldn't affect my case. I am still the same person, the things I have done are the same, there is just a better explanation for them," Eleanor assures, continuing as he nods for her to. "I have a mental health condition. A diagnosable one that you don't know about. A... split personality. Dissociative Identity Disorder, though it's far from a typical case. There's me, who is older, the original personality, from before the Agency, and then the one who was in control until I got pregnant." She pauses to let him think for a few seconds. "I... I hate hurting people; death makes me sick, and I don't like killing. I lost my mind when my parents died, I wasn't strong enough. I have never been strong enough. She has. They hit me down one day, because I couldn't even touch the gun that they wanted me to shoot, and for a few seconds I was unconscious, then when I woke everything was numb, like I wasn't in control as I stood up. She picked up the gun and shot the man who had knocked us down.

"We found we could talk to each other, and we could decide who was in control. Ellsie is what we named her; she held the reins for years. Born out of pain and death, she loved the life we led. Hurting people made her feel safe, important, needed. She kept me alive, kept us both alive. And in doing so, lost herself to violence." Suddenly clenching her jaw, then relaxing, Ellsie smirks. "I think you'll find I did not lose myself. I merely found my way. Nora needed me, and so I provided, I made life easy for us both. If it wasn't for me, she would be dead in a ditch. Maybe I enjoy watching the light fade from people's eyes too much, maybe I find it soothing to carve a cross on my victims' foreheads, but I live only to keep us safe. Why do you think she ended up in your grasp? I could have easily ripped the control from her, but she wanted to have our daughter, she wanted a way out of that life. I would do anything for her, so I agreed, even if I knew I would miss my life.

"Adelyn, and Nikolas, they kept her out of her shell. They made her want to live and be in control, so I allowed for her to live her way. I came out when she needed me to, when she was scared, or tired. I was the reason she found solace in training. I do try to get her to eat as much as I can, but I couldn't shelter her from much of the psychological damage they inflicted, so often she ignores me. I would never hurt our child; she is the only other thing I love. I must say, I did let myself be conformed by her rules, and I only take full control over her when absolutely necessary, or when she chooses. I won't kill if she doesn't want me to, unless there is no other option, but it isn't our way to kill civilians, only those who work for the Agency. Promise.

"I don't really know how to be nice to people. It's hard for me to trust anyone, really, while Nora allows for more leniency. I try to learn how to be nice, I must admit that Nikolas helped a lot in that department. And Dr Nolan has been helping us to understand each other better, not to argue and fight for control as much. Can you understand why I need to release the pent-up violence that runs in my blood? Nikolas would usually let me fight him, and as you know I spent a lot of time taking it out on my punching bag, but without him here, and knowing I do not train as much as I would normally need to, I go to fighting rings to get my energy out. I refuse to bet; I refuse to take any money. No-one sees my face and I don't kill them. Normally I'm not this beat up, either. I just had a fight with a new friend of mine. We're pretty evenly matched so they had us fight blindfolded."

Kenichi nods, still mulling over what she had told him. But his eyes stay kind, to Eleanor's partial surprise.

"That, oddly, explains much," he sighs. "We were just thinking you were bi-polar, and insanity was on the table for a few weeks, but this makes much more sense. I don't know how I didn't see this before."

It's amusing to see the slight huff Eleanor makes. Insanity probably should have still been on the table. She wasn't actually insane of course, but it can appear that way when you start seeing things.

"I am very good at hiding it. We've spoken of having to be perfect, have we not," Eleanor breathes. "Michael caught onto something for a little bit, but he quickly forgot about it. Luckily. Nikolas, he noticed much quicker, and we decided to tell him. He never even thought of sharing that with anyone, he knew telling him was important to me so kept it quiet."

Kenichi smiles, offering for her to come closer – Eleanor does, silently allowing him to start cleaning her face.

"Is there any way to quench the bloodlust, without attending underground fight rings?" he asks carefully, rolling his eyes as she hisses in pain. "I thought you were tough."

"You surprised me. And I tried other things, before I started. Captain was alerting more, he does it less when I do this," Eleanor replies. "I enjoy it. Usually, I don't get this bloodied up, but it's much harder to see a fist flying for your face when you literally can't see. And unfortunately, I'm right at his fist height."

"Did you end up winning?" Kenichi questions, laughing as she looks at him in surprise. "What, am I not allowed to ask?"

"I won. He may be bigger and stronger than me, but I can move quietly. I've fought blindfolded many times," she answers in amusement. "I just thought your question would be who he was."

"Would you answer, or would you tell me it's none of my business?" he challenges.

"Likely the latter," Eleanor admits. "You seem weirdly unbothered by the whole split personality thing."

"It makes sense. Somehow justifies your actions a little bit."

He sits back, finished with cleaning her face and placing two wound closure strips on a cut on her jaw.

"Was your nose broken?" he frowns, attention on the continually purpling feature.

"Yeah. I reset it when I got out to my car," she shrugs, "I'm very good at resetting noses."

"How is there not any permanent damage?" he asks incredulously.

"You tell me. You're the Doctor."

Kenichi rolls his eyes, glancing at the bear still sitting in her lap.

"Is that the one from..." he starts.

"Yeah. It helps me ground myself when I don't need Captain jumping up and crushing my legs or internal organs," Eleanor answers softly. "And the lavender helps as well."

"I didn't know you still had it."

Eleanor pauses for a second.

"I still have it all."

Eleanor only tells two more people that she has a split personality, that being Lahash and Lerajie, though they had suspected as much well before she tells them. Kenichi keeps her secret, not willing to breach her trust in him. Even in the face of saving her, they kept that secret to themselves.

It's something I know she was always grateful for, especially as he also kept that she had been going to fight rings a secret until she had to reveal it. He was never happy about it, but like most things when it came to her, he understood why and let it slide.

Chapter 25

Eleanor grits her teeth against the hot wind as she climbs out of her car.

"I'm not allowed a gun licence," Eleanor warns as Lahash leads her towards a shooting range. An uncharacteristic stab of fear makes Ellsie pause. "Instability and all, no one in their right mind would let someone with my conditions shoot a gun. Not in this country at least."

"These guys owe me, and if I need to stop you, I can," he assures. "No matter how many times you shoot me, you cannot kill me."

With Captain lingering at her side, Eleanor looks up to her friend. Lahash ruffles her hair affectionately, succeeding in breaking her tense expression. But she still hasn't prepared herself to walk in.

"I haven't shot a gun in a long time, I don't know how I'll react," she insists. "Is there not somewhere quieter? Less populated?"

Lahash chuckles at her as he replies.

"You don't want to take us to your house yet, so no. We've hired the entire thing out, only the owner will be there besides us," he says. "If you don't want to, we can go somewhere else but figured you might like to have a little practise. And..."

He trails off, glancing around the empty parking lot with apprehension. It's midday, the late spring heat causing waves of heat distortion on the tarmac. The building in front of them is the largest of the otherwise residential area, not a single person visible from their position.

"And what Lahash?" Eleanor mutters, sharp tone drawing his focus.

"The Daemones are getting increasingly more common to spot in the streets," he returns. Clearly, this was something he hadn't wanted to bring up yet, turning away from her in irritation. "We were going to tell you to stop fighting underground, but you've done that anyway. There isn't enough to be worried, but I think it would be wise to start carrying a gun with you."

"They're in the streets?" Eleanor questions, eyes growing frantic in a second.

If he had known her longer, he would have been scared by the panic in her normally fearless self.

~

I certainly was. Even though I know what happens after this, watching the growing instability in her stronger half, designed to control her emotions, is terrifying. So much could have gone wrong. So much could have changed in this story that we may never have been gifted a second chance. If she didn't have support, if she didn't have her Fallen Angels, I'm not sure she would have made it to 25.

~

"Only in the really populated areas," he assures. "I don't think they're looking for you, but they are there. Paying people off, from what Lerajie can tell. Collecting information from long term agents. Things that would appear normal but…"

"But the Daemones don't do jobs like those. They're hoping the face traces will find something, or hoping it might draw someone in hiding out," she finishes. "Lerajie needs to be careful, they want attention, and they can't have it."

The calm on Lahash's face does its job in tempering her worry, enough that Captain remains watching her but does not intervene.

"She knows. But we need to send them a message that their increased activity only creates risk to us. The Generals know better than to create attention around a pair of Fallen Angels. Especially one who is in the fold," he assures. "Now, are we going to go inside, or can we go back to the air conditioning in the car? It's too cold to stand out here arguing."

Huffing, Eleanor walks towards the building, waiting only for him to unlock the door. A woman stands behind the desk, glancing up as the two walk inside, her appearance harsh in every way except her expression as Lahash greets her with a smile. He walks directly up, focus on the door behind the owner's shoulder. Barely refraining from laughing at the look on the woman's face as Eleanor sticks close to the Fallen Angel's side, she watches money pass over the bench.

"Is this the favour I owe you?" the woman asks, voice gravely. "Risking my license to let someone shoot?"

"No one will know, the whole point of coming here is to make sure it's a secret," Lahash assures. "Record her as Lucy."

The woman concedes, the red light over the door flicking on as she waves them through. They slip inside in silence, Eleanor taking the handgun he passes her with only a second's hesitation.

It's cold in her hand, taking more effort to hold than she remembered. But muscle memory prevails, her fingers checking the safety and empty chamber on instinct. Her fingers run over the individual parts methodically checking each piece as Lahash gets his own out.

"They were always very meticulous in teaching you lot to shoot," he notes. "I'm betting you could pull that thing apart and put it back together. I guess it saves them the risk of having a gun break on assignment if the agents can identify damage before use."

"Slaves are expensive, and a broken gun would cause undue risk to our lives," Eleanor mutters.

Her face is shadowed in the locker room, but the fatigue in her tone shocks him. The look in her eyes as she glances up to watch his own expression worries him more.

"They'll pay for it, Eleanor," Lahash promises. "They won't survive what they have coming for them."

"Where do you get all these ideas?" she asks in reply, taking a handful of rounds from the box he offers forward. "It's not like anyone can do anything about them, we don't know where their base is, and we can't be sure they won't just kill us all if we find it. No one can take down that many ACEs."

Lahash merely raises an eyebrow, leading her further into the building.

Shooting ranges stretch out in front of her, little cubicles facing paper targets. Eleanor dons the orange earmuffs, loading the gun slowly. Focus drawn on the task at her hands and the long passage she will be shooting down, she doesn't notice Lahash merely watching her from the wall. With a depth of analysis that would challenge her own, Lahash measures every little movement she makes.

With her reluctance to enter, he thought she might show more anxiety. But her hands are perfectly controlled as she slots the rounds into the magazine and Captain doesn't argue as she sends him out of the room with a quiet command. Her tone has turned, thick with German and carrying an almost deadly waver. Perfect form raises the gun to face its target, silence overwhelming the range as Eleanor takes a breath.

Three rounds fire in quick succession, Eleanor only pausing to switch to a single arm fire for another three rounds. A final three rounds are fired from her non-dominant hand, each landing within a centimetre of the other. She places it down, turning to him with faultless poise.

"Motherhood did not take away my ability to do my job," she says, detached from the words in a way he had never seen. "I will always do what I need to, don't doubt that."

As she stares him down, Lahash can see the danger in her eyes. He can see the power. He can see the echo of her ancestors that would drive her to greatness. Any doubts he had vanish, smiling at Eleanor with a matched dominance.

"I never will again," he nods. "Regina Tenebris."

Chapter 26

Christmas. The time for family and love, presents and giving. Eleanor never really was fond of the event but made an effort for Adelyn. But of course, with no family other than each other –Kenichi planned to arrive a week later, after visiting his own family – they were more than happy to accept an invite to a Christmas Eve party at one of the Adelyn's friend's houses. Neither of them are particularly close to this friend, but most of the town would be there.

Eleanor stands by herself in the living room, drink in her hand. Someone, a man, is sitting at the piano across the room. Eleanor had been watching that piano for a while, trying to will herself to play it, but not daring to walk over. Now someone else was sitting there, about to start playing.

In her mind she wasn't in that room, or even in the country. Not as the music starts.

Captain alerts, pawing at her leg until she shakes her head and reaches down to scratch his head. But her eyes, studded with tears, don't stray from the man at the piano. He is no one important, but as her head spins over and over again, she can't help but watch as he continues to play.

Rachel walks over, seeing her stressing out – the woman had grown quite adept at reading Captain's cues. She follows her eyeline as she arrives at Eleanor's side.

"Are you good?" she asks.

Eleanor nods quickly, breath coming out in a deep sigh, "he just reminds me of someone I used to know."

The woman looks over to her in confusion. Eleanor had not mentioned someone who used to be in her life since her arrival. Not to these people.

"Do you believe in soulmates?" Eleanor asks, turning towards her friend.

"I guess so... never really thought about it," she shrugs. "Why?"

"I had mine." Her fingers rise to touch her throat lightly. "He saved my life."

In so many ways...

"What happened to him?" Rachel asks, still watching her girl carefully.

"I was in danger, he went to protect me," she starts. "We haven't seen him since. I only know he's alive from the books he sends me."

"What was his name?"

Eleanor pauses, thoughts sticking to her head as she answers.

"Nikolas."

One word, a round sound rolling off her tongue. She had said it before – she knew that – but saying it to her friend was different. Somehow, she didn't feel the guilt she thought she would feel when she uttered the name.

The night continues, but Eleanor waits until most of the party have left to walk over to the piano. Her fingers brush over the keys, a tear rolling down her cheek. It had been so long. So very long.

Her fingers ached to press melodies into the ivory keys, hear the sweet song dance through her ears.

"Do you play?" Donna, whose house they are at, asks.

"I used to..." Eleanor replies, voice almost lost to the deep emotion.

"Feel free to have a go, it hasn't been used much since my eldest daughter left home."

Eleanor nods weakly, thanking the woman as she reaches forwards and finds a piece of music. A reasonably difficult one. Donna walks away, allowing the obviously distressed girl space. She could sense a lingering emotion in Eleanor's words.

Eleanor plays, for the first time in two years.

The song plays blue and grey, dancing over the party's heads as they glance over at the girl. She had not lost her ability, playing like a long-practiced pianist. Tears roll down her pale cheeks as she plays, heart aching like it had finally been released from its chains. The weight that lifts is almost a curse, the shame seeping in. Captain sits, confused, next to her. He realised that this was her own way of coping, but still wasn't sure if he should intervene.

Adelyn hadn't heard her mother in so long, she had almost forgotten what it was like to hear her play. But as the three-year-old hears the piano, she walks over, wide eyes watching her mother. She climbs up so she's standing on the seat, leaning her head on her mother's shoulder.

Eleanor doesn't feel her daughter there, she feels Nikolas, leaning on her shoulder. Nikolas playing beside her. Playing the bass clef while she played the treble clef. Smiling as she finished.

The music stops as she turns to pull Adelyn into her lap, using her hair to hide the sob that breaks from her. She missed him so.

A man steps out of the back of the room, focus on the mother and daughter.

"Uncle Keni!" Adelyn calls as she glances up, Eleanor letting her child run to him.

"I thought you weren't coming for another week?" Eleanor asks, body refusing to turn around.

Not allowing herself to break out of the tight binds her emotions had put her in.

"I wanted to surprise you," Kenichi replies, picking up the child and walking closer. "Thought you might like some company."

Eleanor stands up, walking into his chest and wrapping her arms around his middle. He still holds Adelyn with one arm, the other returning Eleanor's hug.

"Merry Christmas, Ellie," he whispers, before letting her go.

Eleanor steps away quietly, easily finding her host standing not too far away. She says a polite farewell and a brief apology as she starts to leave. Within a few minutes she has said goodbye to anyone else she cared to and gathered all her things. Kenichi waits at the edge of the room, still holding Adelyn as she starts to drift off to sleep.

They drive in different cars, Eleanor arriving back at her house before he does. Adelyn is deeply asleep as her mother places her in her bed, only just stepping onto the main floor as Kenichi walks through the door. Numbly her feet carry her to him, letting herself lean into his arms and tuck her head into his chest.

"Why does it hurt so much? It shouldn't hurt this much after so much time," she whispers, eyes shutting tiredly as he runs a hand over her head.

"Because you loved him," Kenichi answers softly. "You still do."

"I want to be able to play; I miss playing. But whenever I think of doing it, all I can think of is when we did it together," she adds. "It hurts to remember. But it hurts even more to realise it's just a memory."

"Probably, but that doesn't mean you shouldn't do it. Playing piano is such a big thing for you, I think that continuing to play will help to alleviate the pain of missing him. It may hurt to start with, but it will get better," Kenichi replies, taking a deep breath as she sighs in acceptance. "Pain can be fickle like that."

"I threw a blanket over the piano in the attic," she admits quietly. "So I couldn't see it. Like how I hide my artworks in boxes. I can't bear to see any of it."

"That's okay. You just need to learn how to manage it," he shrugs. "When do you plan on going to sleep?"

"I'll stay up a little while longer, I have to put out Adelyn's presents," Eleanor replies. "You can go to sleep if you'd like. I was just going to read my book."

Kenichi steps away with a grin, pushing her lightly to the couch facing the television.

"We are watching the Grinch," he says, turning on the screen and putting the sound down before he finds the movie.

He sits next to her, chuckling as she rolls her eyes.

"This is a children's movie," she chastises.

"Correct, now be quiet and watch. Maybe we can absorb some of the snow to cool us off," he returns, then in a low whisper, "where'd you hide her presents?"

Eleanor huffs lightly, pulling an ottoman over with her feet.

"In the tub closest to the door in the attic. She knows not to go through those," she answers eventually.

By the end of the movie – as Kenichi suspected – Eleanor had fallen asleep, head leaning on his shoulder. Making sure to lie her down carefully, he retrieves the presents and places them under the tree in a neat pile. He lifts Eleanor to take her to her own room, resisting the urge to roll his eyes at the pillow with a shirt on it before moving to the guest room.

Both the Beck girls wake to chocolate milkshakes – the Australian summer was too warm for the heated alternative – and pancakes, which are devoured within minutes as Adelyn begs to open her presents.

Eleanor is surprised as she opens a box, a pair of ivory pointe shoes laying underneath a small card.

"You mentioned you knew ballet, thought you might like to take a refresher course," Kenichi explains. "Seeing as though you haven't done it for years."

Eleanor smiles faintly.

"Thank you," she says.

While at the Agency, she was adept enough to be a ballerina, well-practiced on pointe. No doubt she had grown quite rusty in the time since her last lesson.

Eleanor enjoys her lessons more than she thought she would. And the dance instructor was firmly amazed at her lingering ability after four years. More so, her brilliant ability to take and apply corrections almost instantly. She was almost begging Eleanor to return as she finished the last of her lessons.

Instead, Eleanor enrolled Adelyn into the woman's classes, having been subjected to her daughter's begging ever since she had let her sit in on a lesson. She loved the classes, and quickly became a favourite of the teacher.

Chapter 27

The Dunkler Bischof sits at the dining table, sifting through the files of people that need killing as if they were expense reports. Beside him, a 12-year-old Eleanor is filling page by page in literature analysis. The exercise is designed to foster a better understanding of the languages she is learning, each book of varying language, and the corresponding essay is to be written in a language separate to that again. Then it was to be read aloud for assessment, incorrect pronunciation or grammar would be corrected and the essay must be started again. More than two mistakes was cause for punishment. As she got more and more fluent, grading began. It was never an issue for her.

Quietly, she turns towards her Vater, confusion written across her face.

"May I ask a question?" she says in quick German.

"As long as it isn't about the themes of that book, you must analyse it yourself," he responds.

This wasn't an actual rule, he had made it up so she wouldn't discuss the many novels she read with him. He wasn't a particular fan of classical literature, much preferring just killing people and getting it over with.

"It isn't," she says. "What is the French word and gender for a small boat?"

He answers almost instantly, not even lifting his eyes from the files.

After a few moments, he adds, "you've already finished your essays for this week. Why aren't you doing your other work?"

Now Eleanor doesn't look up to respond.

"Finished it all. I wanted to work on my French and Spanish so I'm doing another."

"Of course you are," he grunts. *"When you're done, I'll show you what I'm doing. Might encourage Sebastian to finish quicker."*

"Yes, Mein Vater," Eleanor grins quickly.

~

"I'd like to talk about your relationship with the Dunkler Bischof, your trainer," Dr Nolan begins. "It appears very peculiar when you consider where you were…"

Eleanor rolls her eyes, but gestures for the psychiatrist to continue.

"You two were incredibly close, would you say that was correct?" Vanessa asks. Receiving an affirmative answer, she continues, "is it usual for trainers and their students to be close, as you were?"

"I wouldn't know," Eleanor shrugs. "We never got to see how they interacted. I'd guess probably not, but I have a weird way of getting attached to people."

"What was his response to that?"

"He was always distant, to begin with he was cold and harsh but as I got older and he figured out what was… different within me, he got kinder. Past the age of ten he never raised a hand to me outside a training ring, though he rarely did it before. By twelve he disobeyed orders and saved my life when he was supposed to eliminate me," she replies. "He's done it twice more since then, both after I got pregnant."

"When did you start calling him Mein Vater? And why?"

Eleanor must think for a second, before answering, "around when I was 11, it just felt better than calling him Schutz or sir. I was getting into the swing of missions by then, so he had taken a small step back in teaching and just began guiding me a lot more. Sebastian was a slower learner than me, so it took longer before he started to do the same with him."

"He and Sebastian weren't as close?" Vanessa assumes.

"No. He was still kinder to him than I imagine many ACEs were to their trainees, but he certainly allowed me more leniency than Sebastian. Our handler treated me much worst though, Ellsie's attitude probably didn't help, but he had a strong hatred for me from the beginning."

Dr Nolan takes a breath, considering which potentially hazardous question pattern to follow. In the end it appears she chose not to try revealing the toxic nature of their relationship – figuring an existential crisis or complete loss of trust would not benefit Eleanor's healing – instead heading towards the idea of family.

"Was there something about him that reminded you of your birth father?" she asks.

"I can't remember," Eleanor whispers, head tilting and lips pursing. "I don't remember him. He worked a lot, I think. The only solid thing I have was that he and my mother had an argument about religion. She thought he was faking his faith. He was always slightly uncomfortable in churches. I only remember that because it was always him who took me outside when I'd start crying, he'd console me."

"Why churches?"

"I don't know, but I've always felt it as well. Judgement and distaste for no reason. Maybe it has something to do with Angeli Terra... or Nikolas, but it's always been there," she answers quietly. "The church on Angeli Terra was the worst. I've learnt how to hide it though."

A few moments pass as Vanessa takes a few notes, the silence growing uncomfortable.

"I remember my mother being incredibly intelligent. She could always figure out problems between people with ease. If there was such a thing, she would be an empath. With my father it was harder though, I don't think she could see it as easily with him. She is much clearer in my mind than he has ever been," Eleanor says, breaking to the silence as the therapist suspected she would.

"That's interesting. It seems they were an odd match..."

Slowly, Eleanor nods. The clock tower a few blocks away chimes, signalling the end to their session.

Eleanor leaves with a quick farewell.

Chapter 28

21, one of the important birthdays in a person's life. I don't really understand why it's a big deal in Australia, seeing as though their drinking age is 18 anyway, but it is. Huge parties, stories from your closest friends and family. A huge cake.

But something in Eleanor snapped, as she became 21. Almost as if it just hit her, that her parents were dead. Her sister, dead. That she had no childhood friends. She had no happy stories.

And she just… snapped.

Eleanor glances around the café table. Amy and her husband. Rachel. A few others she had come to know since she arrived in Australia sit with her. Adelyn was outside, playing with her friends, while they all sat around talking over drinks to celebrate her 21ˢᵗ birthday. Captain is tucked at her feet, waiting calmly.

But as Eleanor starts to dissociate, he climbs to his feet, pawing at her leg. Slowly, she gets up, shuffling out into the cooling air. Her eyes are glassy, completely ignoring Captain who continues to alert her. Her breath chokes in her throat, tears threatening to spill over the edges. She drops to the ground, landing on the concrete steps that lead to the carpark.

A breathless, soundless scream breaks from her, the tears falling freely now. Pain, aching deep within her heart. Amy and Rachel run outside as they see her drop, stopping abruptly as Captain attempts to wriggle under her arms. Her long fingers grip her hair, face hidden behind her arms as she doesn't react to his movements.

Slowly, Rachel edges down to where she is seated, surprised as Captain allows her to get close enough to touch the girl.

"What's wrong, Diana?" she asks carefully, trying to sit her up a little straighter.

Eleanor doesn't reply, harsh sobs, curling her even further inward. Captain is still trying to pull her arms out of her face as she lets out another not quite scream.

"Diana, speak to me. What's wrong?"

The girl just inches away from her touch, red eyes open wide. Her phone rings, Captain backing out of her lap so Rachel can reach it. The caller ID reads Dr Nolan.

"Hello?" Rachel answers quietly, frown deep.

"Who is this?" the woman on the other end of the line asks.

"Rachel. I'm a friend of Diana's, who are you?"

"Her therapist. I was just calling to say Happy Birthday," Dr Nolan says cautiously. "Why hasn't Diana answered the phone?"

Eleanor starts to mumble something beneath her breath, unintelligible to her friend.

"She just started shaking out of nowhere, crying and choking on her breath..." Rachel answers. "She's muttering something, but I can't make it out."

There is a pause on the other end of the line.

"Can you please try and figure it out?"

Rachel nods, though to herself as the woman on the other end of the line cannot see her. After a few moments, she answers.

"They're dead. She just keeps repeating that..."

Dr Nolan sighs, thinking as quick as possible as Eleanor continues to shake.

"If she's able to be moved, which she probably won't, take her somewhere quiet. Keep Adelyn away, this is something she doesn't need to know about," she eventually says. "When I hang up call the contact on her phone called Lucy, get her to come down. You will have to send her your location, and it may take a bit for her to get there, but it should only be an hour and a bit."

"I can do that," Rachel replies, "but who is she?"

"A friend of Diana's who understands what she is going through," Dr Nolan says. "Now, do as I suggested please."

The call hangs up, Eleanor still rocking catatonically on the steps. Rachel glances to Amy quickly, eyes worried.

"Her therapist, she said to keep Adelyn away. I'm calling a friend of hers that lives an hour away. Apparently, she will know what's going on," she says quickly. "Can you make sure Riley keeps Adelyn busy for a bit?"

With an affirmative nod, Amy disappears. Rachel stays at Eleanor's side as she scrolls through her contacts, finding the only one called Lucy, right next to another named Lachlan. Also the only two without a last name.

She picks up on the third ring, and it doesn't take long before she says she is already on her way. It wasn't hard for her to figure out why the assassin had suddenly broken down. The ways in which many blocked out grief was not an unknown area for her, nor how it could erupt so suddenly. Lerajie had seen it many times over many years.

Eleanor is unable to be moved, completely locked off from the rest of the world. Captain still lays in her lap, head stuck under her chin and up onto her shoulder. Amy and Rachel wait in worry, watching from a few metres away as Eleanor rocks back and forth.

The screaming has stopped, her breathing now even, but the blue pools of her eyes see nothing. Lerajie arrives on a motorbike, parking it quickly before she strides over to the girl's side. As she crouches down, the two women frown to each other, she is not the type of person they were expecting. The tattoos were certainly a deterrent.

She skips English, speaking in German as she gently pulls Eleanor's hands away from her face.

"Can you focus on me?" she asks softly, cautious not to use her real name. "Regina Tenebris..."

She almost blinks in recognition, letting her hands stray away from her face. But her stare holds blank.

"You've never let yourself grieve, have you?" she continues, German rolling easily off her tongue. "You shouldn't bottle stuff up, you can't do that to yourself, trust me."

Almost as if the German was finally weaselling into her brain, Eleanor's chin tips towards her just in the slightest, the shaking renews with fervour.

"You need to let it all out, you need to let yourself feel," she instructs softly, pushing her hair out of her face.

"I can't..." she whispers in her comfortable German as well, a bare flick over her eyes telling her enough. "They're dead," she chokes.

Quietly Lerajie calls Captain off her friend's lap, assuring him with a pat as she moves to pick up the shaking girl.

"What are you doing with her?" Amy finally interjects, stopping her before she can lift her fully.

Lerajie continues anyway, only turning to face them as Eleanor settles in her arms.

"I'm taking her somewhere a little more private. She needs to get it all out, and she can't do that with people watching her," she answers calmly. A practice that assassins and immortals alike had mastered. "Just behind those trees. When she can hold a sentence, I can take her and her daughter home. Unless you know how to speak German you will be of no help."

"Adelyn needs someone with her," the woman counters. "She won't be able to understand her mother."

"Adelyn is fully capable of translating German herself, and her mother will only be able to fully process her emotion when she is at home, safe," she answers. "If you don't mind..."

Amy nods slowly, watching with careful eyes as Captain trots off after them.

As they round the trees Lerajie slowly lowers her to the ground, crouching in front of her and keeping a hold on Eleanor's hands – she tries to hide her face still, letting her hair obscure her vision – until she lifts her eyes to find Lerajie's.

"Eleanor, you need to let it out," she tells her, the German a comfort to her. "Just speak, I don't care what you say, just speak."

"I can't speak. Speaking hurts me," she whispers, eyes casting away again. "They get mad if I speak about my parents."

"They aren't here anymore. You don't have to worry about them," Lerajie assures her. "You can talk about your family."

Her bottom lip trembles, whole body shaking as she moves her weight onto her knees, shuffling so her face is hidden in her friend's shirt. She keeps her arms close, relaxing ever so slightly as Lerajie wraps an arm around her.

"I nearly died with them," she starts, barely a whisper. As if opening the floodgates. "It was only at the last minute that they spotted me, dragged me out to where they had vans. I could see it all. The other children blindfolded and gagged, guns in the arms of the adults they were dragging me towards. Smoke was stinging my lungs, I couldn't breathe, couldn't think. I was trying to get out of their grasp, but I couldn't. I was begging for anyone to help me, but no one did. There were sirens, people shouting. As soon as I had been thrown into the van, they shut a metal grate and started to drive. They didn't even shut the doors.

"The second round of bombs went off a second later. I saw it all. They hadn't had time to blindfold me. I could see, I could see people running from the fires, covered in the flames themselves. I could hear them all screaming. Gunshots. Sirens. Screams. Someone climbed into the back of the van a few minutes after. I couldn't understand what they were saying. I was numb. I felt nothing as they jabbed me with a sedative.

"The other children couldn't understand. Didn't understand. But I did. I knew what happened. They beat those who cried. Kept beating them until they stopped. They didn't care if they had managed to pull themselves together or were unconscious, or dead. I was just numb. I couldn't move with the fear, the grief. Then all of a sudden, I did. I grabbed a gun and shot two men dead. I wasn't sad anymore, I wasn't numb. I was just okay. In a moment. As if everything in me turned off.

"And I kept it off. That switch stayed firmly in place until... Adelyn. But I still couldn't let myself think of them. I couldn't think of them. Not in the way I needed to. I... I told Nikolas my tears for my parents had long since dried. Because they had. I couldn't cry for their loss. I couldn't. Mein Vater told me I couldn't. I did once, I asked my handler where they were buried. I didn't eat for three days..."

Her voice trails off, weak. Scared in a way. She was shaking so badly Lerajie thought she might melt out of her arms. But Eleanor's eyes stay brutal, staring blandly into space.

"I... never could talk to Nikolas about it. I didn't want him to see me that way. This way," she admits. "I had to make sure he only remembered me as strong. Not this weak, pitiful being... I don't even know where they were buried, if they ever made it back into this soil. If... if Kate was buried beside them.

"I killed her. I knew she was my sister, but I killed her anyway. I killed her. And they killed my mum, my dad. They killed them. She never knew them; she never knew me because I was taken away. By them. They ruined everything. And I worked for them. Willingly. They won. They won."

Ever so gently – as not to startle her – Lerajie takes her face in her hands, making her hold her eyes.

"They did not win," she tells her. "You are alive. You have a daughter. You have your freedom."

Eleanor tries to look away, but Lerajie keeps her grip on her jaw. Forcing her to focus.

"You have a life. You think if they won you would be able to have friends? They win by you believing that they are stronger than you are. They win when you admit defeat," she enforces. "Eleanor you are winning. You are surviving. You are stronger than they are."

"I murdered for them. I was willing," she chokes.

"Maybe. Maybe you enjoyed it as well. But you knew no better," Lerajie says. "What matters is that you are here now. You made the choice to leave. You were willing to die for what you did. You're better than I have ever been. Eleanor, you chose to leave that all behind, now you must grow from it. You cannot block it all away, it doesn't help. Emotions fester when they aren't allowed to breathe, holding in your grief makes it hurt more in the long run."

"But it's easier to hold it in," Eleanor whimpers. "You can't get hurt if you hold it in."

"Yes, you can," Lerajie tells her. "It may suffice to start with, but it will come back to stab you the minute your back is turned. It took me hundreds of years to figure that out, to be able to get over my anger at the Angels who threw me out. For me to realise that it was that rage that had got me sent away, not even mine. Your grief will cripple you. Don't make the mistakes we all made. You only have four years left of your life. Live it happy. Live it without the weight of grief on your chest."

Eleanor's eyes clear, body relaxing slightly as Lerajie releases her face. Four years. She had four years to live. Such a different punishment to the Fallen Angels, yet so similar in the same way. They both understood, knew what it was like to come from where she had, to do what she had done. To know just why it hurt her so much to have happiness. Lerajie, Eleanor knew, had seen things that Lahash hadn't, she had been subjected to many of the things Eleanor feared. But she still lived happy.

"Thank you," Eleanor murmurs, voice still weak. "I'm sorry, that shouldn't have been so bad. I don't know what happened. Thank you for coming. I know Rachel called you, but you didn't have to come."

"Of course I did, Eleanor," Lerajie returns kindly. "I cannot just string a friend out when they need me. You should be glad Lahash was not around. He's much more protective of you than I. He worries about you after you come to see us."

The Fallen Angel was changing the topic, drawing her mind away. Eleanor could cry at home but here was not the place.

"Why? It's not like I am anything special..." Eleanor frowns softly, head tilted to the side.

Lerajie chuckles as she shakes her head, "you are more special than you realise. And though he will not admit it, he will miss you deeply when you go away. It has been a very long time since we've had a friend as true as you. It's been a while since I've heard him laugh like he does now."

"He doesn't, have any other emotions..." Eleanor asks cautiously. "Other than friendship?"

"No," Lerajie assures gently. "He only does hook ups. When he was thrown out, there was a human girl he gave everything for. She rejected him when she saw him after. Refused to let him see the child he had sired. It was an Angeli, but his wings were featherless. A slave of the Angels as punishment for his misdemeanour. When she died a part of him did to. He hasn't loved anyone since."

A sad smile pulls onto Eleanor face, Captain finally managing to wiggle into her arms.

"The holocaust messed him up more than he'll admit. The Angeli being around meant our kind were being hunted and the ones that were safe weren't making a good name for themselves," she shrugs. "With so much conflict so focused on an area, we saw a lot of our past acquaintances, and some of them were not in their right mind. We heard rumours the Nazi's were experimenting on some of us, which is when we split up. I only found him again in 1998."

"How do you deal with all the pain?" Eleanor asks softly, fingers running smoothly through Captain's coat.

"You let yourself feel it, the only way it doesn't consume you is by letting it do it's harm and growing from it," Lerajie says, finally switching back to English. "Now, you need to go assure your friends I'm not going to abduct you. I'll get Captain to retrieve Adelyn. If you wouldn't mind, I'd like to keep an eye on you for a bit. Lend a shoulder to cry on. Is that okay?"

Eleanor nods, pulling herself onto her feet.

She speaks in only semi-certain Latin, "you have my trust. Both of you do."

"You learn fast. Now go on," Lerajie grins, giving the girl a few seconds to translate before pushing her out towards the shop.

Rachel runs forward to greet her, hug tight.

"I'm sorry. A lot just hit me at once," Eleanor whispers. "I hope I didn't ruin your evening."

"Never," Rachel assures, grinning as she pulls away. "Amy doesn't like your friend very much."

Eleanor has to stop herself from chuckling.

"Of course she doesn't," she breathes. "I better go talk to her."

Amy is eyeing off the Fallen Angel as Eleanor steps in front of her.

"You okay?" Amy asks instantly.

"As okay as I will be," Eleanor shrugs. "Lucy's going to hang at mine for a little bit to give me a hand."

The caution flashes in Amy's eyes.

"Are you sure she's safe?" she questions quietly. "We've had people on our radar with those tattoos. They always disappear as soon as we get near them."

"She is perfectly safe. And you will say nothing to your boss or my American friends about your worries. I wouldn't let her anywhere near this place if I didn't trust her," Eleanor assures. "I can protect myself; I promise."

Nodding in acceptance, Amy squeezes Eleanor's hand lightly.

"Call if you need anything, okay?" she offers. "I'll see you at drop off on Monday."

"See you then."

Eleanor glances to the almost set sun, shuffling into the still bustling restaurant to grab her bag. Adelyn joins her as she gets back to the front of the store, hugging one of her mother's legs the second she sees her, only letting go as Eleanor picks her up and lightly kisses the side of her head.

They pause at Lerajie's motorbike, telling her to follow them before slipping into their car. Taking her time to explain who Lerajie was, Eleanor makes her daughter promise not to tell anyone who she is. It was important to protect her privacy if she wanted hers protected.

Lerajie stayed the night, Eleanor managing to show her some of the artworks she had painted. There was an entire box devoted to the bombing, and she knew that looking through them all would help her. And it did. As if the slightest weight was lifted from her shoulders, Lerajie left her smiling the next day.

Chapter 29

Eleanor knows she shouldn't be here. But she felt she had to. She had to see it with her own eyes. 15 years since the Beck family went on holiday to Berlin. 15 years since one returned, only to die herself eight years later. 15 years.

All because of a post on someone else's Facebook page, seen over a shoulder. So many questions answered.

Her black wig is indistinguishable from normal hair and falls in front of her face as she slowly steps out of the car. The church is how she remembers it to be, small and old, and still standing by some miracle. She's glad there aren't any cameras, Kenichi would be mad if he saw her there, and the Agency would likely notice her too. This would certainly show up on their radars.

Her contacts are dark, the dark eyeshadow around her eyes helping to conceal their presence. Eleanor had also coloured her eyebrows in to help hide the incriminating ashen colour. She took no chances. Even though it's still quite warm, she wears a black turtleneck and long blue jeans. Captain hangs at her side, on full alert as she peers into the assembly.

It's nearly full, with only a few seats still empty near the back, but she can't let herself step into the holy place. Confident she could hear sitting outside, Eleanor slides down, head lolling back to lean against the stones framing the door. Her fingers tremble as Captain slides into her lap, head pressing up to her collar.

Eleanor listens in silence, daring glances inside as the pastor speaks. Her mother had frequented this church, often bringing her family with her. Having been a very popular family, she had no problem believing all the people seated inside cared about them. The stories people brought forward, they stung Eleanor, weakened her. When they mentioned her, she had to try hard not to break into a laugh. The emotions coursing through her are nearly driving her into delirium. Her head is spinning, yet at the same time everything is clear. Every little noise, every word. Each bug and swale of rock. Each person.

Perfect clarity matched with near-complete frenzy.

She moves away as the service starts to wrap up. Slipping quietly across the road, Eleanor stands in the shade of a tree, watching as people leave the church. The pastor, having seen her sitting outside during the ceremony, finds her with his eyes, frown clear as she stands perfectly still under the tree. Captain sits on her feet, watching as well. No one approaches her, all willing to stay within their own circles.

Eventually they all leave, moving to their homes, or to the pub, Eleanor didn't know. Didn't care. The sun has begun its descent as the last person leaves. She moves dully towards her car to retrieve a bouquet of roses, violets and irises and she crosses back over the road. The tremor in her hand is unnoticeable as she crouches in front of the monument. Her name sits with her family's. The flowers take their place at the base, Eleanor's pale fingers running over the engraved text. With one last breath, she stands, head snapping to the side as someone stops behind her.

"You could have come inside," the Pastor says, voice kind. "We would not have minded."

He had no idea who she was. Thought she was just a normal person.

"How did you know the family?" he asks, stepping a little closer.

"I was a friend. Of Kate's," she answers softly. "Like sisters."

"It was such a shock, when everything happened. How one family could have such a terrible turn of fate, I cannot understand," the Pastor offers.

"Yes, such terrible luck," Eleanor breathes.

"Eleanor would have just turned 21, and Kate would be turning 18," he muses.

"Do you think the theories Eleanor is still alive have any merit?" Eleanor asks, finally turning to face him.

The man's smile is faint.

"Maybe. They never did find her body," he answers. "The thought of what may have been done to her, though... if she is alive, I would pray healing on her soul."

"Yes..."

Eleanor moves off quietly, neglecting to say goodbye. He doesn't stop her, only watching as she climbs into her car, Captain in the passenger seat, and drives away.

She couldn't bring herself to visit their gravestones.

Chapter 30

Eleanor tries to keep her nerves down as the two motorbikes stop in front of her home. Of course, Lerajie had been here already, but it was Lahash's first time. Adelyn was squirming on her hip, watching the two approach. Eleanor places her down gently, keeping a hold of her hand as the two Fallen Angels stop at the end of the walkway to her house.

"I brought a teddy," Lahash starts. Nervous, Eleanor realises. "I assume you want to check it..."

Eleanor smiles softly at the purple bear held between his tattooed hands.

"I trust you," she says, kicking her head to Adelyn beside her.

He smiles, crouching down and offering the toy forward to the child.

"Hello Adelyn," he says kindly. "I'm Lachlan. I got this for you."

Shyly, Adelyn takes the teddy off him.

"Hello," she says. "You're Lucy's friend. The one who Mummy doesn't want me to tell anyone about."

"I am," he smiles.

"She's nervous..."

Eleanor rolls her eyes, tapping her head lightly.

"What do you say, Adelyn?" she reminds, smile light.

The child thanks him but her large eyes are clearly on the tattoos on his hands. Curious, not scared. He offers his hand forward carefully, eyes watchful as the four-year-old runs her fingers lightly over the wing stretched along his thumb. Then she lightly runs her fingers over the halo, head tilting slightly.

"You have the same..." she blinks, glancing back to Lerajie, who was watching the interaction with interest. "Exactly the same."

Lahash glances up to Eleanor, asking in Latin, "how much does she know?"

"Enough. She'll understand what you mean," she answers.

Turning back to the child, Lahash says, "that's because we are both Fallen Angels. We are branded like this as a punishment."

"But they're pretty..." Adelyn murmurs.

"That's very kind of you to say. Many don't believe the same though. They're made to mock us," he tells her, gesturing to the halo. "We used to have real Halos, and wings just like this." He flips his hands to face her, the wings appearing to flap for a few seconds. "It's to remind us of all we lost in the decisions we made. People used to treat us badly for them. But they don't anymore, its more normal to have tattoos."

Adelyn smiles at him, finally letting go of his hand.

Lahash stands quietly, ignoring the grin Lerajie sends him as Eleanor gestures for them to head inside. She orders Captain to stay with Adelyn as she slips into the kitchen, watching him as he follows her to the couch. Offering drinks, she pours herself a juice and passes over two beers to each of the Fallen Angels.

But Lahash's focus is on the shelf of special books, gifts from Nikolas. His fingers are about to trace over the spines when he abruptly pulls his hand back, sending Lerajie a quick look.

"Where did you get these?" he asks Eleanor, gesturing to the collection as she steps closer.

"They're from... him. Why?"

With another skittering glance to Lerajie his eyes land on her once more.

"His Aspect, does it include the ability to mentally shield?" he questions.

"I think so. He blocked his brother from compelling me once. And he mentioned he did the same thing to himself," she answers cautiously. "Why?"

"These books are blocking anyone from supernaturally finding this place. From using your connection to find out where you live," he explains. "Including him. He could easily find where you were if he wanted to, but these books are stopping him. A barrier for if his control breaks. Do you carry one with you? You should."

Eleanor frowns, the little crease between her eyebrows increasing as she steps a little closer. Lahash looks to Lerajie again as Eleanor runs her fingers down the spines.

"Don't touch them. They'll alert him a Fallen Angel is in his Geminae's house. Same with Daemones," he says. "One thing you can always count on with the Angeli, they will do anything they can to protect the ones they love."

It's as he walks towards Eleanor's dining table, that something clicks in her head, Eleanor jogging over to catch up to him.

"How can you feel it? Michael couldn't," she questions, glancing between the two in suspicion.

Lerajie answers with a grin, "Lahash was once a charm breaker and creator. The slight bit of his Aspect that remains means he can feel when things have been altered. Has saved our asses many times."

"Yet another taunt at what we used to be," Lahash mutters, glancing between the women for a second. "Now, I was told of a knife collection. Let's not pretend I'm here for any other reason."

The two girls roll their eyes, Eleanor leaving him in the living room and slipping around her house like a wraith. By the time she finishes, about 15 blades are dropped unceremoniously on the dining table. Eleanor leaning back into her seat as the Fallen Angel starts to rifle though the lot.

"Do you not worry about Adelyn finding and playing with one?" Lerajie mutters as she tests the sharpness of a stiletto blade.

"They're all in places she cannot get to," Eleanor assures, raising an eyebrow as Lahash swings an extremely ornate longsword.

"Usually when I see these, they're blunt," he notes. "This one is surprisingly well equipped for battle. Though you'd likely get laughed off the battlefield."

"What can I say, I'm a fan of decadence," Eleanor giggles. "That one was a whim, I prefer daggers. Much easier to use."

"It is fit for a queen," Lerajie nods, lips pulling into a knowing smile. "Regina Tenebris, perhaps."

Chapter 31

The air deep underground where the Daemones build their bases remains in a constant state of stifling dampness. Many of the bases are as old as the colonisation of America, and as such have the bare minimum of new technologies possible.

Nikolas is sitting with his legs stretched out in front of him as the General of the American Daemone sector approaches, the man's fearsome face taught.

"How sure are you that agent 828 died?" the General questions, beady black eyes flicking over Nikolas. "What chance is there that they lied to you?"

With no chance at escape, Nikolas forces himself to push his face into pain, rather than horror, as the General keeps his beady black eyes on the exiled Prince.

"I felt her heart stop in my arms, I felt the breath leave her lungs. I felt her die." Nikolas returns, the tremor in his voice easy to create. "Are you going to question me?"

"I'm not questioning you, Princeling. I understand that's what you thought happened, that the pain you felt was because she died. Maybe it was and my gut feeling is wrong, but I feel like you should be much more unstable than you are," the General says.

"First off, I am in no way stable. Second, she was human, and I am not full Angeli. The bond was there but it was never as strong as it could've been. Or would've been if we had more time. But the pain I felt... there is no way she was alive," he argues, desperation succeeding in changing the General's approach.

"How long after she died did you leave?"

Cautiously, Nikolas replies, "less than an hour. She was my safety, with her dead Angeli Terra could do whatever they liked with me."

"So, it's possible they revived her and told her you had run away? Causing you to inadvertently hurt her which would have triggered the pain..." the General suggests. "She could still be alive, Nikolas."

He shakes his head slowly, voice tight with emotion.

"As much as I wish that could be true, I know that she is dead. I know it like I know I will be suffering for it until I die. They knew what they were doing sending her to school again that day, they knew it could cost her her life. They didn't care." With his jaw set, Nikolas rolls his head back and forth as he bites out the words that were not entirely false. "I tried to keep her from going but I failed, and she lost her life because of it," he says. "My Geminae is dead, and we can't do anything to fix it."

Regarding Nikolas with a sceptical glance, the General finally nods.

"We're going to keep looking into it, so if you think of anything arrange a meeting. If we find anything I'll come tell you," he concedes. "Until next time, Princeling."

Watching him leave with a stinging glare, Nikolas reaches out with his mind. A quick swipe of the General's mind wipes out the lingering suspicion clouding their conversation. The use of his Aspect tires him, and Nikolas drops his head back to stare at the roof as the thumping in his head slowly returns to normal. Slowly he sits back up, placing his head in his hands to compress the overwhelming urge to scream as every ounce of his self-control is channelled into not smashing something.

This wasn't the first time someone had brought up her still being alive. Originally, he had merely wiped the thought before it could get too deeply implanted, but they often found it again as if they had forgotten for a while. That was dangerous though. Why would they forget something so important, so he was left seeding doubt and protecting his own life at the same time.

For now, they didn't know where she was, or where Adelyn was. That was what was the most encouraging. They couldn't figure out if Eleanor was alive, so finding her was an entirely different game.

But being unable to find Adelyn, who they knew was alive and would be with her mother if Eleanor was, meant they were safe for much longer.

But while the precipice draws ever closer, Nikolas would not let himself fall. He would not give in.

Chapter 32

Deep in the depths of the Angeli prison, nestled in the dormant volcano in Angeli Terra, unrest is stirring. Wings, black as night, flex to touch the edges of their cells, eyes coloured in madness start to open again for the first time in centuries. The Fallen can feel the shift in the air, the presence of watching eyes upon their world. Quiet, melodical murmurs echo though the vast cavern like a prayer, prophecies remembered in the oldest of minds.

The Azazel – the prison head – visits the prison's dark layers for the first time since their last inmate joined them, listening to the song they preach into the darkness.

"Our Queen," they whisper. "Our Queen has risen. She shall finish our mission."

Azazel, tattoos heavy on his hands, lets out a horrified breath. He does not tell his King of the development as he should, asking only one question of the mad.

"How?"

One cell answers; their most recent arrival.

"Kimaris, she did not go to war purely for the sake of the human race," the general sings. "She had something to hide. Something that will save the world. Save us."

The chant begins again, loud enough the castle begins to tremble. The disgraced Angels of night are put back into their slumber with a simple spritz of gas.

The new moon is high, the three faces sitting around a small glass table barely visible. With Adelyn just put to bed downstairs they keep the lights off, content to talk in the cool moonlight, the only disruption the buzzing of springtime cicadas. Eleanor is swirling her drink, a long-necked beer like her companions, taking the occasional sip.

"What can you tell me about the Angels? Obviously, there are Fallen, but are there others?" she asks, attention turning to the pair.

Lerajie begins quietly, smooth voice peppered with hints of stress.

"There are the Angels, divine beings that never leave their city in the skies. They have Ward Keepers hiding them from discovery just as Angeli Terra does. If it ever was breached, a message would be automatically sent to every actual Angel on Earth. They are led by the Archangels, who are gifted with the ability to create and destroy their subjects," she says, looking to Lahash to finish.

"They are the light, the supposed 'good' of the world. The Dark Angels balance that out. With gifts more powerful than the Angels but numbers far fewer they were always feared. It put pretty much all of them in prison right about when Lerajie fell. It didn't help that more often than not, the Dark Angels ended up completely insane by the time they reached maturity, their power often corrupted their minds," he explains, refusing to meet either of the girl's eyes. "As far as the Angels are aware, there are no Dark Angeli, nor any Angeli descended of the Archangels. But there are rumours that there is a bloodline – very diluted and barely perceptible – currently on Earth."

Eleanor frowns at the speculation, looking up to her friend.

"The Daemones would kill thousands to get their hands on that person..." she mutters. "Do they know it exists?"

Cautiously Lerajie replies, "they'd know it as folklore. But their recent increase in strength suggests they might have started believing it. And might have some idea who it is."

"That's problematic."

They can only agree with her.

"What about the Daemones... they're half-blooded right? Who leads them?" Eleanor continues.

"On Earth they lead themselves. A General for each continent, plus a few extras in highly populated places and of course the leader of the Berühmte Söldner," Lahash replies. "But those Generals are supposed to be working to return control to the true Demons. Due to their vulnerable emerging from their underground city – you know it as Hell – they don't risk emerging without protection from the Angeli. Their leaders haven't emerged for millennia, not since they lost one of their own."

Puzzled, Eleanor gestures for him to continue. He only does so once Lerajie has shrugged permission.

"Like there used to be seven Archangels, there are seven leaders of the Demons," he explains. "Six Kings and one Queen. But their Queen went after the Angels a long time ago, lost the fight and ended up so deep in the Angeli prison there is no chance of escape. Since then, they haven't dared to surface. Some Lords of Hell have, some of whom are Fallen Angels themselves, but never the Kings."

"You said used to be seven Archangels, there is only six in the Angeli Chapel..."

Lerajie cuts her partner off before he can answer.

"There was a Dark Archangel. She was to be killed by her equals for her ideals and took the rest of us out with her. No one really knows what happened to her, but she is gone," the Fallen Angel replies. "She was good, they were power hungry. Just as always."

Eleanor lets silence fall over them, fingers playing with her bottle as she thinks.

"You've gone unusually quiet," Lahash muses, flicking his blonde eyebrows as Eleanor huffs.

"Just considering," she replies, "though I think I may have come to a decision."

"What decision, darling?" Lerajie drawls, smirking ever so slightly.

"To tell you what to do to ensure you won't get found because of me," she answers softly. "I removed the note a while ago, but... there are cameras all over this house. I always replace the feeds once you have gone, but if I get taken, I won't be able to do that. If I disappear, you cannot come and check on me. Message me, call me if you'd like, but you cannot come here. You will appear on their radars, no one should be in my house in my absence, and they would come for you. I will try to get word to you, if I can, but if I do not, you must forget me."

The Fallen Angels glance between each other, displeasure clear on their faces. Eleanor has no suspicions on who speaks first.

"That is not something easily done, Eleanor," Lahash murmurs, eyes worried. "You are the first true friend we've had in centuries. You cannot expect us not to try and save you. Or at least to find out where you have gone."

"I do expect it, because you must. They will see you on the cameras, find you. Michael will take you away. I will not let you do that. Just because I am lost does not mean you two need to be locked forevermore in that god-awful prison. Do not come to find me. If I disappear, you disappear. Leave the country, make a new home," Eleanor orders, face stretched taunt. "I am sorry, but the longer I stay here the more likely it is they will find me. If they find me, and take me, there is nothing you can do. If they find me and I have to leave, I will inform you, I promise. You cannot let yourselves fall into their grasp. I could never forgive myself."

The pair sit in silence, looking between each other. Silent conversation; only flicks of the eyes and ticks of the head. Eleanor tries to follow the expressions on their faces, but the night shrouds the finest movements from her enough that she remains unaware of their decision until Lerajie finally speaks.

"We will not come. We will break your phone with messages, but we will not come searching for you," Lerajie assures. "But if you need help, we will give it to you. Without a thought. If they come for you, call us."

Eleanor nods, but Lahash sees her eyes skittering away. She would not put them in that danger. No, they could not be anywhere nearby when Michael came.

"Thank you, for being my friends," Eleanor says quietly, "not many can accept me so fully. Especially the wilder parts of me."

"The wild parts are the fun parts." Lahash grins. "We are honoured to be your friends, Regina Tenebris."

Lerajie smiles quietly, rolling her eyes as Eleanor shakes her head lightly.

"Why do you call me that?" she asks, curious. "Queen of the Dark..."

"Just for fun," Lahash winks, "thought it fit."

Eleanor drops her head back in amusement, chuckling slightly with Lerajie. There was more to the story, Eleanor could tell, but she didn't prod. With the Fallen Angels, she had always found it impossible to get a straight answer from them if they didn't want her to know something, but somehow, she trusted that it was never important enough to push the problem. Instead, she watches as Lahash stands up to lean against the railing.

"Can I have a hug?" she blurts, pale blue eyes on Lahash.

With a raised eyebrow, he opens his arms. Eleanor walks slowly into them, letting her whole body collapse into him as she gets within reach.

"Any particular reason?" he mutters as his arms wrap around her in a bear-like hug.

"A girl can't like punching people and hugs?" Eleanor returns, grinning. "And you look like a giant teddy bear."

Behind them, Lerajie laughs.

"I've never heard anyone call him a teddy bear," she chuckles as Eleanor finally steps back.

"There's a first time for everything," she shrugs, "even if it's entirely true. He gives the best hugs."

"Oh? Really?" Lerajie asks, grinning.

"Yes," Eleanor answers, matter-of-factly. "You hug better. But I do much prefer extended cuddles with Nikolas, preferably in the middle of the night, he's just a little too thin for bear-hugs."

It is impossible to miss it as both Fallen Angels roll their eyes, glancing between each other knowingly. It takes everything in her to not peg cushions at their heads.

But her muscles freeze for a second, eyes catching on a figure in the dark. She shakes it off a second later.

"I've noticed you've been jumpy recently..." Lerajie mutters, eyes landing on Eleanor. "Even here."

She bites her lip nervously.

"You want to explain that to us?"

Lahash is cautious with his tone, reading her as she turns away.

"I am scared," she shrugs, eyes staring off into the abyss. "Of them."

"Who, Eleanor?"

"The Berühmte Söldner. The Daemones. Losing Adelyn," she lists, turning back around. "Michael. Dying. Such a long list."

"You're allowed to be scared."

"I shouldn't be scared, though. I was trained not to be scared. But I am still, so scared," she admits.

Lahash walks forward to her, pulling her into his chest with one arm while the other holds her head still.

"They are terrifying. They can hurt a lot of people, and they could hurt you. But here, you don't need to worry about that. You can let it fall into a small, inconsequential part of your thoughts. It might not go away, but you can work to make it quieter. Less significant," he tells her, hand stroking her head softly.

"All the tiny voices in your head telling you that you need to always be watchful, the ones terrified of the people in your past life," Lerajie continues. "They don't run your life. You can trust us; we've been through this all. Every single person who has ever escaped away from anyone abusive knows it. Letting them run your life leads nowhere good and as hard as it may seem, you can teach yourself to let them all go. It takes time, and persistence but being around people who can help you is extremely beneficial."

"What Lerajie is trying to say," Lahash follows, chin resting on top of Eleanor's head, "we're always here for you. Whenever you need to talk, or rant. Punch something... or cry. Tell anyone how you're feeling. We understand. We know what it is like."

"You are our best friend and, in that way, we love you. We want only the best for you, we want to see you happy, truly happy. We will always help you," Lerajie adds, stepping in and hugging Eleanor's other side. "Whenever you need it."

"Thank you," Eleanor whispers, still leaning into Lahash.

"We should go home. Even Captain is already falling asleep," he says, gesturing to the dog splayed on the deck. "You need rest, Eleanor."

"Drive safe. I'll see you in a few weeks," she answers softly, finally stepping away from them both. "Do not forget what I have told you."

"We won't."

Chapter 33

Time passes, Adelyn grows, and Eleanor stabilises just a little more. The winter flies past uneventfully, and yet another year Eleanor lives, but lives alone.

That Christmas two more tattoos join her existing ones. An ankle each.

On her still banded right is a linework bouquet, consisting of only four flowers. A rose the highest, a violet and iris sitting just a few millimetres beneath, and finally a lily. A mother, two daughters, a granddaughter. Rosalie, Eleanor Violet, Kate Iris and Adelyn Lily Beck. It was always my favourite of her tattoos, closely followed by the phrase on her finger. I've drawn those flowers many times, in margins of books, corners of military reports. As I study her life more and more, I find myself drawing them more often.

Baz had asked little questions about the irremovable black band, taking the answer of it reading her vitals with only a few seconds of pause.

On the other ankle she got a simpler pattern. The southern cross.

Adelyn had grown independent in her horse riding, now able to ride by herself. On this instance, Kenichi was visiting for Eleanor's 22nd birthday and had tagged along to Pony Club. He understood little but was happy to keep an eye on Adelyn while Eleanor enjoyed her own ride.

Tucker is cantering smoothly around the sand arena, Captain laying casually in the corner as always, while Adelyn is trotting around a small course of jumps on Angel with Kenichi watching. When Adelyn lets out a scream, clutching her arm tight as she rolls onto the ground, her mother instantly pulls up. In a few seconds she is off her horse, someone already moving to grab Tucker as Eleanor runs towards where Kenichi is already tending to the girl. Captain beats her there, but Kenichi turns to him as he arrives.

"Do your job," he growls, gesturing towards Eleanor standing about ten metres away.

She had stopped moving, head twitching as her eyes stayed solely on her daughter. Just as Captain arrives, she starts swaying on her spot. Her eyes roll back into her head, and she faints – fortunately still wearing her riding helmet. Captain waits until she has hit the ground before moving to check over her.

"Great," Kenichi mutters, turning back to the pale, crying child. "We're going to need to go to the hospital, for your arm, okay? It might be broken."

Kenichi finishes helping Adelyn to her feet before he turns to Eleanor with a grimace. Adelyn nods in understanding, but her focus is towards her mother, face clouded in worry. Amy – having caught the wayward pony – joins them now, crouching at the child's side.

"Is Mum okay?" Ady asks meekly, taking the very cautious hug Amy offers her.

"Just a little spooked," he explains kindly. "Is the jumper in the car?"

Adelyn nods in answer, following quietly and staying a step back to let the doctor look Eleanor over. With Captain placed between Eleanor and everybody else, Rachel is the only one who can approach having already put Tucker and her own horse in their yards.

Kenichi looks up to her as Eleanor groans slightly.

"In Eleanor's bag, on the passenger seat of her car, can you grab me the jumper that's in there? Please." he asks, smiling weakly as the woman nods and jogs away.

Eleanor sits upright just as Rachel arrives back, Kenichi quickly taking the jumper and placing it over her head.

"Breathe," he instructs. "It's likely that Ady has fractured her arm; she will be fine. Are you good?"

Weakly, Eleanor nods, sliding her arms into her jumper and making to stand, but Kenichi stops her for a second, eyes cautious.

In German, he asks, "can you please tell me?"

"I am fine, the flashes have stopped, and the old break in my ulna has stopped burning," she answers, mimicking his language. "And I would like to get my daughter to the hospital, please."

Kenichi nods in approval, giving her a boost onto her feet. Immediately, Eleanor moves to Adelyn and gingerly wraps her arms around her daughter's small frame, careful of the still unsecured arm. Adelyn snuggles closer almost immediately, hiding her teary face in her mother's neck.

"Does it hurt badly, Baby Girl?" Eleanor asks, keeping her on her hip as she takes the reins to her pony with her other hand.

"Yes," Adelyn whimpers, glancing down to her pony for a second. "Is she hurt? She fell badly as well."

"She's fine. Looks a little sorry, if anything," Eleanor assures, getting the pony to walk herself into her yard. "Not sure how we're going to get them home, though. Do you think you can handle an extra 40 minutes?"

Rachel interrupts as Eleanor places her saddle on the fence.

"She doesn't have to. I have a paddock they can stay in tonight and two spare spots in my float," she says. "If you take all your gear, I can take the horses. Just don't want to mix up our stuff."

"Are you sure?" Eleanor checks, holding a palm out to the still worrying Captain.

"Absolutely, arm breaks are painful," she says, "and you both need to be checked for concussion."

"Thank you. I'll call you later about picking them up, depends on how long the hospital takes." Eleanor sighs. "Go sit in the car, take Captain. I'll be there in a minute."

Adelyn takes Captain's lead in her good arm, walking slowly towards the car. With quick orders to Kenichi – as he splints Ady's arm – Eleanor moves to her own horse, and they are gone within five minutes. The drive is quiet, Adelyn still in shock. Captain keeps his head on the girl's lap, Eleanor content to snuggle herself deep in her jumper. His jumper.

"Can you do the talking? They'll listen to you," Eleanor says as they walk into the Emergency Room, Adelyn resting on her hip.

Kenichi agrees, leading them towards the triage desk. Captain gets a few glances as Eleanor keeps his short lead in her hand, she had put on his vest before they entered the hospital to limit the number of questions. Within a few moments they are sitting in the uncomfortable waiting room chairs, filling out the forms.

Eleanor's eyes meet a light green pair exiting the building, surprise in both as the Fallen Angels pause. But Eleanor shakes her head lightly, willing them to keep walking before Adelyn sees them. They do, luckily, making it out the doors just as Adelyn looks up. Her phone receives a message a few seconds later.

Lahash
Is everything okay?

Eleanor
Fine. Ady's horse fell and she might have broken her arm. But Kenichi is here, so you need to stay away.

Lerajie
Are you okay, though? You looked a little seedy.

Eleanor
I have a hard time when she's sick or hurt. Passed out earlier.

Lahash
Captain didn't pick up on it?

Eleanor
No, he was checking on Adelyn. Made the wrong choice. I'm fine though.

Lerajie
You might be concussed...

Eleanor
I had a helmet on, but I'm not.

Lahash
When does the doctor leave?
I'll bring Adelyn a get-well-soon present.

Eleanor
In a few days, I'm sure she'd love that.

Lerajie
Message us the results later. Tell Ady we're thinking of her.

Eleanor
Will do. Thanks guys.
What were you even doing here?

Lahash
We were helping a lady get help and kept her company until her family arrived. See you soon.

"Who are you texting?" Kenichi asks, drawing her attention away.

"Just Rachel, she was saying the horses made it to her place fine," Eleanor lies, the words so smooth he doesn't even notice.

"That's good. Have you finished with the forms?"

Eleanor nods slowly, passing them over with ease. It takes only a glance for Kenichi to lower the page, the pair settling into the wait.

Two hours later they are finally taken in to see a doctor, Captain laying under the chair Eleanor sits on. Adelyn stays perched in her mother's lap, still cradling her arm, quiet with the pain. Kenichi had already checked both the girls over for concussion, so they waited only to get an x-ray of Adelyn's arm, and hopefully a cast.

In all, the visit takes four hours, the group making it home as the sun sets with only a brief detour to collect the float. The horses are returned the next day, Adelyn spending a good hour doting on her little mare. Kenichi leaves three days later, letting them be alone once more.

And, as promised, Lahash brings the child yet another toy, doting on her wildly as Eleanor talks with Lerajie.

At least Eleanor knew that when she had to leave, they would keep an eye on her daughter. The Fallen Angels would protect Adelyn, even if it was from afar. They would be there for her if she needed it, they would honour Eleanor's friendship to the ends of the Earth.

Only Adelyn noticed their presence when the Daemones attempted to end her family. She was indebted to them, but they refused to take any acknowledgement. They were like that.

Chapter 34

The storm had rolled in too fast, thunder beginning before anyone even realised it was even a possibility. Eleanor, having let Adelyn go play with the town's children, is completely unprepared as the first big clap sounds and makes everyone in the tavern quieten in surprise.

In an instant Captain is on guard, standing in front of his patient in warning. People nearby frown as they see the pure terror that fills the 22-year-old's face. She ducks her head as the next clap reverberates, calling out hurriedly for her daughter.

When she starts to move, the dog barks, loud and clear. She doesn't listen, trying to push past, but the dog barks louder, growling as she tries to push past. Adelyn realises the problem the minute she hears him bark and starts running towards the area however she is further away than she thought.

Amy's husband reaches out to Eleanor in a hope of calming her down, but she grabs his wrist and uses it to spin him onto the ground in a heap. Captain raises his guard even more, snapping at his owner as she attempts to move away, running around to stay on her facing side at all times.

By this time Adelyn has gotten close enough to know what she had to do. The now five-year-old sneaking to her mother's bag and pulling out the sedative enclosed in an EpiPen container. The protocols that had been taught to her ever since she could walk and talk, at the forefront of her mind. She comes up behind her mother, making eye contact with Amy as she does so.

"You're going to need to catch her, watch her though, she might panic," the girl says, before stepping closer. "Cap, down," she orders, small voice strong.

The dog complies, dropping to his stomach as the girl swiftly moves in and jabs her mother in the thigh. Amy is there in a second, using Eleanor's shock to pin her arms behind back and holding the thrashing woman there until she slumps. Captain attempts to go to Eleanor's side, but Adelyn orders him down again.

Everyone is still watching as they lower her to the ground, Amy looking at her incredulously.

"Should I be particularly worried?" the woman asks the child, who has finally let the dog walk over and sit on alert at her side.

"No, it's why we trained him to respond like that," Adelyn shrugs. "If she touched another person, he would have started to get everyone away and continue to block her off from moving until I arrived or until someone picked up her phon—"

As if on cue, the mobile phone in her bag rings, the girl rushes over and picks it up.

"Adelyn speaking," she tells it.

"Are you and your mother okay?" Kaylee asks.

"Yes, we were caught unawares in a storm at the tavern. I wasn't close and Mum freaked out, Cap did his job and kept her stationary until I used the sedative," she responds.

"Are there any injuries?"

Adelyn looks over to her friend's dad, mouthing 'are you okay'. He nods in return, smiling reassuringly.

"No, there was one encounter, but he is fine."

"Did she reveal anything?"

"No, but they are going to ask questions."

Splotchy raindrops start to fall, the thunder continuing.

"Tell them she lost her parents in a bombing as a child, get Amy to drive you both home and put her in bed. Don't lock the door, stay close for when she wakes up. When she does, video call Kenichi," Kaylee instructs her. "If her friend asks questions, you can answer the ones about why, or what the other precautions are, for if you aren't there. We can trust her. Is there anything else?"

"No," Adelyn answers confidently, "Captain is really on edge though..."

"Just reassure him Ady, talk to you later, okay?"

"Yes, goodbye."

Adelyn ends the call and moves back over to her mother, running a hand over the dog's head.

"Can you please take us home?" she asks Amy. "I've been told to get her home and wait until she comes to. She should wake before we get back."

"Are you going to be alright?" the woman checks, watching the child carefully.

"Yes, she's had episodes like this before, but usually she hides it better," Adelyn replies. "If we know a storm is coming, we make sure we're alone."

"What was that about?"

"There... she lost her parents in a bombing very young; the thunder scares her. Especially with so many people around and me out of sight. We usually try and drown it out with a movie, or she calls our friends overseas," Adelyn answers slowly. "She doesn't cope well around this time of the year... evening storms and all."

"Who was on that phone call?"

"Kaylee, a friend from America."

The woman nods, easily picking up her friend and gesturing for Adelyn to grab the rest of their stuff. After quickly talking to her husband, Amy leads the way to her car. Adelyn takes the passenger seat while Captain and Eleanor sit in the back seat, the latter carefully leant against the window by Amy's husband before he takes their own car home. Amy starts to talk as they pull away.

"What happens if you can't get close to her?" she asks, keeping her eyes forward until the girl pulls out their car keys.

Adelyn opens a clip on the bottom, having to use a little force to get it open, revealing a small button.

"It is wired into her anklet, shocks her just enough to knock her out."

"What if she had her car keys on her?"

The girl holds up her necklace, opening the locket and clicking it once.

"It takes five clicks for this one to work."

"That anklet is the one which reads her vitals?"

"Yeah," Adelyn answers.

Amy sits quietly for the next few minutes, before asking one last question.

"For a terrified person her defence was very... accurate. And the ease she put him down..."

Adelyn sits silently, head tilting a little bit.

"I don't know... You need to ask her about that," she eventually says as they turn up her driveway.

Just as they do so, Eleanor starts to come to, the drug keeping her sluggish enough that there is barely a reaction as Amy leads her into the house.

Once Eleanor is settled into bed, Amy waits for her to wake, staying close to Adelyn as she watches her mother. It doesn't take long for Eleanor to figure out she's home, but her hurried breaths continue. Adelyn passes the computer over to her mother, smiling weakly as Eleanor takes it, kissing her daughter's head lightly. Once Adelyn has left and shut her door, Eleanor looks to the screen. Amy slips out quietly before she is noticed.

"I want you to breathe," Kenichi starts, voice soft through the microphone. "Evenly, I should have specified, I want you to breath evenly." After a few minutes of coaching, she starts to breathe normally, and Kenichi starts to talk to her. "So talk to me, what happened?"

"I, I didn't realise that the storm had come, and... the second I heard it..." she trails off. "All I could think about was getting Ady and hiding. And someone grabbed me, I don't know who, but I snapped, and they were on the ground. I was panicking, and Cap, I mean he was doing his job perfectly. Then I woke up here."

"The man was Amy's husband; he is perfectly fine. And Adelyn jabbed you with the sedative, Amy drove you home," Kenichi fills.

"I thought, I had been getting it under control," Eleanor whispers. "At least in public."

"That's okay, Ellie. No one expects you to be perfect," he assures.

"But I haven't lashed out for ages."

"Progress is rarely linear, we can always expect there to be setbacks," he shrugs. "Today it was this, but tomorrow we'll be moving forward again."

Eleanor bites her lip anxiously, hand straying to her throat as she looks past the computer to the end of her bed.

"Did they ask questions?"

"They did."

"What do they know?"

"Your parents were killed in a bombing; you were just scared. Amy knows it was your band that alerted us, and that it can electrocute you. She doesn't know it has a tracker in it."

She nods tiredly.

"I'll have to talk to her," she mutters. "Has there been any news?"

"Another attack, still under the radar. He says happy, late birthday," Kenichi says. "Along with an untranslated special edition copy of the Phantom of the Opera."

In front of Kenichi, Eleanor doesn't hide the pain on her face. Running her hand through her hair, she looks back up to meet his eyes. No matter how many times she gets the books, the loss still burns in her chest.

"I'll post it tomorrow," he tells her. "You doing alright?"

"I guess. I'm not good, obviously," she breathes. "I'll survive. I always manage."

"That's okay. I'm here whenever you need to talk," he reminds her. "Have you been feeling sick? Stuffy head, running nose?"

"No. It was after the anniversary though. But I think I'm a little more relaxed this time around, and with an extra horse to ride I've been able to stay busy enough..."

Chapter 35

"**R**iley's bags are in the ute tray," Eleanor tells Amy, as Adelyn's closest friend goes home from a sleepover. The meet up spot, the park. "I'll go and try to separate the little misfits."

The woman chuckles as Eleanor turns away, making for the playground. As Amy pulls the small bag out of Eleanor's otherwise empty tray, she notices the black compartment, camouflaged into the edge of the space. Hidden. Professionally hidden.

She finds the latch with more than a little effort, stepping back in surprise as it falls away from the edge. Two handguns. Two suppressors. Four fully loaded magazines. A black, full-face mask. Twin blades. A set of throwing knives. Two daggers. A pair of bladed brass knuckles. All items illegal to carry in the country. The kit of a mercenary.

Amy takes the two daggers, shutting the case and the tailgate. She walks to the front of the car, face serious as the children run up. Riley goes to her car without noticing, but Adelyn stops, eyes already having found her mother's daggers.

The ASIO agent notices Eleanor's flick of a hand, her service dog moving immediately to Adelyn and moving her away. Keeping himself between her and the child. A protective movement. Eleanor follows him just slightly, placing herself in front of her daughter. In the moment she can't believe how she never noticed the precise things Captain is trained to do.

Eleanor finds the blades as well, face staying perfectly neutral as her eyes move back up to find her neighbour's.

"I believe you and I need to have a talk," Eleanor instructs. "Do not call your employers, the minute my name arrives on their system your boss will call you off. He knows I am here, and they will protect me. Take Riley home and come to mine when James gets home. I will answer any questions you may have, then."

"Who are you?" Amy replies, still defensive. "What are you doing here?"

"I am here to live in peace and raise my daughter. Who I am will have to wait," Eleanor answers. "I cannot do this here, too many people could be listening. And Adelyn doesn't need to hear it all now. That is for later in her life."

It's clear the child is confused, glancing to her mother. She thought having the weapons was a normal thing, and while she knew a lot about her mother, she didn't know all the terrible parts. Not yet at least. Amy realises that, stepping back in acceptance.

"I'll be there at 11. Make sure you're home," she says, setting the two knives on the front of Eleanor's car.

The assassin chuckles, eyes tired.

"I couldn't run if I wanted to. They know my every step," Eleanor mutters, waiting until her friend has entered her car to move to her own.

Eleanor puts Adelyn in her room, turning on a movie on the TV in her room. The sound kept loud enough she can hear it from upstairs, to ensure Adelyn doesn't decide to listen in. Captain stays with the child as well, ready to protect her. When Amy arrives, Eleanor is waiting outside her door, keeping a careful eye on the gun in her friend's hand.

"That is not necessary," she says. "I will not hurt you. You are my friend."

"And you are trained to kill, I'd say, so I'm not quite sure I can trust your word," the woman replies snappily.

Turning her back, Eleanor moves into her house, sitting lightly on the dining room table and waiting for Amy to shut the door behind her. Almost for the first time, the ASIO agent notices the blades dotted around the building.

"Your name isn't Diana Evans…" she starts, staying on her feet in caution.

"No. We needed to change it, so my former owners didn't hear of me," Eleanor answers slowly. The title was Dr Nolan's suggestion, to call them her owners instead of employers. "They think I'm dead."

"You are a spy…"

"Why do you think that?" Eleanor replies, curious to hear her explanation.

"You move perfectly, I don't think I've ever seen you stumble. You never talk about your childhood. You have more muscle than a normal girl your age, and you have a suspicious knowledge of languages," Amy says. "You can case an area in a few seconds, and you always keep yourself in positions of escape. You never seem to feel pain and react badly when Adelyn gets hurt. You are suspicious of most people. You have a case of weapons hidden in the tray of your ute. Makes me wonder why someone like you needs a service dog…"

"My nerves are fluctuating. For me to keep a hold of myself I need to lock off my emotions, which is bad for everyone involved. And I can't keep it up around Adelyn," Eleanor answers. "I do truly need Captain." Her eyes wander for a second, falling upon the place she hides her notebooks. "I'm not a spy. When I was active, I very rarely just collected information. I'm more of a high-profile mercenary."

"Captain is trained to protect Adelyn. And to protect others from you…"

"He is. Downside of being taught to kill since you were six, your fight response is incredibly deadly. If I lose control he is trained to take me down. And if people come for me, I need him to protect Adelyn. If she is safe, no one can break me."

"Who would come for you?"

"The Berühmte Söldner. Any number of evil forces. I did a lot of bad things in my youth, for them. And I was good at it. I've pissed them off just a little bit too much."

"You have two handguns. Those are illegal to carry. Along with the other weapons."

"I have three handguns, in my car. One is under the driver's seat. And I have permission," Eleanor says. "If I hurt anyone innocent, then I die. That is the terms of my life. But they want me under their supervision, that involves me being able to protect myself from attack."

Amy frowns, placing her gun down on the bench next to her.

"You said my boss would block any investigation into you. Who is supervising you?"

"The National Agents of Protection in America, primarily Colonel Nancy Randall and her strike team. Kenichi works for her, as do all my American friends that you know of."

"Whose orders mean Mike Burgess can't look into you? An American Colonel doesn't have jurisdiction here."

"I stood trial for my crimes in front of the International Criminal Court, Australia cooperates fully with their actions. They found inconclusive evidence towards my motives so allowed seven years for me to gain proof of change, and so they could control the political nightmare it would create. I have until my 25th birthday, when my likely sentence of death will be carried out."

Amy visibly pales, glancing towards the stairs. Through the walls and floor, she looks at Adelyn.

"She doesn't know. She knows I'll go away but doesn't know how or why. Not yet. I beg you not to tell her."

"What's your true name? And what is hers?"

After a pause, Eleanor answers, "I am Eleanor Beck, she is Adelyn Beck. They didn't know her name, so it was safe for her to keep it. The last name was my mother's maiden name."

"You said earlier they knew every step…"

Eleanor shows the band on her ankle.

"Doesn't just read my vitals. The shock is there to control me. If I try to run away, they can incapacitate me until someone arrives. I try and take it off the same thing happens. And it tracks my location. They know every step I take," she answers. "The last time I was free I was six. So is the life of a forced assassin."

"How am I supposed to believe you aren't just trying to complete some mission?"

"Everyone always asks that…" Eleanor muses, eyes glancing away. "I've been here four years now. Longest I've ever spent on a mission was a month. Someone of my calibre doesn't do the long game. That is for the lesser assassins. I had the opportunity to kill an entire royal family, but I didn't. And it's not just because I loved one of the princes…"

"A Prince?"

"The man I said was supposed to join me, he left to help hide me from them. The man who came to your party last year was his older brother, demanding to know where he was. I have no idea," Eleanor shrugs. "Is there anything else?"

"Exactly how many illegal weapons do you have?"

With a laugh Eleanor lists them off, with the places redacted of course. As she finishes Amy sits down, rubbing her forehead.

"You cannot tell anyone this, it could kill me. Can I trust you?" Eleanor finally asks. "Are we friends again?"

"Yes, and yes. I will tell no one," Amy assures. "Does anyone else know?"

"Rachel doesn't, if that's what you're asking," she answers. "And I will tell you no more. I have people I have to protect as well."

The woman nods, smiling softly. Eleanor visibly relaxes as she does, glancing down the stairs.

Adelyn would find out eventually, but for now she just wanted her daughter to be able to have a childhood.

Chapter 36

USA, 17th August 2022

A man stumbles into the compound, pushing past the security guards at the doors to collapse in the atrium. A pair of twin blades clatter over the white tiles, released from his grip as he falls.

The face is bloody, lip cut, eye bruised. There is blood leaking through the back of his grey shirt, the knees on his pants covered in mud and blood. The guns trained on him seem to have no effect as he tries to get up, eyes finding the Colonels as she walks out to find out what the commotion was.

"They know. They know," Nikolas chokes, silver eyes bloodshot. "They're going for her."

It takes a moment for the woman to realise what he means.

"Eleanor. They know where she is?"

"I came as fast as I could, but they knew I was hiding her," he answers. "You need to help her."

The team run in a second later, Kenichi in front as he breaks into the clearing. An alarm is going off on his phone, he holds it out for the Colonel to see.

"She's on her own."

Ten minutes earlier, 7:13pm Makarrata, Australia – at the local shop.

"Ady, do you want to go out and play?" Eleanor smiles, glancing at her daughter's empty plate.

The girl nods, leaning up to press a kiss to her mother's cheek before skipping away. Eleanor watches her go, chuckling to Amy as the girl disappears. Captain shifts at her feet, allowing himself to take the extra room Adelyn had opened.

"Are you planning on doing anything for the holidays?" Eleanor asks as she picks at the last of her dinner. "We – of course – aren't going anywhere..."

"We were thinking of making a break for the snow, cheapest tickets are now and there is still a little snow left. Owen wants to try and find some Brumbies—" Amy chuckles "—but we haven't decided yet."

"That sounds fun. Adelyn loves it when I read her the Silver Brumby books, I'm pretty sure she pretends our horses are Brumbies some days," Eleanor sighs, before her face contorts into a frown.

As if someone is calling to her across the room, her head snaps to the side, turning back with horror written over her features.

Something flashes through the glass at the back of the dining area, up on the hill behind them. A moment later she sees the little red dot, pointed directly at her. Its pair is on her chest.

For half a second, she considers it as just seeing things, but the thought passes quick enough.

She launches her body down underneath the table, swearing loudly as there is a quiet smash of glass and a tranquiliser dart sticks out from where she was sitting. In an instant she turns to her dog.

"Go to Adelyn!" she orders, sticking a special patch on his vest.

'Run and Hide'. Adelyn knew what it meant.

"Now, Captain!"

The dog is away in a few seconds, slipping out into the dark. Now Eleanor starts to rifle through her bag, finding the entrance to the false bottom.

"What's happening, Diana?" Amy asks, bending down to look at her.

"They've come for me," Eleanor answers, out of breath as she pulls out the handgun. She pops up for a few seconds, scouting the area before ducking back down. A few people are watching her, but she ignores them. "There's a sniper on the hill, I can count four others, two in the carpark, one in the bar, one on the steps. There will be a lot more. Keep your head down and make sure the children are safe. Don't let them tell anyone where Adelyn has gone, not even yourself."

Shoving earplugs in her ears, she turns to face her seat, almost screaming as she spots the Daemone with ink black eyes looking down at her through the glass.

A shot goes off a second later, the man falling to the ground. Now the people around her yell, ducking away from her as she fires at the sniper, confident she has hit her target as she takes a step up onto the bench seat and jumps through the already smashed window. Two more bullets go to the two in the carpark, before she gets to her car.

The four magazines go into the waistband of her pants, one of the silencers being wound onto the nozzle of her gun. She takes the brass knuckles and slips away, more assailants already moving in. Eleanor moves swiftly, eyes already on a woman clambering into her car. The shots she fires are now much quieter, barely pops as she takes out any of the Daemones who spot her. With little care she rips the woman away from her car and takes her keys. With Ellsie in control, the terror running through her veins sharpens into focus: deadly focus.

Everything is quiet now, the people in the restaurant already gone silent. There is no sound of Adelyn screaming, which meant she had made it away before they found her. There was nothing Eleanor could do for her daughter anymore, so she pulls out of the shop and races away. Twelve motorbikes pull out as she makes it to the road, close on her tail as she presses the accelerator for more speed.

Amy has made it to the children, Riley in her arms, Adelyn nowhere in sight. They all understand not to tell anyone where she has gone as men descend on them, guns raised as they look for the precious child.

Eleanor is swerving on the road, trying her hardest to keep moving as the motorbikes start to fire on her. The back window smashes and she ducks, firing blindly behind her. At least one gets hit, taking enough of the others out that she can get a bit of space. But as she rounds a corner, a kangaroo jumps out of the bushes.

"Hello, old friend," the Colonel greets, eyes locked on the jet lighting up on the runway as she speaks on the phone.

"Colonel Randall. How nice to hear from you. To what do I owe this pleasure?" Mike Burgess replies, looking around his family table to ensure they are quiet.

"Eleanor Beck has been attacked, she is currently on the run, however we fear for her safety and her daughter's," the Colonel replies. "You need to get a team over there. We cannot lose her."

"I understand," he grunts, standing immediately. "I assume you will be joining us..."

"My team are just lifting off, should be 18 hours. I'll message the jet's details in a minute. They are going to be coming in hot, please make sure they make it into the country," she answers. "Do not go looking for the child until they arrive, she will not come out unless it is them."

"Anything else?" he asks, moving for his jacket.

"You need to stop all movement to and from the country other than our plane. With her in their grasp anything could happen," Nancy orders. "She can't be taken out of the country. Be careful."

"I will."

Eleanor manages to climb out of the wrecked car, head spinning. Blood trickles down her face, and her left shoulder is dislocated. Popping it back in, she keeps only one of the brass knuckle sets, and her gun as she rolls out of the car. Another groan breaks from her lips as she lands at the bottom of the hill, mud covering her clothes. But she gets up, running into the darkness.

The Daemones are close behind her and, injured, she can only move so fast. She can't brace the gun with her other arm. Blood clouds her vision as she fires behind her, pushing her legs to run faster, faster. But they keep coming.

Her reload is sloppy, slow. She fires again. Runs. But soon they start firing back, tranquiliser darts stick into trees as she dodges.

Fires. Reloads. Runs. But soon her head starts to swim, limbs refusing to lift fast enough to keep her in front.

Fires.

Falls.

Eleanor tries to push herself back up, but three darts hit her, the sedative working quickly. Her head is swimming. Swimming. Swimming.

She fires wildly, hitting at least two before she tries to turn the gun to herself, but with her consciousness failing, she cannot pull the trigger before she falls to the ground.

"Now, now, Kitten. Is it really that bad to come home?"

Zach and Kaylee pilot the jet, half an ear listening behind them.

"Any developments?" Kenichi asks the Colonel.

From the phone in her office, she answers, "her vitals spiked; she was seriously injured but managed to start running. She just lost consciousness." Nancy swears. "And we just lost all data from her band. They've broken it off her."

Kenichi glances at the beaten Nikolas, who's cursing loudly, resisting the urge with everything in him to punch the side of the jet. He drops to his knees, fingers tight in his bloodstained hair as he screams. Inside, the doctor was feeling much the same way.

"Adelyn?"

"Her tracker puts her in the middle of the bush next to the shop. Signals a little sketchy so I'd say she's in a cave. Her vitals still read strong, scared but okay," the Colonel answers. "Captain is with her."

"Call us if anything changes?"

"Of course."

1 hour later.

Three black SUV's pull into the small shop, followed by three vans. The vans unload first, moving through the building with guns raised. The hostages in the corner scream as they enter, but Amy recognises their badges, sighing in relief as they take out the armed assailants.

"Are there more?" an ASIO agent asks, looking towards Amy as she pulls out her badge.

"Many. Most of them are out the back, trying to find Adelyn, but her mother took off down the road," Amy explains.

"There is a team there already, however we have lost the tracker on the woman. Approximately how many are there?"

"20 or 30, I'd say. But a fair lot left about 45 minutes ago. There will probably only be ten or so left."

He nods, gesturing for his team to follow him out of the area. Men in suits come in next, quickly setting about evacuating the civilians and taking them somewhere safe for questioning. Rachel sticks close to Amy, still in her café uniform.

"What's happening? Where's Diana?" she asks quickly.

"Gone, by the sound of it. She had bad people after her, and apparently they found her," Amy answers, Riley still crying on her hip. "I'd say it will be a while before we see her again."

"Why are ASIO involved? Why not the Military or Police?"

Amy doesn't speak for a moment, sighing heavily.

"My guess, witness protection or political asylum," she lies. "There is a lot we don't know about her."

Rachel stays quiet as she is led toward the rest of the staff.

I remember this day so clearly in my mind. Everything happened so fast, but I can still remember it all. Everyone was worried, scared. But I think a part of me understood that if Adelyn stayed hidden, Eleanor would be able to withstand it.

But withstanding isn't particularly surviving.

Chapter 37

By the time the jet lands on the straight strip of road the sun is high in the sky. The team emerge, Michael in his normal white uniform while everybody else wears the NAP black. Kenichi and Nikolas make it to the shop first to be met by the ASIO agents.

Only a few people from the night before remain: Amy and Rachel among them. The former had sent her kids home with her husband, waiting anxiously for permission to search for the still missing Adelyn. She runs over as the pair burst in.

"They won't let us look for her," she says, glancing at Nikolas for only a few seconds before returning her attention to Kenichi.

"That was our orders," he answers. "It wasn't safe for her to emerge until we were here."

The woman nods, attention turning to Nikolas again.

"What happened to him?"

"I failed to keep her safe," he growls. "I warned them too late."

Surprise contorts Amy's face, looking him over once more.

"You did the best you could," Kaylee offers as she joins them. "But right now we need to find Adelyn. There isn't any coverage more than 20 metres out that way, so we need to search the old-fashioned way."

Rachel walks over, tired eyes now wide.

"We'll help, she can't have gone far," she says.

They walk systematically, each person spread apart. They keep the search party small, understanding that Adelyn won't know their voices. It's Kenichi who finds one of the Daemones with an EpiPen stuck in his leg, one of Eleanor's sedatives. He starts calling louder as he spots a trail of blood leading down beneath the track he was walking on. The blood stops as he gets to a rock shelf, no more of the liquid continuing in any direction.

"Adelyn! Captain!" he calls, looking for any movement in the area around him.

If Adelyn was hurt, Captain should come to lead him to her, but if he's hurt, Adelyn may not want to leave him.

"Uncle Keni?" a small voice asks from close by. Below him.

"Adelyn?"

"Yes."

He looks around again, unable to find her.

"Where are you?"

Directly out from the edge of the rock, a head pokes out, blood on her face. He jumps down the ledge a second later, finding the pair hidden in a cave tucked into the shelf. Captain is barely breathing behind where Adelyn stands, hands covered in blood and terror written on her face.

"Where's Mum?" she asks, voice weak.

She had been crying, no... she had been bawling.

"We don't know," Kenichi answers truthfully. "What happened to him?"

"Shot. It was quiet. They didn't hear. I stabbed him with the sedative, and have done it twice more since then," she answers. "I put pressure on it as soon as I could get him down here. It stopped bleeding a few hours ago, and he's barely breathing."

The doctor nods easily, stepping forward to take the girl in his arms while he runs a hand over the dog's coat.

"He should be okay, seems like it's only a flesh wound," he assures her. "We're going to get out of here now, okay?"

Adelyn nods weakly, arms wrapped around his neck.

"I've found her," Kenichi says into his radio. "I need two stretchers following the trail I took."

"Is she okay?" Kaylee asks after they receive confirmation.

"Yes. Captain got shot though, and she's been keeping a Daemone unconscious on the trail," Kenichi replies.

Everyone is waiting as they emerge from the trees, Adelyn still buried into his shoulder. She had started crying as they made it onto the trail and continues as Kaylee steps up and takes her quietly off him. The doctor moves to examine Captain properly, flicking half an eye to Adelyn as she sobs.

"I want my mum," she whimpers, tears running down her face.

"I know sweetie, I know," Kaylee comforts, rocking her slightly as she starts to walk down to the club room. "We're trying to find her, I promise."

"Is Captain going to be okay?"

"He should be, you did an amazing job keeping pressure on his wound," Kaylee says, placing Adelyn on one of the café chairs. She keeps a hold of the girl's hands as she crouches in front of her to wipe her tears. "I'm going to get you some food and water, then I'm going to go try and find anything that could lead us to your Mum. Nikolas is going to keep an eye on you for us, since he's not supposed to be involved with any investigation. I need you to make sure he doesn't sneak off, is that okay?"

Adelyn nods weakly, glancing over at the man sitting across the room. He has his head in his hands but glances up as he feels Adelyn's eyes on him. He waves slightly, lips twitching up into a smile as Adelyn waves back.

Kaylee slips out, allowing for the child to fully look at him.

"You're the one Mum mentions, aren't you?" she asks quietly. "Who keeps giving her books."

"Probably," he replies, voice gravelly. "Does she keep them?"

"They have their own shelf in our bookcase," Adelyn answers. "She cries whenever she gets one."

He looks away, head moving back into his hands. Kaylee slips in quickly, giving Adelyn breakfast before she leaves again, moving out with Zach and Michael to try and track where Eleanor may have gone.

"What happened to your face?" Adelyn asks, eyes barely lifting from her food.

"The people I was hiding your Mum from weren't too happy when they found out what I was doing," he answers. "I'm fine, just worried about Eleanor."

They both go quiet; Adelyn continuing to munch on her toasted sandwich. She stands up as she bites into her third quarter, eating it as she walks over to him and offers out the last piece. He looks up in surprise, taking it quietly as she pushes it forward again.

"Thank you," he smiles, taking a bite as Adelyn sits down on the other end of the couch he is sitting on. "You've grown a lot since I last saw you."

"It has been four years," Adelyn mutters, sending him a look he swore he could see Eleanor in.

"I see you lack none of your Mother's sass," he returns lightly.

Adelyn rolls her five-year-old eyes.

Kenichi walks in a few hours later, having taken Captain to a veterinary clinic. The dog is to stay there for observation for a day before they can put him into quarantine to fly over to America. He stops in surprise as he finds both asleep; Nikolas sitting up with his head resting against the wall and Adelyn with her head using his leg as a pillow. He leaves them be, joining the team as they scout out her house which is surprisingly untouched. After a little while they return to pick up the pair along with Kaylee, who had stayed with them.

Kenichi brings the teddy on Adelyn's bed with him, the one from Lahash. Though he didn't know that.

They receive word that a single, unauthorised aircraft managed to get out of the country while it was locked down. It shot down the military escort sent to turn it around.

Chapter 38

Blearily, Eleanor blinks into consciousness, eyes having trouble focusing on the room around her. Her head is heavy, thumping. Limbs leaden. The familiar urge to throw up catches her as she sucks in a mouthful of musty air.

She really hates sedatives.

Now, as more of her body regains consciousness, the nerves along her body start to work again. Her shoulder is burning, aching with a fury she grits her teeth against. The tightness in her chest, she realises, isn't fear – for her emotions hadn't caught up to her body yet – but likely bruising and muscle ache from her crash. In the same way, one leg is throbbing. There is a distinct feeling of stitches above her eyebrow... and a needle in her arm.

As if her body finally regains control over itself, her eyes flick around the room. It's stone. Damp. Silent. A single red dot blinks from the corner – a camera – and light shines from the other side of the almost black bars. She's locked into a chair, metal cuffs almost painfully tight on her wrists and ankles. At least her arm is held immobile.

An IV runs into her arm from a stand to her side, the clear bag clearly tagged 'fluids'. Eleanor goes to scream, but the cloth gag in her mouth muffles the sound, leaving her to choke on her sobs in brutal quiet. For a few minutes, that is all that fills the room, until – finally – heavy, booted footsteps echo down the corridor outside her little room.

"Ah, you're awake, I see," a man grins as he stops in front of her. "I must say, the damage you did to yourself in your attempt to escape me was impressive. I have to wonder if you were trying to get yourself killed."

Still gagged, Eleanor settles for glaring with all her might towards the man. His eyes are the same ink black of all the Daemones, greasy black hair slicked back off his face. All the features structured along the gruff angles of his face are harsh and mean. A face that would haunt her dreams.

A sword hangs from his hip, so tantalising to her, but so far out of reach.

"Well, I wanted to be the one to welcome you back into the Berühmte Söldner. It's not often one of my ACEs avoids me for long." My ACE. "Or kills one of my Handlers." My handler. "Mind you, I cannot fault you for that; he was not a nice person, even apart from the fact he oversaw the sending of people to kill others."

Eleanor has to stop herself from rolling her eyes.

"Dunkler Bischof, however, he appears to have a soft spot for you," the man grins. "Not only did you escape, but you managed to corrupt two of my other ACEs. My, my. You are skilled, but if you weren't, I wouldn't have bothered to retrieve you." His horrid eyes run over her body. "This is very one sided, let me in."

Without any argument, the lock pops open. As he steps up to where she sits, Eleanor can't help but flinch away, eyes mistrustful. He grips her jaw tight, forcing her to meet his eyes. Finally, he removes the gag. Eleanor snarls at the man – wishing to be able to pull away, but the grip is too tight, and the head rest holds her from the other side.

"Who even are you?" she hisses, throat tight as he exposes it.

"I was rather disappointed when I heard about your throat being slashed, thought for sure you were dead," he says, spare thumb brushing over the scar. "Should've known when your little boyfriend showed up surprisingly sane you had managed to keep kicking."

"You seem to know a lot about my life."

"I know everything about all my ACEs, Kitten," he grins. "I guess the sedative hasn't quite worn off yet, from what I've heard of your ability to discover exactly who my agents are, I would have thought you'd have figured me out."

"Yeah, I generally don't respond well to sedatives – headaches and all. And I'm pretty sure I'm concussed as well," Eleanor mutters, eyes shutting in a display of pain.

"The fact you managed to get as far as you did was quite amazing. How about I just tell you?" he was obviously taking much glee in her pain. "I'm the one you've been working for all this time. The one you've been killing for. The one who you belong to."

Eleanor does a good job of keeping the shock off her face, raising a lazy eyebrow in response.

"You're naïve if you think I'm not going to plaster your face all over every screen the minute after I get home."

"You're naïve if you think you're getting out of here any time soon."

"I'm going home. You have never succeeded in keeping me locked up."

"My underlings have never succeeded, no. But you've never been held by me. I don't take any chances, not with you. You will train more agents, you will teach them to do as you have, and maybe in a few years we can discuss assignments."

"I will not."

Her cheek burns as he draws his hand away.

"Will you work?"

"Never."

Chapter 39

They tried many things to break Eleanor Beck. Starvation. Beatings. Electric shocks. They threw her around like a sack of meat. Then they would give her a few days break, to heal so they could start anew.

And with each new attempt, they asked the same question. Their endgame.

Will you work?

And she always answered no. They had trained her not to break under physical torture, trained her well enough that they knew she would not give in.

So, they brought in a third party.

Sebastian walks into the room she has been dragged to. He looks healthy. He looks worried. For her. Surprise filters on Eleanor face as he runs to her, brushing the hair out of her face.

"Nora, what are you doing here?" he breathes, hugging her tight as she relaxes for just a second.

"I cannot work for them again, Seb," she whispers. "My baby, she deserves better from her mother than that. I cannot do this again."

After a pause he nods weakly.

"I know, Nora. I know," he sighs, burying his nose into her hair. "I don't want you to. Schutz told me you looked happy out there, I believe him."

"You would love her. Adelyn. She's a sassy little thing," Eleanor chokes.

"Course she is, you're her mother," he chuckles. "They're going to torture me to break you, Nora. Don't cry, don't break. You do not deserve this life."

Eleanor looks away, eyes tearing up.

"I heard you fell in love with a Prince," Sebastian says. "Good upgrade."

"I loved you, I did."

"I know," he breathes. "Do not cry. You're a Princess now, Nora. Princesses don't cry."

Eleanor nods, gripping his hair in her hand.

"You would take torture for me?" she asks, throat tight.

Sebastian chuckles, holding her close for one more second, "I would do anything for you."

Daemones come into the room, pulling him away from her. Behind them, the man she had seen many times over the past few weeks. The commitment was almost scaring her now.

"Did you tell her what we discussed?" he sneers, eyes on Sebastian.

"Yes," he lies. But the answer is so smooth no one can tell. "She doesn't care. I told you, she only used me as a plaything."

"We'll see about that, won't we Loverboy," the man grins, eyes raking over Eleanor as two men pull her to her feet.

Sebastian manages to hold in any sounds of discomfort to begin with, but soon enough he starts to break, screaming in pain. But he doesn't beg for them to stop, he just cries as they whip him, then electrocute him. Over and over.

And Eleanor holds her head high, refusing to let tears fall. She watches as they torture her first love, knowing that he understands. They both know she would do the same for him, and she knows that she cannot join them again, she wouldn't allow herself to.

Don't cry, he told her – so she doesn't. Not a single tear falls, she doesn't break as they expect her to. She would not break.

From what I have been able to find, they repeated this sequence for a week, before they finally released poor Sebastian and went back to the drawing board. Eleanor would not break, she refused to with every inch of her being.

For Adelyn, she would take anything they threw at her.

What came next was much, much worse. It tore her apart. Made her an empty shell of a person, but she still would not break.

She would not.

Meanwhile, two weeks later…

"Are there no leads on her location?" Nikolas growls, stalking around the room. "How is there nothing!"

"We are trying our hardest," Kaylee counters, glaring at him from the kitchen of the manor house. "They're well set up, all the scans we do of the Alps show nothing but rock. They must be deep beneath the mountains. Or they could not be there at all."

"Does the prisoner know anything at all?" Kenichi tries. The man Adelyn had knocked out had turned out to be the only surviving Daemone. "You've spent hours with him."

"The Berühmte Söldner are very protective of their location," Nikolas mutters. "He only knows they had to get her to a plane at that airstrip. No idea where they went after that. It's the same for all the missions he's done before. Get to a place, no memory until he wakes up in a compound."

The exiled Prince rubs his temples, dropping in exhaustion onto the couch.

"We've already hit all the bases I know about. The Agency have no presence there though, and there are no records of any other bases. She isn't in America, I could feel her when she was here, but then again, they likely have Malum lining wherever she is so I can't find her," Nikolas continues. "All the faces I remember from the Balls are either protected or know nothing. And the attacks have stopped."

Kenichi sighs, offering the man a cup of coffee as he moves towards the glass doors. Nikolas takes a swig out of the cup, savouring the burn as it moves down. With Michael already in his room, Kaylee walks over to where his little brother sits, hand squeezing his shoulder kindly.

"We'll find her," she tells him. "I know we will."

Pulling a tight smile, Nikolas glances up.

"I can feel her pain. They're doing horrible things to her," he says. "And I can't stop it."

"She's strong," Kaylee assures.

Nikolas bites his lip as he replies, "I worry she's not strong enough."

Chapter 40

Three weeks, it takes, for any new leads to pop up. Three weeks of torturous silence.

The house was unsettled, mostly from the clash of Nikolas's desire to find Eleanor and the child's complete bewilderment at where her mother had disappeared to. The horses are set to be brought over, but they take time to organise, so Captain is left to babysit the child once he has fully recovered from his brush with death. Only Eleanor's second horse stayed in Australia, Rachel keeping her with her herd as Eleanor's house remained empty.

They had taken everything of importance out of it, leaving many of the walls empty. They did not expect Eleanor to go back any time soon, if ever.

Now, about that lead…

The parcel sits on the interrogation room table. It has already been cleared for mechanical parts, so it isn't a bomb. But the compound does not get mail. More specifically, Nikolas didn't get mail, at the compound, from someone without a return address. Under the close watch of the team, he slowly starts to cut off the end. Electing to pull the packaging away instead of pulling out the contents, the small bundle slides onto the table with ease.

A pelt, folded to fit into the package. Nikolas unfolds the red fur carefully, gloved hands running over it.

"It's a fox pelt," Kaylee realises, stepping closer. "Why did you get a fox pelt?"

"Kleiner Fuchs," Kenichi and Nikolas answer together, the former continuing as Nikolas flips it over. "Eleanor's trainer called her Little Fox in German. I'd say this is from him."

A rough shape is drawn onto the skin side. With 16 black dots spread across the inside space, and one bigger in the top right quarter, it takes a few seconds for Kenichi to recognise the shape of Germany with its state capitals.

"Find me a map of Germany," he says. "There's one too many dots."

Zach returns after a minute with a computer, the map online. They all watch carefully as Kenichi starts to place small stickers over each dot he finds on both the maps. Until one is left, sitting just off the Czech Republic border.

"What's there?" Nikolas asks, glancing across at the map.

"Nothing, looks like just a forest," Kenichi answers, "there are a few small districts in that area, nothing big."

"Perfect place to hide a base," Kaylee notes, "I'll look over it with the satellites, get permission to do a fly over with Zach's jet. If that's from an ACE, I think it would probably be a good idea to check it out."

She walks out a few seconds later, followed by Zach as he goes to start planning the flyover. With only Michael, Kenichi and Nikolas left in the room, attention finally draws to Nikolas, who is sitting completely silent with a hand over the spot.

"There's something there," he murmurs after a few moments. "When I focus on that location, something repels me. I don't want to push too hard in case they have any Fallen Angels who might sense my presence, but there is Malum hiding something there."

Chapter 41

The team move silently through the dark, pausing in the tree line as they look out at the entry port. Their dash is quick, Nikolas glancing to his brother as he stabs his toe into the dirt, meeting a layer of black stone.

Nausea hits them both at once, but they force the feeling away as they turn back to the team.

"Our Aspects aren't going to work," he warns. "Not well enough to be useful."

"Good thing we can fight then," Michael returns, guns ready.

Nikolas had refused to pick one up, opting for his blades instead. They glint in the dark, leather grips warm in his hands.

The door swings open, a bullet meeting each of the guards posted inside the door. All the guns have suppressors on, drawing no extra attention as they move into the descending stairwell. Splitting up the team at the bottom, they are careful to keep quiet as they continue to move through.

Zach follows Nikolas who leads them onwards, relying on his gut as they weave through the myriads of corridors. They continue moving deeper as alarms start to sound, more and more Daemones and Berühmte Söldner agents crossing their path, but none stand a chance against the exiled Prince. While Zach has to reload, Nikolas continues to swing his swords, cutting down each with little care.

"Do you know where we are?" Zach asks eventually. "Are we going to be able to get out?"

"We have taken out most of our problems already," Nikolas answers lowly. "And to get out you just follow the bodies."

"But why are we so deep?"

"Because they keep their prisoners furthest in, give them more time to stop them in case of escape," Nikolas says. "I'm following my gut, which will bring me to her."

"She's here then?"

Nodding in affirmation, they finally meet a door at the end of the corridor. It doesn't open as Nikolas puts his shoulder into it – seemingly locked – but the guards dead at their feet have keys. The first four cells are empty, damp stone stained with vomit and blood. The next has a woman, curled up tight against the corner.

Eleanor.

The key to her cell turns and she flinches away, hiding her head behind her bare legs. Zach stays away as he radios the others, Kenichi waiting in the jet. Meanwhile Nikolas carefully slips into the cell, seeing his Geminae barely covered with a bloodstained singlet and tattered shorts as he gets within reach. The clips to his cape release, the fabric held out carefully in his hands.

Eleanor flinches again, tucking away tighter as he crouches next to her.

"We've come to get you out, Dulce Meum," he whispers, using one hand to brush some of the hair away from her face. The touch floods relief into his veins. "You're safe."

With tremor in her voice, Eleanor glances towards him slightly.

"Nik?" she asks.

"Yes."

Lightly he starts to wrap the cloak around her, using one arm to lift her slightly as it passes under her for the second time. As he lifts her fully, keeping her pressed close to his chest, Michael and Kaylee run in.

"An underground train left just as we found it," Kaylee says as her eyes find Eleanor. "No one important is here anymore. We need to get out in case it blows."

Nikolas just nods, stepping out of the cell and gesturing for them to lead. As he glances down once more, he notices Eleanor is completely unconscious, breath still shaking as they move swiftly out the way they came. With the deadweight in his arms, Nikolas stays out of any confrontations, focusing on Eleanor.

Her face sports bruises, skin grey and hair filthy. She is thinner than he has ever seen her, collarbone sticking out from her chest. At least he knew they hadn't attempted mental altering – a technology they were still perfecting – as he does a silent scan over her memories, only long enough to ensure there was no damage.

The shockwave hits them as they run onto the jet, throwing Kaylee the final few steps. Zach takes the joystick, letting Michael help Kaylee to her feet. She ignores his attempts to see if she's okay, moving directly to Eleanor who is still held in Nikolas's arms.

"She was scared of me when I came in, flinched away as I moved closer," Nikolas murmurs, sitting down and settling Eleanor on his lap. "They must have been..."

He swallows in pain, brushing some of the hair out of her face. Kenichi steps closer as he does so, looking over Eleanor with a quick clinical eye. The hollowed cheeks and pale skin shock him the most, they had spent so long ensuring she ate that he found it hard to believe she would starve herself.

"They'll pay," Kenichi offers, "maybe not straight away but they will pay."

Nikolas nods, still silent as he traces over the scar on her throat.

They would pay.

Upon arrival back in America, Eleanor goes directly into the medical centre, still unconscious. They wire her up with fluids, pumping as much of the nutrients she is missing back in through IV. A new band goes on her ankle. But she doesn't wake.

They keep Adelyn away, assuring her that her mother was safe, but she wasn't well, so the child had to stay in the house. Of course, Nikolas nearly never leaves her side, Kenichi watching over her from afar, too cautious of the Angeli's reaction if he got too close to Eleanor. Kaylee had been the one to warn him to stay away after Michael allowed her to read Anastasia's most recent correspondence.

After two weeks, she wakes briefly, reacting poorly to the situation in which she wakes up. When she is calmly back unconscious, they decide to move her to the manor to put her in her bed. Confident she would wake up not too long after, and with Eleanor breathing fine on her own, she will be connected to no machines when she wakes up.

Nikolas barely leaves her side, ordered not to heal her to not risk increasing their connection. They didn't want her to become more physically dependent on him while she may be so unstable.

Chapter 42

Slowly, Eleanor swims to the surface of consciousness. She is somewhere different, more comfortable. It's peaceful, quiet – no more beeping machines and blinding white. But there are two people talking, arguing. The weight near her feet shifts slightly as her eyes blink open. Head pounding wildly, they shut again in pain. Stupid sedatives.

"You weren't there for her," one of the pair growls, Kenichi she believes. "She was a disaster after you left, we were worried she wouldn't make it through."

"I had to keep them away!" the other rebuts. Nikolas? "They realised she was alive two years ago, found her location a few months after that. I was the one who hid her."

"There were other ways, she nee—"

"She needs you both to shut up," Eleanor groans, voice gravelly from disuse.

Both men start to move towards her, but as she tenses Captain jumps up and stands over her, stopping both from touching her.

"Leave," she mutters. "Both of you leave, please. Don't argue, just... Leave."

With a look between each other, both step away, starting to move towards her door. Nikolas takes the longest, watching as Captain steps off Eleanor to allow her to ease herself upwards, sniffing over her anxiously.

"Get Kaylee, please," she says. "I'm sorry."

They disappear, Eleanor slowly letting out a breath as she makes it to a seated position. Captain lays himself over her thighs, head on her stomach as her hands find his fur. She's licking her bone-dry lips as Kaylee slips into the room, pulling the door shut behind her. A glass passes to Eleanor, the cool water like gold on her lips. Eleanor savours the flow down her throat, taking small sips until the glass is empty.

"I'm... sorry that happened. I couldn't handle them being so close," Eleanor says, voice weak as she returns to stroking Captain's head. "I don't know what happened."

"I do," Kaylee offers, sitting lightly on the bed. "Post traumatic stress. We already know you have those reactions to some things; it just appears this has been added to the list."

Eleanor looks away, "so I'm even more crazy..."

"Not crazy. You have never been crazy," Kaylee tells her. "We'll work through it, we always do."

"If I'm scared of Nikolas and Kenichi, I'll be scared of them all," Eleanor says. "It's paralysing."

Her fingers twitch over her stomach, playing a quiet melody.

"Fear often is. We'll start slow, build it up. We can work through it, I promise," Kaylee offers, running a hand over Eleanor's hair. "You are strong, you can overcome fear."

Biting at her lips, Eleanor leans back into her headboard, hand pressing to the centre of her chest.

"How long was I... there?" she asks softly, eyes glassy.

"Three months, and you've been unconscious for two weeks," Kaylee answers. "We haven't let Adelyn in to see you yet, thought you might need to be fully aware."

Eleanor nods, patting Captain as he asks for more attention.

"Who washed my hair? It was filthy..."

"Nikolas. It seemed like quite the task with you unconscious, but he managed," Kaylee answers. "He was having a hard time seeing you like that. Some of the nurses at the compound washed the rest of you. Kenichi was saying it was actually beneficial you stayed unconscious because your body needed time to recover."

"And my house, in Australia?"

Kaylee smiles easily now, settling properly into her seat.

"All your valuables and important things have been brought here; some went into storage. Your newer mare, Carly, is with Rachel. She was more than happy to keep training her. Tucker and Angel are about to be released from quarantine here. They should arrive here in two days," she explains. "They all know enough that they haven't been asking questions, but you really should call them, just to ease their worrying. And you got a bunch of calls which hung up when they couldn't reach you, Kenichi turned off your phone so it would stop ringing in the middle of the night."

"Okay. I'll get that to stop," Eleanor sighs, raising an eyebrow as Captain starts to bop her with his nose. "That took a while... Can you get me some food, please? And tell the boys to stop loitering outside, I can't see them yet."

"Sure," Kaylee nods, moving towards the door. "Anything in particular?"

"Not porridge or bread."

Finally alone, Eleanor lets her head loll to the side, face blank. There is little on her mind, for once, eyes just focusing on the daybed against her wall. She swings her legs to the side, standing carefully. As she steadies herself against the bedside table, her head spins, but within a few seconds she takes her first steps forward.

While her legs are weak, they are still able to carry her to the window, more than happy to lay out on the thin cushion. Kaylee finds her staring out the window, Captain laying on the floor beneath her. Taking the food with little acknowledgement, Kaylee leaves a few minutes later, pulling the door to, a tiny gap keeping the cameras running.

The two boys turn towards her as Kaylee re-enters the living room, Nikolas still with his head heavy in his hands.

"How is she?" Kenichi asks, tracking the woman as she sits lightly on the kitchen stool.

"Not tops. I think it will be a bit until you two are able to go in, though," the woman answers. "It's not just you though, it's all humans of the male gender. It scares her. Be glad she could form enough of a sentence to tell you to leave and didn't just freak out."

"Because of what they did?" Kenichi follows, glancing at Nikolas for a second.

"I'd say so. That can scar people pretty badly," she says. "We won't push her. If that means letting her stay in her room for a while, then that's what happens. If she comes out, don't start any interaction, stay away. And I'll give her phone to her so she can ask me for things. Might ask Nancy if I can stay off other duties for a bit, at least until she can be in the same room as you guys."

The doctor nods, leaning back in his seat as Nikolas stands, stalking off towards the library.

"He's not doing well," Kenichi mutters. "Doesn't help that Michael keeps arguing with him. I think some part of him wishes he had his brother to help him through this…"

"I'll talk to him. What's done is done, and Michael needs to grow up a bit."

Nikolas is not doing well, not at all. He wants nothing more than to hold his Geminae close, force all her worries away. But alas, that cannot be done. So instead, he spends his hours blaming himself.

Adelyn follows Kaylee into her mother's room a few hours later, waiting for Eleanor to acknowledge her before she runs over and launches herself forward. With a tight laugh, Eleanor catches her daughter, hugging the child firmly as Adelyn grips her.

"I was worried I'd never see you again," Adelyn whispers, keeping her head pressed to her mother's chest.

"So was I, Ady," Eleanor replies, glancing to Kaylee only for a second as she slips out of the room. "But you being safe is all I care about."

"Don't go again. Promise me you won't," Adelyn tries.

Eleanor sighs, kissing her daughter's head.

"I can't promise that. I wish I could, but I can't," she says, opting for the truth. "But I'll try very hard, okay?"

Adelyn doesn't reply, bitterly burying her head into her mother's chest and gripping her shirt in her small hands.

Eventually, Adelyn falls asleep in Eleanor's arms, happy to finally have her mother home. She doesn't understand why Eleanor refuses to leave her room, looking between the other adults in confusion as they talk in hushed tones. Kaylee spends the most time with her, keeping her busy and distracted as Eleanor sorts through her mind, trying to regain control.

When she finally gets her phone back, she texts Lerajie. Brief and terse, she writes, 'I am safe. I won't be coming back anytime soon. Can't talk, not safe or smart. I'm sorry. Goodbye.'

She doesn't read the response.

Chapter 43

One morning, a week after she wakes, Kaylee finds Eleanor's room empty. Quietly, she checks around the house – Adelyn's room, the piano, the library – only to find each place empty. When she finally stops in the kitchen, Nikolas raises his scarred eyebrow, surprisingly calm compared to his usual attitude.

"You're looking for Eleanor?" he says, nodding down to the stables. "She woke up before anyone else and slipped down there. Just got on Tucker."

Sure enough, the pinto stock horse is being ridden around the paddock, Eleanor sat atop him. She is still too skinny, and the horse is obviously being gentle, as they do all sorts of exercises. Even though he was eating breakfast, it was obvious Nikolas was tracking every movement the pair made, all the while attempting to look as if he wasn't. It was a failed attempt, but Kaylee gives him credit anyway.

"What has she been doing all this time?" Kaylee asks, eyes now on Eleanor.

"Brushed him for a while, tacked him up. The stable hand on today is female, so that's fine anyway. She spent about half an hour lunging him – that was explosive – but once he calmed down, he was fine," Nikolas answers without hesitation. "Captain has stayed at her side the entire time... he's very protective of her."

"That's why we bought him for her, she needed someone to take care of her when she couldn't," Kaylee shrugs. "He's loyal to a fault."

Michael steps off the bottom step as she finishes speaking, raising an eyebrow as he spots Eleanor outside. It only takes him a second to notice Nikolas's indirect gaze on the girl, rolling his eyes as he moves into the kitchen.

"She has finally emerged!" he chuckles, biting into his apple. "How long have you been stalking her?"

Defensively, Nikolas answers, "I'm not stalking her. I'm watching in case she has any problems; Tucker was wild earlier."

"Which you know because you've been up for... two hours?"

Refusing to respond, Nikolas just rolls his eyes, eating the last spoonful of his cereal and placing the bowl in the sink. He settles onto the couch with a book, keeping Eleanor in his view.

Later that morning, when he sees her finish with the horse, Nikolas slips into the library to allow her to pass through the house undeterred – everyone else was at the compound for a meeting. He waits until he's sure she made it upstairs to move back to the kitchen.

A ham, cheese and tomato toasted sandwich sits on a plate in the kitchen, a quickly written note sitting on top.

'You like it with tomato, right?' it starts. 'You didn't need to be worried, Tucker would never hurt me... badly, though I appreciate the thought. Thank you for staying away, I'm sorry. Eleanor.'

He chuckles lightly, moving it aside to eat the thoughtfully prepared food, writing a response as he does so. The paper is slipped under her door, and Nikolas slips into his room only moments before Eleanor pokes her head out in surprise.

'I do like tomato, though I'm fine without if you don't want to prepare it just for me. I will always be worried about you. You have nothing to be sorry for, Dulce Meum. I will stay away until you approach me.'

She smiles softly, the note settling folded on her bedside table. Adelyn runs in moments later, chattering away about this and that as she did most days. Eleanor listens, but a part of her mind wanders as she glances out her door and to the one across the hall.

"Can we go on a ride tomorrow?" Adelyn eventually asks, "I saw you riding Tucker earlier..."

"I think it's supposed to rain tomorrow, but whenever the sun is out next, we can," Eleanor tells her daughter. "Don't want to get caught out in the rain..."

"I don't mind," Adelyn tries, almost desperate to ride the next day.

"But Angel will. And Captain. It's our job to keep them happy too," she corrects kindly. "And Tucker should have a day off. So not tomorrow, but if it's clear the day after we can."

Eleanor knew everyone would be at home tomorrow and making it out without confrontation would be extremely hard. It was mere coincidence it was also supposed to rain, luckily.

Adelyn agrees quietly, staying laid out on her mother's bed. Captain, of course, is in between their feet, watching Eleanor dutifully. With a quick few swipes on her phone, Eleanor offers it over to her daughter, eyebrow raised. The child takes it without a thought, opening a game to play.

"Keep the sound low, I'm going to draw, okay?" Eleanor says, walking over to grab a few things and shut her door as Adelyn nods.

When there is a short knock on her door later that day – around dinnertime – Eleanor closes her novel, having switched entertainment when Adelyn went to watch TV. She opens the door just an inch, glancing up and down the empty corridor. Only a pizza box waits on the floor, a note placed lightly on top of it.

Eleanor checks the flavour quickly, finding an assortment of her normal favourites. It seems Nikolas had decided to bring her dinner as repayment for making his lunch.

Moving back inside, Eleanor pulls out the artwork she had finished earlier in the day, writing a note in the top corner. She rolls the parchment and tucks it into Captain's collar, taking him to the staircase and letting him sniff a piece of cloth.

"Go find Nikolas," she tells him, pointing down the stairs.

Just as the dog returns, a laugh echoes up from downstairs, surprising Eleanor as she darts back to her room. A slip of paper emerges from beneath her door a good while later, the note passing system seeming to have been adopted by them both.

'Best portrait of Michael I think I've ever seen.'

It was not anatomically accurate, let's say that.

Chapter 44

Once the rain that had arrived early the next day finished, Eleanor took Adelyn on a ride. All had gone to plan, and she encountered no one else in the house.

Kenichi and Nikolas had noticed her slipping into the gym late at night to exercise, sometimes even entering the room in the early hours of the morning. They didn't mention it, much like Kenichi never mentioned the notes he often spotted waiting for Nikolas. A female doctor had looked her over after she had woken up, but he still reviewed all her reports, and knew Eleanor had made sure he did. A part of him had realised pretty quickly that even though he and Eleanor had been close for the past four years, Nikolas would be the first one she would get close to. It stung a little, but he understood how connected they were, even when Nikolas wasn't there.

I've talked to Kenichi a lot since I first learned the truth about Eleanor, because I was deep in the dark for quite a while after… He finds someone for himself, eventually. Eleanor never meets them, but I'm sure she would like them just as I do.

~

Eleanor pulls her door shut behind her, using it as a barrier to stop her from slipping back to the safety of her room. Captain watches her intently as she glides down the staircase, pausing just before she steps off in hesitation. Kaylee – still on babysitting duties – and Nikolas are both in the living room, the former in the kitchen and the latter watching TV. Adelyn is sitting near him as well, turning around as she hears Eleanor step down onto the floor.

"Mummy!" she exclaims, staying seated as Eleanor smiles softly. "What are you doing down here?"

Stepping slowly across the closer Eleanor answers.

"I was just going to play piano," she says.

Nikolas only tilts his head slightly to the side, keeping his eyes off Eleanor, but still tracking her movements. He knew she needed to get herself ready before he would look at her fully. But her eyes are fully on him as she steps a little further in, glancing at Kaylee for half a second before returning to analysing the back of his head.

With a huff to herself, she makes herself walk – not stride, nor run – across the room, disappearing into the corridor a few seconds later. Nikolas tips his head slightly in surprise, turning back to the television before Adelyn notices. But his eyes keep straying back to the doorway as the piano starts to play, sound dancing through his bones. When Adelyn is fully absorbed in the television, he eases up, about to slip into the corridor when Kaylee steps up next to him for a second.

"Where are you going?" she asks softly. "You know you can't put that pressure on her yet."

"I'm not going to go inside," Nikolas assures softly. "Just sit outside the door to listen... please?"

After a few seconds' pause, Kaylee nods, stepping away to sit with Adelyn as Nikolas edges to the door. He glances inside for only a second, before sliding down the wall. It's easy to lean his head back into the wall, sound waves lulling him into peace. He tries incredibly hard not to let the tears building in his eyes fall.

When the piano finishes, staying quiet, he startles.

"Nikolas?" Eleanor calls softly, staying perfectly still.

He is hesitant as he replies, voice tight, "yes, Dulce Meum."

"What are you doing?" she asks, the tone in her voice obviously urging him to stay out of sight.

"Just listening, I like hearing you play," Nikolas admits. "I can go if you'd like..."

"It's okay. When I can't see you it's nice to be close," Eleanor breathes. "I do miss being close to you, it isn't my choice."

"I know," he mumbles, a slight choke in his voice. "Suppose it's punishment enough. I am sorry for leaving, but it was necessary."

He can hear her shift, hear her feet padding across the floor. Feel her stopping directly opposite him through the wall. Hear her shirt rustle as she slides down the wall.

"You're not sorry," she says, voice clear in his ears. "And I don't expect you to be. I made the same choice when I was 16, I cannot fault you for it. I just missed you, really badly."

"I missed you more than anything," he admits. "I thought Incaendium may have a different reaction..."

The nickname for her other half comes as a surprise. But Eleanor doesn't take long to respond.

"She'll bite your head off eventually, figures the separation is punishment enough for now," she chuckles. "She's been quiet recently. Our bond was, injured, when they... tried to use Sebastian to break us. It didn't damage her, but it blunted her ego. I think it scared her more than she'll admit."

"Is she listening?"

"Always. Commentating every second of this conversation," Eleanor giggles.

"What is she telling you now?"

There is a chuckle in his tone as Eleanor huffs.

"That I should grow a pair and kiss you," she whispers.

"Not the greatest advice machine then?"

Now Eleanor laughs, having to bite her lip as Captain perks up, looking at her in surprise.

"She speaks truth, but unfortunately my mind is still my downfall."

The silence settles between them, Nikolas's fists tight as his sides. He would kill them all, he swore. Every single one of them would die. But first he would offer her the chance. She deserves her own vengeance.

"We will work through it, promise," Nikolas says, trying his hardest to make his tone light. "Trust me, I have a personal stake in the outcome."

"Oh, I'm sure you do."

Eleanor stands quietly, moving back to the piano. Nikolas leans back into the wall, eyes shutting in bliss as his Geminae Animarum continues to play.

He moves away only as he hears a car pull into the garage, Eleanor waiting a few seconds for him to make it out of the corridor before slipping out. Making it to the stairs just as they walk into the foyer. Kenichi cocks his head as he looks at Kaylee.

"New development?"

"Seems to be able to handle walking through a room with Nikolas in it. Talked to him through a wall as well," the woman replies. "Didn't look at him though."

"Progress is progress."

~

By the end of the month, Eleanor can tolerate being in the living room with any of the men, but her room was still closed off, and in smaller spaces she would only tolerate Nikolas and Kenichi. She could hold a conversation with the former, and small snippets with the latter, but she had never gotten close enough for physical touch.

Chapter 45

"Kenichi, Kaylee, I need to talk to you..." Eleanor says, glancing around the room. Adelyn and Nikolas are the only other people in the living room, but Eleanor adds, "alone."

With a glance between them, Kaylee leads the way towards the library. Eleanor hangs near the shut door, Captain sitting on her feet and watching the other two as they perch on the leather lounges.

"What's up, Ellie?" Kenichi asks, secretly glad she had even approached talking to them in such a tight space.

"I need to be looked over, by a doctor," Eleanor breathes. Her hands shake. "Though I have a feeling it may need to be a specialist."

Frowning, Kenichi nods for her to continue.

"I haven't had my period since I got back," she whispers. "I'm not pregnant, I remember what that felt like. I think it is something else, but I need to be sure."

Captain rises to his feet, placing his nose under Eleanor's twitching hand as she waits for a reply.

"What type of specialist?" Kaylee asks softly.

After a pause, Eleanor answers, "fertility."

~

They found and took her to one the next day, by pulling some strings to get her in quickly. The results, however, would take a while. They determined she was not pregnant, and there was no physical damage to her reproductive system. But there was something amiss, or so the specialist had said.

~

The medical report sits on her bed. Eleanor's eyes glaze over as she reads it again, only a few words making sense to her.

Positive. Artificial chemical. Irreversible. Zero percent chance of impregnation. Possibility of surrogate IVF.

Captain pushes into her lap, pulling her out of the trance that had taken over her. Her teeth bite hard on her lip for a few moments, head tilting in thought. Then she slides out from underneath him, walking in silence to her door. With her hand hovering over the handle, Eleanor takes a breath before stepping out.

The house is dark, quiet. Asleep. Eleanor's knuckles wrack against the door, the girl hovering silently as it pulls open. Nikolas frowns as he sees her looking up at him, hands wringing over her stomach.

"Can I come in?" Eleanor asks, stepping through as he opens an arm inward.

He stops the door just before it shuts, allowing for privacy but also an out for Eleanor if she needed it. She waits nervously in the middle of the room, eyes on him as he looks her over.

"Something's wrong, you're upset," he says softly, staying away.

"I need a hug, Nik," Eleanor replies softly, walking closer.

She stops a meter away from him, eyes flickering nervously. Finally, she takes the final step, pressing her head to his chest as her arms wrap around his waist. A breath leaves her as he carefully moves his arms to wrap around her shoulders, ensuring they stay away from her waist. Lightly his hand fits to the back of her head, holding her close.

"What happened, Dulce Meum?" he whispers, chin resting on the top of her head. "You've been quiet for days."

The calm beat of his heart warms her, the steady pressure of his hand on the back of her neck soothing.

"I..." Eleanor bites her lip. "It's hard for me to tell you, if I'm being honest."

He takes a chance with stroking her hair, but she doesn't move.

"There is nothing you can tell me that would change things," Nikolas offers, "and I won't tell anyone if you don't want me to, you know that."

"But it is still hard for me to tell you. It wouldn't change how you see me, but it changes things if we ever find a way to be free of our death sentences," she says, pulling away ever so slightly to look him in the eye. "I've been missing my periods since I got back so I went to a specialist with Kenichi and Kaylee the other day."

Eleanor pulls away fully, moving out of his arms as she lightly sits on his bed. He moves over with her, offering a hand to hold as he sits down.

"They... When a female ACE graduates at 18, they sterilise them, to ensure no unwanted children are born out of our line of work," Eleanor continues, linking her fingers with his. "It seems they did the same to me, to make me even more of the agent they wanted. Being unconscious allowed them to do whatever they wanted with me."

Nikolas squeezes her hand lightly, the urge to pull her into his arms stronger now than ever.

"I cannot bear another child, never can. The chemical sterilisation is irreversible," Eleanor says, looking at him once more. "Even if we earn their respect, earn freedom, we can never have a family, children."

Eleanor almost withdraws her hand as Nikolas stays silent, but he opens his arms, offering for her to move closer. To his surprise she does, shifting her weight into his lap and tucking her head under his chin. Captain finally lays at the edge of the bed; the need for comfort that drives Eleanor closer to Nikolas outweighing her fear. She could deal with it for now. But she knows he is being extremely careful only to touch her in safe places, and even she realises that he must.

"I don't care, Dulce Meum," he says, holding her tight. "I don't care about any of that. You have Adelyn; we have Adelyn. And as long as we have each other that is all I care about."

A loose chuckle breaks through Eleanor's lips, forming into sobs as she buries closer to his chest. He keeps his arm around her shoulders, hand on her arm. The urge to wrap her legs around his waist and hold her as close as possible as she cries is almost unbearable, but he settles for cuddling her close. And with her arms tucked into her chest, Eleanor savours the proximity, the touch she had been aching for for weeks now... for years.

"I don't know why it hurts so much. It's not like I planned to have another child before my execution," she whispers.

"Because you are a brilliant mother," Nikolas offers. "Having Ady saved your life. For you it's another closed door. You like having options open to you and this is one close to your heart."

With a few blinks, Eleanor glances up to him for a second before lowering her eyes.

"Why aren't you upset? It's like you don't care..." Eleanor mutters, the slight slip of Ellsie through her wall. "I'm sorry. That's rude."

Nikolas chuckles lightly.

"It's fair," he says. "I'm not... upset. Furious that they did that to you, very. I'm a little disheartened, but I know that there are always other options. And I do care what you feel about it, I always will. But this is not my time."

"Thank you."

With a smile to himself, Nikolas keeps Eleanor in his arms as she begins to stare into space. Eventually, her eyes drift shut, head still tucked under Nikolas's. He waits for a few minutes, before oh-so-carefully lifting her up. Captain follows loyally as he walks into her room, laying her out on her bed. Once she is carefully tucked in, he steps away, moving the papers off the bed. He ignores the open sketchbooks, forcing himself to begin walking out of the room. Nikolas pauses to glance back at her; she is still blissfully asleep, Captain curled at her feet. He slips out before his control can break, shutting the door softly.

Ever slowly, Eleanor became more confident. The news had left its mark, that they knew, but through it she had grown able to be closer to people. Sitting in rooms with anyone, talking to everyone. Though not as close as that night, she could touch Nikolas and Kenichi, and they her, but only on her hands or through her shirt. Little things.

It wasn't until she was much older that Adelyn found out why her mother had changed. They kept a lot from her, until she turned 16.

Chapter 46

Small feet run down the staircase, Adelyn stopping in front of her mother with a phone extended. Eleanor frowns, not taking it immediately.

"Lucy called, I accidentally answered, I know you said not to," Adelyn whispers in German, extending it. "She needs to talk to you. She sounds scared."

Reluctantly, Eleanor takes the phone, taking a breath before lifting the phone to her ear.

"Hello," she says softly.

"Eleanor, you're okay!" Lerajie answers, the frantic tone obvious in her voice. "Lahash, he wouldn't accept your message, said it was too cryptic. He wanted to check out your house, see if there was anything there, maybe try to contact your Geminae."

Abruptly, Ellsie takes over, standing and pacing away from her seat.

"He did what!" Eleanor growls, switching to German.

"He thought he had got away with it, but the man you showed us photos of came with an American assault team yesterday," Lerajie explains, keeping to the changed language. "He ordered me to run, I was only just able to get to a phone. They took him, Eleanor."

"And they just walked in the door," Eleanor hisses. "I'll fix it, I promise."

"Don't let them lock him up…"

"He will be back with you within the week, free as can be," Eleanor assures. "I've got to go."

Eleanor turns on Michael, Zach and Kaylee as soon as the phone disconnects, jaw clenched tight.

"Adelyn, can you go sit in the library with the door shut, please?" Eleanor says, sending her phone with the child. As the door shuts, her glare returns to the trio. "Where have you been?" she asks, feigning interest.

"Just the compound," Kaylee answers.

"And before that? You've been gone for three days."

"Down in Florida, had some Daemones to handle," Michael says.

"I would have thought you knew not to lie to me," Eleanor growls, stalking forward.

But Nikolas steps up to stop her, hands lightly on her shoulders as he steps in her path. He incorrectly figured he was the best one to try and stop her fury.

"Incaendium, watch it..."

"Get out of my way," she returns with a violent push past as she swiftly pins Michael by the neck.

A knife presses to his gut, when she acquired it no one knows, but it stays pressed against the skin.

"Have you told Angeli Terra?" she says. "Do not lie."

"No." Michael coughs. "I was going to in an hour or two."

"Where is he."

"Compound," Kaylee answers, hand lightly on Eleanor's shoulder. "We can take you now, there is no need for violence."

Backing off, Eleanor raises her hands in surrender, hair flicking out of her face.

"We go now. But someone needs to stay with Adelyn," Eleanor says, breath evening out only slightly. Ellsie still held tight on the reins.

Zach volunteers, and within a few minutes everyone else is spread through two cars, Kenichi and Nikolas with Eleanor, Kaylee and Michael – once again – together. The doctor doesn't make it very far into the drive before breaking.

"Who is it? And who called you?" he asks, glancing across at her.

With a sigh, she answers, "Lachlan, the friend I would spar with. His... partner called, told me. They've kept my identity secret for years now, I owe them this much."

"They know who you actually are?"

Eleanor chuckles.

"Of course, they know a trained assassin when they see one. And only a Berühmte Söldner ACE could take one of them down."

Now Nikolas frowns from the back seat.

"Why would Michael have called Angeli Terra?" he questions, suspicious.

"Because he is a first generation Fallen Angel," Eleanor answers softly. "His true name is Lahash, hers Lerajie. They've been running together for thousands of years. They're good people."

Nikolas is still cautious. Even more so, perhaps.

"Do you know why they fell?" he asks.

"Lahash because of a woman, a child. He never saw them again. Lerajie... disobeyed them somehow, fought against them, she never told me what happened, but she was not the only one. They don't really like to talk about their first years," Eleanor says. "Be nice, Nikolas. They are the first friends who are truly mine. They understand my bloodlust. It's only because he was worried about me that Lahash even got caught."

With the finality in her tone, both men shut up.

They follow closely as they are led through the compound, entering the interrogation room with her. Lahash lets his shock show, eyes flicking up and down Eleanor's form for a few seconds. She knew she was still skinnier than she used to be, skin paler. That there was a haunt behind her eyes. It was scarily familiar to him.

Eleanor rushes forward, brushing his golden hair out of his face to inspect it. Beaten and still bloody, Lahash tries to move his own hands to her, but they meet the ends of the chains attached to his feet.

"I thought I told you not to go back to that house," Eleanor mutters in Latin. "You promised."

In shame, Lahash glances down.

"Your message was so cryptic, and you wouldn't answer my texts," he replies. "I was going to try and contact... him." The Fallen Angel glances to Nikolas, standing wearily in the corner. "I see you've been reunited."

"Yes. But after my time being tortured by the Berühmte Söldner I have some additional issues. I'm going to need you not to touch me too much once I get you out of these chains," she murmurs. The contact with Michael had been purely adrenaline based, Ellsie possessing more control than she had now. "You aren't going to Angeli Terra."

Lahash chuckles as Eleanor steps away.

"Glad to hear it, but how do you plan on doing that?" he mutters, glancing at the one-way glass.

"I have my ways…"

She steps away fully, turning towards Nikolas, who is half grinning, half frowning at her. A part of him loved seeing her so confident, so in control. Another worried why it didn't come out more often.

"I didn't know you could speak Latin," he says in English, drawing attention away from Lahash.

"I learnt. Thought I might as well figure out what you keep calling me," Ellsie fires back, smile just behind her lips for only a second. "I need you to stay in here for a moment, keep the door shut."

Before he can argue, she slips outside, making sure the door is shut as she moves into the viewing room. Michael glares, but not as hard as she does, holding a hand out.

"They can't hear us?" With a negative answer, Eleanor continues unhindered. "He's walking out of here free; I don't care what you say."

"I can't do that, Eleanor. I am the Prince of Angeli Terra, and it is my duty to protect the world from his kind," Michael returns.

"He is harming no one, just living his life. Complain about it all you like, but he is my friend, and I promised him and his partner that I wouldn't let them end up in that hellhole of a prison," Eleanor hisses, fists clenched. "I doubt Nikolas would like to hear about your little visit. What you accused us both of. The risk you put on my location… I won't tell him if you let Lahash walk."

"Is that all you have to barter with? Telling Nikolas something," Michael teases.

"Oh, did I forget to mention Anastasia and I have been talking recently… she's expecting a child, isn't she. I wonder how her hormones affect her anger," Eleanor returns, watching as Michael's face pales. "Of course I could easily break him out, but I rather like where I am right now."

Kaylee steps forward from the edge of the room, interrupting the argument.

"Michael, it's not worth it. It's obvious he's done nothing wrong – is it really that hard to let him go?" she says, an odd look present in the gaze they share.

Begrudgingly, he hands over the keys, watching in annoyance as Eleanor grins and walks out of the room. Kaylee bumps his shoulder lightly, smile soft. Wrapping an arm around her, Michael lightly kisses the top of her head.

"Who are you more scared of? Anastasia, Nikolas or Eleanor?" Kaylee chuckles.

"Honestly, Anastasia and Eleanor are a tie. Would not want to make them both mad, I don't think I'd survive," he huffs.

Inside the interrogation room, Lahash stands up, amusement clear as Eleanor enters victorious. With her permission, Captain moves to greet him, tail wagging wildly.

Not trusting anyone else, Lahash rides in the car Eleanor drives, Nikolas stuck in the back with Kenichi and Captain as the Fallen Angel is ordered – by Eleanor – to take the front seat.

"Is Lerajie okay?" he asks, concern clear.

"Yes. She's the one who called me," Eleanor answers. "You'll be back with her as soon as possible."

Lahash smirks, "want to get rid of me, Regina Tenebris?"

"Never," Eleanor grins, eyes flashing to Nikolas for a second. "Just don't want there to be any problems."

To her surprise, Nikolas huffs, muttering something beneath his breath.

"What was that?" she hisses.

"I said, is there a reason for there to be problems," Nikolas says, clearly irritated.

Watching the encounter from his seat Kenichi raises an eyebrow.

"No, you possessive ass," Eleanor mutters. "We are friends, nothing more. You know that. I waited for you; I will always wait for you. I merely looked at you because I like to, I was talking about Michael."

Backing down ever so slightly, Nikolas sighs.

"What did you threaten him with?" he asks.

"Telling you and Anastasia something he doesn't want you to know. I won't tell you what until Lahash and Lerajie are completely clear from where he found them," Eleanor answers, before adding softly. "You know I wouldn't have done anything with anyone else, right?"

Ever so slightly, Nikolas tilts his head, asking for permission to speak into her mind. With a nod, he does.

I trust you. But I did find it hard to believe you wouldn't have, seeing as though it was horrible of me to do that to you,' he says. *'And he is undeniably attractive, I mean did you see his jawline?'*

Eleanor has to stop herself from laughing out loud, keeping her eyes on the road.

'Do you have a crush on Lahash?' she teases. *'I'm sure I could set something up...'*

'I do not, and don't you dare,' he answers. *'Are you telling me I'm wrong?'*

'No. It's undeniable,' Eleanor chuckles. *'Though you're better.'*

'You flatter me.'

"You can speak aloud, you know," Kenichi mutters, "it isn't nice to exclude people from your conversations."

"Especially if it seems so very amusing," Lahash adds teasingly, "or is that a blush on the assassin."

"I wouldn't want to boost your ego," Eleanor returns, glancing at the now grinning Nikolas. "We're nearly back. You can take my room tonight; I'll steal his couch."

"You'll steal my bed, I'll take the couch," Nikolas says, "but there are other guest bedrooms."

"They all have no bedsheets," Kenichi explains, "and it's the maid's day off."

"Then she takes my bed," he says, turning to Eleanor. "You and I both know you'll end up on the floor if you sleep on the couch."

Lahash can't help but grin, eyes landing on Eleanor as she cracks her jaw in annoyance.

"I thought you said you enjoyed extended cuddles with him?" Lahash chuckles in German, remembering Eleanor mentioning Nikolas not speaking the language. Softer, he continues, "what happened?"

"A lot of crap," she whispers. "I can barely stand male touch, only those I'm truly close to can get away with it. But it's still limited."

Offering a kind smile, Lahash turns forward again as they drive up to the manor. As they move inside – behind the other pair – Nikolas sidles up to Eleanor's side, leaning down to whisper to her as they walk through the stone entryway.

"Extended cuddles, huh?" he says, grinning as she freezes and looks at him. "You're not the only one who learnt a language in the last five years."

"And only now you decide to tell me?" she mutters, walking forward again.

"Had to get some surprise out of you."

With an annoyed shake of her head, Eleanor moves into the living room to find Adelyn standing in shock, eyes on Lahash. Her blue eyes find her mother's, question clear.

"It's okay Adelyn. They know," Eleanor says, laughing as her daughter launches herself at the man.

'They're close,' Nikolas notes, still hanging at her side.

'He brought her most of her toys. She loves him,' Eleanor replies. *'And he dotes on her more than anyone.'*

'What is it with you two and melting the hearts of powerful people,' Nikolas chuckles.

'Just charismatic.'

Chapter 47

Lahash makes it back to Lerajie without problem, both disappearing within weeks. They kept their phones on them, however, a channel so they could organise to say goodbye in the years to come. Time was ticking for Eleanor, she only had two more years.

As if life was repeating itself, Eleanor and Nikolas started to wake each other up during nightmares. They don't spend the night holding each other, merely sit on the bed and talk, but the old pattern was emerging. Eleanor felt comfortable enough to fall asleep while he was sitting next to her, but Nikolas knew to slip back to his room.

His nightmares were worse than they used to be, causing him to wake up in a sweat nearly every night. Often Eleanor woke when he did, but she stayed away, knowing if he needed company he would come in. If she heard him leave the house, she'd leave her light on. A beacon.

Nikolas slips in the door, shutting it silently behind him as he moves across the room. Eleanor stays deep in sleep as he moves over. Curled around a pillow, facing out with her hair falling over her face, she looks at peace. He has promised himself that he would just check she was there, but he can't stop his hand as he reaches out to brush the hair away from her face. Twirl a piece with his finger. His control slips slightly, the finger running smoothly down from her temple to her chin, following the curve of her jaw. He is about to turn away, to leave the room before he can't step away, but Eleanor shifts just slightly. Captain watches him from her feet.

"What's wrong, Nikolas?" she murmurs, only the small movement of her lips to show the sound had come from her.

"I was just checking you were still here," he replies, own voice low from sleep.

She nods just slightly, fingers tangling on his, just for a few seconds before she pulls the hand back.

"I am..."

He is about to step away, remembering their current situation, but she huffs, snuggling into her blanket before speaking.

"Lie down, Nik," she says, "you won't get back to sleep otherwise. Just stay on the other side, please..."

Nikolas doesn't argue, slipping in the other side of the bed and settling into the pillows. Much like Eleanor, he grips a pillow under his arm.

"Only for tonight," she whispers, "I still need space."

"I wouldn't expect anything else," he replies, "thank you."

Eleanor doesn't reply, shifting ever so closer and letting out a breath as she pushes herself into sleep once again.

She wakes to Captain's face in hers, the dog trying hard to get her attention. With a tired glance at her clock, she eases up. It is significantly later than she normally wakes up, Captain is obviously desperate to go to the toilet. With only half a glance at Nikolas, still asleep on the other side of her bed, she slips out her door in her pyjamas. Regretting the decision not to change as she passes through the already occupied living room, Eleanor leans on the glass doors to wait for Captain.

Adelyn finds her mother quickly, happy to be taken into her arms. Conversing quietly between them, Eleanor only glances at the rest of the room for a few seconds, eyes rolling at the smirking Kenichi. He walks over with a glass of water just as Captain finishes, blocking Eleanor's escape.

"You slept in late..." he notes, watching her in amusement. "I notice someone else is also missing."

Sending Adelyn off, Eleanor turns to him in annoyance.

"What's it to you," she says. "He just slept on the other side of the bed, no touching. But I guess the presence allowed us both to get some rest."

With a soft smile, he adds, "and you just forgot to get dressed?"

"Forgot I had slept in, Captain needed to go out," Eleanor answers. "I was too lazy to."

With a heartfelt chuckle, Kenichi steps out of her way, Eleanor quickly making her way back up the stairs. Nikolas rolls over to face her as she walks in, arm flopping off the bed.

"Morning," Eleanor says, smile tight. "Sleep well?"

"Yes," he answers groggily. "What time is it?"

"Nine."

He raises an eyebrow, glancing her over as she moves onto the other side of the room.

"How long have you been awake?" he asks, clearly intent on staying in the bed.

"Not long, Captain woke me up."

"Is that my shirt?"

Rolling her eyes, Eleanor doesn't answer as she grabs clothes to change into. She slips into the bathroom and emerges shortly after with a hairbrush in her hand. Not long after she sits down to start, Nikolas eases out of the bed and appears behind her. The message in Eleanor's eyes is clear as she looks at him through the mirror and hands him the brush: be careful.

Nikolas is extremely so, the brush moving slowly through her hair. He warns her when he knows something is going to pull slightly, apologising profusely. Once the brush is sliding through without interruption, he takes a hairband off the handle and gives it back to Eleanor. When the plait is finished, he steps back to give her space.

Eleanor stands, leaning in for a side hug for just a moment before shifting away. For only a second, Nikolas's hand runs over her waist, accidentally. Her jerk away is violent, Captain arriving at her side seconds later and shoving his head into her hands.

The flash of terror only takes hold for a few seconds, before she's calm enough to turn back to him. It's clear he's sorry, watching carefully as Eleanor takes a few breaths. Only once she smiles weakly at him, does he speak.

"Sorry, I wasn't expecting you to move so quickly," he offers. "You want me to go?"

"No, you're fine," she says. "It's good for me to have exposure."

She drops back onto her bed, rolling her head back to expose her throat. Dutifully, Nikolas sits on her vanity bench, watching carefully as Eleanor's eyes find his.

"Why did you come in last night?" she asks softly. "What dream drove you in here?"

He sighs, answer quiet.

"A bad one, that involved you back in their hands... I just had to check you were okay," he says. "I am truly sorry, for the effect of what I had to do ended up having on you."

"I can forgive you," she breathes, voice distant as her fingers stroke patterns on the pillow at her side. "Ellsie is a little tougher, but she understands enough not to bite your head off."

Nikolas laughs slightly. Ellsie seemed to always make him laugh.

"I got the feeling she would like to whoop my ass," he chuckles. "I assume you are the one stopping her?"

"Of course I am. Without her taking full control of us, I can't quite handle it," Eleanor admits. "I'm a broken cog in the machine. Hell, I can only sleep properly near you but can't stand your touch."

"We'll figure it out," he promises. "We always do."

"You always do, I'm just along for the ride."

"That's a lie."

Before Eleanor can argue against him, Captain jumps up onto her bed, nose bopping against her thigh. After settling the dog with a salty glare, her eyes fall on Nikolas.

"Why must you always raise the scarred eyebrow?" she mutters as she stands, ignoring his grin.

"Habit," he answers. "Why does your dog take such joy in telling you to eat?"

With a huff, Eleanor answers, "because he's a pain."

Both share a rare smile as they descend the staircase.

Chapter 48

Eleanor is once again hidden away in her room when Zach approaches Nikolas in the living room. Even though they are the only ones in the house, Nikolas is still surprised as Zach asks to speak to him, especially as the usually uninvolved team member leads him outside. The warm August winds run over their faces as they get far enough away from the house that no one – especially Eleanor –would be able to hear them.

"I want you to understand that this isn't me telling you what Eleanor talks to her therapist about," Zach starts, gazing across his property as Nikolas's focus snaps to him in a moment. "I'm sure she does tell you stuff – seeing as though you two love keeping secrets from the rest of us." Before Nikolas can argue Zach fixes him with a no-nonsense stare. "Honestly, none of us care that much about that, we don't need to know everything. But what we do need to know is if Eleanor is going to have a breakdown and do something rash."

Nikolas snorts as he lazily walks towards the nearest tree and leans up against it.

"I feel like you lot should have a handle on that by now," he says, brain caught between defending Eleanor and admitting that a breakdown was in fact possible at the moment. "And as you said you've read her therapy files; you know what to look for."

"The thing is, we don't really," Zach replies, maintaining a calm that is frankly rather impressive. "I know a little about how Berühmte Söldner can react in high stress situations… my sister is paraplegic because of it. It's the same reason that I know how tough their torture can be. You worked for the Daemones, so you'll know a little, but I don't think their actions even scratch the surface of what the Berühmte Söldner can do to people. My sister described them as livewires, honestly, I think that's the best way to explain it." Zach takes a moment to try and read Nikolas's expression – one that had grown almost infinitely taut throughout the rather one-sided conversation. He finds no indication of the reaction Nikolas might have, other than that he didn't particularly like this conversation. "We are all being careful to slow everything down for Eleanor, it's something we have been doing for a while though. Slowing things down should allow her to make rational decisions, but sometimes that falters... as we saw with the Fallen Angel."

"So, you dragged me all the way out here—" Zach snorts at Nikolas's expression of indignance "—to tell me that Eleanor needs time to process things?" Nikolas questions. "Because I'm kind of aware of that."

"No, I came out here to tell you, that if Eleanor starts to feel pressure from anything, it could be extremely easy for her to snap. Especially after the recent developments," Zach corrects, willing his response to make it through to Nikolas. "She's scared of a lot of things, I— we really don't want her to do something that would jeopardise her position here or her position with Adelyn. Unlike the others, who want to just keep her in, I honestly think she needs something to do, to keep her mind focused on one thing, rather than The Thing. You and I both know this whole delayed sentencing thing is a sham, I'm just worried that they will pretend it's not and get her into a worse situation."

Nikolas slowly nods, gaze landing firmly on Zach's for the first time... possibly ever. The exiled Prince cracks his jaw as his gaze slips up to the manor for a second, before finding Zach again.

"Currently, she's concerned by... other things, but I will keep an eye on it. Once she gets more comfortable with me, I'll start training with her again, that always helped," he says. "So you know, Eleanor has always been fully aware that she may die, or even that she may have to continue working for the rest of her life. The reason she complies, is because it will keep Adelyn safe. The only reason she didn't break under the Berühmte Söldner's torture is because Adelyn was safe.

I don't want her to have to lose the life she's built, but if she thinks for a moment that Adelyn is no longer safe here, no one will be able to stop her. Not even me."

Wind whistles up through the trees, blowing Nikolas's hair across his forehead, but his gaze doesn't slip from Zach as he considers Nikolas's words. Slowly, Zach looks back up to the house, and then slowly brings his gaze back down.

"I know." His lips pull into a grimace, as if he's pushing away a headache. "Look, I don't want Eleanor to suffer. All I'm saying is that Eleanor is a whole new breed of unstable, a level that we have no chance of understanding or controlling. You might be able to. If you notice anything, let us know, and we'll adjust to suit her needs."

With a silent agreement from Nikolas – who makes no indication that he plans on returning to the house immediately – Zach begins to walk away, back up the hill. Stopping only as Nikolas calls out after him.

"She will never be stable, and the more we try and control it, the worse it will get."

Zach thought no words had ever been truer.

Chapter 49

A lot of people proved extremely useful to Eleanor's plight in her last year, in her last few months. Friends of old, friends of new. She was responsible for a lot of evil, yes, but it seemed she attracted a very particular type of person.

Powerful.

She softened the heart of the Dunkler Bischof. Made friends with the Princess of Angeli Terra. Earnt the undying loyalty of two Fallen Angels. And she was the last call for help from a very powerful woman.

Living in a penthouse apartment, wife to the District Attorney of New York, a far cry from High School.

Eleanor is walking up from the stables when her phone rings. The blank caller ID makes her pause for a second, but slowly she raises her phone to her ear.

"Hello?" she answers, sliding into the house.

"Eleanor is that you?" the woman on the other end of the line asks, voice stressed.

Holding a finger up to Nikolas – who was asking who it was – as she says, "yes. Who is this?"

Seemingly, a sigh of relief comes through the line.

"Skylar Demorae, from Gravenhal High… you said I could call if I needed to," she explains. "It's been a long time."

"It has," Eleanor notes, eyes flicking to Captain for a second as he worms closer to her. Slowly she lets her muscles relax. "Why have you called, Skylar?"

Having just entered the house, surprise flicks onto everyone's faces, Nikolas moving closer to listen to the other side of the conversation.

"I need help," Skylar admits. "Your kind of help..."

"What kind? Because I am not allowed to partake in contracted killings."

Eleanor could only assume the girl had figured out exactly what she was or was told by her mother when Skylar's father went to prison. They were adults now; the sugar-coating was gone.

"I know. And I wouldn't ever want to make you break your deal," Skylar assures. "My wife was the one who suggested I call. I'm sorry for telling her, but we have no secrets and when everything started happening, I had to tell her why."

Calm as ever, Eleanor replies, "that's fine. What is happening?"

"My father. He got out early, on parole for good behaviour," Skylar says. "And a few weeks later my mother popped up for the first time since I left for college. She started trying to get close to me, but I wouldn't allow it, not after she refused to answer my calls for years. After a few weeks she disappeared again and shortly after that my house started getting way too specific threats for our security detail to ignore..." Small murmurings on the other end of the line give Eleanor a chance to put the phone on speaker and sit down. "I should probably add that my wife is the New York DA, so threats are normal, but these ones kept coming, and we noticed we were being followed. The detail has been constant since she was involved with a gang bust earlier this year."

Eleanor had heard about the bust, but the information was irrelevant.

"What made you think you were being followed? Specifically?" Eleanor asks, pads of her fingers playing out tunes as a small crease forms between her eyebrows.

"We kept seeing the same people behind us, alternating each day. Our detail was ordered not to engage, but they confirmed each person was carrying a handgun," Skylar explains. "Then I started seeing my father and mother... watching us. When Arthur, my twin, called he told me he thought he was going crazy, seeing people following him.

He hasn't been in a good way since high school, but he's clean and we still talk often. We called in a favour and got him moved into a safe house. And now we can't move our family because they sent a note forbidding it... enclosing one of my brother's eyeballs."

Kaylee swears in surprise, perching across the table as Eleanor cracks her jaw.

"Was there any symbol on the letter or any signature?"

"Yes. It was on letterhead with a symbol like the Nazi SS bolts but as a two-pronged fork in a circle. It was signed by my father," she answers. "Back in high school when everything went down, you said they didn't choose to do what they did, well I think you may have been wrong about that, because they certainly seem like they are choosing to make my life a living hell now."

"I have a feeling they are pressuring you so you will call me, and likely distract you from other things happening. Is your wife working on any high-profile cases currently?"

Skylar laughs tiredly.

"Of course she is. It's her job description," she says. "But yes, we have a few gang cases going. One or two with that symbol. What is it?"

"The Agency your parents work for, and I am running from. A bunch of people you don't want to mess with." Eleanor outlines, evading the question as much as possible. "You said family, who do you live with? I don't need names, just general please."

"My wife and our son."

"Who else knows or has the power to intervene?"

"My wife's father is an Army General, he's worried about us. Our security detail and the police know but are doing nothing," Skylar answers.

"Does the General know you're calling me?"

There is quiet at the other end of the phone for a few seconds, Nikolas watching Eleanor carefully.

"He knows I'm calling an old friend who has connections in the NAP and has experience with people like my father," Skylar says. "He won't intervene; his word holds no sway in New York."

"Okay. Message me so I have your number, and I will sort out getting up there. We'll talk more once I get there, it's not safe to talk on unsecured phone lines," Eleanor says, "I have a feeling they aren't just harassing you because of your wife's job, but because we were friends. I kind of pissed them off."

"Course you did," she chuckles. "Thank you, Eleanor. I hope to see you soon."

"I made a promise," Eleanor says softly. "See you soon."

The line breaks, Eleanor lightly tucking her phone into her pocket. Kaylee is the first to speak, eyes concerned.

"You aren't allowed to work like that," she says, blonde hair curled over her shoulder.

"I am allowed to stop the Agency from hurting civilians and getting to me. That is what this is," Eleanor answers easily. "They want me."

"How do you know? Her father may just want revenge... or they might want to stop her working on a case," Zach tries, watching from across the room.

"Her father failed the Berühmte Söldner, the only reason he isn't dead is because of her connection to me. He'd do anything to keep his life, and that includes trying to scare Skylar into drawing me out and torturing her brother, which is illegal in this country," Eleanor explains. "If it was for a case they'd threaten her wife, yes, but they would have realised by now it was fruitless and organised to have her killed then gain control over her replacement, not go through the estranged brother-in-law. They want me."

Quietly, Nikolas asks, "then is it really a good idea to go?"

The worry in his silver eyes keeps her from snapping, opting for a weak smile.

"I have to," she sighs. "It's my fault they're in danger, and they won't hesitate to harm her family more. Annoyingly, their theory that I won't let them get away with threatening my friends is correct. I'm going."

Nodding in acceptance, Nikolas continues, "who is going with you?"

Before anyone can interject, Eleanor speaks.

"You and Captain can but no one else," she says. "You lot can monitor us from here, but I need free reign with the Agency. And with Adelyn here, I will be able to... cope." Her eyes flick between Nikolas and Kenichi. "Captain is trained to keep crowds clear of me and I am good at slipping through the back alleys."

They all look between each other, eyes cautious. But slowly Kenichi nods, pulling out his phone.

"You will need a badge off Nancy, we'll figure out everything else," he says. "If you want to go, then you can, but you need to be careful. At least be able to say goodbye..."

For a few seconds, Eleanor looks to the staircase, mind following up to where Adelyn was in her room.

"I have no plans on dying early," she says softly. "Don't you worry."

Chapter 50

"It's been a while since we've talked, how are you going, Eleanor?" Dr Nolan starts, smiling through the computer screen from her office in Australia.

"Terrible, but you know that." Eleanor's answer is curt.

Vanessa fixes her with a look.

"You know that's not how we answer," she reprimands, "try again."

Bitterly, Eleanor does so.

"I'm still feeling the effects of being recaptured in a way that is harmful to my everyday life. I am still scared if I get touched unawares by Nikolas or Kenichi and freak out if it's anyone else. I am not sleeping well at all."

"Thank you. Now, I hear you are wanting to go to New York, how do you think that will go with so many people around? You have never liked crowds."

Eleanor's eyes roll as she looks beyond the screen. Alone in her room, no one else is listening, but her eyes still flick around to ensure she is alone.

"I don't like crowds when I am the focus of them, I can handle using them to disguise myself." Slowly she returns her gaze back to her psychiatrist. "I am usually okay with accidental bumps, and Ellsie will be in control the majority of the time, she can handle most of it."

"Do you think it will be safe to fully release her in New York?"

Once again, it was clear Dr Nolan had been given a list of questions to get answers to. By now Eleanor was used to it.

"Yes, but I'm still going to hold a little bit of control until we enter a fight with them. It's too exhausting on us for her to hold complete control for too long. But I trust her to do the right thing, especially with Nikolas there to keep us in check."

Eleanor regrets mentioning her companion the second she does so, watching as the doctor clearly changes focus.

"Yes, I heard about your very strict decision for only Nikolas to accompany you. Any reason why that choice was made?"

"I won't be able to work to my full efficacy – as you put it – with anyone else with me. They will just put up too many rules and interfere with my way of doing things. But they believe – and so do I – it's probably a bad idea for me to go alone, and Nikolas understands the way in which I work. We understand each other and are the best option to complete an infiltration as a pair."

"No other reason?" Vanessa prods. There is a glimmer of friendship as she asks the obvious question.

Eleanor huffs slightly before she speaks.

"I do want to try and spend some time with him. I enjoy his presence, and we have a lot to catch up on," she says, eyes narrow. "Is that what you wanted to hear?"

"Only if it's the truth," she reminds. "But yes, I do appreciate your admission of your feelings."

"Is there anything else left on that list of yours to quiz me on?" Eleanor mutters in response, head leaning back on her headboard.

"Just one thing." The woman had long given up on lying to her. "How will Ellsie cope with being so close to Daemones? Interacting with them? We have discussed her loss in personal confidence before, but after recent events I feel the need to check back in with her in that regard."

Eleanor sits up, perfectly straight as she looks to the woman. It's the pads of her fingers that tap on her leg, not her nails.

"I'll survive," she assures, a waiver of uncertainty in her tone. "Hopefully facing them and overcoming them will allow me to overcome my own issues. But even if I have a problem, I will have Nikolas with me and..."

"And you trust him to keep your secret?"

"I trust him to look after me."

"Like you trust him with Nora?"

"I will never trust anyone with Nora, not fully. She is my heart and my true being..." Ellsie looks to where a painting of Nikolas watches her kindly. "But yes. The trust I hold in him is almost unparalleled."

"Almost? So how many else equal it?"

Such an innocent question that throws Ellsie off balance.

"Not quite to the same extent, but Mein Vater and Kenichi do come close. Sebastian as well."

Dr Nolan is unaware as she asks her next question.

"Did you come into contact with the Dunkler Bischof or Sebastian while you wer—"

"I am not here to talk to you about that," Eleanor interrupts. "Please – can we not?"

Vanessa bows her head in apology and lets the topic go.

Kenichi slides into the room just after she finishes, sitting lightly on the end of her bed. Suitably, Eleanor rolls her eyes, letting the timing settle as coincidence to avoid conflict. She starts before he does.

"Why did you come to America?" she asks, watching him closely.

"I came to America because I believed I could help more people here than anywhere else. I could get into the federal agencies since my parents spent a little time in America when I was young, so I have dual citizenship. Otherwise, I likely wouldn't have bothered trying to get myself accepted," he shrugs. "This country needed help, so I came to provide it."

After a few seconds pause – Kenichi clearly finished – Eleanor frowns.

"What did you come in to ask me?" Eleanor asks, voice odd.

"I just wanted to talk. We haven't been able to since you came back, and I've missed our weekly conversations," he admits, finally squeezing her hand back. "And to tell you you're very brave. I would never have the courage to continue on like you have."

"I can only do it because I have people to help me. You have no idea how much you've helped me over the years," Eleanor murmurs, moving close enough to rest her head on his shoulder. "I may be closer to Nikolas now but remember that I will never forget everything you've done for me."

"I won't."

He lets her rest there without interruption for quite a while.

Chapter 51

Adelyn is suitably confused as to why her mother was going away, but with promises to talk every day, she allows it. It is the best option, though. Eleanor needs to focus, and Adelyn needs to be safe.

Finally biting the bullet, Eleanor starts training with Nikolas, Ellsie often holding the reins as they spar. It quickly becomes apparent she has lost little of her skill, and after a few days she is back to her normal fighting self. Nikolas, however, ends up on the floor rather frequently, but Eleanor is more than happy to let him practise with her, quite enjoying throwing him to the ground (in a loving, passive-aggressive sort of way).

They leave after five days, driving to avoid being stopped at the airport. Both have new uniforms and hidden in the trunk are their weapons, guns and ammunition and both their sets of twin blades along with an assortment of other deadly devices.

When they finally park in the city – Eleanor having been a few times on missions, and Nikolas having never – they walk to the arranged meet up spot in Central Park.

~

The city that never sleeps reaches up above her on every side. So many people, so many eyes. So many witnesses.

One target. Two bodyguards. An injector of Nox grasped in her hand, tucked up into her sleeve.

The target is getting out of his car; she moves into the intercept path. Half-run, make it look like you're hurrying. Three, two... contact. The needle goes straight into his stomach as she runs into him. Her drink goes over his shirt, ice cold to disguise the little prick. Such a shame, it tasted great.

Apologise, apologise. So many apologies. But get out of there. Quick, quick. The timer runs in her head. 20 seconds until he collapses, she's away in ten. She is lost in the crowd by the time his bodyguards turn to find her again. Slipping through the alleys, lost to the thrum of the city.

A senator dead.

~

Eleanor stands quietly on the edge of the path in Central Park at the arranged meeting point. Her hair is pulled into a tight bun, one hand holding Captain's lead and the other brushing against the dagger hidden beneath her skirt. The pleats hide the weapon, and with her preferred longer skirt length, she could move without worrying about uncovering it. Due to the heat, she is wearing a singlet top, scars visible as she waits.

Nikolas watches from a hundred meters away, monitoring the situation carefully. He has already marked the security detail loitering in the park, focusing as a blonde walks up next to Eleanor.

"You're alone?" Skylar frowns as she stops next to Eleanor, eyes flicking around the park.

She doesn't see Nikolas.

"No, my friend is just being a lookout," Eleanor replies. "He'll come over once I give him the all clear."

"You have come to help? You're allowed to?"

For the first time, Eleanor's gaze flicks to her old friend.

"Yes. They even gave me a badge," Eleanor assures. "We need to get back to wherever you live, to ensure we are alone. Are you comfortable with that?"

"Of course," she answers, "do you want to ride with me, I have a car..."

Making her agreement clear, Eleanor begins to follow Skylar, Nikolas joining their side with their bags piled into a shopping cart. Skylar raises an eyebrow as he carefully places them all in the trunk of the new car, staying in the front seat as both Eleanor and Nikolas slide into the back.

No one speaks until they finally make it into the apartment. Nikolas hangs close, eyes watching Eleanor carefully as they walk into the slightly sunken, pristine living room. The entire apartment is about as modern as you can get, all shades of white and grey excepting the odd artwork or photo. Their host's clothes fit the theme, minimalistic and sharp.

Another woman now stands with Skylar, both quietly talking to each other. The woman has blonde hair, so light that it's almost white, that falls into a well-kept bob, bright blue eyes settling where Eleanor waits. She's slightly shorter than her partner, more cautious as well. It's her that sends the little boy – around nine – to his room. He's adopted, Eleanor remembers, his significantly tanner skin an obvious dissimilarity to either of his parents. Ryder is his name.

"Welcome to New York," the woman smiles, "you know Skylar – obviously – but I'm Emma, her wife."

Eleanor's lips pull into a kind smile, but the expression doesn't reach her eyes as the women step closer.

"I'm Eleanor, this is Nikolas and Captain. He's a service dog to assist me with some issues I have," Eleanor replies. "He won't be a bother, I assure you."

"That's fine," Skylar assures, beginning to walk closer. "Is there anything we need to be aware of or not do?"

"I can moderate things myself," Eleanor replies, "and Nikolas can as well."

Skylar's green eyes turn to the man, a smirk clear as she looks him up and down.

"I see you've kept him around... good choice," she grins, her wife clearly rolling her eyes.

"He does have some uses other than eye candy," Eleanor replies, Nikolas's head snapping to look at her in surprise.

Ellsie just sends him a smirk, turning her attention back on the two women.

"I am going to be blunt. They will know I'm here already, but I suspect that is why they even started bothering you," she says. "Your cases wouldn't warrant such threatening; they would just kill you. However, your father—" Eleanor looks only at Skylar "—must have made a convincing case for his use in recovering me through you that they didn't kill him the moment he stepped out of prison. Your mother likely was brought in after the idea was proposed, to weaken you and attempt to get close. The Berühmte Söldner utilise family dynamics to manipulate those in power, and often plant families in areas of interest, usually the parents are both agents, the female often a sleeper agent, and the children know nothing to ensure they do not release vital information and are known for their entire lives instead of being missing until the age of eight."

Skylar does a better job of hiding her surprise than her spouse, who is clearly alarmed.

"How do you know these things?" Emma asks, cautiously.

"When I first met her, Eleanor was detained by the National Agents of Protection, and I was one of the people who testified for her in front of the International Criminal Court. While not pardoned, she has been given time to live before her sentence is confirmed," Skylar explains, attempting to ensure her wife stays calm as Eleanor continues.

"As a young child my parents were murdered and I was taken by the Berühmte Söldner, I trained to be one of their top tier agents until I got pregnant with Adelyn," Eleanor says, voice void as she speaks. For a second Nikolas moves to take her hand but pulls back as he remembers her likely reaction. Captain however shifts to paw at her leg, Eleanor holding a palm at him quietly. "I was working on and off in the field for six years, between age ten and sixteen. Plus a few when I was younger, but they were fully supervised due to my slight instability."

A frown forms on Emma's face.

"Instability?" she asks carefully.

"As a child the line between fear and bloodlust was almost non-existent. Until I was sixteen, the strength was what I leant on. But I am now stable enough," Eleanor breathes, pinkie just brushing against Nikolas's. "However, when they discovered I was alive and managed to retrieve me, only a few months ago, they sought to restore the instability to set me out on the world. Unfortunately for them I have a reason to hold on, so instead they just royally messed up my head."

"That is why I am here," Nikolas explains. "She needs something to hold on to, and since bringing Adelyn here is the worst idea in the world, I will have to suffice. Not to mention I do have some uses, as Eleanor put it, other than being eye candy."

~

I never really got to see much of Nikolas in his prime. He spent so much time focusing on Eleanor and helping her find security in her situation that everyone kind of forgot that he was a power of his own. He was born a Prince of the Angeli, and time would show that no matter his father, he was just as powerful as any of them and Ellsie sure brought out the confidence in him.

~

Skylar chuckles lightly, gesturing for the pair to sit while her wife slowly recovers from the shock.

"Let's make a plan, shall we?"

Chapter 52

First rule in fighting the Berühmte Söldner: make sure you haven't already lost.

So, in one day, all of Skylar's security detail are locked in a room. Then each one is taken out of the room and checked over by Eleanor – for the tattoo, with a UV light – and unknown to anyone else, Nikolas runs a scan over their minds. Congratulations were given to Emma at the conclusion, for not a single one turned up corrupted. With the staff cleared, all attention turns to tracking Agency movements.

Eleanor keeps her head down as they walk the streets of New York, Captain loyally flagging her as she ensures to stay off the busiest sidewalks. Nikolas tracks her from across the street, marking the people around her as she follows those sent to watch Skylar. For the first few hours, Nikolas had kept a close eye on anything that might set her off – Zach's warning forefront in his mind – but this is easy for her, it always has been. With Ellsie in control, they have no problems with accidentally bumping anyone and being by herself on the sidewalk allows for her to work at her best. Just another woman in the bustling city of New York.

They both stay out late after Skylar finally returns to her house, under the protection of her own guard. And, of course, the agents lead them back to the same place each night. It was almost too easy to stay hidden in the city, or perhaps the care Nikolas was taking in tracing through their minds allowed them to know all the plans in motion. And ensure no one noticed they were being followed.

In such a populated place, they couldn't risk carrying any weapons openly, so only blades were tucked away on them —a gun drew too much attention and was a finite resource. That didn't stop a myriad of daggers bring tucked in waistbands or hidden holsters. Eleanor generally wore skirts and dresses to utilise the shapeless fabric, where Nikolas almost exclusively wore a trench coat to hide his. (Both Ellsie and Nora – still semi-present in their body – noticed how much more at home he seemed in the heavy black coats. Much more than when they first truly encountered him).

It was on their sixth night stalking the Agency that Eleanor had her first confrontation. But not in the way they had expected.

Nikolas, as always, is walking across the street from Eleanor when he notices her pause at an alley. Through the sounds of the city, he cannot hear why, and the lack of light meant he could not see what her eyes were so intensely focused upon.

'What is it, Incaendium?' he asks into her head.

'A girl needs help, I am going to give it to her,' Eleanor replies. *'I can handle it myself, and don't try to stop me.'*

'You know I don't want to, but you could get in trouble. From the actual authorities,' Nikolas warns. *'Be discrete, please... and try not to kill them.'*

'Remember what I told you, about that gala? With the girl who I saved and let me leave? I don't feel that guilt anymore, not like I used to. People like this don't deserve to live.'

'I know. Just try not to let them know who you are.'

Nikolas regrets the words as soon as they come out of his mouth, inwardly wincing as Eleanor replies.

'There is only one way that happens...'

The disconnect from her mind is obvious, the implication as she shuts him out. Two men are in the alley with a girl, and both snap their heads in Eleanor's direction as she steps closer. Captain is hidden around the corner, sitting on the street so the men couldn't see him. Eleanor tucks one of her daggers to the inside of her arm, hand turned to hide it. Both men relax fully upon seeing her, misjudging her with ease.

"Scram," one hisses, the closer one. "This isn't your business."

With half a glance to the girl cowering on the damp ground and the man hovering over her, Eleanor shakes her head.

"I don't think I will," she replies, keeping up the weakling act.

In the shadows, the two men glance between each other in surprise, but seem to reach an agreement as the one behind stands.

"It would be much more fun if we had one each," he muses roughly, preparing himself to walk towards her.

"I don't think tonight will be much fun for either of you," Eleanor says, "I'm afraid you may not even see the sun rise tomorrow, or is it today yet..."

As one finally steps into her range, Eleanor easily swipes his legs landing him on his ass, the second man falling for the same trap. With both picking themselves up, Eleanor has time to whistle, Captain running towards her in an instant. But she sends him to the still shaking girl.

"He'll keep you safe while I dispatch these two," Eleanor tells her kindly, before her jaw sets and she turns on the two men. "Don't watch."

The fight is short, Eleanor easily triumphing over the two men as her blade glints in the barest light. One is dead quicker than optimal, the last looking towards her in terror as she pins his throat to the wall. The dagger is pressing to his stomach as Nikolas appears at the end of the alley, frown clear as he looks over the situation.

He starts to walk forward as he catches the remaining man's attention.

"Stop this bitch!" he tries to call, "she just murdered my friend!"

But Nikolas just looks towards where Captain stays standing over the girl still on the floor.

"He isn't going to help you," Eleanor whispers, voice sickly sweet. "No one can..."

She is quick to step away as his body sags in place, letting it fall to the ground. He's dead before his head can hit the pavement, a dagger in his eye. Pouting, Eleanor turns to Nikolas, throwing her own dagger into the man's chest for good measure.

"You're a spoil sport," she mutters, leaning down to pluck the evidence from the corpse.

"And you couldn't have left some fun for me," he returns, a violent spark in his eyes. "I hate men like that as much as you do."

With a lingering glance at him, Eleanor steps slowly towards the girl, calling Captain away as she crouches gently in front of her. The girl flinches away for a second, wide eyes on the blood splattering Eleanor's clothes.

"I'm sorry you had to see that," she offers softly, tone turning rough a moment later, "but they deserve much worse. Do you need anything? Help getting to a hospital?"

Weakly, the girl replies, "I'm fine. I can get home okay..."

"Why don't you want to go to hospital? Your arm looks quite hurt." A glance towards Nikolas. "And other things," Eleanor smiles. "We have no problems helping you anywhere you need to go."

"The hospital takes too long, and I'm not beat up enough for their attention," the girl shrugs, keeping her eyes away, "and I wouldn't want to bother you."

"It is no bother," Nikolas says, "and we work for a defence Agency, we can get you in quickly."

Doubtfully, the girl nods, preparing herself to stand. Eleanor helps ease her to her feet and shields her from Nikolas for a few seconds until she shakily nods once more. In that time, Nikolas has managed to shove both bodies into half-full dumpsters, all without getting blood on himself as he walks back toward the two girls. On sub-conscious assessment of his Geminae, he shrugs off his trench coat and holds it out to her.

'You're covered in blood, Incaendium. Take it,' he enforces, propping up their charge while Eleanor reluctantly pulls it on.

The coat swamps her but does the job of hiding the blood on her clothes as she quickly rubs her face off with the inside of the collar. Hesitating to get her permission, Nikolas finishes wiping the blood off her face, turning up the collar to hide the rest on her neck. Eleanor knows the girl notices his slight hesitation but ignores the curious look as Captain bumps his nose against her leg.

"I know buddy," Eleanor whispers. "I'll get something on the way home."

Slowly, they start making their way to the nearest hospital, the girl supported on Eleanor's arm. It's Eleanor who hangs with her as Nikolas walks up to the front desk, badge ready in his hand. With him now gone, the girl braves asking Eleanor a question.

"Why are you doing this?" she asks, eye's flickering over her saviour's face.

"I've been in the situation. The only thing I couldn't give would have stopped it," Eleanor answers quietly. "It has messed me up pretty badly, but I can't let it happen to another person."

"Why did he?"

A fair question, Eleanor figures, as there has been little affection between them.

"We loved... we are very close, he understands more than anyone how much it affects me," Eleanor answers. "He holds a lot of unreleased anger towards those who did it to me, and he cannot release it on them. Trust me, those men are lucky it was me who got to them first."

Both fall silent as Nikolas walks back over with a nurse hot on his heels. The badge had done its job, it seems. Eleanor hands over the girl, Captain tucked calmly between her legs. He only gets half a glance from the nurse as Nikolas takes his place back at Eleanor's side.

"We will check in with her treatment tomorrow morning, we hope to hear good things," he says, beginning to turn away when the girl speaks up.

"Thank you," she says, smile soft. "You're good people."

Both incline their heads before walking away, leaving the girl in safe hands.

She gets a package the next morning, a new set of clothes with a note. Her hospital bill fully paid. I tracked her down many years later to get her account. She was forever grateful.

Chapter 53

When they walk into Skylar's apartment, all lights are out already. Having had dinner on the way home, they go directly to the room they are sharing – Skylar had assumed, and they hadn't bothered to correct her. Eleanor calls dibs on the shower, emerging 20 minutes later in one of Nikolas's shirts and a pair of three-quarter length tights. He is sitting on the pull-out couch-bed – they swapped nightly – eyes glancing over Eleanor as she lightly lowers herself onto the bed.

"Did they land any hits on you?" he asks softly, silver eyes looking up through his lashes at her.

"No," she answers, her eyes refusing to find his. "I'm fine."

Unlike their normal, comfortable silence, this one is frigid. Steely.

"I heard you talking to that girl..." Nikolas starts, hands locked together tightly. "You said loved. Past tense..."

Swallowing tightly, Eleanor looks away, "what are you asking, Nikolas?"

Nikolas swings to lay back on his couch, throat bared as he swallows. From her place on the bed, Eleanor can't help raking her eyes over the pulled skin, the lump in his throat. She has to force herself not to let her eyes trace down his arms.

With a snap, she focuses back on his head, blinking rapidly.

"Nikolas, I..." she starts, hands in her hair as she sighs. "I didn't know what I was saying. I didn't know what I... Ellsie wasn't sure what I wanted said. We don't know what we wanted to say. Or what you felt…"

He looks over in surprise but stays horizontal.

"What is it you feel?" he asks, taking a gamble as she stands abruptly.

Eleanor paces back and forth, eyes hanging on him for a few seconds each pass. Sitting up, Nikolas finally meets her eyes, gaze quickly shifting to her bit lip for a second before he returns to looking her in the eye.

"Nikolas, you know this is hard for me," she breathes, dropping on the seat next to him.

He tightly smiles, hand resisting the urge to brush her hair out of her face.

Eleanor cracks her jaw, looking away as she blurts, "I do love you. I never stopped loving you and will never stop loving you. For those four years everyone kept telling me I was allowed to move on or have flings. My therapist even suggested it as a release for Ellsie, but I refused. I couldn't do that. Each night I slept I had to have something that smelt like you. And those notes you left meant more than you could ever realise."

Lightly, Nikolas releases a choked breath, eyes glancing towards her for a few seconds. She is still biting her lip, blue eyes flicking between the floor and his clasped hands. The room too silent for either of them. The silence lets in the rush of thoughts rampant in their heads.

"I put a ward on those books…" Nikolas says, mind still turning over.

The urge to pull her into his arms and kiss her was getting dangerously close to overtaking him, the prince tearing his eyes away as a last-ditch attempt to control himself.

"I know. Lahash sensed it a while ago…" Eleanor admits.

"Did you enjoy them? I tried to get special copies and different languages."

Eleanor bolts to her feet, stalking across the room, pausing for a second before she turns back.

"Don't deflect, Nikolas. Please just, respond," she snaps, a hand in her hair. Ellsie had pulled into control, admiration reflecting in her eyes before she pulls back again.

His eyes hang on her for a moment, throat bobbing.

"I missed you every single day, each day I had to argue with myself not to leave and find you," Nikolas says. "And even now, every bone in my body aches to hold you close and kiss your worries away, but I cannot." He sits there with his head in his hands, language falling into Latin. She was glad she had spent the time to learn it. "I have this inexplicable need for you, for your love and attention and I cannot bear to see you in pain. I love you more than anything else. I was going completely crazy when they had you, when we found you, I wanted nothing more than to hunt them all down and do horrible things to them, but I had to resist because you needed me more. I will always give you what you need, and if that is space then that is what you will have. But know, if I move away, or I am quiet... if I act like I don't want to be around you it isn't because I do not love you, it is because I do, more than you could ever know. And sometimes that is a little hard for me to bear with you so close, so I detach myself. But I love you, My Sweet Wildfire. I do."

Tears stud Eleanor's eyes, her face slack as every ounce of her focus is put into turning over each and every word he says. It takes a few seconds for her to fully comprehend his words, head tilted slightly in thought. Slowly she walks closer, thin hand reaching out to brush the hair falling over his face, staying in place as his silver eyes meet her blue.

"Thank you," she breathes, unsure of any other way to acknowledge the admission. "I'm sorry it has to be this way; I wish it didn't. With all my heart I wish it didn't but know that I love you. I love you so much."

Carefully, Nikolas eases to his feet, smile faint as Eleanor allows herself to lean into his warmth. Her arms wrap around his middle, eyes shut in bliss as his wrap lightly around her shoulders. Being so careful not to hold her too tight, Nikolas lets himself find the back of her head, fingers entwining in her hair. Even that makes Eleanor tense slightly, but she forces her hackles down, breathing deep. For a few seconds they just stand there, before Eleanor tilts her head back, exposing her throat as she looks up at him. The only vulnerability she can stand.

Nikolas looks down, meeting her eyes. The longing is obvious, the love. Daringly, he lets his fingers trace over her throat, and the scar that sits there. Even now his hands are soft, bare of callouses. So unlike hers.

The touch makes her shiver, but she stays perfectly still. Holding his stare, Eleanor starts running her fingers over his back, tracing the ridged whiplash scars. To her surprise, he shivers slightly, eyes narrowing as he stays perfectly still.

"For the sake of me getting any sleep tonight I ask you not do that," he warns hoarsely.

Eleanor steps back, head returning to its natural position as Nikolas lets her out of his arms. Apology quiet, Eleanor starts to drift towards the bed, sliding into her side with ease. Adjusting the long pillow running down the middle of the bed, she looks back at Nikolas. He is still watching her, weak smile on his lips.

"If you keep on the other side, you can sleep in here," she says. "You're too tall for the couch."

"I don't have to. I can survive," he replies. "And I'll only do it if you aren't sleeping on the couch."

So cautious, so chivalrous.

"Nikolas," Eleanor warns, Ellsie breaking through. "Get in the bed."

"Shower first," he interjects, smile only a tad teasing.

Only a few minutes later, the prince fulfills her command. The Geminae fall into sleep only moments later.

Chapter 54

Eleanor wakes early in the morning, slipping out into the penthouse living room. Methodically, she moves through each of her blades, cleaning and sharpening them all. Each one is back in their sheath and put away by the time Skylar wakes and joins her.

There is a deadly twitch in Eleanor's manner, like a live wire without anyone to cut the power. But Ellsie knows how to deal, moving into stretches on the cold tile floor. Even still, the assassin tracks every movement in the room, keenly aware of the blade held to her wrist by a leather holster.

"You guys came back late last night," Skylar says, breaking the silence in the room.

"Had to make a detour," Eleanor says quietly. "Sorry if we woke you."

"Not at all, I just saw the notification then," Skylar assures, green eyes tracking her old friend. "Are you confident you know where they are?"

"Yes," Eleanor smiles. "We will talk strategy once everyone is awake."

"And what of my brother…"

Eleanor can't help but chuckle at the concern on Skylar's face, memories of the time she had spent with them before everything had happened at the forefront of her mind.

"He'll be there. On hand in case they need to give you motivation," Eleanor replies, eyes flicking to the entrance of the corridor for a second as Captain runs out. "Once we get inside and disable the base we will recover him."

Carefully, Eleanor leans down to give her dog a pat, short nails running down his smooth head. Within a few moments, he bops his nose against her thigh, tail wagging. Rolling her eyes, Eleanor walks to the kitchen, grabbing a plain piece of bread and shoving it in her mouth – all while glaring at the mutt.

"Thank you for doing all this, I know you would prefer to be with Adelyn while you can," Skylar murmurs, gaze soft. "Are you scared?"

Eleanor bites her lip, even Ellsie glancing back towards her room.

"A little," she answers. "I've spent my entire life trying to keep myself alive… it feels wrong to go to death so… powerlessly. But at least I'll have Nikolas at my side, to hold my hand. I'm tough, and it's necessary."

Shrugging roughly, Eleanor turns away. Her face pulls to greet Emma a moment later, stepping out of the kitchen. She flips her hair back out of her face, fingers running through as Captain shoves his head into her hands. She's still patting him as Nikolas enters, eyes running over her for a moment before he turns to greet their hosts.

"Neither of you are working today, are you?" he asks, gliding past Eleanor just close enough for his fingers to brush over her shoulder.

"We aren't," Emma smiles, "but Ryder has a friend coming over for the day, he'll be here soon."

He nods, Eleanor barely glancing up as he sits next to her.

"Once they are settled, we can talk," Nikolas says, silently offering a hand to Eleanor under the table. "Eleanor and I need to have a chat first."

Now Eleanor turns to look at him in surprise, meeting only a warning glance before he turns to talk to their hosts. Eleanor barely follows the conversation, slowly – tentatively – sliding her fingers into Nikolas's waiting hand. A gentle hold that does more to ground her than she realises. Eventually, their hosts slip away, likely to wake their son, allowing for the pair to move to the couches.

"You woke up very early this morning," Nikolas starts, speaking in easy Latin. "You're very on edge."

Minutely, he presses a penny into her spare hand, closing her fist loosely.

"Last night was a wild one, the fight didn't last near long enough to satisfy me. And heartfelt conversations always set me on edge," Eleanor shrugs, looking away quickly. "You only see the wild me, Meine Geliebte. Me unleashed. You are not used to me when I am tame. Me in the time between fights is different. My blood sings for violence, Nora understands that. That's why she allowed for me to go to the ring fights, because without the violence I cannot control myself. And she's in hiding, too emotionally tired to be in control. It will be okay; I will be fine."

"Is there anything I can do to make this easier?" he asks softly, extending a hand to her again.

"Just stay close, you calm me..." Eleanor takes a deep breath. "...and lets just get this over with. That base is only going to be more annoying the longer we leave it."

"I know, Incaendium. We will get you back to Adelyn as soon as possible," he assures, touch soft as he runs a thumb over her knuckles. "Promise."

Mouthing a soft thank you, Eleanor looks back to where the family are re-entering the main room. Ryder had not taken a liking to the guests in his home, even though Eleanor had tried her hardest to help the child warm to her. However, her efforts were not completely in vain as he sits on the couch opposite them, squeaky voice offering morning salutations. In her best display of sanity, Eleanor responds as she would to Adelyn, the mask falling on easily.

Only a few minutes later, Emma gets a message, disappearing from the penthouse apartment though the elevator.

"Is there anything I should know about Ryder's friend?" Eleanor asks softly, placing herself near the back of the room.

"Not really. He's just Ryder's friend," Skylar shrugs, barely looking up from where she's cutting fruit. "A little quiet, his parents fight a lot. We take care of him some days."

Her tone is sharp in warning and Eleanor ducks her head in submission.

"Apologies," she says. "It's part of my nature to question everything. Even children."

"That must be tiring," Skylar replies kindly, as if remembering why Eleanor was there.

"It gets that way sometimes, yes. But it has kept me alive."

They both fall silent as Emma walks back in with a small boy at her heels. Completely unassuming in nature and looks, the boy smiles at both Emma and Skylar before walking to where Ryder is grinning at him. He only allows himself a quick glance at both Eleanor and Nikolas, before returning to his friend. While a frown forms on Eleanor's face, she lets it be as the two children run out of the room.

They wait an hour and a bit until they all sit at the glass topped dining table. Paranoid as ever, Eleanor clearly places a device on the table, staying silent until a little red light starts blinking.

"That blocks any communications from leaving this floor," she explains briefly. "Everything said now is kept quiet until after we are finished. We only need to talk with you two for about 20 minutes, then we'll sort out all the little details ourselves."

"Do you have enough to go on?" Skylar asks immediately. "Are you sure my brother is there?"

"Yes, and yes. We know which building it is, got the schematics off Emma's city hall contact," Nikolas answers. "Hidden behind the others you pulled out, so they won't think to move. And they would have kept Arthur close for ease of access."

"They loath to admit the two of us could take down an entire base. They think we'll wait for back up like good little NAP agents," Eleanor adds, eyes rolling. "There will be a warning sent to all public security and government agencies on first contact, sent by our Colonel. At that time, you both – and Ryder – will be in this apartment and your security detail will be in the room with you. Anyone who isn't cleared will not be allowed into the apartment."

The two women look between each other quickly.

"Are you worried about an attack back on us?" Emma asks cautiously.

"While we aren't here, not particularly, but it is possible," Nikolas says, failing at keeping his eyes from straying to Eleanor's throat.

Skylar does the same, swallow evident.

"They came for you at school as backlash because of the ships, didn't they?" she realises, face paling.

"They did. And I was sloppy because I had jumped off a cargo ship and got dragged back to shore on a grappling hook the night before," Eleanor says, ignoring the quick reprimanding glare Nikolas sends her. "This time it will be easier; we can orchestrate it all."

"In the unlikely case either of us falls unconscious, an alert will be sent to the local police and NAP agents to move in from their perimeter," Nikolas adds. "But that is highly unlikely. It is only in triggering the counterattack that we need your participation."

Now both women frown, hands clearly linking under the table.

"How do you plan on doing that?" Emma asks cautiously. "This is one of the most populated cities in America."

And so, they start to explain their plan. Talking quickly and precisely, the women interjecting as soon as they lose track of the conversation.

Eleanor is acutely aware of the two children entering the room, silencing everyone with a look. Once they have left, with a glass of water each, she starts to speak again. Explaining everything, ensuring everybody was caught up on the plan. But Nikolas notices her distracted nature, the half an eye she keeps on the corridor. Her distinct silence whenever she catches a flash of a child.

As promised, the conversation only lasts for about 20 minutes. And as they all move away from the table, Eleanor places herself in clear view of the corridor, eyes waiting for any movement as she quickly starts to search through her phone.

'What are you thinking, Incaendium?' Nikolas asks, keeping his face still as he sits at the other end of the couch.

'There's something off about that child,' she replies softly. *'He is too cautious of us, much more than he should be, and I got the distinct feeling he was listening to what we were saying. For two children they were surprisingly quiet.'*

'He could just be cautious of new people. Some abused children can be like that,' Nikolas says, careful to keep his tone neutral. *'What are you doing now?'*

'Researching. Hoping I get lucky and there is a record of missing children I can access from here that match his description four or five years ago,' Eleanor says, jaw setting in annoyance. *'There is not. But I have other tests.'*

With a light roll of his eyes, Nikolas glances behind him as the two children are called into the living area for lunch. But ever cautious, Eleanor watches the new boy, analysing his movements as he slips into the seat next to his friend.

In Latin, Eleanor speaks to Nikolas, "we are going to discuss our plans for entering the compound in German. But keep your mind keyed into mine just enough so I can talk to you that way."

He nods, turning back to face her. Eleanor does so as well, keeping the boy in her periphery.

"There's three entrance options, correct?" Nikolas starts, German still accented compared to hers.

"Yes. From the street, alley and roof. Of course we could go in a window but that complicates things," Eleanor answers. "I say we don't enter from the alley, but from the street behind. Ensure we are as quiet as possible in entering. There will be lookouts, but at 8pm they should be bleary and bored. We enter as discretely as possible, so no cape. And until we get inside, we'll have to hide our twin blades."

The chatter in the kitchen is quiet, trying to be polite as they talk to each other. Emma and Skylar are frowning – the only faces visible from Eleanor's position – clearly not understanding what they are saying. Ryder had turned to look at them to start with, but had gone back to his food shortly after, but it wasn't any of them that she was worried about. Only the little boy who hadn't turned around in confusion, and who had tilted his head just to the side in an attempt to hear better.

"Coats? Mine can be hidden under a trench, but you'll either have to hide yours in a bag or give them to me until we get inside," Nikolas suggests, "and you'll need to hide your jacket."

"A duffel will work, and I can get two guns inside that way. The Daemones won't see us coming," Eleanor grins, eyes acutely on the boy as he tenses slightly. "I mean, they train the ACE's to be the best at infiltration, but they often don't think about making sure they don't end up training their downfall."

'Talk to Skylar, tell her to get Ryder a few meters away from that kid,' Eleanor instructs, eyes locked firmly on Nikolas's. *'Trust me, he's listening to our every word, understanding it. There's a very strong chance he has been placed close to Ryder to get an in with this household.'*

'I will. But you cannot attack him. He is only a child, Ellsie,' Nikolas warns, holding steady under her gaze.

'I'm aware. But agents at this age are flighty, and I can likely talk him down. Get her to lock down the floor as well,' Eleanor returns. 'He isn't returning to his carer.'

Eleanor begins to speak in German again, eyes watching the group in the kitchen carefully. Skylar covers her surprise well, shifting to lock down the floor with a discrete press of the button under her kitchen counter. Nothing noticeable happens, only the light blue light on the elevator going dark. Ryder is instructed to get something out of the fridge, Eleanor taking her opportunity as soon as the child is behind his mother. Emma frowns only slightly, drifting to her wife's side.

"You would think the Berühmte Söldner would be smarter than sending an underage agent to gather intel around an ACE," Eleanor muses, still speaking German. The boy freezes in his place. "Especially one who is possibly the most paranoid agent on this planet."

Nikolas tracks her with his eyes as she stands and walks into the boy's view.

"Can you three please get behind me?" Eleanor asks in English, eyes flicking to the family for only a second. "There is nothing to be scared of, I just need to keep him isolated."

The child does a good job of looking to Emma for support, measuring her to be the weaker one between the two. Eyes pleading for help. But all three do as she asks, Nikolas sliding in next to Eleanor, Captain trots over as well. Eleanor places him in front of the family. Her eyes now meeting the boy's.

"You are aware any devices you could be wearing are disabled?" Eleanor says, voice blunt as she looks him up and down. "They cannot hear you. They do not know what is happening. They have no control over you now."

"They always know. Traitor," the boy hisses, seemingly surprised as Eleanor crosses her arms.

"Do they not teach you respect anymore?" she returns. "You do not talk back to an ACE. You do not even meet their eyes."

"You are no ACE. ACEs do not give mercy. ACEs are not weak." But the boy is unsure.

Nikolas straightens slightly, eyes narrowing.

"If she was merciful," he starts, speaking in German. "She would have killed you already. Do not mistake this kindness as weakness. It takes power to stand up against those who seek to tear you down."

Eleanor keeps to the language, conscious of the family behind her.

"And if I were weak, do you think they would bother sending in a mole to try and glean information? If I were weak, they would not be afraid of my plans," she says, voice too sweet. But she continues softer, in English. "I can get you out of there. I have managed years without them finding me, and they care not for a child. Only for those who wish to destroy them. We can find you a place like this one, with a loving family that can take care of you. You wouldn't have to do their bidding. You would not have to kill."

Eleanor steps forward slowly, movements smooth and hands still with perfect grace as she offers a hand to him.

"Do you want that?"

In a flash the boy has grabbed the knife he was eating with and is holding in out in front of him. But his hand shakes, wide eyes fearful. The muscles in Nikolas's hand pull taut as Eleanor steps closer, physically holding himself back as Eleanor reaches once more for the boy's hand.

"You will never have to do anything you don't want to. You can eat as much as you'd like, and find out all your favourite things," she says, a real smile forming on her lips. Ever so slightly her head tilts. "You can have a pet, and as many toys as you'd like. Did you used to have a pet? Maybe we can find any family you might have... a cousin, or your grandparents? You can go to school, make as many friends as you'd like. Most people out here are kind. They won't hurt you."

Slowly Eleanor reaches around the boy's hand, holding it still as she carefully takes the blade out of his hand.

"Do you remember what cake tastes like? Ice cream? Have you ever been to the beach, smelt the salty sea air?" she says, stepping slowly closer as she slides the knife out of reach. "The stars in the country are so pretty, like a million little fairy lights in the sky. You can't really see them in the city, though. And they have this thing they call a disco, where everyone is dancing to the same music without a care in the world. There are so many movies to watch, not like the ones we see, I promise. Ones where everything turns out perfect in the end, and ones where they find a new family if they lose theirs. There's so many I can't even name them all."

"Can I have pizza?" the little boy asks, hand trembling in Eleanor's.

"Of course you can, and they have this thing called fizzy drink. Personally, I don't like it – it makes your tongue all bubbly – but a lot of people absolutely love it." Eleanor smiles. "I wish I could show it all to you, but I'm not going to be around forever, so someone else will look after you. But I promise with all my heart they will be good people who understand what has happened to you and they will show you the world. This country can hide you, so they never find you again and you never need to worry about the Berühmte Söldner ever again. But I know it can be hard to forget it all, I know I'll take the memories with me until I die, but after a while you learn to grow around it and eventually you barely notice it's there anymore."

The boy nods quickly, Eleanor stepping forward to offer a hug. Carefully she holds him close as his face buries into her shoulder, hand running over his head in repetitive movements. He's crying, the group behind her realises as she turns towards them, eyes focused mainly on Nikolas. There is a heartbreak in her eyes, unresolved pain he had barely glanced before.

In four years of therapy, she never even touched on the normalcy she had lost. She made sure Adelyn had everything she ever asked for, and no one had ever asked why that was.

Eleanor's eyes shift to Skylar, whose son was still tucked behind her legs.

"Can you call Child Protective Services, please?" she asks. "Make sure they send someone you will know." Turning to Nikolas a few moments later. "Can you try and get a NAP agent to accompany them?"

Skylar nods quickly, pulling out her phone and stepping away to make the call. Now moving to his other mum, Ryder watches Eleanor and his friend carefully, confusion clear in his gaze. Eleanor lets Emma take care of him as she quietly moves to the couch, sitting the boy in front of her as she stays in a crouch.

"You are very brave," she tells him, holding his hands between them, "and it may get scarier still, but in the end, you'll find somewhere you belong. If I can do it, you can too. You just have to learn to trust people worthy of your attention and ignore those who are not. Don't be afraid of speaking up if you're worried or scared, everybody is here to help you. And you need to tell people the truth, your truth, not anyone else's, that's the only way they will learn to trust you too."

The boy's teary face nods, barely meeting her eyes as she speaks.

"What is your name?" Eleanor asks softly, "not your code, not your name for this mission, the name your parents gave you. Do you remember?"

After a moment's thought, he shakes his head.

"Okay then," Eleanor accepts, running her hands over his head. "That's okay. We can find it out - the internet is amazing."

Weakly, the boy smiles at her, the relief in his shoulders palpable.

Chapter 55

The elevator dings, a loud echo drawing the attention of the room. Almost subconsciously, Eleanor tucks the boy behind her back, keeping him out of line of sight as the steel doors slide open. A woman steps out, tall but stocky. Dark skin; straight, black hair. Mulberry lipstick.

"Lana?" Eleanor blurts, eyebrows furrowed. She hadn't seen or heard from her closest high school friend since she had left for America.

"Eleanor?" the woman replies, stopped dead just out of the elevator.

Nikolas – in his sweeping assessment of the friends – notices Skylar grinning from the other side of the room, trying her hardest not to laugh. Lightly, he steps up to Eleanor's side and brushes his fingers against hers, just enough of a touch to draw his Geminae back to reality.

"It's been a while," Eleanor says with a strict smile. "What odd luck we're all here at the same time."

"I must admit, I have done a bit of work with Emma before, our jobs often end up mixing," Lana replies, finally stepping forward. "Though it is quite surprising to see you, last I heard you were going to call me."

"I couldn't risk someone tracing your calls. I was in hiding until the end of last year," Eleanor says. "I'm sorry, but Skylar only had my phone number in case this happened. You wouldn't have needed my particular help."

"Is Adelyn here? Is she still with you?" Lana prods, brown eyes scanning the room again.

"She is my daughter, yes she's still with me," Eleanor answers shortly, "but she's back in Washington DC. I can't bring her on assignment."

Lana nods slowly, stepping fully into the living room as Skylar finally approaches. Carefully, Eleanor steps aside, the little boy standing perfectly straight at her side.

"Emma called me because I work at Child Protective Services. She said there was a boy, who had been kidnapped..." Lana says, directing her words to Skylar. "Is this him?"

"Yes. By the same people who took Eleanor as a child, and attacked the school," she answers, allowing Eleanor to take over.

"He's nine or ten, doesn't remember his name. Has been gathering intel off their son for a few months I'd say. There will be someone assigned as his handler that will probably attempt to recover him, but you cannot let him go back to them." Eleanor pauses looking down at the child. "He needs protection, a new life with people who can help him learn to live normally. Children taken by the Berühmte Söldner have a lot of... issues, mentally. He needs a stable home that can adjust to any outbursts or meltdowns, keeping in mind they may be violent."

Lana nods, careful as she approaches the boy. It's obvious her manner is practiced; lowered shoulders and open arms offering no threat. It was the same way that Kenichi had approached Eleanor in the beginning, as if they were walking towards a wounded tiger. He stays in the perfectly straight and still posture taught to all in the Agency – but his face fails to hide his nervousness, the quick blinking of his eyes, the twitching of his jaw.

He doesn't run as Lana starts to talk to him, introducing herself in the same calm and kind manner she had greeted Eleanor so long ago. There is no attention on Eleanor as her hand shakily raises to her throat, even Nikolas doesn't notice the anxious movement until Captain slips to his owner's side, pawing her leg lightly.

"I know Buddy," Eleanor murmurs, hand held out to his nose.

Nikolas steps a little closer to her, hand extending just the slightest. Eleanor doesn't take it, mouthing a weak assurance as her attention turns back to Lana and the boy.

"Is it okay for me to take him to my office? We can set him up there and keep him safe until we can find out more," she asks, legs still bent in a crouch. "Since he's been surrendered, we have to do research before we can return him to anyone, and if he doesn't want to go, he doesn't have to."

Eleanor nods in acceptance, stepping towards the child in silence. As she kneels quietly at his side, he folds into her opened arms, pulling back only as she releases him. But she holds him within arm's reach for a few seconds, smile soft.

"Tell them the truth," she says, voice oddly void. "They can only help you if you tell the truth. It may be scary, but the only way you can move forward is by being honest."

He nods quickly, hanging on every word she says.

"What about the bad things I have done?" he asks, eyes flicking to Lana quickly.

"You can only get the help you need by telling them," Eleanor says, refusing to glance to Nikolas for support. "Trust me, I've been through it all before. It does get better."

The promise hanging in her eyes seems to be enough for the boy to step away, small hand fitting into Lana's. She guides him backwards, stopping a few metres away.

"My phone number is still the same, call sometime," Lana smiles at Eleanor. "It would be good to catch up."

"I will," Eleanor replies. "Make sure he gets to a good home, please..."

Lana promises, slowly guiding the boy to the elevator. Once again – with the focus on Lana – no one notices Eleanor's hand raising to her throat, the other curled in Captain's fur to keep it from trembling. Air puffs in and out of her mouth at a rate of knots, the flick of panic in her eyes clear only to Nikolas, who turns to look at her in worry.

Eleanor is speedily walking – refusing to let herself run – out of the room, Captain on her heels as she pushes into her bedroom. Nikolas is quick to follow, long legs catching up enough to get inside before she tries to lock the door. However, Eleanor hadn't even bothered, the water system kicking on as soon as he steps foot in their room. Carefully checking for any discarded clothes – of which there are none – Nikolas walks toward the bathroom. Captain is whining, pawing at the closed shower screen door as he walks in.

Eleanor is sitting on the floor of the shower fully clothed, steaming water falling mostly over her legs and arms, leaving angry marks on her skin. Her head is held in one of her hands, dry hair slowly dampening in the spray. Obscured, her other hand is wrapped tight around her throat, only the haphazard rise and fall of her back showing any movement.

Nikolas edges Captain out of the way of the water, trying his hardest to assure the dog as he slides the door open. The hand he reaches out with retracts quickly, a hiss breaking through his lips. His fist punches the water off quickly, eyes staying locked on Eleanor. The action gets a reaction out of her, the assassin's head weaving in phantom pain.

"Leave it on," she croaks. "It keeps it quiet."

Reluctantly, Nikolas opens the lever again, but he adjusts it to a cooler setting immediately. Face grim, he realises he can't move to help her in the small shower cubicle without the risk of triggering her. Instead, he drops into a crouch, a hand on the door frame to balance himself.

"Eleanor, what is it?" he asks, eyes refusing to leave her.

Not a sound escapes her, not until Captain jumps into the water and places himself in her lap. The service dog does his job, getting her hands onto him and keeping pressure on her body.

"I was already on edge," Eleanor whispers, voice still choked. "The boy and Lana were just one thing too many."

Nikolas nods slowly, aching to step in and hold her. But – with white knuckles gripping the door – he stays where he is.

"Seeing Lana reminds me of school, the last time I worked. Nearly dying..." she explains, head weaving slightly in distress. "That makes my throat hurt. Ellsie is too edgy right now to do any good until tomorrow."

"Is the plan too stressful? Because we can adjust..." Nikolas offers, lips waiting slightly pursed.

Distinct from the weaving of her head, Eleanor shakes it in dismissal.

"The plan is fine. I just need to get control over myself," she says. "Talking to you helps."

For a second, Nikolas pauses, before he smiles.

"Course it does, no one could resist this charisma," he teases.

In surprise, Eleanor looks up at him, a weak, annoyed smile pulling onto her face. Nikolas just grins, shifting to sit properly on the floor.

"You're not funny," she says, but the slight smile remains.

"I'm hilarious."

It's the dead serious look on his face that makes Eleanor chuckle lightly.

They don't spend much more time sitting on the floor, Nikolas monitoring her emotions until he deems it safe to turn off the water. By that point, Eleanor is soaked through, taking the advice to change. When she emerges from the bathroom in fresh clothes Nikolas is lain out on the bed, one arm under his head and the other holding an open book.

He barely glances up as she appears, continuing to read as she tentatively walks over – Captain laying out on his own mat, clearly aware they didn't want to touch him while he was still wet. Though it surprises him that she doesn't pick up a sketchbook or novel, Nikolas doesn't let it show as she climbs onto the bed and slowly shifts closer to his side. Eleanor places her head on his chest, keeping both her arms wrapped tight around herself as she leans into his warmth – acutely aware of how perfectly still Nikolas has gone. He forces himself to keep his arm tucked beneath his head, to keep her escape option open.

The slight – accidental – brush against her mind gives him all the motivation he needs, the churning, nervous energy surprising him as Eleanor makes herself exhale and relax. In a failing attempt to act casual, Nikolas starts to read again. After a few minutes, he goes to turn the page, eyebrow raising in surprise as Eleanor reaches out to stop him. A few seconds later she flicks the page over, hand returning to her chest.

"Do you need me to catch you up?" Nikolas asks softly, glancing down for a second.

"No. I've read it before," Eleanor replies. Blunt.

Very cautiously, Nikolas asks, "do you want me to read to you so you can rest your eyes?"

For a few seconds, Eleanor is silent, before she faintly nods.

"That would be nice."

He starts without further encouragement, using the exercise to keep monitoring his Geminae, curled at his side. A deliberate brush against her mind while he is reading surprises him also, as Ellsie is much more present than he would have thought, her own mind soothed by the proximity. Meanwhile Nora is just listening, blocking away any thoughts of their position.

Nikolas forces himself out of her mind.

Chapter 56

*S*kylar asks no questions as the pair emerge only for dinner, keeping her confusion as far from her eyes as possible. Although she had glimpsed small shifts in Eleanor's behaviours, she had never suspected anything of the magnitude the breakdown earlier that day had suggested.

Many years from this point Skylar seeks me out; to resolve some unasked questions she would never be able to ask her friend, still torturing her mind. I answered what I could: what happened in the five years between their interaction, whether asking Eleanor for help was a good idea. But I could not answer one question.

Was Eleanor insane? Mad? So mentally unstable it wasn't safe for her to be operating like she was? They all meant the same thing.

Many people worried that with more time, Eleanor may become so. I have always hated thinking of her as unstable, I always worried that I may have stopped her from getting the help she needed.

But at this point in time, I believe she was not insane, just scared, scarred, and broken. The Daemones had messed something up inside her head, made her fear their power. Their power over her. But she realised late that night – as she lay in strained consciousness – the only way to conquer her fear was to face it.

And to face it, blood would have to be shed. Lots and lots of blood.

The Berühmte Söldner did not care to retrieve their lost agent, that was true, but they wouldn't let the blatant challenge to their power go unanswered.

The bomb they set off didn't do much damage – for them at least – only taking out five of the bridges between Manhattan Island and the rest of the city at a time where there weren't too many causalities. But it is a message. A warning to the District Attorney and her assistants.

Get off their backs. Stop working with their rogue agent. Stop messing in their business.

Emma is informed by the NYPD first, of course, receiving a phone call just after dawn. Eleanor finds out next, receiving a message from Kaylee – still down in Washington – asking if she was involved. From there, everyone wakes.

There is a brief meeting with their hosts, setting a quick plan before Eleanor and Nikolas return to their room. While not what they had hoped for, they weren't in the worst position. They still held an advantage; they still could work with their plan. But the base would be in full flurry, everyone would be awake and a lot of the Daemones would be out, surveying all the powers of the city.

That would seem like an advantage, but Eleanor and Nikolas knew better. It would be an easier infiltration, yes, but once they were in there and the alarm was raised, all the agents would flood back in and trap them. That is unless they can fight their way out. Nikolas is confident, having further developed his fighting techniques in the last five years and trusting Ellsie to keep Eleanor safe.

However, it was clear to Nora that her normally more courageous half, was worried. Ever since the original plan had been set, Ellsie had been quiet – reserved. The reliance was gone. To work properly, as they both had acknowledged many times Ellsie needed complete control, but of course, complete control was only ever given if Nora believed Ellsie was stable. Currently, such was not the case. Dr Nolan had touched on it a few times, but they both did a good job of hiding the residual fear that echoed like a phantom pain whenever they saw, or talked, or even thought of anything related to what happened to Ellsie. The scar on her throat was merely a physical reminder, there every day to taunt her for what had happened and highlight what she might have lost, and did lose. But the fear that held in her chest was not of marred skin.

It was of the Daemones. The Berühmte Söldner. Those who sought to hurt her.

And it had just worsened ever since she had been retaken by them.

For once, Nikolas hadn't noticed her reluctance, mistaking it for her aversion to touch. It finally dawned on him as she walked back to their room after speaking with Skylar. He noticed the ticks for what they were.

Her fingers played not because she was nervous – although they often did – but because her mind was churning, mapping all her movements to the second. Reassuring herself that she would win. And it was not the nail tapping that Nora would do, but the light pads of Ellsie's thin fingers. Ever perfect. Ever discrete.

Her back stays straight as a plank, shoulders back. Pushing herself into the open to spite herself. Lips pursed, face neutral otherwise. The slight crease between her eyebrows only just noticeable.

It was the picking up of a dagger that makes him finally intervene.

"Incaendium, you can talk to me, you know..." he says, peering at her as she snatches the knife by the handle and throws it back into the air. "I'm not blind; you are nervous."

"I'm fine, Nikolas," she returns, throwing her blade higher in the air.

With almost unnatural reflexes, he steps in and snatches it mid-air.

"We are about to break into the lion's den, Eleanor. I need to know you are going to be focused," he reinforces, staring her down as she cracks her jaw.

"I have been out of the field for almost five years, I just need to prepare myself," Eleanor returns, her words biting at his insistence like a chihuahua, savage but ineffectual.

Nikolas lets her stalk away, embedding the knife into the door frame as she attempts to leave.

"Do not walk away," he hisses, the Latin falling out through his annoyance. "You need to sort yourself out and going out there will not do that."

"Because you're the expert on me, right?" she growls, ripping the knife from the wall and striding back over.

Instantly, Nikolas backs off.

Using that tone with an assassin wasn't his smartest choice.

"No, I'm not," he says softly, "but I have been in your position. And I know that being around people you don't fully trust can put you on edge."

"I trust them. Why do you think I'm here?" she mutters.

"You trust them, maybe, but you are not nearly close enough to them to allow yourself to embrace what you are feeling," Nikolas offers.

His eyes watch her like a hawk, tracking her movements as she finally drops onto the bed – leaving her legs hanging off the edge as she lies back.

"You sound like our therapist," she says, still playing with the knife in her hands.

"Is that a problem?"

Eleanor pauses, tossing the knife lazily onto the floor as she grumbles at the ceiling.

"No... Dr Nolan generally has pretty good ideas."

Slowly, Nikolas moves so he is lain next to her – staring at the ceiling.

"What would she want you to do now?" he asks.

For a second, Eleanor goes completely silent in voice and body, the type of deathly silence that haunts the dead or lost. And she certainly wasn't the former.

"You get nightmares, about the fight at the high school, don't you?" she replies, head turning to look at him.

"Among my most frequent, yes."

"I don't..."

Nikolas frowns, glancing back at her. Their eyes meet in the middle, a scape of winter loss.

"I have waking nightmares during the day; like wraiths taunting me."

"Wraiths aren't amongst the supernatural beings actually on Earth..."

Eleanor drops her head to the side, fixing Nikolas with a stern expression that he only meets with a half-smile.

"I'll get glances, out of nowhere. Just for a second," Eleanor continues, lips almost muted. "Daemones. Agents. People I've killed. Chasing me but not. Adelyn never notices, and when Captain does, I brush it off. But it shakes me. Enough to not even tell Dr Nolan. I do not need to add schizophrenia or hallucinations to my list of mental conditions."

An annoyed huff leaves Nikolas, Eleanor rolling her eyes weakly as he lifts a hand to hold her chin – the touch barely a finger under her jaw.

"You need to talk to people when things like that keep happening," he sighs.

"I like to talk to you when things like that happen…" she says, "but you weren't there."

His face softens, thumb stroking against her bottom lip so light it's barely a touch.

"I'm sorry, Dulce Meum…" he whispers.

"I know." Eleanor chuckles weakly. Recalling a conversation she had with Lahash before he had left to reunite with Lerajie, Eleanor continues, "Lahash had an explanation for it, thought it might be an echo of the angelic blood you used to save me. It might have been punishing me. They couldn't be sure though. But it doesn't change the fact they all scare me… and it wasn't just the Daemones. If it was them, I might understand it better, but it was my sister I saw when they took me. It was Kate, just as I last saw her; young and beautiful with two bullets in her head."

She releases a shaky breath, looking away and pulling out of his grasp.

"I had never feared anything. Nora has, but not me," Eleanor admits. "But these thoughts, visions, keep me up day and night, keep me from laughing or enjoying myself. And make me worry about confronting them, especially now. I know I can do this; I know I'm good enough to do it. That's why I don't understand this. Why am I scared to go into that base?"

"Knowledge of past success can alleviate the fear but sometimes it can turn into a greater fear of failure. In a twisted endless spiral…" Nikolas says. "I know that for a fact."

With a breath, Eleanor sits up, flexing her fingers.

"How do I fix it?" she asks.

"Face the fear, find it within yourself to overcome it. Have someone at your side that can help you," Nikolas suggests, following her lead and keeping his eyes on her.

Ever watchful.

"Who did you have?" Eleanor whispers, fingers out stretching slowly towards him.

He doesn't answer immediately, locking his hand with hers.

"You."

Eleanor's eyebrows raise in surprise, lips pursing slightly. Of course, Nikolas just sends her a crooked smile.

"Not a word," he mutters. "Now. We need to change; do you want the bathroom or this room?"

Now she fixes him with the look.

"You think I don't know you're just going to spend the entire time looking at yourself in the mirror if you get the bathroom?" Ellsie teases.

"And you won't?"

Chapter 57

With new roles, comes new outfits. Nikolas's fighting gear has changed little, merely a remake of his original after it had been destroyed, but Eleanor's – while mostly the same shape – has had a redesign and a few major adjustments.

Where it had previously been fully black, now there are swathes of green throughout. The vest piece is one such spot, solid green that matches Nikolas's uniform perfectly. But where his is detailed with silver, hers is gold. Minute etchings of embroidering and lining. Truly, Eleanor doesn't know why they bothered; her job was to not be seen.

The vest includes a hood, slim and curved to allow for full peripheral visibility. It follows down her back, silhouetting the stylised arrowhead. It rests flush to the black that creates the rest of her jacket. The tailcoat style mimics her original jacket, sleeves reaching down to loop around her thumb. Five windows are cut out along the inside of each of her arms – two on her upper arm and three on her lower – and follow the curve of her arms, covered in spider-silk mesh to give her skin a little bit of air. The protective mesh fills in the space left by the vest, covering the area around her throat as well. The fabric is made to withstand a glancing blow of a blade in the attempt to stop her from being injured badly again.

Stitched along her pants – the same black as the outer jacket – are a myriad of holsters. Throwing daggers on her right thigh; gun on her left. A band on her anklet allows for a hidden blade under the pant leg, and the pressure points are all heavily reinforced.

A belt wraps around her waist, with room for two spare magazines, two daggers and up to three cylindrical objects. Two loops sit on each side for her twin blade holster to connect to, along with two on her back to stabilise it.

Her heavily worn in combat boots haven't changed, however. Somehow the boots she had been wearing on capture had managed to survive long enough that she could still wear them now. In the heel are two tiny pins, and still tucked underneath the sole is a flat blade.

Placed on top of her new uniform is a quick note; 'Don't wreck this one – Colonel Randall.' Eleanor had no plans of letting it get a single scratch.

With her hair woven into a tight braid down her back, she leaves the hood down for now, and her mask sits in her hand. Silently, she had been debating with herself whether to wear this piece of her history. To wear it would further enforce her previous life, remind everyone of the things she did, what she was a part of. But to not could lead to her overloading. She couldn't figure out whether being locked off from her emotions was a positive or a negative. She had never been able to figure it out.

But in the end, she chooses to wear it, at least while in the base.

Stubbornly, it stays in her hand as she lightly knocks on the door to check Nikolas is dressed. Once receiving a positive response, she steps out. Their uniforms fit together brilliantly, like two sides of a coin. While hers was more muted and stealthier, his was loud and attention seeking. The garb of a Prince.

"Is the cape really necessary?" she mutters as she grabs the two bags of weapons.

"Is the mask?" Nikolas returns, slotting his own twin holster in the drape of the cape.

Eleanor assigns him the point for that one.

"Should we organise the weapons here or out there?" she continues. "We need to arm them at some point."

"But they'll distract us. We need to make sure we have everything…" Another point.

"Do we give them a gun or a knife?"

"Both."

"You're full of good ideas today," Eleanor chuckles, catching the holster thrown to her and attaching it to the front and back of her belt.

"Just more used to preparing with more people around me than you are…" Nikolas shrugs.

He lets her lay out all the weapons in two halves, quickly discovering the pattern she is laying out. Equal on each side, it allows them both to grab what they preferred. The guns sit beneath the blades, empty magazines next to the corresponding bullets.

"You want throwing daggers?" Eleanor eventually asks, a thin silver set next to heavier, double sided – thus more evenly weighted – set.

"I like the double sided," he replies shortly.

"Good, I like the other ones. Grab those, your twins and guns, then we'll figure out the rest," she follows.

They both start moving immediately, the throwing knives sliding into their places. Next are their individual pairs of blades.

Eleanor still uses the slightly curved, black and green blades, while Nikolas has managed to keep track of his own long blades – the detour was necessary in his escape, but the thought had come to him more than once, of the changes he would have to make if he had left them behind.

Then, methodical as ever, Eleanor starts to count in the bullets to her magazines, checking each and every one. Nikolas is significantly less practiced, shoving them in with little care – he is not at all surprised when Eleanor snatches them off him and rechecks the load. As if in a practiced trance, she moves through checking his handgun then her own, pulling sections apart and putting them back together.

Captain – curled on the floor watching the effort – clearly huffs as she passes the gun over. And much to Eleanor's annoyance, Nikolas chuckles as well, double checking the safety and locking it into its place.

"I need to make sure they work," she mutters, finishing her own gun and tucking it away.

"I know. It's just cute to see you babying me."

"I'm not sure cute is the right word for preparing a gun to shoot."

"We're not exactly normal people."

Having checked and loaded two more smaller handguns, Eleanor flicks her gaze back up to him in annoyance. A pair of identical gold, two pronged and wavy daggers slip into the belt of her jacket before Nikolas can argue.

"I don't like prong blades anyway," he smirks, taking two interlocked blades and sliding them into his belt.

A stiletto slips into the secret holder on her ankle.

One of the two collapsible staffs tucks into Nikolas's belt.

The other goes to Eleanor.

"Your one doesn't split," Nikolas teases, lining the rest of his belt with weak explosives and smoke bombs.

"I like it that way. Are you taking anything else?"

The last of her spots go to two smoke bombs.

"I'm good. You?"

Eleanor just holds out an earpiece.

As they both press them into their ears and pack away the unwanted weapons – leaving two guns and three daggers for those staying at the house – a silence falls. Eleanor can't help but let her eyes flick to her bag, finally giving in as the last duffel bag is zipped up. Her keepsake box is in the same condition as the last time Nikolas saw it.

From a pocket, Eleanor pulls out the locket she had been wearing, letting it pool in her hand. She swaps it with the necklace in the box. Small, gold, a drawn bow and arrow. Holding it tight for a few seconds before replacing it, then the photo of her family comes out, next to a photo of Adelyn.

Captain moves to her feet as she returns them as well, sniffing her hand gently. Nikolas only steps closer as she pulls out the blood covered dagger. It turns in her hand slowly, the only sliver of silver on the perfectly sharp edges. Lightly, Nikolas's fingers brush over her shoulder, the other hand reaching out to turn her head to him. She turns before he can touch her pale skin.

But he merely holds her eyes with his, expression calm. Kind... Loving.

"I wasn't going to bring it..." she breathes, the furrow between her brows just visible.

"I wouldn't have minded. I know it's your way of coping," he replies, face still perfectly relaxed.

"People call it psychopathic."

He shrugs lightly.

"Psychopathic... not quite. You just have weird tendencies to cope with trauma," he assures. "But it's strong of you to let that part of your habits go."

Eleanor lets the knife return to the box, turning into his arm and resting her head on his chest, tucked in under his shoulder. It's awkward with all the weapons attached to them both, but Nikolas keeps an arm around her, holding her still. Eleanor's arm wraps around him lightly, breath even as Nikolas allows himself to duck his head and breathe in her hair.

"I wasn't babying you earlier..." she whispers.

"I know."

It honestly surprises Nikolas when Eleanor doesn't draw away, instead pressing closer.

"I just needed to make sure you were going to be okay," she continues. "I was worried for you."

"I know."

"The handle of one of your daggers is jabbing me in the stomach."

"I know."

"When I step back my collapsible baton is going to release."

"I know."

She looks up in humour, smirk playing on her lips.

"Those things really have sensitive releases, don't they?"

"You haven't been smashed in the balls by one."

"Can you grab it for me?"

Very carefully, Nikolas moves one arm in between them, grasping the small collapsible rod in his large hand. Eleanor steps backwards, hanging carefully as Nikolas turns the switch back over. When he lets go, they both let out a breath and a giggle.

"Would it be okay if I kiss the top of your head?" Nikolas asks quietly.

Eleanor nods stepping forward once more and leaning her head into his hand. Her eyes shut in relaxation as he kisses the top of her head, fingers twisting at her side. Oh so slowly, Nikolas pulls away, tipping her chin up to see her eyes.

A frown appears as his thumb brushes lightly over the scar just above her eyebrow.

"How haven't I seen this before?' he asks, gaze returning to her eyes.

"Got it when I crashed the car... it isn't very obvious," she shrugs. "I guess we match now."

Nikolas chuckles, hands still cupping her face.

"I love you," he whispers. "Both of you. Always."

"I love you too," Eleanor replies, a flicker of both Nora and Ellsie in her eyes. "Now we just have to stay alive."

"We will."

Chapter 58

Horrified is probably the best word for the look on the family's faces as Eleanor holds a gun out to both women.

"Are those necessary?" Emma asks cautiously, watching as Skylar takes hers and removes the magazine.

"Yes. As much as I trust your security team, you need to be able to defend yourselves," Eleanor replies shortly. "I am also giving you all, including Ryder, a knife in case they get within close quarters. But that shouldn't happen if you shoot them before they can get to you. Aim for the throat and head if you are a half decent shot – I assume you both have handled guns before – or the heart is your next best shot. They might not feel the pain, so shoot them dead."

"And if these run out?" Skylar asks, ensuring the chamber is empty before pushing the magazine back in.

Despite the nervous looks on both of their faces, it's clear they both know their way around a gun.

"Our room has the rest of our weapons, the bullets for those are sitting on our bed. Don't use the explosives unless it's a smoke bomb," Eleanor instructs. "Your security team are split between the staircase and here, and the elevator is completely off. Let no one in except for us."

"We know," Emma mutters. "Are you leaving soon?"

"Imminently," Nikolas steps in, handing over the three daggers. "Make sure Ryder has one, just in case. They aren't terribly sharp but be careful."

They nod, glancing between each other slowly.

"Thank you for following this through... it is a bit more than I had expected to ask of you," Skylar says, eyes staying mostly on Eleanor's face. "Please remember that I will testify for you again, if they decide to revisit your sentence."

"It's okay, and thank you," Eleanor replies, head inclining slightly. "Just keep in mind what it would do to your reputation to be supporting us. I wouldn't want any harm to you, ever."

"Nonsense, Eleanor. You are my friend. If I can help keep you alive then I will."

The grateful turn of Eleanor's face is one not often seen, pure in intention.

From her pocket, a phone rings. Pulling off one of her gloves to answer, Eleanor turns away ever so slightly.

"Are you about to head out?" Kenichi asks, tone muted.

"Yes. We plan to initiate contact in 15 minutes," Eleanor answers, eyes locking on to Nikolas. "I assume you all are patched into our earpieces."

"We are. Though no one is listening until you send out the signal... if you have things you want to say to each other," Kenichi assures. The ever so slight tease in his tone throws Eleanor off. "I just wanted to make sure you are okay."

"I am. Fully. And I am confident in our success," she says, still holding Nikolas's eyes. He nods in assurance and encouragement. "Could I please talk to Adelyn, if she's nearby?"

"I'll get her now, she's in Nancy's office," he says, then quieter. "Nora's not too nervous?"

"Muted but fine. She trusts my judgement and seems to be encouraged by the fact I am being cautious," Eleanor shrugs. "You have a copy of my will?"

"I do... but I will not need it, understand me, Ellie?" he warns, the pause in his movements clear. "You need to let us all say goodbye, properly."

"I understand. I have no plans of cutting my time with my daughter short. And I need to give my thanks to you in person," she says. "I will survive."

"Do not survive, Ellie. Live."

A door opens through the line before she can reply, the phone being passed into younger hands.

"Hiya, Mummy!" Adelyn calls.

"Hey Baby Girl," Eleanor replies, softening almost immediately. "Are you okay? Not hungry at all?"

"I'm good. How's New York!"

"Busy. I have to go now, but I just wanted to tell you I love you..."

"I love you too. Can you talk tomorrow?"

The hope in Adelyn's voice shakes her mother.

"Hopefully, if not I will see you in person the day after. I promise," Eleanor says. "Now, be good for Kenichi and Kaylee."

"And not Michael!" Adelyn recites, eliciting a chuckle.

"Exactly. Love you Ady."

"Love you, Mum."

Eleanor hangs up the phone, rocking on her heels for a second before stilling and returning to her strength. Face tight, but fists relaxed at her sides. She turns back to face the family, chin high.

But nothing can disguise the single tear that had rolled down her cheek. She ignores it though, letting the water stain her cheek as she looks between them all. Then her gaze turns to Nikolas, determined and strong.

"Shall we?" she breathes, lips perfectly still.

Every part of her perfectly held.

"We shall. Any last questions?"

"We are all good. Stay alive, will you?" Skylar offers, hand holding tight to Captain's led as Eleanor starts to turn away.

"I plan on it."

Chapter 59

Kenichi takes the phone back from Adelyn as the child holds it out expectantly. As he tucks it into his pocket, she catches his eyes with a concerning level of accusation as he moves to turn away. The gaze – one that reminded him so clearly of her mother – makes him pause, a frown developing on his features as he watches the six-year-old.

"What is it Ady?" he asks quietly, squatting down to meet her eye to eye.

The child holds her expression as she huffs, arms crossing indignantly.

"Why are you making her do it again?" she asks.

Kenichi balks, failing to hide his reaction.

"Your mother was the one who decided to go help her friend, Adelyn. She's perfectly safe," he replies, trying his hardest to keep his tone even.

"Don't lie to me," Adelyn snaps. "She only ever has that tone when she is scared. My mother doesn't get scared easily. Why are you forcing her to be scared? She doesn't want to be scared."

"We aren't forcing her to do anything," Kenichi responds, his tone even, face kind, and yet he knows Adelyn doesn't believe him. Honestly, he's not sure if he believes himself. "Your mum will be fine. She knows how to handle herself, and she has Nikolas to help her."

The child sighs, turning away from Kenichi and moving back to her seat on Nancy's couch – where she had been told to stay earlier that morning. Adelyn says nothing more, but sits, glowering at Kenichi with her arms crossed until he reluctantly leaves the room.

He walks immediately to the mission room, joining the rest of the team and Nancy as they watch over the security cameras in the building. They have nothing to do yet, but once Eleanor and Nikolas are in, they will be keeping a close eye on them. Kaylee sends him a questioning glance as he walks in, perplexity almost tattooed on his face.

"Something wrong?" she asks, gaze running over the screens as if to find the issue herself.

"Not with Eleanor and Nikolas, no. Eleanor's... stressed but otherwise fine. No sign of a breakdown," Kenichi replies as he takes his seat near the microphone that is hooked into their earpieces, right next to Nancy. "It's just Adelyn. She was being very accusatory."

Nancy narrows her eyes and turns her focus onto him for the first time since he came in.

"Accusatory of what?" she asks tersely.

"Us forcing Eleanor to do things. She knows what her mother is doing, to some extent," he says. "She asked me 'why are you making her do it again?'. If I didn't know better, I would think she remembered the high school."

"She can't have, she was a baby," Nancy responds instantly, but a little of the doubt that lingers in Kenichi is mirrored in her eyes as she turns her attention back to the screens. "Anyway, she's just upset, it will be fine once Eleanor is back."

After a pause, it's Kaylee who responds.

"We better hope so. If Adelyn doesn't trust us, there is nothing keeping Eleanor here," she says quietly.

Chapter 60

"**T**wo minutes to initial contact. Patterns mapped. On next opening we will engage," Eleanor mutters. "Clear?"

They don't bother to hide in the shadows, midday sun high above them. The constant thrum of people crossing in front of the alley is enough to hide them in plain sight. Anyway, it's not like they didn't already know they were coming.

"Clear," Colonel Randall replies. "Are you both prepared?"

"Fully," Nikolas replies.

"Sentries just passed, once more and we move," Eleanor follows. "Could we keep chatter on your end limited please?"

"Understood."

Eleanor finally takes her last free breath, beginning to lift the mask towards her face. But across the alley her eyes lock with Nikolas's, holding for just a second.

'*You are the bravest person I know,*' he calls into her head. '*Don't forget that.*'

The thanks in her eyes are clear as she finally fits the mask onto her face. Like a film between them, the final drops of Nora slip away, leaving only the assassin.

"Ten seconds to window," Nikolas mutters, watching as the sentries make their pass.

"Preparing to engage."

Eleanor pulls her daggers from her belt, prepping them easily. The mental clock ticks in her mind.

Four. Three. Two...

The metal is cold against her forearm – even through the fabric – constantly reminding her of their presence.

"Let's go."

They dart across the nearly empty street, slipping into the opposite alley with ease. The two guards are down within half a second and Eleanor steps away smoothly. The blood dripping slowly off her daggers is red, the two men human. Carelessly, she kicks one onto his front, exposing the tattoo on his lower back.

"Agency grunts," she mutters as they take place on either side of the door.

"Switch to guns for infiltration," Nancy says through their comms. "They will likely know you're already there."

The weapons had already been switched in Eleanor's hands; her daggers wiped on one of the corpses.

"This isn't my first rodeo, Colonel," she growls, head nodding just slightly to Nikolas.

He kicks the door open with ease, stepping out of the way for Eleanor to take point. Ellsie is a significantly better shot, and fires without a second's thought, keeping the gun up as she takes out the last guards. These bleed black. And stay down.

"There are multiple sectors here," Nikolas mutters as he moves in behind Eleanor.

With his swords drawn, Nikolas watches the doorway they came in while Eleanor starts to move further into the complex. Apart from the occasional gunfire or clash, it remains quiet. As suspected, the base is nearly empty as most agents are out in the streets waiting for a public response, so it is an easy path in. For a few peaceful seconds, they can have a break, Eleanor reloading her gun for the last time and returning it to her leg. Now she draws her swords, swinging them easily.

"It's been a while since you've used those, hasn't it?" Nikolas says, watching her like a hawk.

"To kill people, yes. But I am in no way rusty..."

"Is this the best time for this?" Nancy mutters. "You have hostiles inbound."

"Which we are going to have to deal with in a moment, let us catch our breath," Eleanor quips, taking a few slow breaths.

Her mask pops off for a few moments, sending a look towards Nikolas, who merely chuckles at the expression. After a few seconds, the mask goes back on, the measured, conservative breaths returning.

Nikolas pushes into the stairwell, ignoring the annoyed hiss Eleanor makes at his roughness as he starts to edge up the levels. They needed to get to the top, where Arthur would undoubtably be kept.

The path is easy up the first level, before a grenade lands at Eleanor's feet. With quick profanities she kicks it down to the level below, dashing up to the next landing. Nikolas raises an eyebrow as she flinches away from the explosion.

"We need to get into close quarters, there's no way to win a fire fight from below," she huffs.

"I am aware," Nikolas returns, kicking his head in annoyance as the Daemones stomp on the floor above them. "You good to cover me?"

Ellsie rolls her eyes, taking one of his magazines and tucking it into her own belt. Her own goes into her handgun, flicking the safety off and edging out from the corner. With a nod she steps out fully, Nikolas dashing up behind her. Her shots are quick as she steps up the staircase, continuing to fire as Nikolas greets the first Daemones that step out to stop him. They carry wounds from Eleanor's gunfire, so are easy to take down.

Only when Nikolas is fully into the group does Eleanor stop shooting, keeping the burning hot handgun in her hand as she joins him in taking out their opposition. By the time they've finished, the gun is empty, cooled enough to safely slide it into its holster. Upon drawing her swords, she moves to enter the corridor in front of them. Nikolas catches her arm, eyes locking on hers through her mask.

"You can do this," he tells her quietly. "No matter how many people stand on the other side of this door, you can take them down."

Her nod is short, confidence masking the lingering fear in her eyes.

"Come now, Meine Geliebte, of course I can," Ellsie grins, caressing his face gently. "Let's have some fun..."

Nikolas lets himself meet her with a cocky smirk. You don't become a Daemone Major without some affinity for the fight.

Eleanor is the first one to step into the corridor. Facing her are Daemones, followed by a selection of the Berühmte Söldner. She finds her first target within a second, stepping up with blades swinging.

Her swords do not stop as they meet flesh, sliding like butter. Nikolas steps in behind her, handling the few agents who had slipped in behind them. But Eleanor can only see those in front of her, taking a step back for every few bodies. There was no need to gain ground when they kept stepping up to meet her.

Her blades are singing, meeting more and more fates. A Queen of Darkness, leading them to her grasp. For a few brief moments, Nikolas can turn to watch her dance. There is not a single falter, each step as fluid as a ballerina. But the door handle twists once more, and he must pull his eyes away. No guns are fired now, instead each fighter carries their choice of daggers, knives or brass knuckles.

"Are you killing them all?" Michael calls through the earpiece, the first person to speak other than Nancy.

"Mostly. They don't get up and become an issue if they're dead," Eleanor hisses in a thick German accent. She falters just enough for a set of brass knuckles to slam into her ribs, knocking the air out of her. "Be quiet, you are distracting—" her swords extend, following their ornaments to the ground "—me."

Tone measured, Nancy speaks carefully, "Eleanor..."

Ellsie bites back the profanity, stepping onto the defensive. With the thrum of the fight, she manages to get enough time to slide her swords back into their place, returning for a few seconds with her fist before the collapsible shaft is extending in her hand and she is fighting again.

"There, as long as I don't manage to hit someone hard enough to kill them with a pole, they'll live," she growls, the interference barely impacting her fight.

"Thank you," Nancy replies. "Nikolas, you as well."

With only a grunt in response, he swaps to his poles as well. He is without anyone to fight now, turning to watch Eleanor as she makes it to the last few lines of defence. The blockade must have been working.

But Eleanor is not stopping, in fact it appears her movements are not entirely her own as she finishes the last few men. Ellsie was a brilliant fighter – that was not to be ignored – but as she knocks out the last of them, the shake in her hand and tremor in her step does not stop, instead growing with each moment of immobility.

The bloodlust that had built up for five years, the last of it that she couldn't get rid of by sparring.

The deadly, dangerous bloodlust that could take out a corridor full of trained assassins within a few minutes.

"The building is clear, we will retrieve Arthur and leave momentarily," she says, voice rock hard.

Eleanor refuses to look towards Nikolas as he edges closer, merely returning her pole to its place. But her hands still tremble, the only physical manifestation of her restraint.

"Incaendium..." Nikolas starts, "it does not rule you."

"We need to retrieve Arthur."

Her response is short, and her voice hard, but a thick wall comes over her face as she turns the door handle into the torture chamber the Berühmte Söldner had left Arthur in.

Within sits a man, blonde hair stained with blood, tall build lessened by the exhausted sag of his shoulders. A bandage sits over one eye, many more covering his arms and legs. The chair he's tied to is sturdy, but he is only tied with rope. Without even looking up, Arthur flinches away from them.

"Stay holding the door," Eleanor orders as she moves to step in. "Do not let it shut."

Nikolas complies with a frown.

"Do you want help?"

Her withering glare is answer enough, but still she speaks.

"Not at the risk of getting us both locked in a room they could easily gas us in."

Arthur seems to waken slightly as Eleanor steps closer and draws a pair of daggers from their places on her leg. One presses lightly to his chest in warning as the other starts to cut the binds. To be most annoying, it seems, Arthur thrashes wildly, only stilling as Eleanor growls in annoyance and the blade on his chest draws a dribble of blood.

"I am trying to save your life, dimwit," she snarls — a slip of the hardness Nikolas had seen in the hall slipping in as she shifts the dagger up so the tip hovers just off his throat.

"Sure doesn't seem that way," he returns, but stays perfectly still. "You look like a slightly more colourful version of them."

"The uniform is very practical; however, I can assure you I am in no way one of them anymore. Your sister hired me to save your life and get her out of the mess your parents have created. I am holding a knife to your throat to ensure you do not attack me. Can you promise you won't?"

A tremor hovers on Eleanor's tone, like it was paining her to be so passive. While no one else notices it, Nikolas frowns as the first binding is cut.

"Only if you tell me who you are…"

"She was your prom queen," Nikolas interjects, finally drawing his attention, "and she's saved your life once already, you can trust her to do the same again."

With his eye opened wide in surprise, Arthur looks back over Eleanor, finally seeming to recognise the eyes behind her mask. His nod is subtle, but enough for Eleanor to cut him free entirely.

"I thought you were dead," he says as he drags himself to his feet. Eleanor watches expectantly, glad she doesn't have to assist him. "Last I heard you were bleeding out on our gym floor. You know they never quite got the stains out."

Eleanor ignores him as she steps back out of the chamber and into the hallway. Her focus is undivided upon the unconscious bodies around her. Unconscious, not dead. With a start Nikolas realises what exactly she is restraining herself from doing.

"There are medics waiting outside," Nikolas says quietly to Arthur. "Head down, we'll be behind you in a minute."

Arthur frowns, but upon seeing the tremble in Eleanor's step as she inches down the hallway, ducks down a side passage and into the elevator contained within it. Only once he is out of sight does Nikolas turn to Eleanor again, catching up to her in four smooth strides.

"It does not rule you," he remind her quietly.

"That is where you are wrong, Prince. It does rule her," a male voice calls though the building's intercom.

Both Eleanor and Nikolas recognise the voice instantly, the younger freezing with every inch of her being, and the elder closing the final distance to her side. On the other end of their earpieces, not a single person can place the voice.

"It rules her every step. It's what made her the perfect little mercenary," he continues. "Turn her onto a crowd, have just one person initiate contact and no one in the crowd would escape. All she would do is just… kill."

As if the voice is trapped inside her, Eleanor shakes her head, trying to rid herself of the torturous tone.

"But then there was this… sickness," he growls.

Deep inside, the disgust in his tone cuts her.

"Such filthy weakness. Poisoning my beautiful little Kitten – I've been watching for longer than you believe, little one. It did so hurt me when you refused my offer."

Beside her, Nikolas flinches as Eleanor's fist slams against the wall. Her yell borders on a scream, but her feet stay anchored to the ground they stand on. And as the sound is left to reverberate around the room, every other piece of her joins them in terror-locked stillness.

"The first time I heard of you I was surprised… the little girl that couldn't pick up a weapon – they told me this, you see – 'she just snapped' they said. 'Killed two men within a minute', they were amazed." He chuckles, letting his grin be heard through the speakers. "You improved so very quickly; I knew you would flourish under the Dunkler Bischof. There was always something about you, I know what it is now."

Finally beginning to catch on, the team on the other end of their earpieces eerily quiet. Listening to every word.

"Each year I watched you learn, watched you grow," he continues. "It saddened me immensely to order the Dunkler Bischof to take you out. Twelve was so young to lose such an adept fighter. Hearing you had failed was more surprising though."

"You sent a child into a maximum-security prison," Eleanor croaks, shivering at her own words. "What could you expect?"

"I expected the world from you. My little Kitten."

The name makes her shudder, finally looking to Nikolas for help. He offers a hand for her to hold.

"And I got the best, in some ways. You never broke, I guess I should've known we wouldn't persuade you when we brought you home. I never really understood why you left us that first time. You could've raised your child if you wanted… we just wanted you with us. At home," the man says, voice taking a softer tone.

"It sure didn't seem that way when you kept sending people to kill me," Eleanor calls, the blue of her eyes glazed like a lake on a foggy morning. "I never wanted to kill you, little one. I only wanted you with me." He adds harshly. "With us and no one else. You belong to us. You are one of us." Then softer again. "We could have forgotten about it all."

"No, you couldn't," Nikolas replies, hand holding Eleanor in a grip completely opposite to his tone. "You forget I worked with them, they never forgot what she had done. Even when they thought she was dead."

"I don't forget things, Prince. I was the one who got you your place back. I knew what you felt. I know the allure she holds for powerful people." For a moment Eleanor starts, but there was no way for him to know about Lahash and Lerajie. They had been too careful.

"You know nothing," the Geminae say in sync.

"I know everything. I know you love this all, Eleanor. You love the fight, the blood. You love to kill."

Hopeless, Ellsie's eyes turn to Nikolas through the mesh of her mask.

"I don't," she chokes. "I promise I don't."

Only Kenichi can understand the desperation in her tone, the only other one to know of her separate personalities.

"You can't let it go. You can't fathom stopping. You can't stop being one of us."

Her breath is short as Nikolas turns her to face him fully.

"Don't listen to him."

"I'm not. He is nothing but a liar. If he meant it, he would be here, rather than across the world. I trust you."

Slowly Nik slides his hand to rest on her shoulder, edging close to hold her head steady.

"Look at yourself. You still wear our uniform; you still fight like us. You still wear your mask. You are still one of us, nothing can change that."

"You are not," Nikolas promises, sliding her hood back.

"They don't understand you. They can't help you. They just want to make themselves feel better. Give the broken girl some time to be human. Let her lose who she is." The disgust in his tone is clear, and back in Washington DC, they shift in realisation. "Rip her away from her destiny."

They begin to worry.

"I am with you, always," Nikolas whispers, nose brushing against the side of her mask.

"They will never be able to see you as anything other than a murderer. They will never trust you. Just look at your ankle. After seven years, they still track your every movement. They are not your family. They do not care. We are, we do."

Very slowly, Nikolas moves to find the small catch of her mask.

"I see you," he murmurs. "I've always seen you."

"You don't have to leave them behind. There is more than enough room for your Prince and your daughter," the man says. "She doesn't even have to become like you, if that will bring you home." He pauses for a moment. "She can live pure."

"But never free," Eleanor snaps. "A criminal of this world, a prisoner of yours."

"Not forever, little one," he promises. "Your world is not long for its freedom."

Finally, Kenichi speaks, voice crackling over the

"You chose this life so she could live free, Ellie," he whispers. His words so very cautious. "So she could breathe fresh air. So she could grow into a beautiful little girl. So she could live in a world with opportunities. You may not have much time left, but you can help us keep it that way..."

His words cut her, the reminder of her time limit hard to hear. With promise in his eyes, Nikolas releases the front of her mask. Letting it fall to the ground with its other half.

So carefully, he runs his bloodstained fingers over her pale cheek. So lovingly, he lowers his head to rest against hers.

"Join us and we can promise she will live, Eleanor," the man calls, rather lucky Eleanor couldn't get her hands onto him. "They can promise you nothing."

"We can do it. You can do it, Incaendium," Nikolas murmurs.

She swallows, still gloved fingers raising to hold the back of his neck, melting into his hold as his arms wrap around her body. He holds her steady as she sways in her place.

"Come home, 828."

Three numbers. Eight hundred and twenty-eight. The nail in his coffin. Perhaps if he had chosen a different way to say it, they may have gone.

~

We will never know. I always have to remember when writing these recounts, that Eleanor was not perfect. She was not driven by her moral compass, as many heroines are. She merely wanted to keep all she loved alive and safe. In a different world, she may have gone back, and this world would have been lost.

~

Eleanor brings her eyes to Nikolas's, only a few centimetres separating them. She kisses him slowly, holding the embrace as she makes her decision. Between them, they form a plan.

They separate a moment later, finding the camera in the hall.

"Where have the agents gone?" she asks.

Play the game.

"They'll bring you home. All you need to do is meet them at the docks."

He believes the charade.

Nancy speaks quickly through their earpieces, "they have hostages. Important ones..."

Her unsaid words hang heavily on the line.

"They will see me soon," Eleanor promises, eyes still locked on the camera.

They only flick away as NAP agents enter the hall. The pair nod to them as they walk out, stern acknowledgement. Nikolas watches Eleanor as they wind down to the waterfront, pride shining in his eyes.

Forgotten, the mask stays on the floor.

Chapter 61

With the sun still high, they don't bother concealing their entrance to the docks, easily able to step through the police line and continue deeper into the compound. All is quiet but for muffled shuffling ahead of them and their own footsteps.

"You were terrified of him…" Nikolas says quietly. "Did he ever…"

Ellsie sighs softly, looking over to him quickly.

"No. But he was always the one there after all of it, telling me I could stop it all. Hard to hear it again," she says. "Really hard."

Nikolas offers an arm out to her, smile soft as she slides the two steps over to tuck under it for a moment.

"If it helps at all, the leaders of the other factions don't like him all that much. It's only that they dislike you more that they're putting up with him," he replies.

Cracking a crooked smile, Eleanor moves out from under his arm and straightens herself again. They were coming up on the agents and their hostages, keeping their hands clear of weapons as they step out onto the waterside.

Five agents are waiting to greet them, the other hostages behind them. Their entire focus on the pair, standing steadily at the entrance to the clearing.

"So, you're the reason they've gotten so strict," the ACE at the head of the group sneers. He's young, maybe just 18 but not older.

Barely seasoned and aching to prove himself.

"Probably, I do like to cause them pain," Eleanor returns with a grin. "Apparently for all their control they still can't manage to get their ACEs to stop being cocky assholes."

The ACE's face turns, growing defensive as Ellsie flashes him a grin.

"You're one to talk," he growls. "Decided to come running back to us, have you?"

Now Nikolas glances down to her, the pull on his lips only just visible.

"Why is it that you think I want to come back?" Eleanor sighs, noticing the agents behind their ACE glancing between themselves. "I've been treated with nothing but disgust since I became an ACE."

Confusion flicks onto the other ACE's face, but the emotion is concealed quickly enough.

"More so, why on Earth would I take my daughter into that environment?" Eleanor continues, sliding a dagger out of its place and examining the blade.

"You yielded, you agreed to come with us," the ACE barks, met only by Nikolas's grin.

"Whenever did we do that? We cleared that building completely, then we were given the location of more agents with hostages, so we moved to here." He glances to Eleanor as she looks up at him. "We never agreed to anything."

Before them the ACE freezes. He was only told he had to bring them a few minutes before, he was not prepared to take down an Angeli Prince and the ACE who had killed so many of his own.

"The people at the other end of our earpieces would prefer we didn't kill you." Eleanor smirks. "And my bloodlust has been sufficiently quenched that I can accept that, but we need those hostages, and I need to account for five Berühmte Söldner agents by the end of today. Dead or alive. Fighting or surrendered."

The ACE's face turns to hostility as Nikolas watches the other agents, eyes narrowing slightly as they signal to each other. He places a quiet finger on Eleanor's arm as they raise their guard, giving her a look of his own.

"Berühmte Söldner do not surrender," the ACE sneers, pulling a gun on them.

Eleanor merely smiles, eyes refusing to glance behind him. The other agents have pulled knives, edging closer. One nods to her, keeping her head bowed in question.

"How old are you? I don't remember your face – and I remember faces – so you mustn't have graduated," Eleanor queries, keeping her focus forward.

"I will when I bring you in. I will prove myself, and I shall graduate," he replies.

"So, you have no useful information?" Eleanor chuckles. "Great. That means you can die."

Nikolas looks down on Eleanor in surprise, but her gaze stays forward, refusing to flicker as the agents shuffle the last few steps forward. Now Eleanor holds a hand on his arm, stopping him from shielding her as the agents move onto the attack.

One agent knocks the ACE's gun arm down while another swings a sword through his neck, taking it off in a clean sweep. The head rolls to Eleanor's feet, body dropping shortly after.

"Well, this is an interesting development," Nikolas muses, hand settling on the middle of Eleanor's back.

The pressure is steady, keeping her in place as the agents take a step back and drop to one knee. Nora is returning now, regarding the agents with a tilted head.

"Königin der Dunkelheit, wir gehören dir," the woman says: 'Queen of Darkness, we are yours'.

Eleanor's focus snaps to Nikolas in that moment, translating quicker than he, but the surprise covers his face a moment later.

"Explain this. I am no queen," Eleanor orders, focus turning back to the agents.

"There are superstitions, among the lower agents. From well before the Berühmte Söldner were created," one says.

Upon gaining no useful information, Eleanor sighs, stepping away from Nikolas.

"Get up," she says, moving to step past them. Her words are soft, eyes cautious. "Don't speak any more of this, it is false. I am a murderer. I am insane. I am no leader, nor will I ever be."

"You know the evils of this world, and you have conquered them. You live, you give us hope. Do not discount yourself."

Ignoring them, Eleanor steps towards the hostages, releasing each with a flick of her knife. None are harmed, but all quickly jump away from the clearly bloodstained woman. They form a group behind one woman who stays facing Eleanor.

"Who are you? Why are you here?" she asks quickly, eyes cautiously on Nikolas still blocking the exit.

"We are agents for the National Agents of Protection, you were put in danger because of our interest in the District Attorney and her family. The Berühmte Söldner don't take lightly to threats, and we are exactly that," Eleanor replies.

"National Agents of Protection don't carry your weapons…"

Clearly the woman knew her government agencies.

"No, they don't," Nikolas cuts in. "We're specialist agents, internationally trained. The Colonel is fully aware of our specific talents. The best way to fight fire is with fire."

The hostages go quiet, taking the answers with suspicion.

Finally, police run in, guns high until they assess there is no threat. Handcuffs are slapped onto the remaining agents, and they are led out, Eleanor and Nikolas following closely. As they exit the docks, they edge off to the side.

"Are we clear to finish duty?" Eleanor asks, fidgeting with the edge of her tailcoat.

"That was a clever trick, pretending to be returning," the Colonel replies, ignoring Eleanor's question. "Never do it again."

"They won't offer again," Eleanor mutters. "Those four agents need to be kept under protection; the agency won't want them spreading whatever they were going on about."

"And what is that?" Michael cuts in, suspicion clear in his tone.

With Nikolas bristling next to her, Eleanor offers a hand. He takes it quickly.

"How should we know?" he replies. "Neither of us were ever in the lower circles."

There is a pause on the other end of the line before Nancy sighs.

"The brother has been moved to the nearest hospital, accompany Skylar there and you can go back after that. You can take your earpieces out now," she says. "Wrap up and get back here quickly."

"Yes Ma'am," Eleanor replies. "Tell Ady I'm uninjured, I'll call her tomorrow."

"Are you uninjured?" Kenichi asks.

"Comparatively, yes. Don't confuse her with specifics. All she needs to know is her mother is safe, which I am."

"Then we'll hear from you tomorrow."

"Yes," Eleanor replies, pulling out her earpiece a moment later.

Nikolas does the same, offering to pull her close the moment after. She does so gladly, taking the kiss he plants in her hair with a little smile.

Chapter 62

They change and shower just enough that they aren't obviously covered in blood before taking Skylar to her twin. Once there, they only stay for a few minutes – Eleanor growing increasingly annoyed by the looks Captain is receiving – before making their way back to the apartment. Bullied into getting street food, they are still finishing as they enter the apartment.

Captain settles himself onto the bed, ignoring the food they place on the table. Nikolas watches her carefully, frown clear as she winces leaning down to pick up her pyjamas. Finally, he steps in front of her, catching her arm lightly.

"You haven't taken a full breath since we finished," he says quietly, accent prominent as he grows sleepier. "What's wrong?"

Eleanor ignores him completely.

"Your shoulder is bleeding," she says. "Do you want me to stitch it?"

"I asked first..."

"You're bleeding..."

"Eleanor..."

"Nikolas..."

From the corner, Captain – nearly asleep – growls slightly. He was used to their bickering by now, and Eleanor's behaviours were familiar. But he was too tired to bother getting up, Nikolas could deal with her, he figured.

As far as he dares, Nikolas lifts Eleanor's shirt to see the growing purple bruise. He runs a thumb lightly over it, the featherlight pressure making Eleanor wince.

"Your ribs could be broken," he mutters, raising his eyes to hers as he drops the shirt.

"I know what broken ribs feel like." Eleanor's tone is harsh. "They're just bruised. I'll be fine. You won't be if you let that get infected."

"Focus on yourself for a second. If it's broken it could puncture your lung," he returns.

"It's just a bruise," she sighs. "Blame your brother if you'd like, but I'm fine."

Rolling his eyes in amusement, Nikolas rolls his shoulder to test the cut. It's clear it stings more than he lets on.

"Take your shirt off," Eleanor mutters, "and sit on the bed."

"I mean, if you want me to..." he teases weakly, complying as she gives him a Look.

Eleanor disappears into the bathroom for a second and returns with a first-aid kit in her hands. Her eyes stay stubbornly on his face as he pulls his shirt off and tosses it on the ground. With quick and nimble fingers, she removes the blood weeping out of a deep and troublesome cut on his shoulder.

They are both quiet as she disinfects it, stitching it shut and placing an adhesive gauze strip over it. Her fingers linger though, brushing over his shoulder lightly. Nikolas shivers, leaning into the touch as Eleanor lets herself lower her head to rest it on the bare skin. Her arm gently wraps over his chest holding them close as she brushes her nose over his jaw.

He takes her hand gently, kissing it lightly.

"I'm proud of you," he says quietly. "I hope you know that."

Eleanor is quiet, waiting for him to continue.

"You let it all go, stood up to them. I know what that mask meant, why you continued to keep wearing it," he says. "You let it all go today. You should be proud of yourself."

She smiles lightly, squeezing his hand in thanks. Loosening her grip, she shifts back to sit against the headboard, smiling as he follows shortly after pulling a shirt back on. They both slide into their places, sat close to each other's side. Very slowly, Eleanor leans up to kiss him, their lips holding together for a moment before they pull away.

Nikolas's thumb waits on her cheek, hand cupping her neck lightly.

"Look at me, kissing a queen," he grins, leaning back.

Eleanor groans as she rests her head against his chest, eyes staring into space. They are quiet for a moment, the crease forming between Eleanor's eyebrows.

"This isn't the first time someone has called me Queen of Darkness..." she finally murmurs. "I hadn't thought of it until now."

Shifting slightly, Nikolas looks down at her.

"What do you mean?" he asks. Quiet.

"The Fallen Angels I'm friends with, they call me Regina Tenebris. They've never said why but Lahash is very superstitious," Eleanor says. "Do you have any idea what they might be talking about?"

Nikolas pauses for a few seconds, scanning back through his own mind.

"Deep in the royal libraries I remember reading something that mentioned a dark queen as a part of the Great Falling," he eventually says, massaging her shoulder lightly. "It was followed by the imprisoning of nearly all the Dark Angels. The queen they mention was not named, but from what I remember, she was never caught."

"What are you taught about Dark Angels?"

"That they're Angels who are gifted with dark and powerful gifts. Some say they are cursed by the six kings of hell and their queen; others say they are blessed to do what others cannot," he answers. "We don't know much anymore, books on the Dark Angels are few and far between. I never dared to look at them, not when the King hated me so much."

Eyebrows creasing, Eleanor pauses to think, the pads of her fingers tapping out songs on his chest.

"If anyone asks, we have no idea and have never heard the name," she eventually says. She frowns, an unbidden thought raising to the surface. "Does Angeli blood appear on blood tests?"

"Not really... it can be seen when blood is examined under a microscope – like a mutation in the blood – but small amounts can easily go undetected." His hand stops for a moment, frowning lightly. "Dark Angel blood is much harder to detect, almost impossible even. Only their kin can discover dormant Dark Angel blood. Kin being Dark and Fallen Angels. I'm sure your friends would have said something."

"The King's Aspect?"

"Limited to Daemones," Nikolas assures. "Really it's rather useless on an island with a warning system."

With a slow nod, Eleanor reaches behind her to pick up her notebook and pencil. Nikolas watches absently as she sketches out each face, easing it from her hands as her eyes droop into sleep.

Chapter 63

They leave immediately after the press conference the next day. Undoubtably, their faces would be plastered across the news by now, but they cared little. The time for hiding was over.

Nikolas drives, leaving Eleanor to stare out the window as the scenery whips past. The lavender bear sits in her lap, the weight a comfort as her fingers fiddle with the purple fur. Her other hand is linked loosely in Nikolas's between them, head resting back against her headrest in relaxation.

She only returns her focus to the car as her phone rings, frown appearing as she reaches to pick it up.

"Who is it?" Nikolas asks as she continues to stare at the Caller ID.

"Amy..." Eleanor replies in a confused whisper. "My old neighbour."

"You should answer it..."

"I haven't spoken to her since... since the night they took me."

"Even more reason for you to answer it."

Nikolas does well to keep his face neutral as she glares over at him.

"She'll be calling because she saw me on the morning news..."

Infuriatingly, he just shrugs, eyes returning to focus on the road ahead of them. The call goes to voicemail, but the phone stays in Eleanor's hand. It rings again a few seconds later.

"I get the feeling she will keep calling until you pick up," Nikolas murmurs, pulling the car into the shoulder. "And we aren't going anywhere until you talk to her."

"Why must you be so annoying?" The words are irritated but without the usual stinging threat that Eleanor's interrogative questions usually held.

"Because you would stay hiding away from the world otherwise..."

Their eyes meet, silent words passing quickly between them. Eleanor's thumb swipes the call open.

"Hello," she answers, phone to her ear but eyes still on Nikolas.

"Diana, my god I thought you were dead!" Amy almost yells. "I tried for weeks to call you after those friends of yours disappeared, tried to talk to them even but no one ever said anything about you or Adelyn. Then suddenly you pop up on TV, healthy and fighting things! Why didn't you tell anyone!"

"Everything has been a bit of a mess recently..."

"A mess? Enough that you don't call me to at least tell me you're alive! Or text, just something, Diana! Or should I call you Eleanor now, seeing as though EVERYONE here knows," she continues. "We figured it was a bad sign when they flew Angel and Tucker over but not Carly. She's doing well, by the way, Rachel has been training her."

"I know..."

It's quiet for a few moments, before Amy changes topic.

"I though you said you weren't working anymore," she says, seemingly calmer now. A tension still holds in her voice, though.

"I wasn't. When they took me, it took a few months for me to be recovered enough to even enter a room." Her hesitation is clear, fingers lacing back into Nikolas's silently. "It took a while for me to recover – I'm still recovering – but an old friend of mine needed help. I had promised it to her years before. She testified for me at my trial, so I owed her that much... and they were only bothering her because of me so I had to handle it. It was good for me to face them anyway."

Amy is silent, breath the only sound coming through the phone,

"I couldn't find it in myself to call any of you," Eleanor murmurs. "I got thoroughly messed up, and up until this last week I think I was kind of operating in a catatonic state. Numb. I'm nowhere near out of it, but I am getting there."

"You don't have to explain yourself. I know it can be hard for you. I just wish you could have told us you were safe. Or even just alive," Amy replies, quiet now as well. "We shouldn't have found out by seeing the news."

"I'm sorry, I should have. I should have talked to more people in general. It was a mistake."

Nikolas squeezes her hand, grip shifting to run a thumb over her knuckles.

"Are you going to come back?" Amy asks, almost hopeful.

It's clear Eleanor's words are pained.

"I would love to, but until the situation is fully... handled I cannot return and be safe," she answers. "Hopefully, I can return before my time is up, but until it is safe it just causes unnecessary risk for me to travel to Australia. They know where I would go, and who I might be close to."

A pause, thought.

"Okay, then," Amy whispers. "I'll tell Rachel you're okay, but you should really call her as well."

"I will when I am back at my accommodations. Possibly later this afternoon."

Though she cannot see her, Eleanor is sure Amy is nodding her head.

"And Adelyn can call Riley, if she'd like to."

"I'll pass on the message."

"I hope you can come back home again..."

"So do I."

Both women take a breath, Eleanor letting her eyes fall back onto the roadside.

"Goodbye," Eleanor starts. "Talk soon?"

"Talk soon."

The call disconnects, her phone moving back to its spot in the car door. Nikolas quietly starts the car again, pulling out onto the interstate once more.

"Thank you," Eleanor smiles softly, fingers brushing over his forearm, resting between them.

"It's what I'm here for," he replies softly. "We are in this together, always."

The words hang on the end of Eleanor's tongue, eyes turning back to Nikolas. Her indecision is clear.

"You know, you've done something no one else has ever managed..." she says, head tilting and a playful smile edging at her lips.

"What's that?" he asks curiously.

"Ellsie never once hated you…" Eleanor breathes. "It may have seemed like that, at times, but she never hated you as a person. She has for nearly every single other person we have ever met. Sometimes she warms up to them, but rarely does she skip the hating stage, except with you."

Nikolas raises an eyebrow, kind gaze drifting to her.

"You sure about that?"

"She is agreeing with me now," she assures. "Any hatred you have felt of hers, it wasn't of you, it is of the idea of you. She hates the idea of someone else I can lean on. Of someone that might make her irrelevant. But even she has fallen for you. Even she could not find a way to fault your nature. It came close when you left, but we both understood."

"I'm glad," he says, "because I don't think I'd survive if either of you could find a way to hate me. I think it would break me. Her acceptance means more than you realise."

"Her… love," Eleanor whispers, looking up through her eyelashes at him. "Our love."

"More than I will ever deserve."

"It seems this world is playing in our favour."

Nikolas laughs softly.

"Repayment perhaps."

"Your father would hate to think the Angels were in favour of us."

They both laugh, together, at the absurdity.

Chapter 64

One month later.

Adelyn is curled in her mother's lap, playing on their iPad as everyone sits around the manor's living room. As had become normal, Eleanor sits on one of the single couches, a decaf latte in her hand. Every so often – when the conversation allows – her eyes lock with Nikolas's across the seating area, but other than the occasional looks and quiet conversation that had emerged since their return, the daring interactions had all but ceased.

Overall, Eleanor was slightly more confident around the other men, allowing Kenichi to touch her as Nikolas did – though this was still rather limited. The others could manage accidental brushes but nothing more.

Kaylee had picked up on the silent magnetism between the Geminae almost immediately and had done well to hide it from Michael. But in an attempt to outdo his brother it seemed, the simmering tension between Michael and Kaylee was becoming more and more obvious. Especially in the way he hung around her, the scant touches almost painfully visible as they all relaxed into a seemingly normal life.

Eleanor's head shifts and an eyebrow raises as Nikolas suddenly scowls, rubbing his temple in confusion. His head shakes just slightly to assure her, but it falls on deaf ears as he abruptly stands and doubles over in pain.

"Nik..." she murmurs, standing Adelyn up carefully and moving in front of him. "What's wrong?"

Across the room – walking towards them – Michael drops to one knee, head now in his hands as well. Nikolas groans, grabbing Eleanor's hand as tightly as possible and pressing it to his head. She does well not to pull away in surprise, but Captain does trot over to her side in worry.

Her eyes go blank for a second, Nikolas passing the same images torturing his own mind into hers just long enough to show her what exactly was wrong.

The wards around Angeli Terra reaching out. A message. Quick glances of ships headed directly for an island. A plea for help.

All three return to clarity at once, the Geminae locking eyes as they stand up straight. Nikolas glances to his brother for only a second.

"We can make it, quick enough to help," Nikolas offers, "but you need to protect us if we land on that island. I will not cut her time short because we helped the people who want to kill us."

"You'll be protected. By the size of that armada, they'll need you as well."

Zach finally interrupts them, stepping into view.

"What armada, and who? And what just happened?"

"The Daemone armada. Angeli Terra. And the wards just sent a plea for help to the princes of their land. Michael at least needs to go," Eleanor answers quickly, pads of her fingers tapping quickly on her leg. "I'm sure they could use your help as well."

Adelyn now steps up to her mother, small hand on her leg.

"Will you be safe?" she asks quietly.

"Yes, there is no safer place to fight," Eleanor assures, "and you get to hang out with Nancy for a day or two, okay?"

The small child nods, fingers locking with Captain's fur.

"We'll all come," Kenichi calls, eyes glancing between Michael and Eleanor. "We should get going now, though."

Eleanor picks Adelyn up quickly, holding her carefully to her chest.

"I love you, baby girl," she breathes.

They are already moving towards the cars, Nikolas meeting Eleanor's eyes quickly before jogging up the stairs to grab her box and their twin swords – the only pieces of their arsenal they keep close.

"Are you scared, mummy?"

"No. I'm not."

Jaimie Thomas

Acknowledgements

Writing and publishing one book was a milestone, and now a second feels amazing. As a massive Marvel fan, I have always noticed Australia's disconnect from supernatural and low fantasy fiction and I wanted to bring a bit of fun (if we're calling it that) to our little corner of the world, and So She May Grow allowed me to address that. A lot of the experiences of community within the book are lived experiences, and I'd like to thank some specific people:

To my parents, without whom I could not have written this book. From driving so I could write to deciphering my very odd attempts to figure out a word, nothing in this book would exist if I hadn't had the chances you gave me. Especially to my mother, who, while injured – by my horse... sorry – did all the hard yards formatting this book in every way, and for all the editing work you have done for it. You transformed it from a mess of words to something capable of reading, so thank you.

To my beta readers, Karen Jones and Ruth Goodwin, who put in so many hours reading and improving my books. Your trust and support of my writing kept me moving forward. Between multiple reads – and a very early copy for Karen – you have been indispensable.

To all the firefighters who kept our houses safe in the 2019-20 NSW Black Summer fires. I mention them in this book because they were so important to all of us that were impacted by the Gosper's Mountain fire, just as I know they were and will continue to protect all others impacted by fires around the country. From the volunteer and professional firefighters, out of town crews to the international support teams, we cannot thank you enough.

To everyone from my hometown who supported So She May Breathe and allowed me to keep my dreams of being an author alive, I am so grateful. Whether it's giving my book a chance or stocking it in your shops, without you I couldn't do this.

And to Pony Club Australia, who provides such a wonderful place for people to build connections and be active. Finally, to regional Australian primary schools that allow anyone and everyone to flourish: you may be small, but you are mighty.